"There's only one thing I want to do with you, Brianna MacLeod, and that's kiss you."

She looked up at Cal, biting her bottom lip. "I'm just a little nervous, I guess. It's been a long time. I feel like I did right before you kissed me that summer at Bridal Veil Falls."

He remembered their first kiss like it was yesterday. They'd been swimming at the base of the falls. Bri had climbed up on the rocks, laughing when he'd warned her that it was too dangerous. But the moment he looked up at her that day with the sun bathing her in a golden light, the waterfall sparkling behind her, he'd been a goner.

"Ah, so you feel like you're drowning," he said.

She laughed. "You were the one who thought I was drowning, not me."

"What was I supposed to think? You were under the water a solid three minutes."

"Because I'd lost my bikini top."

And he'd hauled her up and into his arms, kissing her with a combination of lust and relief. A kiss that had sealed their fate. "And here we are, almost a decade later, and I've got you back in my arms. I think that's worth celebrating with a kiss, don't you?"

"I do," she whispered, and went to rise up on her toes to meet him halfway.

PRAISE FOR DEBBIE MASON

"Debbie Mason writes romance like none other."
—FreshFiction.com

"I've never met a Debbie Mason story that I didn't enjoy."
—KeeperBookshelf.com

"I'm telling you right now, if you haven't yet read a book by Debbie Mason you don't know what you're missing."
—RomancingtheReaders.blogspot.com

"It's not just romance. It's grief and mourning, guilt and truth, second chances and revelations."
—WrittenLoveReviews.blogspot.com

"Mason always makes me smile and touches my heart in the most unexpected and wonderful ways."
—HerdingCats-BurningSoup.com

"No one writes heartful small town romance like Debbie Mason, and I always count the days until the next book!"
—TheManyFacesofRomance.blogspot.com

"Wow, do these books bring the feels. Deep emotion, heart-tugging romance, and a touch of suspense make them hard to put down..."
—TheRomanceDish.com

"Debbie Mason writes in a thrilling and entertaining way. Her stories are captivating and filled with controlled chaos, true love, mysteries, amazing characters, eccentricities, plotting, and friendship."
—WithLoveForBooks.com

"Debbie Mason never disappoints me."
—FictionFangirls.net

"Mason takes her romances to a whole new level..."
—CarriesBookReviews.com

"I loved the world of Harmony Harbor and all of the characters that reside there."
—CrystalBlogsBooks.com

"The Harmony Harbor series is heartfelt and delightful!"
—RaeAnne Thayne, *New York Times* bestselling author

"Take another trip to Christmas, Colorado, and you'll be guaranteed a wonderful time."
—*RT Book Reviews*

"Christmas, Colorado, will get you in the spirit for love all year long."
—Jill Shalvis, *New York Times* bestselling author

"If you enjoy multi-layered characters, humor, emotional twists and turns, and heart-tugging romance that will leave you eager for more, I enthusiastically recommend a visit to Highland Falls, North Carolina."
—TheRomanceDish.com

THE HIGHLAND FALLS SERIES
Summer on Honeysuckle Ridge
Christmas on Reindeer Road
Falling in Love on Willow Creek
A Wedding on Honeysuckle Ridge (short story)
The Inn on Mirror Lake

THE HARMONY HARBOR SERIES
Mistletoe Cottage
Christmas with an Angel (short story)
Starlight Bridge
Primrose Lane
Sugarplum Way
Driftwood Cove
Sandpiper Shore
The Corner of Holly and Ivy
Barefoot Beach
Christmas in Harmony Harbor

THE CHRISTMAS, COLORADO SERIES
The Trouble with Christmas
Christmas in July
It Happened at Christmas
Wedding Bells in Christmas
Snowbound at Christmas
Kiss Me in Christmas
Happy Ever After in Christmas
Marry Me at Christmas (short story)
Miracle at Christmas (novella)
One Night in Christmas (novella)

At Home on Marigold Lane

DEBBIE MASON

A Highland Falls Novel

FOREVER
New York Boston

Copyright © 2022 by Debbie Mazzuca
Cover design by Daniela Medina. Cover art by Tom Hallman. Cover art by © Shutterstock. Cover copyright © 2022 by Hachette Book Group, Inc.

Forever
Hachette Book Group
1290 Avenue of the Americas, New York, NY 10104
read-forever.com
twitter.com/readforeverpub

First Edition: September 2022

Forever is an imprint of Grand Central Publishing. The Forever name and logo are trademarks of Hachette Book Group, Inc.

The publisher is not responsible for websites (or their content) that are not owned by the publisher.

The Hachette Speakers Bureau provides a wide range of authors for speaking events. To find out more, go to www.hachettespeakersbureau.com or call (866) 376-6591.

ISBNs: 978-1-5387-0898-9 (mass market), 978-1-5387-0899-6 (ebook)

Printed in the United States of America

OPM

10 9 8 7 6 5 4 3 2 1

This book is dedicated to the memory of my mom and dad, who were the perfect example of a love that was meant to be. They fell in love as teenagers, but life happened and took them on different paths. Fourteen years later, they found their way back to each other. And we're so lucky that they did.

At Home on Marigold Lane

Chapter One

♥

Brianna MacLeod's heart began racing the moment she turned the truck onto Main Street. The pastel-painted wooden storefronts of downtown Highland Falls blurred before her eyes.

It felt like a hummingbird was trapped in her chest, its wings beating frantically against her rib cage in a futile attempt to escape. She couldn't breathe. It didn't matter that rationally she knew that if her heart was beating, she was still breathing.

There was nothing rational about a panic attack. The symptoms didn't respond to reason. They snuck up on you out of the blue when you were performing the most mundane of tasks. Like driving to the grocery store on a bright blue September afternoon.

She needed a distraction and willed her fingers to loosen their white-knuckled grip on the steering wheel. But instead of searching her bag for her phone and clicking on a meditation app, she turned on the radio. It was set to the local news. She went to switch to a station with music—soothing music instead of droning voices—but a familiar name snuck past the panic holding her hostage.

"Dr. Caleb Scott has once again been named Hometown Hero of the Week. Today, while out for his early morning run, Dr. Scott came across a tourist who'd suffered a heart attack while attempting the Blue Mountain Trail. As most locals know, this is not a trail for beginners." The female hosts talked about Blue Mountain's steep slopes and narrow trails before moving on to how Cal had revived the man and then carried him down the mountain. Bri knew the trail as well as she knew Highland Falls' Hometown Hero. He'd saved her life too. Only she didn't think of him as a hero.

When the hosts went on to rhapsodize over Cal and his heroics, Bri switched off the radio and tried an affirmation instead. It was one she'd prescribed to her anxious clients at her marriage and family therapy practice over the years.

"No situation is good or bad." Her pulse continued to race as she turned into the grocery store parking lot. "It's how you react to it that matters."

Apparently her heart had decided that the appropriate response to the number of vehicles parked in the lot was to knock against her rib cage at a nausea-inducing speed.

"Breathe, just breathe. In for four, hold for seven, breathe out for eight." She repeated the pattern as she parked the truck beside an SUV. She shut off the engine and dug in her bag for her phone. Gripping it in her sweaty palm, she pulled up a meditation app, praying it worked its magic.

This shouldn't be so hard. She had a headful of positive affirmations and breathing exercises, two of the very things that her clients had assured her worked well for them. But that was the problem, wasn't it? If last year had proven anything, it was that she had no business holding herself up as an authority on anxiety-reducing techniques . . . or on relationships.

How could she help someone else when she couldn't help herself? Her clients had probably been protecting her feelings when they told her the affirmations and breathing exercises worked. She had amazing clients. *Used to* have, she reminded herself. She'd closed her practice late last year.

She glanced at the customers going in and out of the store, and her pulse, which had begun to slow, began racing again. She couldn't do this.

Frustrated with herself yet relieved at the same time, she shoved the key back in the ignition and started the engine, about to pull out of the parking space. But then her mind inconveniently reminded her of the conversation she'd overheard that morning, and she rested her forehead against the steering wheel. She absolutely had to do this. It was part of her plan to convince her sister, Ellie, that she was fine and that Ellie didn't have to worry about her or protect her anymore.

Bri gritted her teeth and leaned over the middle console, making a grab for her cane. The muscles in her right thigh spasmed, twisting into agonizing knots that had her sucking in a sharp breath. She hadn't thought this through. Her physiotherapy session today had been particularly brutal. Probably because, as her therapist had pointed out several times during the hour-long session, Bri hadn't been doing her exercises.

No matter what her physiotherapist said, her very legitimate reasons for not doing them weren't simply excuses. As far as Bri could tell, the exercises weren't helping. They were also painful and demoralizing. But after today's session, she'd promised to put in the effort. Mostly because she was afraid her therapist would tell her sister if she didn't. That was the trouble with living in this small North Carolina mountain town. Everyone knew her family, and Bri's sordid business.

Another excellent reason not to venture into the grocery store and out of her comfort zone. She'd put her plan into action tomorrow. She glanced at the oversize black hoodie, black leggings, and furry black Ugg booties she wore. She wasn't exactly dressed to be out in public anyway.

Just as she was about to pull out of the parking space, her cell phone rang. It was a ringtone she knew well. Her sister's. Bri glanced at the time, pulled back into the parking space, turned off the engine, and answered her cell. If she didn't, Ellie would worry.

"Hi. What's up?" Bri knew exactly what was up. She hadn't gone directly home after her PT session.

"Where are you? Are you okay?"

At the worry in her sister's voice, a flicker of resentment flared to life inside of Bri. She loved her big sister. She didn't know what she would have done this past year without Ellie's support. Except sometimes, like now, Bri felt...smothered. Worse, she felt like Ellie didn't trust her to take care of herself. After what had happened with Bri's ex-husband, she supposed she couldn't fault her sister for feeling that way. But knowing Ellie had a legitimate reason for being concerned didn't make it easier. Bri had her own doubts to deal with.

She glanced at the grocery store entrance. Two birds, one stone. Forcing a smile on her face in hopes that it would come out in her voice, she said, "I'm fine. My session went really, really well."

She rolled her eyes at her upbeat tone of voice. She sounded downright cheerful. "So well, in fact, that I decided I'd make us a special dinner to celebrate. We'll celebrate you and Nate *finally* rebooking your honeymoon while we're at it." They were scheduled to leave for Scotland next week. Except Bri had overheard them this morning talking about once again postponing their trip. Because of her.

"I thought I'd cook up some traditional Scottish fare. How does cock-a-leekie soup, oat cakes, and trifle for dessert sound?"

"Good. It sounds really good. And so do you," her sister said with what sounded like a frown in her voice. Ellie probably found this cheerful, upbeat version of Bri confusing.

"But I'm not sure now is a good time for me and Nate to go away," her sister continued. "You—"

Obviously Bri hadn't done as good a job selling this new, improved version of herself as she'd thought. "I'm doing great! Fantastic, actually. So stop worrying about me."

"I can't. Stop worrying about you, that is. You died in front of me, Bri. I thought we'd lost you."

Bri worked to keep the images of last year's near-fatal

fall from playing out in her mind. She didn't remember much, but the memory of that day—of running from her abusive ex, her desperate attempt to escape from him— had the power to send her spiraling into another panic attack. She was barely out of this last one. She didn't need to go there again. Not now.

She cleared her throat. "But you didn't."

"Sometimes I feel like we did," Ellie said quietly.

"I know." In a way, Bri had died that day. She wasn't the same person she used to be. She wasn't sure she liked the person she'd become. And as much as she knew her sister loved her, she thought Ellie might feel the same way. "I'm working on being the sister you remember. You just need to give me a little time."

Ellie could justifiably say she'd given her all the time in the world and it hadn't made a difference. Bri had been recovering from her injuries at the family's inn on Mirror Lake for more than a year now.

She didn't give Ellie a chance to respond. Instead, digging deep for the girl she used to be, Bri infused her voice with the spirit of her once optimistic, fun-loving self. "Now off to the grocery store I go. Text me if we need anything else."

"Um, you sound kind of manic. Are you sure you're okay?"

Bri sighed. "You haven't heard it in a while, but that was my excited voice. I'm excited that you and Nate are finally going on your honeymoon, and I'm excited to make you a delicious meal to celebrate." Just not so excited about going into the grocery store to pick up the ingredients.

"I haven't heard that voice in a very long time, Bri. Not since—"

"Oh wow, you should see the gorgeous fall display outside the grocery store." She cut off her sister before she uttered the name of the man who'd broken Bri's optimistic heart and her fun-loving spirit a decade before. And it wasn't Richard, Bri's ex-husband.

She glanced at the apples, pumpkins, and sunflowers on display on the racks beside the store's entrance. "I'll grab a basket of apples and make a pie instead of a trifle. Sound good?"

"Ah, yeah, it sounds great. But Bri, you do remember I inherited Granny's gift, don't you?"

Bri gasped. Her sister was psychic. Something she herself hadn't believed until last year. "You promised never to read my mind!"

"Unless I think you're keeping something from me that puts you in danger. Stop sputtering. I didn't read your mind. But I don't have to, to know you're in pain. I can hear it in your voice, among other things."

"You know what they say: no pain, no gain." Bri opened the truck's door, focusing on the maple trees along Main Street instead of the ache in her leg. In a matter of weeks, the leaves would change colors, lining downtown Highland Falls in a blaze of autumn glory.

"They also say stop putting off your appointment with Cal."

Bri squeezed her eyes shut at the mention of Highland Falls' Hometown Hero.

"It's been more than a year since your surgery,"

her sister continued. "You canceled both your follow-up appointments with Cal. Maybe something's wrong and that's why you're in so much pain."

Something was wrong, all right. Her sister had brought up the one person guaranteed to wipe out Bri's good mood, even if it was a fake good mood. Cal wasn't only Highland Falls' Hometown Hero; he'd once been hers. But he'd broken her heart when he'd broken their engagement almost a decade before.

Some people, her sister included, sometimes even Bri herself, thought it was past time she stopped holding that against Cal. Especially since he'd saved her life last year. But she'd spent the long months of her recovery trying to pinpoint exactly what had happened to put her on such a disastrous relationship path—a path that had led to her lying in a broken heap at the bottom of her condo's stairs in Charlotte—and she'd come to the conclusion that Cal was to blame.

She'd loved him with every fiber of her being. She'd trusted him implicitly with her heart, with her very soul. Something inside her had broken when he ended their relationship with no real explanation, and it wasn't just her heart.

"I have another doctor, remember?"

"It's not the same, and you know it. Mallory is a primary care physician. And just FYI, she also thinks you shouldn't be skipping your appointments with Cal."

"You're not supposed to be talking about me with my doctor. I'm not twelve, you know. I'm twenty-eight years..." She trailed off. She wasn't twenty-eight. She'd lost over a year of her life trying to put herself back together again. "Almost thirty years old, and there's this little thing called doctor-patient confidentiality."

"There's also a little thing called love. As in I love you, and so does Mallory. We're worried about you, Bri."

Well, didn't that just put a pin in the bubble of self-righteous indignation expanding in her chest? "I love you guys too. You know I do. And I understand why everyone is so protective of me, but you have to trust me when I tell you I'm okay." Now she had to start proving that she was, because she didn't need a master's degree in marriage and family therapy to understand why they'd have a hard time believing her.

"You're right. We do."

Bri smiled. That was easier than she'd expected. "Great. I won't be long." Tucking her cell in her bag after disconnecting the call, she stepped onto the asphalt, considering it a win when her leg didn't buckle beneath her.

Leaning heavily on her cane, she closed and locked the driver's-side door, and returned the keys to her bag. "You've got this," she told herself, hefting the strap over her shoulder. She set off across the parking lot at the same time as a ninetysomething woman who used a walker. The woman left Bri in the dust.

A car pulled into the lot, the driver waiting patiently for Bri to get out of the way. Her cheeks heated as she struggled to pick up the pace, nearly falling on her face when the toe of her bootie hit a pothole and she had to put her weight on her injured leg. She fought the urge to turn around and head home.

She couldn't back out now. If she did, Ellie would never agree to go on her honeymoon. She'd never

believe that Bri was okay. Besides, all she needed was a
couple ingredients. Ten minutes, tops, and she'd be out
of the grocery store. Unless she met someone she knew,
especially her grandmother's friends. They liked to talk.
They were also nosy.

As Bri entered the store, she pulled her hoodie over
her head, tucking her long blond hair underneath. She
glanced at the shopping carts on her right and decided
to take one. At least she'd have something to lean on.
Hooking her cane on the handle, she folded her arms,
resting her full weight on the cart. It felt so good that
she might have stayed right where she was if not for the
whoosh of the doors sliding open behind her.

She pushed her cart into the store, admiring the
brightly colored produce in the bins lining the center of
the aisle. The smell of pumpkin spice tempted her to
stop at the nearby coffee bar but balancing the to-go cup
while carrying out a bag of groceries was beyond her, so
she kept moving.

It felt kind of nice doing something on her own
for a change, and she found herself humming along
to Taylor Swift's "Mr. Perfectly Fine" coming through
the store's sound system. Maybe this had been a good
idea after all. She felt almost normal.

She transferred a basket of apples into her cart, spotting the leeks and onions across from her. As she went to
push her cart toward the veggie display case, a familiar
deep voice stopped her cold. Praying she was wrong, she
snuck a peek over her shoulder. The tall, exceptionally
well-built man in green scrubs was as familiar as his
deep voice.

Cal was here.

In the grocery store.

Less than twenty feet away from her.

Searching for her cell phone in her bag, Bri used her body to push the cart toward the end of the aisle. She called her sister, whisper-shouting the moment Ellie picked up, "I can't believe you did this to me!"

"What are you talking about? Did what?"

"Called Cal and told him where I am!" She glanced over her shoulder. He had his back to her, talking to a young mother, who was clearly as entranced by him as her children. Not surprising—the man was a golden-haired Adonis.

"I wouldn't do that. But maybe this is a sign that you should—"

"It's a sign, all right." A sign that she should have gone straight home after her PT session. "I have to go." She disconnected.

Shoving her phone back in her bag, she leaned halfway across the cart. She needed as much weight and forward momentum as she could get. Her already over-worked leg muscles screamed in protest when she picked up her pace but she couldn't stop now. The last thing she wanted was to run into Cal. Mr. Perfect was happily married and living his best life while she'd made an absolute mess of hers.

Bri glanced at her leg as it began to drag. "Don't fail me now," she pleaded, leaning as far as she could over the cart to take more weight off her leg as she rounded the corner.

The cart wobbled and veered to the right. She looked

up. Oh no! She'd taken the corner too wide and was heading straight for a display tower of toilet paper. She tried to get both feet firmly on the floor tiles fast enough to stop the cart but it was too late. She careened into the toilet paper tower, an avalanche of jumbo-sized packages sliding and tumbling toward her.

Surrounded by a mountain of toilet paper rolls, she looked around. No one had seen what she'd done. She felt bad leaving the mess for someone else to clean up, but desperate times called for desperate measures. She had to get out of there ASAP.

She went to steer the cart around the packages but her path was blocked. No amount of shoving through the mound of toilet paper rolls helped. Holding on to the cart with one hand, she leaned over and began tossing them out of the way.

From the next aisle over, she heard two women discussing the benefits of one fiber cereal over another. Their voices were getting closer. She didn't have time to pick up the last package blocking the front wheels of her cart. Grabbing on to the shopping cart's handle with both hands, she gave it a hard shove in hopes of running up and over the toilet paper rolls. It worked. Only it worked a little too well.

The hard jolt and forward momentum caught Bri off balance, and she tripped over the squashed package of toilet paper, the cart's handle slipping from her sweaty grip. She reached for the shopping cart in an effort to regain her balance but her hands grabbed air instead. And that was the moment her leg called it quits and gave out.

Bri, who had become something of an expert tumbler over the past year, leaned back at the last second, falling onto a bed of toilet paper rolls instead of onto her face. She lifted her head and groaned. Her shopping cart was headed for a display rack of jams and jellies in pretty glass jars.

Chapter Two

♥

At the sound of a low groan, Cal looked up from bagging heirloom carrots to see a runaway grocery cart headed straight for a display rack at the end of the produce aisle. He dropped the bag of carrots and ran to intercept the cart, grabbing the front end just before it took out the rack of glass jars. Pulling the cart toward him, he looked around for its owner. His gaze collided with a woman lying on a bed of toilet paper rolls. And it wasn't just any woman.

He'd know those eyes, that face, anywhere. He'd once loved Brianna MacLeod to distraction. It had been the kind of love that changes you, completes you. The kind of love where you don't know how you'll go on when it's over.

He shook off his shock at seeing Bri and let go of the cart, jogging to her side. "What happened? Are you okay?" He hadn't seen her since she left the hospital last year. Not an easy feat in a small town, but then again, it was common knowledge Bri rarely left the inn.

"I'm fine." She wouldn't meet his eyes. "They piled

their toilet paper roll display too high, and it fell over. I tripped over one of the packages." She shrugged as she went to push herself upright. "No big deal."

"How about you let me decide if it's a big deal or not?" He crouched beside her and reached for her foot.

She batted his hand away. "Are you crazy? We're in the middle of the grocery store. You're not examining me here."

He held her gaze. "I wouldn't have to if you hadn't canceled your follow-up appointments with me." If he'd done a recent scan, he wouldn't be as concerned that there were issues with the rod in her femur or the pins in her ankle.

"I knew it! Ellie called you, didn't she? She told you I was here. She told—"

"Your sister didn't call me. Ellie might be psychic, but I doubt she knew you were going to have a run-in with a toilet paper pyramid and that your leg would give out."

If Ellie had the slightest inkling something like this would happen, she wouldn't have let her baby sister out of her sight. She'd always been overprotective of Bri; the entire MacLeod family had been. It used to drive him crazy how much they protected her. He imagined it had only gotten worse since Bri's accident.

If he was honest, he was feeling a little protective toward her himself. Probably because, even though it had happened more than a year ago, he couldn't shake the memory of the day her heart had stopped.

"Who said my leg gave out?"

"Are you telling me that it didn't?"

"I've just come from my physiotherapy session. I overdid it, that's all. I should have gone home instead of coming here." She shoved a package of toilet paper away and put her hand on the floor in an effort to push herself to her feet.

He covered her hand with his and a familiar sensation moved in his chest. She got to him. Even after all these years, she had the power to stir up feelings in him that he had no business feeling with the simple touch of his hand on hers.

Worried she'd hear some of that emotion in his voice, he cleared his throat. "You're not moving until I check out your leg. I need to make sure it's stable before you put weight on it." The words came out clipped, maybe even a little harsh. He couldn't help it. He was angry, angry at himself for having feelings for a woman who'd shredded his heart a decade before.

He lifted his gaze to hers. She wasn't looking at him. She was looking at his hand on hers. What was his hand still doing there? He was positive he'd moved it. He did that now. Too fast, like she'd caught him doing something wrong. Like that small, fine-boned hand had zapped him with a fully charged defibrillator. She met his gaze, a frown furrowing her brow, a touch of confusion in her blue eyes. So it wasn't just him. She'd felt it too.

He bit back the question that was on the tip of his tongue. Why? Why had she walked away without a fight? He'd never gotten the chance to ask. *Too late, dumbass. It was nearly ten years ago. You moved on.* He had, but there was a part of him that hadn't forgiven her for giving up on them. He didn't know if he ever would.

Bri looked up, and the confused expression on her face was replaced with a panicked one. He glanced over his shoulder. An older woman pushed her cart toward them. "Are you all right, dear?"

"I'm fine, thanks. I pulled one of the packages from the bottom, and then this happened." Picking up a package of toilet paper, Bri gave it a squeeze. "Good thing they're as soft as advertised."

She offered the older woman a strained smile before ducking her head and grabbing Cal's hand.

"Please don't make a big deal out of this," she whispered. "I can't let Ellie find out. She'll call off her honeymoon again. I promise, I'll make an appointment for my follow-up. I won't cancel this time." She searched his face, her eyes pleading.

He'd never been able to deny her anything, and it seemed that hadn't changed. "All right." He glanced at his watch and ran through his schedule in his head. "I can fit you in at three." It would take some maneuvering but he'd make it work. No way was he letting her talk her way out of a follow-up this time.

"You don't mean today, do you? I can't come today, Cal. I'm making a special—"

He raised an eyebrow and leaned over, removing the...slipper from her foot. He held it up. "Seriously?"

She grabbed it from his hand. "Fine. I'll come, okay? Now just help me—" She groaned when the store manager hurried over.

He was a big man with a bald head and a booming voice. "What happened here? Do you need me to call an ambulance, Dr. Scott? Did she have a heart attack?"

Bri scowled at the store manager when several customers glanced their way. "No, I didn't have a heart attack. I was attacked by your toilet paper display. You're lucky I wasn't hurt or I'd sue." She wrapped her hands around Cal's forearms, saying under her breath, "A little help here."

He angled his head. "Feisty, aren't you?" He'd never seen this side of Bri.

The woman he remembered had been sweet with a kind word for everyone she met. Even-tempered too. He used to tease her just to get a rise out of her. It never worked. She'd lived in a Zen-like state of mind, looking at the world through rose-colored glasses. A fun-loving optimist who saw only the best in people and in life. He imagined that was no longer the case. She'd dealt with a lot this past year. And not just her injuries, which had been extensive and life-threatening.

"Don't worry, Stan," he told the store manager, who'd looked like he was going to have a heart attack himself when Bri mentioned suing. "No one's going to sue you." He fit his hands under Bri's arms, easing her carefully to her feet.

Stan nodded his thanks, keeping his distance from Bri as he began restacking the toilet paper rolls. Cal didn't blame him. Bri looked like she wanted to sock the store manager in the nose.

She leaned against Cal, and he smelled her familiar lavender and mint fragrance. The feel of her in his arms was familiar too. She looked up at him. "You'd be feisty too if you had to deal with what I do. Thanks to Stan, word around town will be that I had a heart attack."

"I wouldn't worry about it. No one seems to know who you are."

She smiled, a smile that he remembered well. And just like it used to, it took his breath away. He reminded himself that technically she was his patient. When that didn't help, he reminded himself what those first few months after their breakup had been like. Oh yeah, that worked.

"You're right." She tucked long blond strands under her hoodie and then dug around inside her bag, pulling out a pair of sunglasses. She put them on. "Would you mind helping me to my shopping cart?"

He frowned. "You can't walk without your cane? Or is the pain that bad?"

"I told you, I just came from physio. Now are you going to help me or not?"

He offered his arm.

"Thank you." She glanced at him as he guided her to her shopping cart. "And thanks for not ignoring my wishes and examining my leg. I know you wanted to."

"I did. I do. So plan on hanging out at the hospital for at least an hour, maybe two." He looked at her feet. "And do me a favor, don't wear those things again."

"Why not? They're comfortable."

"They're slippers."

"They're not slippers. They're booties."

He shook his head. "They're ridiculous and dangerous. You need something with support, Bri."

"Okay, fine. I won't wear them outside the inn." She let go of his arm and grabbed the shopping cart with both hands, leaning heavily against it. "I guess I'll see you at three." She steered her cart to the produce aisle, glancing at him when he walked beside her. "What are you doing?"

"I'm not leaving you on your own until I know you're okay." He figured she was going to argue so he walked over to the veggie display. "I have a few things to pick up anyway." The bag he'd been filling with carrots was where he'd left it. He picked it up, adding a few more, and then he grabbed a bag of small, colorful potatoes.

Beside him, Bri sighed and then reached for the leeks. She added them to her cart, along with some yellow onions.

"Do you need anything else?" he asked, hoping she was done. He had to run home and get dinner in the Crock-Pot before heading back to the hospital but he wasn't convinced Bri was as good as she was pretending to be.

"A few more things." She glanced at the bags of produce in his hand. "If you got what you came for, you should go. I'm good. Honestly."

"I have a couple other things I need."

"Suit yourself." She rested her injured foot on the bottom rack, pushing off with her other foot while steering the cart with her body.

He lengthened his stride, reaching over to straighten the front of the cart when she nearly took out the endcap turning down the cereal aisle. "Why don't you just tell me what you need?"

"Because I—" She was interrupted by a phone ringing in her bag. Muttering, "I knew it," she pulled out her cell and brought it to her ear. "I'm fine, Ellie." He could hear her sister's anxious voice from where he stood. Bri bowed her head and blew out a frustrated breath. "Does it sound like I had a heart attack? Yes, he's here." She handed him the phone. "She wants to talk to you," Bri said, then pushed off with her one foot and glided up the cereal aisle.

"Hey, Ellie."

"Cal, thank goodness you were there for Bri. How is she? Don't sugarcoat it. Tell me the truth."

Bri stopped the cart, glancing at him over her shoulder as if she knew what her sister asked.

"She's fine," he said, even though he was pretty sure she was far from fine. But Ellie sounded upset as it was.

Bri smiled and mouthed, *Thank you.*

So maybe he hadn't lied just for her sister's benefit.

Ellie scoffed. "Did she pay you to say that?"

"No, she didn't pay me."

"Really? Because take it from me, she is far from fine," Ellie practically yelled down the line, which told him just how upset she was. Ellie was as sweet as Bri used to be. "Today was the first day she ventured out on her own and look what happened. She doesn't get out of bed before noon, Cal. And do you know why that is?"

He turned his back on Bri so she wouldn't see his reaction or overhear his side of the conversation with her sister. "She's not sleeping through the night?" he guessed, keeping his voice low. It wasn't really a guess. He'd noted the dark shadows under Bri's eyes.

"No, she's not, which means I'm not either because I can hear her walking around, and I'm afraid she's going to fall. She has migraines, and she still has dizzy spells, Cal."

"She had a traumatic brain injury, Ellie. It's not uncommon for her to still be having symptoms." Not only had Bri broken her femur and her ankle in the fall, she'd fractured her skull. He didn't tell Ellie that it was possible Bri would have symptoms of TBI for years to come.

"Is it normal that she also can't stand for long periods of time?"

It was worse than he suspected. "Look, Bri has agreed to a follow-up appointment. I'm seeing her later today. I'll run her through a battery of tests and consult with her neurologist, her physiotherapist, and Mallory. I promise, Ellie, between the four of us, we'll come up with a treatment plan that—"

Bri came up beside him, snagged her phone from his hand, and glided past him, which meant she didn't see the woman turning her cart into the aisle. Cal lunged, putting his hands on either side of Bri's, managing to stop the cart before it collided with the other woman's.

Apparently Bri was too busy giving her sister crap to notice she'd nearly taken out the woman.

"Cut her some slack, Bri," he said when she disconnected and shoved her phone in her bag. "Ellie's worried about you, and from what she told me, she has good reason to be."

He fully expected her to tell him to mind his own business, so he was surprised when she said, "I know she is, and I shouldn't have told her off for sharing her concerns with you. It's just that…" She trailed off and looked up at him. He couldn't see her eyes behind her sunglasses but he had a feeling she was fighting back tears. Her voice was thick with emotion. "She won't go on her honeymoon now, will she? I messed everything up. That's all I seem to do these days. I can't do anything right."

"Don't be so hard on yourself, Bri."

"You have no idea what Ellie sacrificed for me, Cal. How much I have to make up for."

"She's your big sister. She loves you. I'm sure she doesn't feel like it was a sacrifice to support you through your recovery. That's what families do." He thought of his own sister. He needed to call and check up on her.

"It's not just what Ellie's done for me this past year. It's...never mind." She pushed her cart to the prepared food counter at the back of the store and removed a barbecued chicken from the glass warming tray. He grabbed one too. He was making chicken stew for his stepdaughter. They'd been eating too much fast food lately.

"You mind if I put this in your cart?"

"Go ahead." She sniffed, swiping a finger under her sunglasses. "I don't know why I'm even bothering making Ellie and Nate a celebratory dinner. It's not like they're going to Scotland now."

"Hey." He lowered the sunglasses. Her eyes were swimming with tears, and his chest tightened. Not only because she was crying but because of everything she was dealing with and how hard she was trying to do something nice for her sister. That was more like the woman he remembered, the one he'd fallen in love with.

"Once we have the results back from your tests and know exactly what's going on, I'll call Ellie and assure her that there's no reason she can't go away." Bri's grandfather lived at the inn, and there were plenty of people in town who'd pitch in while Ellie was away.

"You'd do that for me?"

"Of course I would. As long as you agree to abide by the treatment plan we come up with, I have no problem telling Ellie it's fine for her to go on her honeymoon."

"I'll do whatever it takes, whatever you say, Cal. I promise."

He replaced the sunglasses on her nose, tapping the bridge with his finger. "I'm going to hold you to that."

Bri was quiet as she picked up the last of the ingredients for her Scottish-themed dinner.

"You okay?" he asked when they reached the checkout line.

She nodded and then glanced up at him. "Do you ever wonder what would have happened if we'd gotten married like we'd planned?"

Chapter Three

♥

Bri wanted to take back the question the second it left her mouth. She hadn't meant to blurt it out. It's just that she'd been thinking about their past, about how good they'd once been together. How could she not? Cal was as caring and as kind as she remembered. It didn't hurt that he was also mind-blowingly gorgeous.

Well, that wasn't exactly true. It did hurt. Cal's staggering good looks had succeeded in frying her brain, and she'd just asked the most painfully embarrassing question a woman could ask a man who'd dumped her and broken her heart. The man who was currently staring at her like she'd lost her mind.

"Ignore me. You know how it is. People with TBIs say the darnedest things. These days, I never know what's going to come out of my mouth." It wasn't exactly a lie. In the first few months of her recovery, she had said things that didn't make sense. She'd even had trouble remembering what certain words meant.

Instead of waiting to see if Cal bought her excuse,

she reached into the cart to load her groceries onto the conveyor belt.

"I've got them," he said, leaning around her. He put their items on the conveyor belt and then glanced at her. "I've had a lot of what-if moments in my life, Bri, but I've found it doesn't do any good to dwell on the past. You have to keep moving forward. Take one day at a time. One step at a time."

The smile he gave her was gentle, and she had a feeling he wasn't talking about them and their past but about her. Somehow, he knew that she was stuck. That she didn't know how to move forward with her life. Maybe because she had nothing to move forward to, or maybe because she didn't know who she was anymore. Everything she'd believed about herself was a lie.

And right then, in the middle of the checkout line, Bri realized that, while Cal had broken her heart, he wasn't to blame for the mess her life was in. She was the one who'd missed the warning signs in her relationship with her ex until it was too late. She was the one who'd allowed him to chip away at her confidence, making her feel small and insignificant and, by the end, controlling every aspect of her life.

Bri felt the weight of someone's stare and looked up to see Cal watching her, his brow furrowed. She forced a smile and reached in her bag for her wallet.

"Don't worry about it. I've got it." He nodded at the cashier. "Josie rang us through together."

Bri must have been lost in her thoughts longer than she'd realized. She glanced at their purchases and the total on the screen, adding up her share in her head. Something she could have done easily in the past. It wasn't so easy now. Frustrated, she pulled two twenties from her wallet and offered them to Cal.

He placed a bag of groceries in her cart. "That's too much. Just bring what you owe me to your appointment."

A feminine voice called his name. Bri glanced over her shoulder to see a stunning dark-haired woman wearing a white lab coat striding toward them.

Several shoppers moved their carts out of the woman's way. She didn't acknowledge them with a smile or a word of thanks. Bri had a feeling she didn't notice them. Her attention was focused solely on Cal. Clearly this was a woman who was used to giving orders and having them acted upon immediately.

"Excuse me," she said to Bri, nudging her out of the way to reach Cal's side, a waft of sultry fragrance following in her wake.

"What are you still doing here?" the woman asked him, her voice as sultry as her perfume. "I've been trying to reach you for the last fifteen minutes."

He patted his pocket. "I must have left my phone in the car. I have my pager though. What's going on?" he asked as he packed his groceries and the rest of Bri's into brown paper bags.

"We have a meeting with my mother and the town council at three to present our proposal."

Bri glanced from Cal to the woman she now realized was the mayor's daughter, Raine Johnson. To be more precise, Dr. Raine Johnson-Scott, Cal's wife.

Bri was an idiot. As if Cal had ever wondered what life would have been like with her when he was married to Raine. A woman who oozed confidence and competence.

Bri had no desire to be stuck in the middle of Cal and his wife. "Sorry. I just, um, need to get by?"

Without so much as a glance in Bri's direction, Raine made room for her to get by. When Bri didn't immediately take advantage of the space she'd created—it wasn't that big of a space with Cal standing right there— Raine gestured with an elegant, if slightly impatient, wave of her hand for Bri to pass. It felt as if she were one of the woman's subjects, and not a royal one or a welcome one.

"Thank you," Bri murmured, clearing her throat in hopes Cal would get the hint and move out of the way, but he was thanking the cashier who handed him his change.

Bri prayed that he'd let her walk away without saying anything about her appointment. This meeting was obviously important to his wife, and the last thing Bri wanted was to get on the wrong side of Dr. Raine Johnson-Scott. Bri attempted to maneuver the cart around Cal.

"Hang on a minute," he said, wrapping his hand around the front end of the cart. He placed another bag inside. Then he guided the cart and Bri toward the exit while saying to his wife, "The meeting was scheduled for next week. There's no way I can make it today."

When he didn't receive a response from his wife, Cal glanced over his shoulder. "Raine?" He stopped walking, which meant Bri was once again stuck between Cal and his wife.

The last place she wanted to be. "If you don't mind, I need to get home, and you're holding my cart hostage," Bri said, nodding at his hand.

"Just give me a minute," he said without looking at her.

His wife was looking at her though. "Brianna Evans," she said, walking to her husband's side.

Like she did whenever someone addressed her by her married name, Bri cringed. "No. I'm divorced. It's Brianna MacLeod now."

Technically, both statements were untrue. Her divorce was final in two days' time. And even though in her heart she felt like a MacLeod, in actuality, she wasn't. Months after her accident, her mother revealed the soul-crushing news that Bri was the result of an affair.

"I'm sorry. I'm sure the last thing you want is to be reminded of your ex." She offered Bri a sympathetic smile and extended her hand. "I'm Cal's wife, Raine. We've met before but you probably don't remember. You were heavily medicated for most of your hospital stay. I assisted Cal with your surgery."

Bri shook Raine's hand. "No need to apologize. It's nice to officially meet you. And thank you, both of you, for, you know, saving my life." She took a step back, but Cal had yet to release his hold on the shopping cart. She jiggled it. "I should get going."

Cal took the hint, let go of the cart, and stepped aside. Then he went and ruined her escape by saying, "I'll walk you to your car." He raised his hand when she opened her mouth to argue. "Nonnegotiable. We have a bargain, remember?"

"A bargain?" Raine arched an exquisitely groomed

eyebrow, looking a little less friendly than she had
moments before. "That sounds...intriguing."

Her sister might be psychic but Bri was no slouch when
it came to reading people. She had lots of practice from
her couples therapy sessions. And she was pretty sure
Raine didn't think Bri and Cal's bargain was intriguing.
As evidenced by her narrowed gaze, it was downright
suspicious in his wife's eyes.

"No. Gosh, no. Not intriguing at all. More embarrassing than anything," Bri said, and explained how her
run-in with the toilet paper pyramid, small-town gossip,
and her overprotective older sister resulted in Bri and
Cal's *bargain*. "And that was way more information than
you needed."

Bri had totally overshared but she didn't feel she had
a choice. Just like she was positive Raine was suspicious
of Bri and Cal's *bargain*, she was equally positive that
her initial impression of the woman had been correct.
You don't mess with Raine Johnson-Scott and walk
away unscathed.

"And that's why I have to pass on the meeting,"
Cal told his wife. "I've got a window that I can fit Bri
into today."

Bri wanted to run over Cal's foot with her shopping
cart. Did the man have no idea how important this meeting was to his wife? Bri didn't even know her, and she
could tell. "Don't worry about it, Cal. Just call me when
you have an opening, and I'll—"

"Remind me again when your sister is going away?"

Bri blew out a breath. He was right. Ellie's happiness
and her honeymoon trumped staying on his wife's good

side. Bri also had a feeling Cal didn't want to go to the meeting and was using her as an excuse.

"Darling, this meeting is far too important for you to miss. I'm sure Bri and her sister will understand." Raine tucked her arm through her husband's and smiled up at him.

Bri frowned, wondering what was up with Cal. He didn't return his wife's smile. If anything, he looked uncomfortable. Flustered even.

"I'll let you two talk in private." Without waiting for a response, she pushed the shopping cart through the conveniently open doors, slipping through before they closed.

Instead of leaving the shopping cart where it belonged, she decided having something to lean on while walking across the parking lot wasn't a bad idea. She couldn't afford to stumble with Cal or the other customers looking on.

It hadn't escaped her notice that several shoppers had been sending them curious glances while at least two older women had been straining to overhear their conversation as they'd headed for the exit doors. Bri could only imagine what the gossips of Highland Falls would make of their interaction. It didn't take much for rumors to fly in the small town.

Bri shook off the thought. She had enough to worry about without angsting about what their little tête-à-tête looked like to anybody else. As she walked across the parking lot to the truck, she congratulated herself. Taking the cart had been a good idea. She hadn't tripped in a pothole or held up traffic.

But she had second thoughts once she finished loading her groceries into the truck. She had to return the cart to the store and then walk back across the parking lot with only her cane to lean on. She looked over to where Cal and Raine stood outside the store, talking in front of the sunflower display. It was an Instagram-worthy photo.

If Highland Falls had a contest for most gorgeous couple, Raine and Cal would win hands down. They were perfect together. They...wait a sec, what was that about? Cal was rubbing his fingers up and down his forehead, something he did when he was frustrated and trying not to lose his cool. At least he had when they were dating.

He'd had a lot on his plate back then, taking care of his mom and his sister. He'd had to grow up fast when his father abandoned them. But no matter how much stress Cal had been under, he'd never lost his temper with her.

Then again, that was a long time ago. Nearly a decade changed a person. She was a perfect example. She was so different from the woman she'd been when she was dating Cal that it wasn't funny. It was actually pretty sad. She wished she could turn back time. She'd... "No, I will not beg Cal for a second chance," she muttered when the wayward thought popped into her head and straight out of her mouth—thankfully to an audience of one.

Honestly, her trip down memory lane was seriously messing with her head. Except it wasn't just the memories. It was how her heart had raced when he touched her and how she'd gotten butterflies in her stomach when he'd held her gaze, for just a second looking at her like he used to. Like she was the most important person in the world to him, like he would cherish her and protect her.

Oh my gosh, what was wrong with her? She didn't want a man in her life, no matter how gorgeous or how kind he was. He could be the most perfect man in the world, and she'd want nothing to do with him. All she wanted was a simple life. A little house with a garden and a dog for companionship. She'd be happy on her own.

When she eventually got to the place where she could be happy again. She didn't see that happening anytime soon. She had to heal the broken parts of her, and not just her body. Although that was where she planned to start. If today had shown her anything, it was that she hadn't put enough effort into her recovery. She had to focus on getting better, not just for her sake but for Ellie's too.

And that was the only thing she wanted right now. She wanted Ellie not to worry about her and to focus on making a happy life with Nate. After everything Ellie had suffered because of Bri, she deserved a beautiful life. And Bri intended to do everything in her power to ensure that she got it, which meant she had to stop obsessing about Cal. Cal, who was happily married to a beautiful and brilliant woman. Cal, who was walking toward Bri with a determined stride while his wife looked on, arms crossed and eyes narrowed.

Damn it! Bri grabbed her cane and pushed the grocery cart as hard as she could, sending it rattling across the parking lot directly at Cal. He looked surprised. Bri was surprised too, but probably not for the same reason as

Cal. She couldn't believe she had the strength to push the cart that far and that fast.

"Sorry. I was hoping it would reach the other side and save me the wa—time," she called out. It's not as if she could say *save me the walk* to Cal. Knowing him, he'd make her go directly to the hospital. He'd probably insist on driving her, and at the moment, being alone in close proximity to him was a very bad idea. No doubt she'd blurt out something that would give her wayward thoughts away. There was only so much she could blame on her head injury.

"If you don't mind leaving it at the door for me, I'd really appreciate it. Thanks." She smiled and turned without waiting for his response and got into the truck. She opened her bag and looked for the keys. Unable to spot them under all the crap in her bag, she shoved her hand inside to continue the search. She had no idea how or why she'd accumulated so much stuff. She'd always been an organized person. When her fingers brushed against a jagged metal edge, she blew out a relieved breath and quickly shoved the key into the ignition.

Someone rapped on the driver's-side window. She knew who it was without looking. She considered pretending she didn't notice him and driving away. Which would no doubt draw the same reaction as telling him she wanted to save herself the walk across the parking lot.

She forced a smile and lowered the window, glancing at the front of the store. It looked like he'd returned her cart, and it also looked like Raine was becoming more agitated by the minute. She was tapping the toe of her pretty yellow high-heeled shoe on the asphalt.

Bri used to wear shoes like Raine's, beautiful shoes that added several much-needed inches to her five-foot-three stature. Raine didn't need the added height. Unlike Bri, she wasn't vertically challenged.

Bri forced her gaze to Cal, wishing his looks hadn't improved with age. "Thanks for returning the cart for me."

"No problem." His mouth lifted at the corner. "Glad to know we don't have to worry the muscles in your arms atrophied. That was an impressive push."

"You don't have to worry about my leg either. Despite how it looked earlier, I'm doing much better." Relatively speaking, she was.

"You're not trying to get out of our deal, are you?"

He was right. Ellie was the only thing that mattered. "No, I need my sister to stop worrying about me and start living her life, and you're probably the only person who can convince her I'm okay." She glanced at Raine. "But, Cal, I don't want to cause problems between you and your wife. We can—"

"Bri, Raine and I legally separated over a year ago."

Chapter Four

♥

Bri slowly lowered her sunglasses, staring at Cal with an eyebrow raised. After Raine's performance, Cal wasn't surprised she didn't believe him.

"Does Raine know that you split up? Because it sounded like she very much thinks of herself as your wife. And she's not the only one. According to the Highland Falls grapevine, you two are the most perfect couple in town."

Raine would be happy to hear that people in town had bought their act. "It's complicated." And wasn't that the understatement of the decade. "I don't have time to get into it right now. I thought I could push back the meeting with the town council, but I can't."

"It's okay. I have to make dinner for Nate and Ellie anyway. We can sched—"

"No more excuses, Bri. You can't put this—"

She threw up her hands. "I wasn't making an excuse. You just told me you have to go to a meeting with the town council."

"I do, which is why I asked Mallory to run the tests

for me. She'll coordinate with your neurosurgeon and physiotherapist. The thing is, you need to get to the hospital now."

"I can't go now. I have to drop off my groceries."

"I'll do it for you. I have to run home with mine anyway. Besides that, I'd feel better if you didn't drive across town before you were checked over." It was a five-minute drive to the hospital versus a twenty-minute drive to the inn.

Bri didn't look happy with the change of plans, so he added, "I'll talk to Ellie, and I can almost guarantee that you'll have something to celebrate by the time you get home."

He planned to tell Ellie that, in his opinion, she wasn't doing her sister any favors canceling her trip. She had every right and good reason to be concerned about Bri but Cal had a feeling Ellie's tendency to overprotect her sister, however well intentioned, was having a negative impact on Bri's recovery. The fact that Bri felt guilty for what she perceived as Ellie putting her life on hold for her was only making matters worse.

"If you can convince Ellie to go on her honeymoon without hard evidence that I'm okay, you'd be more than just Highland Falls Hometown Hero, you'd be a miracle worker. You know what she's like, Cal," Bri said as she leaned over to grab the bags of groceries off the passenger seat.

"Yeah, but Ellie likes me. She also knows I wouldn't put your recovery at risk. If that's not enough to persuade her, I'll tell her I'll check in on you every day while she's away." As soon as the words were out of his mouth, he glanced at Raine. She met his gaze across the parking lot, and her eyes narrowed. She hadn't been happy to discover he'd been hanging out with Bri in the grocery store. Raine knew about their past, just as she knew how quickly gossip spread in Highland Falls.

The last thing Raine wanted was for there to be any doubt that their marriage was solid, that they were the perfect couple, the perfect team, to bring a level-one trauma center to Highland Falls. The trauma center had been Raine's lifelong dream.

She'd lost her brother in a car accident when they were teenagers. Raine believed that he would have survived if the local hospital had been better equipped. Cal hadn't been as convinced but he'd agreed to move back to their hometown for his stepdaughter's sake. But after Bri's accident, he'd been as committed to the trauma center as Raine. If he and Raine hadn't been in Highland Falls at the time of Bri's accident, she wouldn't have survived.

"Oh my gosh, do not tell her that, Cal. You won't get a moment's peace. I'm telling you, Ellie will check in with you every day, and not once, but at least three times." She handed him the bags of groceries. "As much as I want my sister to go on her honeymoon, I don't want you to sacrifice your sanity for me."

Cal smiled. "She's not that bad."

"Trust me, she is. I mean, she's a wonderful sister, and I adore her but—" She broke off when Raine walked to his side.

"Sorry to interrupt you two but there are a few things we need to discuss before our presentation, Cal." She gave Bri a thin-lipped smile. "And you have an appoint-ment with Dr. Buchanan to run your tests, don't you?"

"You're right. I do. Sorry for keeping you." Bri reached up to take the bags from Cal. "I'll call Nate and ask him to pick up the groceries."

Cal moved the bags out of her reach. "No, we had a bargain. You're keeping your end of it, and I plan on keeping mine."

"Thank you. I really appreciate it." She started the truck and gave them a self-conscious smile. "Good luck with your presentation."

"You made me a promise too," Raine said.

"I haven't forgotten," he said, watching as Bri drove away.

Last year, he'd put his life on hold for Izzy, his step-daughter. She hadn't reacted well when Cal and Raine told her they were getting divorced. The day after he'd moved out, Izzy started skipping school. Within a month, she was at risk of failing her year. Cal met with her prin-cipal in hopes of turning things around only to learn that Izzy failing her year was the least of their concerns.

Raine had suggested that a move from Washington, DC, to their small hometown might be the change Izzy needed. Cal had agreed it was worth a try. He'd been ready for a change himself, and he'd do anything for the stepdaughter he adored. So far it seemed to be working. Izzy's grades had improved, and she was in a better place. But Cal worried what would happen when he eventually moved out.

Raine elbowed him. "You haven't heard a word I said, have you?"

"About keeping my promise to you? Yeah. I answered you."

"No. What I said while you were preoccupied with thoughts of your ex."

"You're not a mind reader, Raine. I wasn't—"

"No, but I know you. Which is why I said that the only way you can keep your promise to me is to stay away from Brianna MacLeod."

"You can't be serious?"

"I've never been more serious, Cal. It's obvious you still have feelings for her, and if I can tell, so can everyone else. Including my mother and members of the town council. You know, the people whose votes we need to get the trauma center approved and off the ground."

"I don't know what you think you saw, but I don't have feelings for Bri. At least not romantic ones. We have a history together. I care about her. I'm worried about her, and I'll do whatever I can to ensure she recovers from her injuries. The same as I'd do for any of my patients."

"You do not look at your patients the way you look at her, Cal. If you did—"

"Stop," he said as he walked to his jeep. "You're getting worked up over nothing. But I've said it before, and I'll say it again: I don't think it's a good idea that we keep up this charade. It shouldn't matter to your mother or anyone else whether we're married or not."

"Really? My mother and David adore you, Cal. In their eyes, you can do no wrong. The only reason they even considered throwing their support behind me taking over as hospital administrator and spearheading the expansion is because you support me. You believe in me."

"I'd support you and your vision for the trauma center even if we weren't married, Raine. One has nothing to do with the other. You're a brilliant physician, and you'll make an equally brilliant administrator when David retires." Cal opened the driver's-side door, leaning inside to put the groceries on the passenger seat.

"But you're not my mother and you're not David. When they look at me, they see a reckless, out-of-control teenager who got pregnant at eighteen. And it's not as if I can say, 'Don't look at what I did as a kid. Look at what I've done as an adult.' My personal and professional track records don't exactly inspire faith in my ability to stick around or to follow through on a project, especially a project this size. It took three interviews before they hired me at GW, and need I remind you that you're the reason I got the job? If it wasn't for your recommendation, they never would have hired me."

Raine was three years older than Cal and had run with a different crowd, so he hadn't really known her growing up. They'd met in a bar in DC and got to talking. They had Highland Falls and their profession in common, which was probably why they immediately hit it off. It didn't hurt that Raine was beautiful and that Cal had been lonely. Back then, he was a lot like Raine. All he did was work. But he'd wanted more from life. He'd wanted a family.

He'd gotten that with Raine and Izzy. But within two years of being married, he'd discovered his dreams for the future and Raine's were very different. She didn't want any more kids, and work-life balance didn't factor into her vocabulary. She was happiest at work.

The signs had been there from the beginning, but he'd chosen to ignore them. He'd spent his entire medical career at George Washington University Hospital, whereas Raine had worked at four hospitals in four different states. When he'd asked her about it, she'd told him she was a better doctor because of it, and he'd believed her. But it didn't look great on her résumé, and moving around as much as she had, had been tough on Izzy.

"No doubt they rue the day they hired me," Raine continued with an impish grin. "I bet they're still cursing me for stealing away their golden boy. My mother and David feel the same way about you. If they thought I'd messed up another marriage, especially a marriage with you, they'd never trust me with a project this size." And that had been the biggest sign he'd ignored. Raine had been married three times now.

Cal couldn't deny there was some truth to her concerns. When they'd first approached David and Winter with their proposal to turn Highland Falls General into a level-one trauma center, they'd each taken Cal aside to voice their concerns privately, which was how he'd ended up still living with Raine, even though they were legally separated.

"You know what? I'm not as concerned about their reaction as I'm concerned about how this impacts Izzy. When we moved back, I agreed to wait six months before getting a place of my own. It's been over a year, Raine. I'm worried that she's convinced herself everything's good between us," he said as he got into the jeep.

"It's not like we share a bedroom, Cal. Izzy's sixteen, and she's smart. She knows how important the trauma center is to us, and she knows what her grandmother is like. Besides, there are lots of married couples who split up and still live together for financial reasons."

"Yeah, but I'm sure everyone knows why they're living together. I just don't want Izzy confused. I don't want a repeat of last year when I eventually move out."

"Funny how this has just become an issue for you now, Cal."

"It has nothing to do with Bri if that's what you're implying. I've brought this up with you before. Numerous times."

"Not in the past few months, you haven't."

"Maybe because I've had a lot on my plate with Emma." His sister's fiancé had been killed in the line of duty in April. Brad and Em were detectives with the Metropolitan Nashville Police Department, and Em had witnessed the shooting that had claimed her fiancé's life. Cal had spent most of his time off this summer in Nashville, trying to convince his sister to move back home. He was worried about her.

He glanced at his watch. "I have to drop groceries off at the inn and throw on a stew for dinner so I'll probably be a few minutes late."

"Obviously there's nothing I can say to convince you not to go to the inn. Just make it quick. But you don't have time to make a stew. We'll order pizza."

"We ordered pizza last night. Even Izzy's getting sick of it. Besides, it'll take me five minutes to throw everything into the Crock-Pot. If your mother complains that

I'm late, tell her that's what happens when she springs a meeting on us." Unlike her daughter, Winter was a stickler for punctuality. Cal was the same but he wasn't happy with the short notice. He didn't think it was fair that they were expected to drop everything at the last minute. He was actually surprised that Winter expected them to. It wasn't like her.

"I was the one who changed the meeting from next week to today," Raine admitted, pulling a face.

"Why would you do that?"

"To take advantage of you being named Hometown Hero of the Week." She laughed when Cal groaned. "Everybody loves a hero, darling. And we need every advantage to win over the holdouts."

By the time Cal arrived at the town hall, he was twenty-five minutes late for the meeting, and Raine had been burning up his phone with texts. He had a feeling his Hometown Hero status wouldn't save him if the vote didn't go their way.

He walked into the two-story redbrick building, waving to the woman working the front desk as he took the stairs to the second floor two at a time. There wasn't a lot of noise coming from the room at the end of the hall where the council held their meetings. Cal had hoped to sneak in unnoticed but apparently not much was going his way today. Everyone turned when he walked into the room.

The council members sat at a long table in the front of the room, with the mayor sitting in the middle. Four council members sat on either side of her. If Cal read the room correctly—and he knew the council members fairly well—the members to the left of Winter were for the trauma center, while the four on the right were against it. He made the summation based on who looked happy to see him and who didn't.

His ex–mother-in-law—she didn't know she was his ex yet, and if Raine had her way, probably wouldn't for months to come—raised her eyebrow and then cast a pointed look in her daughter's direction.

Raine sat in the front row, looking like she could spit nails as she stared down Harlan Smith, the owner of the *Highland Falls Herald* and the trauma center's most vocal opponent. Harlan wanted the land in question used for a casino, not the hospital expansion that would be required for the trauma center.

Cal and Raine had initially thought the casino would be a nonissue. North Carolina's gambling laws were relatively strict, and casinos were only allowed on Native American land. But apparently the consortium behind the bid had found a loophole that had cleared the way for a casino to be built in Highland Falls.

Cal nodded at several people he knew in the audience while taking a seat beside Raine. The council members went back to huddling in their small groups, like boxers waiting for the bell to ring.

"How's it going?" he whispered.

Raine raised a hand to her mouth, murmuring crossly, "How do you think it's going? You're the charming one, not me. I needed you."

"You can be charming when you want to be." She could but Raine's brand of charm never gave anyone the warm fuzzies. And while she was an incredible surgeon, her bedside manner was nothing to write home about. But Raine's take-charge, don't-mess-with-me attitude would suit her position as hospital administrator well.

She snorted. "I'm not feeling so charming now. Or happy with Brianna MacLeod. If you hadn't gone to the inn, you would have been here to help me deal with Harlan. He kept interrupting me with questions."

"Don't blame Bri. I'm the one who insisted she go to the hospital. And I wasn't at the inn that long." Ellie hadn't taken a lot of convincing to reconsider canceling her honeymoon. As soon as he offered to check on Bri every day—something he didn't plan on sharing with Raine—the strain had melted from Ellie's face. "Izzy got home as I was heading out the door. She seemed upset, and I didn't want to leave without talking to her." Not that it had done him much good. She'd shrugged off his concern, telling him she was fine.

Raine appeared more concerned about Harlan than about her daughter. Her eyes narrowed on the fifty-something man and the three other council members as they broke from their huddle. Harlan tapped a piece of paper on the table. "We're ready to vote, Mayor," he said, sending a smug smile Raine and Cal's way.

"He's convinced them to vote with him, Cal. What are we going to do?"

"It'll be up to your mother to decide. She's the one who'll have to break the tie." Cal had no doubt that's how it would play out. The four local businesswomen and council members to Winter's left were securely in the trauma center's camp. They were also members of the Sisterhood, a group of influential women devoted to the

Highland Falls community. Bri's grandmother, known to everyone as Granny MacLeod, was one of them.

Cal didn't envy Winter having to break the tie. He was pretty sure she'd vote for the trauma center, but it was a big risk for her to take, given that Raine was her daughter and Winter was heading into an election year—issues Harlan had raised every chance he got. Cal had little doubt the man was going to throw his hat into the mayoral ring.

Winter glanced at the three men and the one woman on her right and briefly closed her eyes. Raine was right, and so was he. Winter would be the tiebreaker, and she knew it.

"Once you've voted, fold your papers in half, and give them to Nina," Winter directed, nodding at the silver-haired Black woman who came to her feet and took her place at the end of the table.

Nina was Winter's right-hand woman and the town's manager. They'd been close friends growing up, and she trusted the other woman to have her back. As a certified public account, Nina was also well qualified for the position. Winter had named Nina town manager a week after she was elected to office.

The two women shared a look that suggested this was a scenario they'd hoped to avoid. But knowing them as well as he did, Cal was sure they had a plan in case of a tie, one that would protect Winter's back. What he didn't know was how that plan would impact their proposal. Five minutes later, they found out.

"Because my daughter has a vested interest in the trauma center, Nina will vote in my place to avoid any perception of conflict of interest." Winter glanced at Harlan. "Are there any objections to Nina voting in my stead?"

Harlan and the council members had a whispered conversation. Then he straightened in his chair. "We're in agreement with the substitution, Mayor," he said, with another smug smile for Raine.

It was common knowledge in Highland Falls that Raine and Nina had a complicated relationship. Nina's son was Raine's first husband.

When Winter got up from the table and Nina took her place, Raine reached for Cal's hand. She was as nervous as Harlan was confident.

"I cast my vote in favor of the trauma center," Nina said.

Raine's shoulders sagged in relief, and Harlan slammed his palms on the table. In the audience, supporters of the trauma center cheered while supporters of the casino booed.

"I demand we vote again with an objective third party standing in for the mayor," Harlan yelled to make himself heard over the mostly cheering crowd.

"Quiet," Nina said to the spectators, banging the gavel on the table. "Your agreement to my taking the mayor's place is on record, Harlan, but I wasn't finished."

Cal didn't like how neither Nina nor Winter would look at them, and he wasn't the only one who noticed. Raine leaned into him, whispering, "Nina's up to something. She's figured out a way to mess with me. The woman hates me."

"She doesn't hate you, and you know as well as I

do how she feels about the casino," he whispered back, giving her hand a comforting squeeze. "She's not going to do anything that would put the trauma center in jeopardy." He hoped.

"Harlan, one of your objections to the trauma center is the infrastructure costs to the town, and it's one we share." She held up a legal document. "The consortium behind the casino would have covered the costs, so we are asking that Dr. Scott and Dr. Johnson-Scott do the same."

"You can't be serious!" Raine objected, rising from her chair. "The casino—"

Cal tugged on her hand to keep her in place. "Calm down," he murmured. While he understood how she felt, she had to keep her cool. Harlan had been looking for any way to discredit them over the past couple of months.

"You will have six weeks to provide proof that the funds have been set aside in trust for infrastructure costs," Nina continued. "If at that time, you can't, the approval for the trauma center will be null and void."

Raine stared at her mother with a betrayed expression on her face when Winter took Nina's place and adjourned the meeting.

Raine turned to him. "How could she blindside us like that? My own mother."

"Don't take it personally. It's not as if we didn't know the infrastructure costs were a concern. We got the approval, and we'll raise the funds." He drew her to her feet.

"Do you have any idea how much money we're talking about, Cal? I have no idea how we're going to raise that kind of money in six weeks." She forced a smile for the petite redhead who joined them. Abby Mackenzie was a famous social media celebrity who called Highland Falls home.

"I do," Abby said. "I didn't mean to eavesdrop, but honestly, one look at your face, Raine, and everyone here knew you're worried about the money and the deadline."

Cal's cell phone rang. He removed it from his jeans pocket and glanced at the screen. It was the Nashville police department. "Sorry. I have to take this." Working to keep his mind from going to worst-case scenarios, he answered while walking toward the door.

"Dr. Scott, it's Lieutenant Graves."

"Is my sister okay?"

"Physically, she's fine. But as you know, I was concerned that she was coming back to work too soon even though she was cleared for duty. Today, my concerns were validated." He went on to tell Cal what had transpired. Em had believed she'd seen a man she suspected was connected to her fiancé's murder and had gone in pursuit, a car chase that her lieutenant deemed an unnecessary risk. And it wasn't the first time. "For Em's own good, I've put her on six months' leave without pay. She didn't take the news well."

"I understand, and I appreciate you calling and letting me know what's going on, Lieutenant." Because he wouldn't have heard how bad it had gotten from Em.

"I'm worried about her, Dr. Scott, and so are her fellow officers. Your sister is well liked and respected. Hell, she's my best detective, and I could use her right now, but she's a loose cannon, and I'm afraid she'll do something she can't come back from."

He had a feeling Em's boss wasn't telling him everything. "You did the right thing. I'll head for Nashville now."

The lieutenant blew out a breath. "Good. I'm glad to hear it. I don't think she should be alone."

"She won't be. I'm bringing her home with me." If he had to drag her kicking and screaming. Cal thanked Em's boss and disconnected. As he headed back into the meeting room, he nearly knocked over Abby Mackenzie. He reached out to steady her. "Sorry. I'm a little preoccupied."

She waved off his apology. "Don't worry about it. Is everything okay? You looked worried when you took the call."

He glanced to where Raine was in a heated conversation with her mother and Nina. Then he returned his attention to Abby. "It was about my sister. I have to head to Nashville, and I'm hoping to convince her to come home with me."

"I heard about her fiancé. If there's anything I can do, let me know."

"Thanks, I...actually, there may be something you can do for me." Abby ran a local charity with Mallory Buchanan called Golden Girls. They matched senior women with affordable housing.

His sister wouldn't have a paycheck coming in, but she also wouldn't want to move in with him. And given his fake-relationship status with Raine, he had a feeling she would balk at the idea of Em living with them anyway.

"I'm going to need a place for my sister to stay for a few months, preferably close to me. You wouldn't happen to know if there's anything available around Marigold Lane, would you?"

"Give me two seconds. I have someone who might be willing to rent." She typed in a number on her phone. "How would your sister feel about living with someone?"

She'd hate it, but Cal liked the idea. He didn't want Em on her own, and living with a nice, sympathetic grandmotherly type might be just what she needed. "She'd be good with splitting costs with someone." It wasn't exactly a lie.

Abby smiled and brought the phone to her ear. "Mr. Jones, it's Abby Mackenzie. I was just wondering if you'd made a decision on your house yet. Really?" She gave Cal a thumbs-up. "That's great. Don't worry about that. The person I have in mind would want to move in almost immediately." Abby paused and then nodded. "I'm sure that won't be a problem. Okay, I'll get back to you first thing tomorrow." She raised a questioning brow at Cal, and he nodded. "We can firm up details then."

"Thanks, Abby," Cal said when she disconnected. "You're a lifesaver."

"My pleasure. The house is 21 Marigold Lane, just down the street from you, so you'll be able to keep an eye on your sister."

"Don't tell her that or she won't move in. She thinks I'm overprotective as it is."

"She's lucky she has a brother who cares. But she

grew up here so she must have friends you can ask to look in on her too."

"The only friend she has who still lives in town is Brianna MacLeod. But they haven't spoken in almost a decade."

"They had a falling-out?"

"You could say that." He glanced at Raine, who was walking their way. He wasn't looking forward to telling her he had to leave. "Thanks again, Abby. I'll give you a call in the morning."

"I'm happy to help, but you'll need my number." She gave him her number, and he entered it into his phone.

"I should be able to confirm when Em will be moving in by then," Cal said, glancing at his phone, which is why he didn't realize Raine was within hearing distance. He'd wanted to break the news without an audience.

"And where exactly is your sister moving?" Raine asked.

"Just down the street from you. Isn't that great?" Abby smiled, then, obviously noting Raine's less-than-thrilled expression, murmured, "Or maybe not so great."

Chapter Five

♥

Bri changed out of the blue paper hospital gown into her clothes and rejoined Mallory, her friend and doctor, who sat on a stool making notes on her iPad. Bri took a seat on the examination table across from her. They were waiting for Cal to arrive and go over the results from her tests. She'd been poked, prodded, and scanned for the last two hours and was anxious to leave. She was also anxious about the results...and seeing Cal again.

She was so used to the dull, heavy weight in her stomach that she hadn't immediately noticed it had been replaced by butterflies in response to Cal's news. At first, she'd wondered if she'd heard him right, and then she'd had trouble believing him. As she'd pointed out, the evidence didn't support his claim. Except he had no reason to lie about his separation. He'd never lied to her in the past. Cal had a reputation for being bluntly honest, something she'd experienced firsthand.

It had taken a moment to recognize the emotion fluttering around in her stomach. She wished she could blame it on nerves, but she was very much afraid it had been hopeful flutters, maybe even excited ones. Definitely not the appropriate response to learning that your first love, who'd broken your heart, was separated from his wife.

Mallory's phone chimed, drawing Bri from her disturbing and inappropriate thoughts. Mallory reached for her phone and glanced at the screen, then swiveled on the stool to face Bri.

Uh, what was with the expression on Mallory's face? She looked concerned. Sympathetic even. Bri's pulse began to race. No, she ordered her brain. This was not the time for a panic attack. If something was wrong, Cal would fix it. She'd be fine.

"There's been a change of plan," Mallory said. "Cal won't be joining us to go over the results. He'll give you a call sometime this week."

"Can't you give me the results?" She was relieved that she didn't have to see Cal but no way could she put off hearing the news. If she had too much time to think, her mind would go to the worst-case scenarios. She'd be up half the night on Google, and the next thing she knew, she'd be exhibiting symptoms for some weird and obscure disease.

"I can, but I think it's best if Cal does."

"How bad is it? Do I have to have another surgery? It's not life-threatening, is it?"

Mallory stared at her with her mouth hanging open. Then she gave her head a small shake and got up from the stool, coming over to take Bri's hands in hers. "I'm sorry. I should have realized coming to the hospital would be a trigger for you. It didn't help that we've run so many tests. I think Cal was just so relieved that

he finally got you in here, he ran every possible test he
could think of."

"So it's nothing serious?"

"As far as I can see from the scans, the rod, plates, and
screws haven't shifted, and the femur bone is healing.
Maybe not at the rate Cal would like to see, but I'll let
him speak to that. I'm not the expert, he is. But there are
a couple of issues that I can address with you." Mallory
smiled and then walked back to the counter. Retrieving
her iPad, she sat on the stool and rolled it closer to Bri.

Here it comes, Bri thought, steeling herself for the
bad news. She clasped her hands in her lap, squeezing
tight. Whatever it was, she wouldn't overreact. Or have
a panic attack.

"Cal mentioned that you're still having migraines and
difficulty sleeping."

"We've talked about that though."

Mallory smiled. "We have, but that was three months
ago. I told you to come back if there was no improve-
ment."

"I have a TBI, Mallory."

"You do, but I think your symptoms are being exacer-
bated by stress."

"I agree. They probably are. But now that my divorce
is almost final, I'm sure my symptoms will—" Bri broke
off when the door opened and Raine entered the room.

"Hi, Dr. Buchanan. I hope you don't mind me dropping in. My husband insisted that I check on Bri." She
rolled her eyes. "You know what he's like with his
patients."

"I don't mind at all," Mallory said. "Cal mentioned

he had to go to Nashville. I hope everything's okay with his sister."

"Did something happen to Em?" Bri asked.

Growing up, Cal's sister had been Bri's summertime best friend. They'd been inseparable until the day Bri had done the unthinkable and unacceptable in Em's eyes—she'd fallen for her BFF's brother. Bri's teenage self hadn't understood why Em hated her for falling in love with Cal. But as an adult, she realized that, from Em's perspective, it must have felt like Bri had abandoned her for Cal.

Raine waved her hand as if it was nothing. "She had an issue at work, and her lieutenant insisted she take some time off. I'm sure she's fine, but try telling that to my husband. The poor darling can't seem to help himself. He has a hero complex. Always ready to rescue a damsel in distress." She gave Bri a pointed look before continuing, "Honestly, it's no wonder so many of his female patients fall in love with him."

Wow, if that wasn't a dig at her, Bri didn't know what was. And she had no idea what Cal was playing at, but clearly, in his wife's eyes they were still married, and she planned for them to stay that way.

"That's great news about the trauma center, isn't it?" Mallory said to Bri as they left the hospital together twenty minutes later.

Bri was giving her a ride home. Gabe had dropped Mallory off that morning, and he was with their kids at football tryouts. Between them, Mallory and Gabe had five boys. They'd welcomed an adorable baby girl last year.

"Wonderful news," Bri agreed. "It sounds like Cal and Raine have put a lot of time and effort into making it happen."

After Raine had delivered her completely unnecessary shot about Cal—as if Bri would misconstrue his concern as anything other than professional—she'd shared the news that the town council had approved their plan to turn Highland Falls General into a level-one trauma center.

"They have, and I'm so happy it finally paid off for them. For all of us, really. The trauma center will be great for the hospital and the community. Although not everyone in Highland Falls feels that way."

"Really? How come?" Bri asked as they reached the truck, and Mallory shared about the owner of the *Highland Falls Herald* and his efforts to have a casino built instead.

"I have a feeling now that the vote has gone in Cal and Bri's favor, he'll ramp up his campaign to discredit them and the trauma center," Mallory added as she got into the truck with Bri. "It's going to be difficult enough for them to raise the funds needed to cover the infrastructure costs through private donations without Harlan stirring the pot."

"It sounds like they could use Abby's help." Abby Mackenzie was a social media rock star. She'd successfully turned around the fortunes of several local businesses, including Mirror Lake Inn.

Mallory's phone pinged. She glanced at the screen and laughed. "Speak of the devil." She turned the phone to Bri. "It looks like we have more than just the trauma center's approval to celebrate."

"Yes!" Bri high-fived Mallory and then started the truck. The honeymoon was back on. It looked like Cal had gotten through to her sister.

Abby was at the inn, helping Ellie figure out if she needed to go clothes shopping for the trip. She'd invited Mallory and Sadie, Bri and Ellie's cousin, to join them. Except technically, Sadie wasn't Bri's blood relative. But the MacLeod side of the family had gone out of their way to assure her that she was, and always would be, one of them.

"I guess I'm going with you to the inn." Mallory's cell pinged again. "They've ordered pizza from Zia Maria's."

"Perfect." Bri drove out of the parking lot and onto the side street, relieved not to have to cook tonight's celebratory dinner. The tests and stress had worn her out. She'd make Ellie and Nate their Scottish-themed meal tomorrow.

She turned onto Main Street and smiled at Mallory. "I should have known Ellie had decided to go on their honeymoon. She didn't text me the entire time I was at the hospital."

Mallory grinned. "She texted me twice."

"Of course she did," Bri said with an exasperated laugh. "But I guess I can't complain. She could have been texting both of us nonstop like she did at my last appointment with you."

"She is a little hypervigilant, isn't she? But in her defense, if I had a sister who'd gone through what you have, I'd be the same. The time away will be good for her. For both of you."

"I think so too. But honestly, unless I make some changes, like figuring out what I'm doing with my life, we'll just fall back into the same pattern as soon as she comes home."

"You're not thinking of moving back to Charlotte, are you?"

"No. Other than my overly protective family driving me crazy at times, I love being close to them, and I really do like living in Highland Falls." She gave Mallory a half smile. "If you can call what I've been doing living. You know, this is the longest I've been away from the inn on my own. How pathetic is that?"

"You're being too hard on yourself, Bri."

"No. I'm beginning to think I haven't been hard enough on myself." When Mallory opened her mouth, no doubt to point out how extensive her injuries had been, Bri said, "I had a good excuse for the first six months. I don't anymore. I'm lucky to be alive, and it's about time I focus on that instead of wondering what would have happened if I'd done things differently. Like what if I hadn't married Richard? What if I hadn't told him I was leaving him when we were alone? I knew—know—better than anyone how dangerous that was but I wasn't thinking."

"What happened to you wasn't your fault. I know you've heard the same question as me: *Why didn't she or he just leave?* As if it's that simple. What they should be asking is *Why didn't he or she stop?* Until we stop blaming the victim and putting the onus on the abuser where it belongs, this epidemic of abuse will continue."

Mallory was right. It was an epidemic. One in three

women and one in four men experienced some form of physical violence by an intimate partner. The statistics were chilling.

"Intellectually, I know that. I'm just not there yet emotionally," she admitted.

Mallory rubbed her arm. "You'll get there. And you know I'm here for you, day or night."

"I do. You've been a great friend, and you're a wonderful doctor. I know that at times I haven't been the easiest patient to deal with, but I hope you know how much I've appreciated your support." Bri was luckier than most. She had a loving family and friends who genuinely cared about her, and she lived in a close and supportive community.

Too many victims of abuse were on their own, dealing with frightened children on top of their own trauma while at the same time struggling to get by financially. So yes, Bri knew how truly lucky she was. And it was about time she started focusing on her blessings and not on everything she'd lost.

"Thank you. I'm just glad you trusted me enough to open up. But I still think you'd benefit from additional counseling."

"Talk therapy works, and I'm comfortable talking to you."

"A support group would be helpful too. I just wish we had one here in Highland Falls." Mallory smiled. "Hint, hint."

Mallory had brought up the idea of Bri starting a support group at her last appointment.

"I'm not there yet," Bri said. She'd lost confidence in

her counseling abilities, and she wasn't sure she'd ever regain them.

"We've had this conversation before so I won't pressure you, but I don't think you'll get there until you get back to work, Bri. Take it slow, take on one or two clients. I have several patients I'd love to refer to you."

She shook her head, feeling a little frantic at the thought of taking on clients but at the same time feeling a deep sense of loss at the thought of never practicing again. She'd loved being a marriage and family therapist. There was nothing more rewarding than being part of someone's journey to a healthier and happier relationship, even if that relationship was with themselves, which was often the key to healing.

"I'm sorry. I said I wasn't going to pressure you but that's exactly what I did," Mallory said.

"Please don't apologize. I know you have my best interests at heart, and I really appreciate it. But right now, all I can focus on is making sure Ellie and Nate get on that plane for Scotland, and that they have the romantic honeymoon they deserve."

"They will if they didn't cancel their reservation at Kincraig Castle. Did Ellie show you the photos? It's incredible."

"The one near Inverness?"

Mallory nodded, and Bri made a mental note to call and make sure they hadn't canceled the reservation. If they had, she'd rebook it and order a welcome basket of champagne and chocolates for their room.

The thought lightened Bri's mood, and she chatted with Mallory about Nate and Ellie's adventurous itinerary as she drove the rest of the way to the inn. As she pulled into the inn's parking lot, she spotted her grandfather and his best friend walking toward them. Jonathan Knight, known to everyone as "the judge," had been renting a room at the inn for so long he'd become part of the family.

Noting her grandfather's dour expression, Bri said, "I'm in trouble now. I've probably made them late for their weekly poker game."

Mallory laughed. "I'll take the rap, but I have a feeling Joe will be as happy as your sister that you had your follow-up today."

"You'd think. But that is definitely not his happy face," Bri said as she and Mallory got out of the truck.

Mallory said hello to Joe and Jonathan and then headed for the inn.

"Sorry I'm late. My follow-up appointment at the hospital went longer than I expected," she said, in hopes the reminder of where she'd been would soften her grandfather's expression. When it didn't, she added in that long-forgotten, excited voice she'd used on her sister earlier, "Isn't it great? Ellie and Nate are finally going on their honeymoon!"

Her grandfather scowled at her as she handed him the keys. "You won't be thinking it's so great when you hear the news that goes along with it."

"Don't be like that, Joe," the judge tsked. "It's a nice thing your daughter is doing."

Bri froze. "What's Mom doing?"

"She's moving in when your sister and Nate go on their honeymoon." Her grandfather pointed at Bri, shooting a triumphant smile at the judge. "See, she feels the same way as me."

Bri could almost guarantee that her feelings about her mother moving in were far worse than her grandfather's. She'd barely been able to look at her mother, or speak to her, since the day she'd revealed the truth about Bri's parentage and turned her world upside down.

Everything Bri had believed about herself had been based on a lie. She'd grieved the loss of her identity. She was still grieving. Her feet were firmly stuck on the second step of the journey through grief: anger.

The judge crossed his arms, giving Bri and her grandfather a look that she imagined he'd used to quell dissension in his courtroom. "Unless the two of you want Ellie to cancel her trip, I'd suggest you make peace with the fact that Miranda is moving in. If you ask me, it's about time you gave her a chance. She's trying to make up for her past mistakes. And if Ellie can forgive her, so can you. Both of you."

The judge was right. Despite everything that their mother had put Ellie through, her sister had somehow managed to forgive Miranda. At fifteen, Ellie had inadvertently learned of their mother's affair and Bri's parentage. In an effort to protect herself and her secret, Miranda had gaslighted Ellie for most of her teenage years.

And Bri had spent those same years trying to figure out why the relationship between her mother and her sister was so fraught. It was one of the reasons she'd chosen family therapy as a career, and why she was desperate to make it up to Ellie for all the years she'd suffered because of her.

"Easy for you to say," her grandfather muttered. Then, releasing a put-upon breath, he shrugged. "What do you think, Bri, my love? Can we put up with your mother for two weeks without strangling her?"

Whenever their mother visited—which thankfully wasn't often, because she worked full-time and lived five hours from Highland Falls—Bri would spend the entire time biting her tongue in order to hold back everything she wanted to say. Her mother's visits left her exhausted and in a horrible mood that lasted for days. There was no way she could live under the same roof with her for two weeks. Except it seemed she didn't have a choice, given that her sister's happiness was at stake.

Unless... "Don't worry, Grandpa. I'll talk to Ellie. I'll convince her that you and I are perfectly capable of managing the inn on our own."

It wasn't as if they'd actually be running the inn on their own. Ever since *Love Blooms at Mirror Lake Inn* had aired on TV—a movie that had been filmed at the inn last year—both the restaurant and the guest rooms were typically booked solid. The increase in business allowed Ellie to hire two cooks, three waitresses, and two housekeepers.

"Good luck with that. I've already tried. Your sister's gotten it into her head that you need more than me and the judge looking out for you."

"Didn't Cal tell her how well I was doing?"

"He did. Even offered to check in on you every day. But you know your sister. She's a regular mother hen where you're concerned. She seems to think the only one better than her to look out for you is your mother."

Bri ground her back molars together. She was a better actress than she thought if Ellie bought that all was well between Bri and her mother.

Her grandfather patted her shoulder. "It looks like we'll just have to suck it up, my love."

Bri nodded, saying a distracted goodbye to Joe and the judge. She had to think of something to convince Ellie that she didn't need a keeper. Her leg cramped on the short walk to the inn, and she gritted her teeth as she used the railing to pull herself up the three steps to the wraparound porch. The wooden rocking chairs with the red-and-black plaid blankets over each arm looked inviting.

She contemplated sitting down, wrapping a blanket around her shoulders, and taking a nap. But thoughts of her mother's impending arrival would no doubt keep her awake. Even the view of the ornamental grasses she'd planted in the garden this spring, their blaze of red foliage gently swaying in the breeze, wouldn't be enough to distract her from her troubles today. She needed a solution to her problem.

Praying one came to her before she saw her sister, Bri entered the inn. A woman was on the phone behind the reception desk. It was one of the housekeepers. The staff was wonderful at multitasking.

Bri smiled and mouthed, *Ellie?*

Entertainment room, the woman mouthed back, giving Bri an excited thumbs-up. The staff would be as happy as Bri that Ellie and Nate were taking their honeymoon. Everyone loved her sister and brother-in-law.

Bri turned to walk through the dining room, pasting

a smile on her face to hide her pained grimaces in case some of the diners glanced her way.

One of the waitresses looked up from laying out cutlery on a table and gave her a sympathetic smile. "Your leg acting up today?"

"Low-pressure system coming in. If you ever need a weather report, just ask me."

The waitress laughed. "My grandmother's the same."

Bri smiled instead of sighing. If the waitress didn't buy her *I'm totally fine* act, there was no way she'd be able to convince Ellie she didn't need a babysitter. But just as she reached the closed double doors leading into the entertainment room, she overheard one of the waitresses telling the cook that she'd found a place of her own.

"Now I have to convince my mother to help me with the deposit," the waitress said, and the cook laughed.

"Your brother just left for college, honey. No way your mother is going to let her baby girl move out too."

"Maybe if she stopped treating me like a baby, I wouldn't need to move out."

Bri smiled. The waitress had given her the perfect way to convince Ellie she didn't need a keeper. Bri took a deep breath, plastered a bright and hopefully convincing smile on her face, and opened the door to the entertainment room.

The four women turned to greet her while sitting on the floor going through what looked like Ellie's entire wardrobe.

"Hey, where's the pizza? I'm starved." She wasn't but Ellie had been worried that Bri wasn't eating enough because she was depressed. "And where's the champagne? I hear we have some big news to celebrate."

She pretended to be looking around for the champagne with that fake smile still on her face when what she was really doing was trying to figure out the quickest way to reach the sofa without tripping over the piles of clothing and falling on her face.

Her sister laughed and reached behind her for a bottle. "I've got it. We were waiting for you."

Seeing Ellie's beautiful face lit up with excitement brought a genuine smile to Bri's face. She wouldn't do anything that might steal even a smidgen of her sister's joy. If she couldn't convince Ellie that Bri and her grandfather were fine on their own, then she'd have no choice but to suck it up.

She mentally crossed her fingers. "Good, because I have some exciting news of my own to share." She lurched toward the leather sectional and tossed her cane, praying she didn't hit anyone with it while at the same time hoping that it looked like she meant to throw herself onto the sofa because she was over the moon about her own news. She stuck her hand in the cushion to keep from falling off.

Rolling onto her back, she turned her head. "You didn't tell them, did you?" she said to Mallory. Bri didn't want her sister to think this had anything to do with their mother coming to stay.

Mallory gave her a *what the heck are you talking about?* look before managing a believable, "No, of course not."

"Good." Bri pushed herself upright. "Now that I've

got a clean bill of health and my divorce is final in two days, I've decided it's about time I got on with my life. So"—she made a *ta-da* gesture with her hands—"I'm moving out."

"You're not moving back to Charlotte, are you?" Ellie asked, a touch of panic in her voice.

"No. I'm going to find a place of my own in Highland Falls. I'll rent at first, of course. Something small with a garden." She searched her sister's face. "You're not upset, are you? I love you, and I love the inn, but I think it's time. Don't you?"

Ellie smiled and nodded. "Even though I'll miss having you around, I'm happy you feel ready to move on with your life. That's a huge step. Have you found a place already?"

"No, not yet. But I'm sure I'll find something soon."

"I might have exactly what you're looking for," Abby said. "There's a house on Marigold Lane for rent, and the owner specifically requested someone who likes to garden."

Her sister clapped her hands. "That sounds perfect, Bri."

Wait a sec. She didn't want to move out now! She was comfortable here. She felt safe here, safe and protected.

"There's just one thing," Abby said before Bri could come up with a believable excuse that didn't sound like she wasn't ready to move out. "The only reason it's available is because Mrs. Randall backed out an hour ago. She decided to move in with her daughter." Abby glanced from Ellie to Bri. "But I do have another tenant for the house. I should know by tomorrow morning when she's moving in."

Thank goodness for small mercies. "It sounds lovely, but I'd prefer to live alone," Bri said at the same time Ellie said, "It's perfect. She'll take it."

"No, I won't. I don't want to live with someone." What the heck was going on? Now her sister couldn't wait to get rid of her?

"Please, for me," Ellie said, making prayer hands. "I'd feel so much better if you lived with someone. I'd worry if you were on your own."

Bri reminded herself she wasn't actually moving out. This was simply an act so Ellie would tell their mother she wasn't needed. Bri could back out the second Ellie left for the airport.

"Okay. If it makes you happy, I'll take it," Bri said with a martyr's smile on her face.

"Great. There's just one thing: the homeowner wants the tenants moved in by this weekend."

"Oh, I couldn't—" Bri began before Ellie interrupted her.

"Yay!" her sister cheered. "I'll be here to help you move in and set up your room. I'm so excited." Ellie turned to Abby. "Do you have the lease agreement?"

Chapter Six

♥

Cal knocked on the door to his sister's apartment. He'd tried calling her a couple of times when he was on the road to let her know he was on his way. She hadn't answered so he'd texted her when he'd stopped for gas and again when he'd stopped to pick up pizza and beer. She didn't respond but she'd read his texts.

He knocked again. "Em, it's me. Open up." He glanced up and down the hall with its pewter walls and gray carpeted floor, then pressed his ear to the door.

He heard the faint sound of voices, which he assumed were coming from the TV. Em had never been overly social and understandably was even less so since Brad died. She'd barely tolerated Cal's presence this summer. Other than the low drone of the television, he didn't hear anything, including Gus—the hundred-pound golden-doodle his sister had inherited from her fiancé.

Balancing the pizza box and six-pack of beer against the wall, Cal dug in his jeans pocket for his key ring. He'd spent so much time here this past summer that Em had finally relented and given him a key. He was about to insert it into the lock when the door opened. His sister stared at him, her shoulder-length hair as dull and as lifeless as her green eyes. She wore an oversize T-shirt that had belonged to Brad and a pair of leggings.

Her eyes narrowed. "I'm not hungry, and I don't need a babysitter."

"I'm hungry, and I never said you did."

She crossed her arms. "Then why are you here?"

"If you didn't want me to come, you should have answered your phone." He gently nudged her out of the way and closed the door behind him.

"Since when have you ever listened to me?" she muttered, turning to walk away.

The one-bedroom apartment was dark save for the light from the television screen and the lights of downtown Nashville twinkling through the sliding glass door that led to the balcony. But he didn't need the lights on to tell him his sister was in bad shape. The apartment smelled like the garbage hadn't been taken out in weeks. She hadn't bothered to pick up after herself either, as evidenced by the clothes and shoes he tripped over on his way to the kitchen.

He went to put the pizza box and six-pack of beer on the island but it was littered with takeout containers and a carton of what smelled like soured milk. With his forearm, he swept the empty containers into the sink. Then he set the pizza and beer on the island and flipped on the kitchen light.

Em rubbed her eyes, scowling at him from where she lay on the couch. "Do you mind? I was trying to sleep."

"Still sleeping on the couch," he said, taking in the pillow, sheet, and blanket.

"What of it? The couch is more comfortable than the bed."

Em sleeping on the couch had nothing to do with the bed being uncomfortable. It had been the same whenever he visited over the summer. She hadn't slept in the bed she'd shared with Brad since he died.

Cal leaned over the island and looked into the bedroom on the right. Gus was curled up on the bed, sleeping on his master's side, his head on the pillow, and Cal's heart broke for his sister and the dog.

She followed the direction of his gaze, and her lips thinned. "Turn off the light. I'm trying to sleep."

"It's eight o'clock." He held her gaze. "Do you have an early shift tomorrow?"

Cursing her boss, she jerked upright, grabbed the pillow, and threw it at Cal. He caught it and walked around the island.

"Graves told me what happened. He's worried about you and so am—" He broke off at the sight of a gun peeking out from under a pizza box on the table.

Em eyed him as he dropped the pillow and picked up the gun.

A muscle pulsed in his jaw, and it took him a minute to calm himself enough to ask, "Why is this out here?"

She searched his face. Then, shaking her head, she grabbed the pillow off the floor, punched it a couple of times, and stuffed it under her head before rolling over on the couch and turning her back on him.

There was only one explanation for that gun being

there but he couldn't make himself ask the question. He was too angry, too scared that she'd confirm his fears. With his heartbeat pounding in his ears, he strode to her bedroom. Gus lifted his head from the pillow as Cal crouched beside the nightstand, opening the door to reveal the gun safe. Keying in the combination, he opened the safe and locked the gun away.

He came to his feet and leaned over the bed, rubbing Gus behind the ears. The dog whined and nuzzled Cal's hand. "It'll be okay, boy. You guys are coming home with me."

"Like hell I am," his sister yelled from the couch. "I'm not moving in with you and your wife."

Em and Raine were both strong women with strong opinions. They hadn't hit it off when Cal had first introduced them. Em had been positive that, given her history, Raine would hurt him, and Raine hadn't appreciated being cross-examined and found wanting by his baby sister.

It was Izzy who'd helped the two women overcome their initial animosity. Em loved Cal's stepdaughter as much as he did and enjoyed spending time with her. And despite how his sister was acting now, she loved him too.

"You don't have to. I found a place for you," he said as he walked into the living room, deciding to wait until the last minute to tell her she'd have a roommate. It would be hard enough to get her on board. He sat on the edge of the coffee table. "And, Em, I won't take no for an answer."

She rolled over to face him. "Too bad. You're going to have to, because I have no intention of leaving."

"You've been suspended for six months without pay. Do you have any money put aside?"

She chewed on her bottom lip, looking around her apartment before returning her gaze to him. "Maybe you can help me out? It's only for a few months."

"That's exactly what I'm doing. I'll cover your rent in Highland Falls but I won't pay for your apartment here."

"What's the difference?"

"About a grand a month, but that's not the point. It isn't about the money." He lifted his hand, gesturing to the clothes on the floor. "You can't go on like this, Em, and I can't in good conscience leave you here on your own." Not after seeing that gun.

"My job is here. My life is here. It's not in Highland Falls."

"Your family is, and your job will be here for you when you get back on your feet."

"My apartment won't be."

"Maybe that's not a bad thing." His sister and Brad had been talking about moving before he died. "We'll find you something else. Who knows, that place you and Brad were looking at might have a unit available when you're ready to move back." He hoped that once she was home for a while, she'd want to stay. She wasn't ready to hear that though.

She pressed her lips together and closed her eyes, a tear trickling down her cheek.

"Aw, Em." He reached over and gathered her into his arms. He wished he knew what to say to take away her pain. She sobbed in his arms for a solid twenty minutes, and all he could do was tell her it was going to be okay and rub her back. She hadn't cried this hard when she'd first lost Brad. She'd walked around in a state of shock.

She pulled away from him, her eyes bloodshot and swollen. "Sorry. I think there might be some snot mixed in with my tears." She picked up a used napkin from the table and wiped at the front of his shirt.

"Yeah, and now you've added five-day-old pizza sauce to it, Freckles."

She rolled her eyes at him using the nickname he'd given her years before. "It's only three days old." She nudged him. "Let me up." Her eyes narrowed at him, and she brought her T-shirt to her nose. "I don't smell."

"No, but your apartment does. I'll clean up while you shower, and then we'll make a list of what's coming with you and what's not."

She glanced at Gus.

"Don't even think about it," Cal said as he got to his feet. "He's coming with us."

Em wasn't a dog person, and Gus, probably sensing that she wasn't, hadn't been a fan of hers. But they'd both loved Brad, who'd rescued Gus from a crime scene when he was four months old, and the two of them had learned to put up with each other.

"If you like him so much, you can take him for walks and pick up his poop," his sister said over her shoulder as she walked through the bedroom to the bathroom.

"No problem." He'd considered taking the dog home with him over the summer but he hadn't liked the idea of leaving Em on her own. He'd paid her neighbor, whose two sons loved Gus, to walk the dog twice a day. He was sure Izzy would be happy to help out. And thinking about his stepdaughter, he pulled out his cell phone.

Raine picked up on the third ring. "You better be calling to tell me you're on your way home tomorrow. We have to get on the fundraising right away."

No *Hi*, no *How is your sister?* or *How was your drive?* Just straight to what was most important to Raine. "No. I called to let you know I'm here, and I should be heading back with Em Saturday morning. And I wanted to check on Izzy. Did she tell you what was bothering her?" His frustration with Raine leaked into his voice.

"If that's the best you can do, I guess I'll have to be satisfied with it. You haven't told your sister that we're separated, have you? Because it's more important than ever that no one knows we're no longer together. Now that Harlan has a window of opportunity, he'll use whatever means he can to ensure we don't raise the infrastructure funds. I still can't believe—"

Cal walked over and shut the bedroom door. The water was running in the bathroom, but he didn't want to take the chance his sister would overhear him. "I haven't told Em, and I won't." He had told Bri though, and that was something he'd have to deal with sooner rather than later. "But, Raine, once the six weeks is up, whether we've raised the funds or not, our fake marriage ends."

"Yes, yes, of course." The call cut out for a second. "I have to go. It's one of the hospital's donors calling me back." And that was it—she disconnected.

Cal scrubbed his face and tried calling his stepdaughter. She didn't answer, so he texted her instead. He started cleaning off the coffee table while waiting for a response. His gaze went to the pizza box, and some of the tension that had released from his shoulders returned, the worry that his sister had been going to take her own life. A worry that was hard to stuff back in the bottle now that he acknowledged what his fear had been.

He scrolled to the number Mallory had sent him earlier in the day—Bri's. The one person who knew his sister almost as well as he did. The one person who would know what he should do or say. Before he could talk himself out of it, he hit Call.

She picked up on the first ring. "Cal?"

Her voice was little more than a whisper. "Yeah. I didn't wake you, did I?"

She snorted a laugh and then continued in that quiet voice. "I'm pretending I'm asleep so my sister leaves me alone. Is everything okay? You sound...off."

"It's Em. Hang on a sec." He walked to the balcony door. Opening it, he stepped out and closed it behind him. "Sorry. I didn't want her to hear me. You know how private she is."

"I remember how private she *was*. I haven't spoken to Em in almost a decade, Cal. Is she okay? Are you?"

"No, to both your questions," he said, and told her about Brad dying in front of Em and how she'd handled it, about her being suspended without pay and what he'd walked into tonight. He shoved his fingers through his hair. "Sorry for dumping all this on you, Bri. I just...I guess I needed someone to talk to. Someone who knows

Em, and someone who has experience treating people dealing with loss and depression."

"Please, don't apologize. I'm so sorry Em is going through this. I can't imagine how difficult this is for her. Or for you. It's not easy watching someone you love suffering and not knowing what to do or say. But, Cal, if you're looking for a diagnosis or treatment plan, I don't feel comfortable offering either. I'm no longer practicing."

"Will you at least tell me if you think it's a mistake forcing her to come back to Highland Falls with me?"

"From what you just told me, it sounded like she acquiesced pretty easily. And that's very un-Em-like. At least the Em I remember."

He smiled. "You're right, and she hasn't changed that much. But without a paycheck coming in for the next six months, she can't cover her rent, and I refused to cover it for her."

"Ah, so there was blackmail involved."

"You think I should have agreed to cover her rent so she could stay here? I'm covering it at the—"

"No, I was teasing. You were always bailing her out financially when we were younger. Remember when she wanted that mountain bike and you told her that if she saved half, you'd pay the rest?"

"Yeah. She'd saved her half and had it spent two days before we were supposed to go buy the bike."

"And you caved and bought it for her anyway." They shared a laugh at the memory, and it reminded him of how it used to be when they were together. He pushed the what-if thought from his head. Like he'd told Bri, no good ever came from dwelling in the past. It didn't mean he didn't have his share of regrets when it came to her though.

"I think Em knows she's struggling and needs help. You're doing the right thing, Cal."

"When you say struggling, do you think she'd...hurt herself?" He couldn't bring himself to say *kill herself*.

"Has she talked about suicide since Brad died?"

He blew out a breath. "No, not to me."

"Did you ask her why she had the gun out?"

"Yeah, and she just rolled over on the couch."

"And you didn't push for an answer." She stated it as a fact, not a question. "I'm not judging, Cal. Sometimes it's tough to ask questions we're afraid to hear the answer to. But I think it's a conversation you need to have. For Em's sake, and for your own. She may feel the need to have her gun close by for protection or she may have simply left it out by mistake."

"And covered it with a pizza box?"

"Well, from the way you described the state of her apartment, it's plausible."

"But not probable."

"If anyone can get Em to talk, it's you. She loves you as much as you love her. Just be open and honest with her. Let her know how worried you are about her and don't be afraid to come out and ask her if she's had suicidal thoughts."

"And if she has?"

"Then you'll get her the help that she needs."

"Would you consider taking her on as a client?"

"First of all, I'm the last person Em would open up

to. Besides that, like I said, I'm no longer practicing. But I'm happy to recommend someone."

He felt like he was being watched and glanced over his shoulder. His sister stared at him through the glass door with an annoyed expression on her face. "I'd better go. Em's out of the shower. Thanks for listening, Bri. I really appreciate it."

"You don't have to thank me. Em and I might not be friends now, but I do care about her. And you saved my life. The least I can do is be there for...I mean, listen when you need a sounding board."

It bothered him to think she felt she owed him for saving her life. More than bothered him, he realized, at the clipped tone in his voice when he said, "You don't owe me anything." He shook his head at himself. "Sorry. I shouldn't have snapped at you. It's just that I don't like you feeling you owe me. That day at the inn, when I— we—nearly lost you, it was one of the most terrifying days of my life."

"Cal—" she began, sounding sad and understandably confused, because he had a feeling he'd just revealed how much she still mattered to him.

His sister was banging around in the kitchen, and he interrupted Bri. "It's not the time right now, but you and I have to talk."

"Don't worry about that now. Mallory said you were going to call and go over the results with me but they can wait. You have enough on your plate, Cal. Go talk to Em."

She disconnected, and he stared at the phone. Bri had to be worried about the results, and yet she'd never

asked. She was more worried about him and his sister.
He couldn't help comparing his conversation with Raine
to the one he'd just had with Bri. And he couldn't help
wondering what his life would have been like if he hadn't
broken their engagement.

Chapter Seven

♥

Bri's brilliant plan had failed spectacularly. Not only was she actually moving out of the inn, but their mother had wanted to be there for the momentous occasion.

Bri glanced over her shoulder, rising up to look over the boxes and mattress loaded in the back of the pickup truck, and sighed. "We have a convoy."

Her sister, who was driving, laughed. "They're excited for you."

"At least someone is," Bri muttered without thinking. Then realizing what she'd said and who had heard her say it, she glanced at her sister. Sure enough, a frown furrowed Ellie's brow. "You can lose the worried face. I meant, I'm glad *you're* excited the entire family decided to join us." Everyone but her father. "I barely have anything to move."

"Oh good. It sounded like you were having second thoughts."

If she only knew. "No. This will be good for me. I've never lived on my own." Her mother had insisted she go to Duke University, a couple miles from their family home in Durham.

Her father was a professor there, and her mother was an administrator. Once Bri had finished her degrees, she'd met Richard. He'd been doing a guest lecture at the university. Her mother had been his biggest fan and cheerleader. Bri had known him a little over six months when he'd proposed to her.

Sometimes she wondered if she'd married him to get out from under her mother's thumb. It wasn't until a few months ago that she'd learned why her mother had been so controlling and protective of her.

"You won't actually be living on your own, remember?" Her sister glanced at her as she turned onto Marigold Lane. "I know you're not a fan of having a roommate, but I think it's great."

"So you keep telling me." Bri leaned forward to catch a glimpse of the house. It was a pretty street lined with sugar maple trees. The two-story homes were tucked back from the road and were predominantly made of wood painted in welcoming shades of yellow, green, and cream. Add in the cedar shake roofs, big front porches, and beautifully landscaped yards, and the area had a warm family feel to it. For the first time since she'd made her fake announcement, Bri felt the tiniest flicker of excitement.

"Has Abby told you who my roommate is? Every time I ask her, she changes the subject."

"No," her sister said. Like Bri, she was leaning forward, looking for the house. "She vets all her clients, so you don't have to worry. I'm sure it's one of the seniors she and Mallory work with." Ellie wrinkled her nose. "Maybe it's a man, and that's why she hasn't said anything. It wouldn't bother you if it was, would it? You basically live with Grandpa and the judge now."

Anything was better than living under the same roof as her mother. Her grandfather had already threatened to move in with her. "I'm sure it'll be fine. Abby said I can have the bedroom on the main floor, and it sounds like the house is fairly large so we won't be in each other's space."

Behind them, someone honked a horn and then the rest of their convoy joined in. Bri shook her head at the noise. "I'm going to get kicked out of the neighborhood before I even move in."

Ellie glanced over her shoulder and waved. "I went past the house," she said, and stopped the truck, shifting gears to back up.

When the house came into view, Bri stared at it with a sense of déjà vu. She'd seen this house with its big front porch and pretty dormer windows before. But she couldn't put a finger on where she'd seen it. She'd never been on this street.

"Oh my gosh, Bri. It's your house!"

That's exactly how Bri felt but she had no idea why. She turned to her sister. "What do you mean?"

"Don't you remember? You had it on your Pinterest board. Here, I'll show you," her sister said, typing on her phone.

Her Pinterest board—the one she'd created when she and Cal were together. Pinning the kind of house they'd dreamed of buying for the family they'd raise together. Four kids and a dog, that had been their plan. It reminded her of one of her grandmother's favorite sayings: *We plan and God laughs.*

Bri reached over, covering her sister's hand with hers. "My Pinterest board isn't there anymore. I deleted it."

"I'm sorry. I shouldn't have—"

"What are you sorry about? It was a long time ago. We were kids." They hadn't been, not really. But that's what Cal had said when he'd broken their engagement.

"I know. It's just that you looked sad, and this is supposed to be a happy day. I didn't mean to ruin it by bringing up Cal."

"You didn't ruin it." She unbuckled her seatbelt, pushing thoughts of Cal and what might have been out of her head. She'd spent far too much time thinking about that since talking to him the other night. He'd texted after he'd spoken to Em, letting Bri know that his sister had admitted she wasn't in a good place but she wasn't suicidal. She hadn't realized she'd forgotten to put her gun away.

Bri had thanked him for the update, noticing the x's and o's she'd added just before she'd pressed Send. She'd deleted them, wondering what had come over her. Cal had texted back that they'd get together this week and talk.

He'd also suggested she massage her leg if she was having trouble sleeping. Ensuring that she didn't get a lot of sleep because she couldn't get an image of *him* massaging her leg out of her head—or his voice when he'd talked about the day he'd saved her life.

She kept going over their conversation, picking it apart, looking for clues as to how he felt about her. Given the feelings their conversation had stirred up inside her, she'd decided meeting face-to-face was a bad idea. Her best course of action was keeping her distance from Cal, and she was fairly certain his wife would agree.

Bri grabbed her cane, hefting the strap of her bag over her shoulder, and got out of the truck. She breathed in the crisp autumn air, inhaling the sweet, spicy scent of fallen leaves and freshly cut grass. The sounds of kids playing down the road and someone mowing their lawn followed her as she carefully made her way up the walkway.

"Bri, wait for me," her sister called out, no doubt worried Bri would trip on the walkway's crumbling cobblestones or the weeds overtaking it. The beds of mahogany-red and golden-yellow marigolds at the front of the house were overrun with weeds too.

Bri ignored her sister and continued walking, something inside of her urging her on.

She didn't know why but it felt important that she see the house on her own. The black wrought iron gate squeaked when she opened it, and she carefully made her way to the front porch. She shut out the sounds of her family and friends unpacking the truck and their vehicles, calling out to her to be careful. All she wanted was a moment of peace and quiet to take it all in.

While the property was somewhat run-down, the exterior of the house didn't appear to be. It looked freshly painted in a warm cream with a welcoming red door. Plump floral cushions graced the old-fashioned porch swing, and she could see herself sitting out there with a book and a cup of tea. The earlier spurt of excitement blossomed into something else, something that felt like hope and new beginnings.

She walked across the front porch, inserting the key into the lock. As she opened the door, she glanced behind her to gauge how much time she had before her family and friends descended on her. She caught her sister's eye and lifted her chin at the family members crowded around Ellie, mouthing, *Give me a minute.*

Her sister smiled and nodded. "Hang on, Granny. You too, Mom. We're going to get everyone organized first."

Nate, who was standing beside Ellie, caught her grandfather by the back of his sweatshirt. "That goes for you too, Joe."

Lucky, Bri thought. She was lucky to have so many people who loved her. Her gaze landed on her mother as Bri went to close the door behind her. She knew her mother loved her too. And maybe one day soon, she'd find it in herself to forgive her for the pain she'd caused Ellie. Thoughts of her family vanished the moment Bri stepped into the house and took in her surroundings.

Off the entryway to the right, hardwood stairs with cream wooden railings led to the second floor. To her left was the living room. A cognac-colored leather sectional faced a gorgeous river rock fireplace with a big-screen TV hanging above the mantel. The walls in the living room and main floor were covered in wood paneling. Some people might find it dark and claustrophobic but not Bri. She loved the warm, rustic feel of the house.

The condo she'd shared with Richard had been stark white with a lot of metal and glass. The furniture the decorator had chosen had been for show, not for comfort, and Bri had hated it. But she'd had no say. Richard had bought the condo without her input. He'd hired the decorator too. She hadn't seen the condo until they'd returned from their honeymoon. Richard had said he'd wanted to surprise her. Another red flag that she'd ignored. She shook off the thought and wandered through the rest of the house, taking in the dining room with its seating for eight.

A small room off the kitchen had been converted into a cozy den with floor-to-ceiling bookshelves overflowing with hardcover and paperback novels. She wondered if her roommate would mind if she claimed this room as her own. They could have the living room. Although sitting by a fire on a blustery autumn night would be nice.

She walked into the eat-in kitchen with its dark wood cabinets, black appliances, gorgeous farmhouse sink, and a table that looked like it had been made from a slab of wood, the knots and rings visible beneath a clear coat of varnish.

Despite the color scheme, the kitchen was bright and cheerful. Sunlight streamed through the window over the sink and the windows that framed the sliding glass door.

Bri went to the patio door and looked out into the backyard. The fenced-in yard was bordered by vegetable and flower beds. As with the gardens at the front of the house, they were overrun with weeds, but sunflowers stood tall along the back fence, pumpkins peeking above the dandelions, apples weighing down the branches of a nearby fruit tree. Bri smiled. She felt like she'd come home.

"Knock, knock, can we come in now?" her sister called from the front of the house.

"I'm in the kitchen," she called back, opening the patio door to let in some fresh air.

She turned at the sound of sneakers squeaking across the hardwood floors. Her sister glanced around and then looked at Bri, searching her face. Releasing a small sob, Ellie rushed forward, enfolding Bri in a hug. "You're happy. You love the house, and the house loves you."

Bri laughed. "I thought you could only read humans."

"You know what I mean," Ellie said, taking a step back from her. "You do love it though, don't you? I can see it on your face."

"I do, and it's a little weird but I kind of know what you mean. The house feels welcoming."

"Exactly. There's—" Ellie began, only to be cut off by their mother, who walked into the kitchen looking like she smelled something bad.

"This is the most depressing house I've ever been in," Miranda said with a shudder. "You can't live here, Brianna."

"I guess the house didn't roll out the welcome mat for Mom," Bri said so only Ellie could hear. Then she forced a smile for her mother. "It's a good thing you don't have to live here then. I think this house is perfect for me."

"Of course you do, dear. You're depressed. Depressed people are drawn to dark, claustrophobic spaces." She walked to the patio door and peered through the screen. "Heaven knows what has made a home among those weeds. If you're absolutely certain you want to stay here, we need to do something with those gardens. I wonder if the homeowner would let you rip them up."

Ellie, no doubt fearing Bri was seconds from losing her cool, intervened. "The homeowner specifically asked for a tenant who would look after his gardens, and there's no one better than Bri for the job. You saw what she did to the flower beds at the inn, didn't you? She's an amazing gardener."

Bri wouldn't go that far, but she loved working in the garden. Her leg didn't feel the same way about it. She had a feeling that all the gardening she'd done this summer was one of the reasons it had been acting up. Well, that and her not doing her daily exercises. According to her physiotherapist, gardening didn't count.

"All right, if you insist on staying here, we have work to do. It's not suitable for someone with a disability. Your walker will get caught on the area rugs and—"

"I haven't used a walker in months," Bri said through clenched teeth.

"Oh, right, I forgot. But you need a seat in the shower and a handicap bar. And we should—"

Ellie took their mother by the shoulders and steered her out of the kitchen. "Why don't you help Sadie unpack Bri's clothes?"

"Oh, that's an excellent idea. We wouldn't want your linen dresses getting wrinkled or your silk blouses put on plastic hangers," their mother said, smiling over her shoulder at Bri.

Bri had given away the clothing Richard had bought for her, which was basically two-thirds of her wardrobe, including her linen dresses and silk blouses.

"Since that job will take her less than ten minutes, we better come up with something else for her to do," Bri grumbled, ticked that her mother had managed to spoil her good mood.

Their grandmother, who bore a striking resemblance to the actress Betty White, walked into the kitchen. "Abby just pulled up. She says your roommate should be here in the next fifteen minutes and asked if we could move the cars. They have a U-Haul, and they'll need the room. It shouldn't be a problem. Nate and Chase are bringing in the last of your things now. Joe's making like Goldilocks upstairs, testing the bedrooms. I think he's planning on moving in with you. Can't say I blame him now that you-know-who has moved into the inn."

"Granny, be nice," Ellie said. "Mom's trying to make amends. She sent you a gift basket on your birthday, didn't she?"

Bri rolled her eyes. She didn't understand how or why her sister always came to their mother's defense. Ellie had to be the sweetest, most forgiving person Bri had ever met.

Agnes sighed. "Aye, she did. But it's not me she needs to make amends with. It's the two of you."

That wasn't exactly true. Miranda had been almost as cruel to Granny MacLeod as she'd been to Bri's sister. Ellie had inherited her gift from her grandmother. Although it worked differently for Granny MacLeod. If she held your hand, she could see your future. Her mother had assumed Granny knew her secret and did everything in her power to discredit her.

"That's why she's here, Granny," Ellie said. "She

knew I was worried about Bri, and she didn't want me to cancel our trip again, so she took time off work to stay at the inn without me even asking."

"Is that what she told you then?" Granny MacLeod nodded as if she wasn't surprised. "You might want to have a word with your father."

"He asked her to leave, didn't he?" Her father wasn't an easy man to read but Bri had sensed he couldn't forgive her mother for her affair. In Bri's practice, she'd counseled several couples who were able to get past affairs, and their marriages were stronger for it. But she'd also had couples in which the betrayed partner used the affair as a weapon. She didn't think her father would, but she also knew his silence would be just as damaging.

"You'll have to talk to your parents. I won't get in the middle of it. But if you ask me, neither of them was happy. They should have ended their marriage a long time ago. Life's short, my girls. Take your happy wherever you can find it." She smiled at Bri. "You'll be happy here. And you deserve some happy in your life."

"Thanks, Granny."

"And you!" She wagged her finger at Ellie. "Don't be fretting about your mother. She'll be fine, and you and that handsome man of yours will have a wonderful time in Scotland. Now that I've seen you settled, I'll be off."

After they'd said their goodbyes and Granny left the kitchen, Bri turned to her sister. "Don't you dare think of canceling your trip because of Mom and Dad, Ellie. I mean it."

Her sister chewed on her thumbnail. "She doesn't

have any friends to turn to, Bri. And it's not like Grandpa will be supportive. I feel like I'm leaving her in her hour of need."

Bri mentally slapped her palm to her forehead at the thought of what she had to do. There was no way around it. "I'm here. I'll stop by the inn every day and…have tea with her or something. She can vent to me, and I promise to be supportive."

"Really?" Ellie hugged her. "You don't know how much I appreciate your offer. You're better equipped to deal with this than me." She glanced around the kitchen. "It completely slipped my mind. You have nothing to eat. I'll head to the grocery store and pick you up a few things to stock your fridge and cupboards."

Bri was about to object until Ellie added, "I'll take Mom with me."

"Great idea. Nate, Chase, and Sadie can go too. I really appreciate everyone pitching in, but I'm sure they have other stuff they could be doing on a Saturday afternoon. And I'm perfectly capable of setting up my own room."

"I'll see where they're at and let them know."

"Don't forget to take Grandpa with you. One roommate I can handle, but not two."

Ellie laughed. "Two? Try three. Grandpa and the judge are attached at the hip. The other day, Grandpa said they're brothers from another mother."

Bri laughed. "He did not."

"He did so." Ellie grinned and took one last look around the kitchen. "I'll be back in an hour with your groceries. Text me if there's something special you want."

As Bri pulled out a chair at the table and sat down to make a list, her brother-in-law walked into the kitchen. "I just got off the phone with Gabe. He mentioned that they've had a couple of break-ins in the area. Probably just kids from the sound of it, but it wouldn't be a bad idea to have bars installed in the basement windows, and there are a couple of bushes outside your bedroom window that should be cut back."

She wasn't surprised that Nate was cautious when it came to home security. He was an agent with the North Carolina State Bureau of Investigation. "You didn't tell Ellie about the break-ins, did you?"

He grinned. "Who do you think made me call Gabe?"

"I'm surprised she let me move in."

"She might have put up more of a fuss if she didn't know that the area has a strong neighborhood watch and that Cal is the captain."

Bri stared at her brother-in-law. "Uh, Cal who?" Please don't be that Cal.

Nate frowned. "Cal Scott. The trauma surgeon. He operated on you."

"Yes. Of course I know Cal." She'd nearly married him. "I just didn't know he lived around here."

"Apparently he and his wife live up the street. They have a sixteen-year-old daughter."

So much for keeping her distance, and so much for Cal being legally separated from his wife.

The rest of her family—minus her mother, who'd left with Ellie—joined them in the kitchen to ask if she needed them to do anything else. It took some convincing, but five minutes later, she had the house to herself.

She was enjoying the quiet when Abby came flying into the kitchen. "Your roommate is here. I wish I could stick around but, uh, I have to get home. Here you go." She shoved a set of keys and what looked like a rental agreement into Bri's hands and then took off out the patio door.

Bri frowned, wondering what was up with Abby, and then she glanced at the paper in her hand. Her eyes went wide. Her roommate was Cal!

Chapter Eight

♥

"Hey, Abby," Cal said, glad of the distraction as he carried two suitcases up the steps of a house that was uncomfortably familiar. He'd walked by and driven past 21 Marigold Lane at least a thousand times, but it wasn't until he pulled up to the sidewalk just now that he realized why it looked so familiar. It had been his and Bri's dream home. The place where they'd raise a family together.

But instead of providing a distraction, Abby offered him a smile and continued sprinting across the yard to the walkway.

"Sorry. I'm late for an appointment," she yelled over her shoulder. "Rental agreement and keys are in the house. Door's unlocked."

"No problem. Thanks for…" He trailed off as she disappeared from view behind the maple trees, trying to brush aside the uneasy feeling he'd had since speaking to Abby earlier.

He'd called while filling up his jeep at a gas station an hour from town to let Abby know their ETA and to ask who his sister's roommate was, in hopes of putting Em

at ease when he finally broke the news that she wouldn't
be living on her own. But the line had filled with static
before Abby had provided him with an answer. Static that
had sounded manmade—or in this case, woman-made.

Cal put down the suitcase in his right hand to open the
door, glancing back at his sister's silver Nissan Altima.
Apparently she was staging a sit-in in protest that the
house came with a roommate.

Picking up the suitcase, he walked inside. A blonde
half-ran, half-hopped, toward him. And not just any
blonde. The blonde he hadn't been able to stop thinking
about for the past two days.

"Bri, what are—?"

She startled at the sight of him and tripped on the up-
lifted corner of an area rug. He dropped the suitcases and
lunged for her, catching her under her arms before she
face-planted on the hardwood floor.

He drew her against him, trying to ignore the wave
of emotion that swamped him at seeing her here in
this house and holding her in his arms. Those long-ago
dreams were messing with his head, and he'd need a
clear one to deal with his sister when all hell broke loose.
"What are you doing here?"

She stepped back and shoved a piece of paper and
keys at his chest. "I'm sorry, but you can't stay here."

"What are you talking about? I'm—"

She went to take another step away from him and
stumbled, sucking in a pained gasp. "Damn it, Bri."
Cal scooped her into his arms and shut the door with
his foot.

Her eyes went wide. "What are you doing?"

"You twisted your ankle and don't pretend that you didn't." He walked into the living room and, bending down, placed her on the sectional.

"Oh my gosh, Cal, I'm fine," she said as he lifted her legs onto the couch, resting her cane against the coffee table.

"Humor me," he said, taking a seat at her feet. "Okay, now tell me what this is all about."

"You can't live here with me."

So he was right. He and Abby were going to have a word if he survived his sister's wrath. "I—" He tried to interrupt Bri but she talked right over him, clearly flustered.

"You might think that you're separated, but your wife seems to feel that you're very much still married." She went on to tell him how Raine had acted when she'd interrupted Bri's appointment with Mallory at the hospital. Something Cal hadn't asked her to do, despite what she'd told the two women. "And Raine isn't the only one who thinks you two are Mr. and Mrs. Perfect."

"Okay, so first things first. I signed the lease for Em. She's your roommate." He glanced at Bri with one eye shut, preparing for her reaction.

She stared at him. "I don't know which is worse: living with you or living with your sister, who hates me."

Some of the tension in his chest relaxed, and he laughed.

Bri nudged him with her uninjured foot. "This isn't funny." She pushed herself up so her head was on the armrest and glanced toward the front door. "Where is Em?"

"Sitting in her car," he said, lifting Bri's feet onto

his thigh. He removed her sneakers and set them on the floor.

"Ah, what do you think you're—" She broke off with a low, breathy moan as he gently massaged her foot while checking her range of motion. A moan that shot straight to his groin. "This is a really bad idea," she murmured, but he noticed she didn't move her feet.

Considering his own response to touching her, he had a feeling she was right and eased her feet off his lap. "I'll get you an ice pack." He might need to use it first.

"There isn't one," she said when he went to get up. "The freezer, fridge, and cupboards are bare. Ellie's doing a grocery run for me."

He sat back down. "So when did you decide to move out of the inn? You didn't say anything about it the other night."

"We were talking about your sister. My issues with my family seemed like nonissues compared to what Em is dealing with. What you were dealing with," she said, and then she told him about her mother moving in and how Bri had used getting her own place as a means of proving to her sister she didn't need a babysitter.

"That didn't work out so well for you, did it?" he said, holding back a laugh he didn't think she'd appreciate. "Might not be a bad thing though. You moving out on your own, I mean."

"I was beginning to think it had been an inspired idea until I found out who my roommate is. Honestly, Cal, there's no way Em will want to live with me. Can't she live with you and Raine?"

"Okay, so that's something else I need to talk to you

about. Raine and I are separated, Bri. I wouldn't lie to you about that. But it's complicated, and I need you to keep it to yourself."

He told her about Izzy and why he'd agreed to move back in with his stepdaughter and Raine, how they'd ended up coming home to Highland Falls, and how he'd ended up agreeing to keep their impending divorce a secret.

"It wasn't supposed to go on for this long. We figured the approval for the trauma center would go through in the spring. But then Brad died and Em needed me, and things stalled with the town council thanks to Harlan. I've agreed to stay quiet for another six weeks. Hopefully, we can raise the funds by then, but even if we can't, I'm moving out."

He looked up from her foot, which he'd been absently massaging as he talked, and he wondered if the stunned expression on her face was due to that or to what he'd just shared with her. At the tension building in his chest as he searched her face, he realized how much he wanted it to be the former. And that worried him.

It shouldn't matter to him what she thought about the status of his marriage. His relationship with Bri had ended almost a decade before. He couldn't, wouldn't, put his heart on the line again. It had taken years to get over her. But even as those thoughts were running through his brain, he knew he'd never gotten over her.

"You think I'm an idiot," he said. If she could read minds like her sister, no doubt she'd think he was. No one but an idiot would consider getting involved with the one woman capable of breaking their heart.

The thought surprised him. Just because he admitted, if only to himself, that there was a part of him that would always be half in love with Bri, that didn't mean he wanted to rekindle their relationship. He shifted on the couch, putting some distance between them.

"No. I've had clients who are separated decide to live together for a myriad of reasons, including financial and for the sake of their children. It's just that—" She shook her head. "It's none of my business."

She was right, and he should let it go. But his heart disagreed with his brain, and with Bri lying on the couch right next to him, talking to him, something that for years he'd thought was lost to him, his heart won out.

No, not his heart. He wasn't an idiot. He was smart, too smart to think a second chance with Bri was on the table or that it would be a good idea to see where it would lead. He knew exactly where it would lead. But like Bri had just said, she had experience dealing with couples who stayed together for their kids. For Izzy's sake, he needed to hear how that worked out.

"Maybe not," he agreed. "But I want to hear what you were going to say. I'm worried about my stepdaughter. I don't want her confused, and if you have any advice as to what I can do over the next six weeks to make the transition easier for her, I'd appreciate you sharing it with me."

"I don't know how she can be anything but confused, Cal. Everyone in town thinks you and her mother are happily married."

"Not Izzy. She doesn't," he reiterated at Bri's doubtful look. "We've made it clear to her that while we're no longer in love with each other, we love her and want the best for her, which at the time was me living under the same roof. But Raine and I don't share a bedroom or do anything that would make Izzy wonder if we're more than friends."

"It sounds good on the face of it. But if Raine doesn't want it getting out, Izzy is having to lie about you guys to her friends."

"She's sixteen, Bri. The last thing she wants to talk to her friends about is her parents' love life. And it's not like they're going to ask if we're happily married."

"Maybe not, but what about Winter? Surely Izzy is close to her grandmother."

"She is, but it's never come up. Izzy would have told us. And she gets why we have to keep it quiet. The last thing she wants is for the expansion to fall through because of us. She wants to be a trauma surgeon when she grows up, and her goal is to work here with me at the hospital." He'd been touched when she'd told him she wanted to follow in his footsteps.

"I'm not sure I understand why you have to keep it quiet," Bri said. "I mean, I actually had a couple in a similar situation. The husband and wife were lawyers who worked in her father's legal firm, and they were afraid he'd fire the husband if he learned they were getting a divorce, so they basically did what you and Raine are doing. From what they told me about her father, I could see their point. But I know Winter—not well, but I do know her—and I can't see her being anything but understanding and supportive about you and Raine splitting up. I certainly don't think she'd jeopardize the trauma center because of it."

"I agree with you. Winter's great. But Raine got it into her head that, because of her professional and relationship histories, Winter learning we were separated would tip the scale against her bid for hospital administrator and her push for the trauma center." To give her context, he filled Bri in on Raine's checkered past. "I honestly didn't think her professional and relationship histories would or should be an issue but I learned fairly quickly that I was wrong. And when you factor in Harlan, who's looking for any advantage or whiff of scandal, it made sense to keep our impending divorce out of the mix."

"Okay, I guess I can understand why you decided to keep your separation quiet. I just hope it doesn't come back to bite you."

Not exactly what he was hoping she'd say. "Did it come back to bite your clients?"

"Big-time. The wife ended up falling in love with the firm's investigator, and the husband ended up falling in love with one of the other partners at the firm. The father sued them both for breach of the morality clause, and because they'd been pretending to be married, he won."

"That's not something we have to worry about. Neither of us is in a relationship or looking to fall in—" He broke off as the front door banged open.

"If you were going to leave me to carry in my stuff by myself, you could have at least brought the dog in with you." Em's eyes narrowed as she put the boxes on the floor. "Who's that?"

Cal glanced from his sister to Bri, who slid lower on the couch and frantically shook her head. He offered her an apologetic shrug. Em was going to find out eventually. "Your roommate."

His sister stalked to the couch and looked down, her eyes going wide. "You!" Her gaze swung from Bri to him, and she fisted her hands on her hips. "What the hell is going on here?"

And that's when Cal realized what he and Bri cozied up on the couch might look like to his sister. "Calm down. It's not what it looks like."

Bri widened her eyes at him, like that might not have been the wisest thing to say.

"Really? Because it looks to me like you were getting cozy with your ex. The woman who broke your heart. He's married, you know. Happily married," she said to Bri. "Or do you even care?"

"Okay, that's enough, Em. You—"

"This isn't going to work," Bri said, and he wasn't sure if she meant living with his sister or keeping the truth about his marriage from Em. Bri cleared that up for him with the next words out of her mouth. "I don't have a lot but it will take time to pack up my things and get everyone back here."

He put out his hand to stop her as she struggled to her feet. "No, you don't have to leave." He looked at his sister, nudging his head at Bri. "Em, tell her."

His sister shrugged. "She wants to leave. She can leave."

Gus slunk around the couch as Bri reached for her cane. She smiled at the dog, and he tentatively came and sniffed her leg. Leaning heavily on her cane, she reached down to pat Gus before lifting her gaze to his sister. "I'm very sorry for your loss, Em," she said, and then walked away with the dog trailing after her.

Cal noticed the edge of the area rug had folded over again and called out, "Bri, be careful." But she didn't need his warning. Gus saved the day, nudging her out of the way.

"Aren't you a smart boy?" Bri said, rubbing Gus's head, and then the two of them continued on their way.

Em watched them go with her brow furrowed. She turned to Cal when they disappeared into a room, the door closing behind them. "What happened to her?"

"She had a near-fatal fall last year. If her brother hadn't asked me to look in on her after she checked herself out of the hospital, she would have died." He told her the extent of Bri's injuries. "It was a miracle she survived the five-hour taxi ride from Charlotte."

"If she was that bad off, why did she leave the hospital?"

"Because she was terrified of her husband."

"He was abusive?"

His jaw clenched, and he gave Em a tight nod.

She stared at him. "You still have feelings for her."

"You'd have to be made of rock not to empathize with what she's been through," he said, giving his sister a pointed look.

"I didn't say I don't feel sorry for her, but damn it, Cal, you can't expect me to live with her. Not after what she did to you."

"You used to be friends. Best friends forever, isn't that what you used to say?"

She rolled her eyes. "We were kids."

"So were we." He raised his hand when she opened her mouth, no doubt to argue. "Look, Em, up until last week, other than to go to her PT sessions and doctors' appointments, Bri never went anywhere on her own. She rarely left the inn. So moving out was a big deal for her, and the only reason she did was because of her sister."

"Why? She and Ellie were always super close."

"They still are, and Ellie is as protective of Bri as she always was, even more so after what she's been through. But Bri feels guilty that Ellie has put her life on hold for her. So this"—he gestured at the house—"was Bri's way of proving to her sister that she was fine and it was time to cut the apron strings." He didn't think it was necessary to add that Bri's mother had more to do with the move than Ellie.

"Sounds like we have overprotective and overbearing family members in common," she said. Then she pursed her lips. "That was your plan all along, wasn't it?"

He held back a smile. "I don't know what you're talking about."

"Yeah, like I believe that. You told me all this to play on my sympathy. You're trying to guilt me into letting her stay."

"You, sympathetic?"

She punched him in the arm. "Fine. She can stay. But she better keep out of my way."

He reached over and pulled her in for a hug. "I knew my sweet baby sister was still in there somewhere."

"I'm not sweet. I'm practical." Em stepped out of his embrace. "She can take care of the dog. What?" she said at his narrow-eyed look. "It was love at first sight. Bri won't mind."

She probably wouldn't, and he didn't want to rock the boat. "Go check out the rooms upstairs. I'll let Bri know she can stay."

"You sure Raine's okay with this? She doesn't seem the type that would appreciate their husband's ex living down the street."

He was pretty sure Raine would absolutely not be okay with this. Not that he would share that with Em. "Why wouldn't she be?"

"If you can ask me that, you obviously don't know your wife as well as you think. Or she has no idea what Bri meant to you."

"She knows. Now go check out which room you want, and then you can give me a hand unloading the U-Haul."

She made a face. "You and your bestie can handle it."

"Josh is here?"

His best friend from grade school lived a couple doors down from them. Josh played college ball and now coached the local high school football team. He was also a volunteer firefighter and recently divorced. Cal had planned to move in with him until he found a place of his own. Josh was the only person other than Bri who knew the truth about Cal's relationship with Raine.

"Yeah, he—" Em broke off when Bri came out of her room with Gus trotting alongside her. Both Bri and the dog froze at the look his sister shot them. "You can stay, but we need some ground rules."

Bri glanced from him to his sister. Cal thought she might tell Em what she could do with her ungracious offer, but Bri surprised him by saying, "Okay."

And while on one hand he was glad that she agreed to stay—he thought it was just the change she needed to move on with her life—he wasn't looking forward to sharing the news with Raine. There was also the fact that he'd most likely see Bri every day, and he couldn't deny that part of him was looking forward to spending time with her.

"I'll let you two work out your ground rules," he said, and headed for the door. Maybe he'd suggest he and Josh go a couple rounds in the boxing ring at the gym after they unloaded the U-Haul. He obviously needed someone to knock some sense into him.

Josh looked up from unloading a couple boxes onto the sidewalk. With his dark hair, blue eyes, and tattoo sleeves, the women loved Josh as much as his players did. Obviously for different reasons. But Josh had been burned badly and wasn't interested in dating.

"So how are Em and her new roommate getting along?"

Cal rubbed the back of his neck. "It's Bri."

Josh nearly dropped a box. "Em's new roommate is Bri? Your Bri?"

She hadn't been *his* Bri for years, but he didn't correct Josh. "Yeah." He glanced at the house. "Maybe it'll be good for both of them. They used to be close."

"So were you and Bri. How's this little arrangement going to—" Josh grimaced when a car pulled up behind the U-Haul. "Raine have any idea Bri is Em's roommate?"

"Nope."

Josh let out a low whistle. "Text me when the coast is clear."

Chapter Nine

♥

"Rule number one, there will be no entertaining in the house," Em stated, raising an aggressive finger. She went to hold up another one. "Number—"

Bri interrupted her. "Are you talking about parties? Because I'm on board with that. But I'm not telling my family and friends they can't drop by."

Em crossed her arms. "Why not?"

"Uh, because they're my family and friends, and I like to visit with them."

"Visit with them someplace else."

Bri pinched the bridge of her nose between her forefinger and thumb. The dull ache behind her eyes was threatening to turn into a full-blown migraine, and her throbbing ankle wasn't helping matters. The last thing she wanted was to admit weakness to Em, but she had a feeling their ground rules negotiation was going to take a while.

"Do you mind if we do this in the living room?" she asked, heading that way in hopes Em would follow.

The old Em would have, but this wasn't the friend

Bri remembered. Em looked the same with her shoulder-length auburn hair and the sprinkling of cinnamon-colored freckles on her narrow nose and high cheekbones. But where her green eyes had once sparkled with mischief and fun, they were now dull and lifeless, shadowed with grief.

"Okay, I'm sorry about your accident and everything, but if you expect me to look after you, this arrangement isn't going to work."

Bri might be less than thrilled to have her ex–best friend as a roommate, but it beat living at the inn with her mother. There was no way she was letting Em weasel out of the agreement. "Do I look like I need someone to look after me?" she asked over her shoulder, pleased to see that Em was following her.

"You look like you're going to collapse."

"I went over on my ankle, and I have a headache," she said as she lowered herself onto the couch, sighing in relief once the weight was off her foot. The goldendoodle rested his nose on her thigh, looking at her with sad brown eyes. She patted the cushion. "Come sit beside me, boy."

"Rule number two, the dog is not allowed on the furniture," Em said as she took a seat at the far end of the sectional. "Gus, sit."

The dog whined, pressing close to Bri's uninjured leg, but he did as he was told. Bri didn't blame him. Em had a commanding cop's voice that matched the hard set of her full lips. She was far more intimidating than she used to be.

Reaching down to comfort herself as much as Gus,

Bri petted the dog. "I think we can work this out without a set of rules. We're adults, and clearly we both would have preferred living on our own."

"No kidding. So whose bright idea was it for us to live together?"

"Trust me, I plan to find out." Abby had some explaining to do. "But unless you have somewhere else to go, we need to make this work, because I'm not leaving." There, she'd said it.

Em raised an eyebrow. "Is that right?"

She nodded. "I was here first, and I really like this house." She'd like it even better if it wasn't down the road from Cal and if it didn't remind her of the life they'd planned together.

She supposed that might also be the reason she liked it so much. The memories of how much she'd once loved Cal seemed to be in the forefront of her mind these days. And while she might not agree with his and Raine's subterfuge, his reasons for going along with it spoke to the heart of him, reminding her why she'd fallen in love with him. He was a good man, kind and compassionate. A man who was willing to put his life on hold to ensure the well-being of his stepdaughter.

He was also a man who could make Bri moan with the simple touch of his fingers on her foot, she thought, embarrassed by the memory. Maybe his sister's rule about no entertaining family and friends at the house was a good one. The less time Bri spent around Cal, the better.

"You may not have noticed, but the house is big enough that we won't get in each other's way," Bri continued, determined to get this over with so she could hide out in her room while Cal helped his sister move in. "You have the upstairs, and if you want, you can have this room. There's a den off the kitchen that suits me."

Em looked around. "Okay. I can live with that. What time do you get up?"

She was embarrassed to tell her. "I've had insomnia since the accident so I sleep in."

"Yeah," Em said without meeting her gaze. "I don't sleep much at night either."

Bri's heart ached for Em, and she wished there was something she could do or say to ease her pain. But even if she could, she doubted her offer of comfort would be appreciated. She could change the subject though. "There's a small patio in the backyard. It's a little over-run with weeds. The flower and vegetable gardens are the same, but I'm happy to take care of them."

"Have at it." The tension in Em's mouth softened, and her lips turned up at the corners. "Brad says I can't keep a..." She closed her eyes, leaving her fiancé's name hanging in the air.

"A cactus alive?" Bri said in an attempt to smooth over the moment. "Your brother used to say the same thing." It wasn't until Em's eyes narrowed in suspicion that Bri realized her voice had softened much like Em's had when she talked about her fiancé.

Someone knocked on the door, and it eased open. "Is it safe to come in?" asked a voice from the past, one she hadn't heard in a long time. Cal's best friend, Josh.

"Of course it's safe, you idiot. Why wouldn't it be?" Em said.

"Oh, I don't know. Maybe because the last time you two were in the same room together, all hell broke loose," Josh said as he shouldered the door open. "Where do you want these, Freckles?"

Bri shook her head. Josh hadn't changed. He'd always gone out of his way to tease his best friend's baby sister. Bri wondered if he had any idea that years ago Em had been in love with him. Em's crush on Josh had actually been the reason Bri had spent so much time with Cal that long-ago summer, inevitably falling in love with him.

Em scowled at Josh. "Just leave the boxes there. I'll take them up later. I'm sure my brother could use a hand with the TV."

Josh set the boxes at the bottom of the stairs and sauntered over. "I'll just hang out with you two for a few minutes, if you don't mind."

"We mind." Em made a shooing motion with her hand.

Josh ignored her and sat down between them. "Cal's talking to Raine. Hey there, fella," he said, leaning over to pat Gus. He lifted his gaze to Bri. "Long time no see. How are you doing?"

"I'm good, thanks. How are you?" She was surprised she sounded normal when all she could think about was Cal talking to Raine, no doubt about her living here. If Raine's behavior at the hospital the other day was any indication, the woman would not be happy. No matter what Cal would have Bri believe.

"I knew it," Em said, launching herself off the couch. She walked to the living room window. "How can my brother be so smart yet so clueless about women?" She didn't have to shoot Bri a pursed-lipped look for her to deduce she was one of the women Em was talking about. Raine no doubt being the other. "I warned Cal she wasn't going to be happy you were living here. But even I didn't think she'd be this upset." Em winced, and Bri found herself doing the same.

"Cal's problem is he assumes everyone is as compassionate and as forgiving as he is," Josh said, glancing at Bri.

Her face heated at the thought that Cal felt sorry for her. "I don't need anyone's pity or forgiveness," Bri said, nudging Gus out of the way so she could stand up.

Em turned on her. "Seriously? You don't think that, after what you did to my brother, you should be begging for his forgiveness? He was beside himself after you ended your engagement. He—"

Bri threw up her hands, tired of being made to feel like the bad guy in their breakup. "You seem to forget that your brother broke off our engagement, not me. If anyone's heart was broken, it was mine." She stood up. "You know what, I don't care what any of you think of me. And I don't care if you stay or go, Em. I'm staying, and you'll just have to suck it up, and so will Raine."

"Sure, just run away when things get tough. It's what you always did," Em jeered.

Bri lifted her cane, pretending Em's jab didn't hurt. "Walking away. I can't run anymore."

The door opened, and Cal walked in carrying three boxes. He set them beside the ones Josh had brought in. Then he straightened, looking from Bri to his sister. "What's going on in here?"

"Nothing," Bri said, and went to move past him.

"Bri was just telling us that you broke her heart, not the other way around," Em scoffed. "Somehow she's convinced herself that you were the one who ended your engagement, not her."

Cal's green eyes darkened as he searched Bri's face, a frown furrowing his brow. "Let it go, Em. It doesn't matter who—"

"It might not matter to you, but it matters to me," his sister said.

"You know what?" Bri said. "It matters to me too. So let's clear this up once and for all so I don't have to be the recipient of your sister's snide remarks or Josh implying that I don't deserve your pity and forgiveness."

"Hey, wait a minute. That's not what I said."

"No, it's what you *implied*," Bri said, returning to the couch before her leg gave out. Cal reached out to help her, and she shook off his hand. "I don't need your help or anyone else's."

"Wow. Talk about ungrateful. He saved your life, lady. If he hadn't gotten to the inn on time, you would have died," Em said.

Bri wanted to bury her face in her hands. Em had changed her mind about sharing the house with Bri for one reason and one reason only: pity. Cal had used Bri's accident to garner his sister's sympathy and guilt her into changing her mind. Bri had little doubt that he'd shared she'd been trying to escape her abusive husband when she left the hospital. It would make her even more pathetic in his sister's eyes.

"You had no right to tell her that, Cal."

"Do you hear yourself?" Em said. "You keep making

everything my brother's fault. If you think I wouldn't have heard about your accident or your ex within a day of being back in Highland Falls, you're delusional. Then again, maybe you are, if you keep holding on to the false narrative you've created about Cal ending your engagement."

Without taking his eyes from Bri, Cal said, "I was the one who ended our engagement, so can you just—"

His sister threw up her hands. "Because she didn't have the guts to tell you she didn't love you anymore, and you being you—"

"Cal, what's she talking about? Why would you think—"

"Oh, come on, are you really going to pretend that you didn't have your mother call him the morning you were going to announce your engagement? I was sitting right there when she called, when she told him you couldn't bear to hurt him but that you didn't love him anymore."

"That's not true," Bri said. "Why are you doing this? Why are you lying?"

Some of the fire went out of Em's eyes, and she looked from Bri to her brother, who'd paled beneath his tanned skin.

Josh released a low whistle. "I told you something was off, buddy. You should have listened to me."

Bri blanched. It was true then. Everything Em had said was true. Her mother had done this. "She didn't want me to move away with you," Bri said, pressing a hand to her mouth, afraid she might throw up. "She wanted me to go to school in Durham. She wanted to keep me close." Bri lifted her eyes to Cal, who hadn't moved. "I didn't know. I never stopped loving you."

"Freckles, give me a hand with the boxes," Josh said as he got up from the couch. Em didn't argue, following him quietly from the living room.

Cal took Josh's place on the couch. Resting his elbows on his thighs, he scrubbed his hands over his face and bit out a vicious curse.

"Why did you believe her?" Bri pushed the words past her emotion-clogged throat. "Why didn't you just come out and ask me?"

He leaned back against the cushions, turning his head to look at her. "Pride, maybe? I'm not really sure. But some of what your mother said rang true. We were young. I was in med school, buried under student loans. I couldn't give you the life you deserved. So I guess she played into some of my own fears."

Reaching over, he gently wiped away the tears rolling down her cheeks. Until that moment, Bri hadn't realized she was crying.

"If you'd said something, anything, no matter how small, that gave me hope I could change your mind when I called that day, I wouldn't have broken our engagement." He held her gaze. "But you didn't. All you said was 'Okay, I understand.'"

"What was I supposed to say? I was in shock. It felt like it had come out of the blue. I…" She closed her eyes, thinking back to the conversation she'd had with her mother the night before they'd announced their engagement.

"What?"

"I didn't do a great job hiding how happy I was that night, and I guess my mother could tell something was going on. I didn't mean to tell her about our engagement, but I was so excited, it just slipped out. I wish I'd called Ellie instead."

"Okay, that explains how she knew but it doesn't explain why you didn't say anything. I'm not casting blame here, Bri. I'd just like to know how your mother was able to manipulate us into giving up on everything we'd talked about, all our plans for the future."

"She did the same to me as she did to you, Cal." She looked away. Unable to meet his gaze when she confessed the fears that had sometimes kept her awake at night. "You were the perfect guy, and I—"

"Come on, Bri, I was far from perfect."

"To me you were. You were so handsome, and so smart, and you had so many big goals and dreams. I'd never met anyone who worked as hard as you or sacrificed so much for their family. You were as good a quarterback as Josh in high school, but your work schedule conflicted with games and practices, and you had to choose between playing and supporting your mom and Em. If you weren't working as much as you were back then, you wouldn't have missed so much school. You would have gotten a scholarship. I didn't want you to have to sacrifice your dreams for your future because of me."

"You were my future. You were my dream. None of them mattered without you." He entwined his fingers with hers and gave them a gentle squeeze. "Sorry. Go on."

How was she supposed to go on after that? She stared

down at her hand in his and cleared the emotion from her throat. "My mother told me I'd hold you back, and you'd come to resent me. She told me you needed someone stronger, more mature. Someone who could be your partner, not someone who was used to being pampered and protected."

"And you believed her?"

"Of course I did. You know what my family was like. For as long as I can remember, they've pampered and protected me, especially my mother and Ellie. I always thought it was because I was the baby of the family. It was only this past year that I found out the real reason." She glanced at him. "You know my father isn't my biological father, don't you? That I'm the result of my mother's affair with Dimitri Ivanov?"

"Yeah. I do. Your brother told me."

She nodded, not surprised that her brother had shared her paternity with him. But there were some things the family had agreed to keep to themselves. "What you don't know is that Dimitri's wife learned about their affair and threatened my mother and my family if she didn't end it with him. Even when she did, his wife had someone continue following my mother. They took pictures of her pregnant with me and made it clear what would happen if Dimitri ever found out I existed. And they weren't idle threats. His wife's family was involved in organized crime."

Cal rubbed his hand over his stubbled jaw. "Yeah, that does put a few things in perspective. But if your mother was so concerned about the threat, why did she let you go to Charlotte and marry your ex?"

"Obviously I didn't know the truth at that point—no one other than my sister did—but I was finishing up my master's in family and marriage therapy and had no intention of living under my mother's thumb forever. I was looking into opening a practice in Charlotte with a friend. My dad backed my decision, and that was a pretty big deal. Around that time, Richard was guest-lecturing at the university. He lived and worked in Charlotte, and I guess in my mother's mind, if I was going to live there, I'd be safer if I had a man in my life, so she became Richard's biggest champion. The ironic thing is, it was because of Richard that my mother reconnected with Dimitri last year."

Bri's phone rang. She lifted her hip and removed it from her pocket. Her sister's name appeared on the screen.

"Sorry, I have to take this," she told Cal, who appeared lost in thought. "Hi, Ellie."

"Is everything okay? You sound off."

She bowed her head and felt Cal shift closer on the couch. He moved her hair aside and began kneading the tension knotting the muscles in her neck with his strong, warm fingers. She glanced at him, and he mouthed, *Don't tell her.*

She nodded, grateful for the reminder. There was no way her sister would go on her honeymoon if Bri shared what their mother had done. "A little tired. It's been a busy day."

"Go lie down, and I'll take care of whatever else needs to be done when I get there. Mom and I are at the grocery store now. Is there anything you need that I might not have on my list?"

Cal, who could obviously hear her sister, stopped massaging Bri's neck. He lowered his hand, smoothing it down the back of her T-shirt in a comforting touch before he came to his feet and walked to the window.

"Whatever you pick up is fine. You know what I like."

Cal turned and mouthed, *Ice.*

"Sorry. I just remembered I need ice."

"Already on my list," her sister said cheerfully. "We'll see you in twenty minutes."

"See you then." She disconnected from her sister and looked at Cal. "I have no idea how I'm going to be in the same room as my mother and not strangle her."

"I'm pretty sure I won't be able to hold back, so I'd better get the U-Haul unloaded before they get here. Josh, Em, come give me a hand," Cal called up the stairs.

At the sound of their footsteps in the upstairs hall, Cal opened the door and then turned to look at her. "I'll be back later. We need to talk."

"I don't think that's a good idea, Cal. Em said Raine was upset. She was watching you through the window," she clarified at his raised eyebrow.

"Raine wasn't thrilled to hear you were living here," he admitted. "But she was more upset that her ex is moving back to town. He's taking over the position of town manager from his mother. Something Winter and Raine's ex–mother-in-law shared with her an hour ago."

It sounded like things had just gotten more complicated for Cal and Raine, and Bri couldn't help thinking of her former lawyer clients. "I guess it's a good thing neither you or Raine are looking to fall in love."

"Yeah, good thing."

Chapter Ten

♥

So, that was quite the revelation," Josh said as he joined Cal at the back of the U-Haul. "How are you handling it?"

"I'm not sure," he said, dragging his sister's boxed big-screen TV toward him. "On the one hand, it doesn't change anything. While on the other hand, it changes everything." He shrugged. "The one thing I do know is I can't be here when Bri's mother arrives." He glanced at the house. "Where's Em?"

"Talking to Bri. She feels pretty bad about how she acted. I think she's apologizing." Josh rubbed his head. "I probably should apologize too. Not for today," Josh said at Cal's raised eyebrow. "I gave her the cold shoulder anytime I saw her in town. I might have called her out about it when she was at the Fall Festival with her family a few weeks after you guys broke up. I'd always wondered about her reaction. She seemed shocked when I told her she'd broken your heart. It makes sense now."

"Yeah. If only she'd told me." He shook his head. "If only I'd told her."

"Her mother has a lot to answer for," Josh said, grabbing the other end of the box.

"She does, but Bri can't confront her until Ellie takes off for Scotland, or everything she's done these past few days will be for nothing." After learning why Miranda had sabotaged their engagement, he could sympathize with Bri's mother, but he didn't think he'd ever be able to forgive her.

And it looked like he wasn't the only one. His sister stalked toward them, her hands balled into fists. "I want to hit something."

"Don't look at me," Josh said.

"I know the feeling, Freckles," Cal said. "But you have to keep a lid on it. Come back to the house with me once we get the last of your stuff unloaded."

"And listen to Raine yell at you for Bri living here? I don't think so. I mean, I don't blame her for being upset, but now that I know what Bri's mother did to you guys, I might stick up for Bri, and that wouldn't endear me to my sister-in-law."

"Why? It's not as if Raine is in love—hey," Josh said when Cal pushed the box into his chest to get him to stop talking.

"What did you just say?" Em asked, her narrowed gaze moving from Josh to Cal.

"Nothing. He didn't say—"

"She doesn't know?"

Cal bowed his head. "She didn't until now," he muttered, lowering the box onto the front porch.

Josh looked from Cal to Em. "I think I need a glass of water." He opened the front door and dragged the box the rest of the way inside.

Cal sat on the step, and his sister joined him. "Raine and I are separated, Em," he said, and then he told her what had been going on for the past year with Raine and with Izzy.

"I can't believe you didn't tell me. Were you afraid I was going to say 'I told you so'?"

"You can say it now." He laughed when she did. "Seriously though, Raine wanted to keep it quiet. She thought the fewer people who knew, the better. And I know you, you wouldn't have been able to let it go."

"You're right about that. But while I don't agree with what you two are doing, I get it. The greater good and all that. And then there's Izzy. Poor kid. How is she handling everything?"

"I thought she was doing okay, but something's going on with her. Maybe you can get her to open up."

"Sure. I can try." She glanced at the closed front door. "Your life just got a whole lot more complicated, big brother. What are you going to do about Bri?"

"What do you mean? Nothing's changed."

"Really? You just found out she never stopped loving you. And don't try and tell me your feelings for her ever went away. You guys were sickeningly in love."

"We were. But sometimes love isn't enough. Obviously, in our case, it wasn't. We let ourselves be manipulated by her mother. We didn't fight for what we had. You'd think if it was worth fighting for, we would have." He stood up and held out his hand, pulling his sister to her feet. He slung an arm around her shoulders as they walked to the U-Haul. "This wasn't exactly how I envisioned your homecoming. How are you holding up?"

"You always do that, you know. You put everyone else's needs before your own, and it's about time you stop."

"Old habits die hard, I guess. But I'm okay, Freckles. You don't have to worry about me."

"Fine. I won't worry about you if you don't worry about me."

"I'm your big brother. It's my job to worry about you."

"I'm almost thirty years old, Cal. I'm not the little girl whose scraped knees you used to bandage, or the girl you protected from the schoolyard bullies, or the one who always came to you for money when she was short." She made a face. "Okay, so maybe I'm still that girl."

"I'm sorry. I shouldn't have held that over you to get you here. I would have paid for your place in Nashville if I thought that's what was best for you. But it wasn't, and I think you know that. You need to be with people who love you."

She nodded, looking up the road, where a couple of kids were playing basketball. "Do you remember when we were here last year, helping you and Raine move in?"

He smiled at the memory. "Yeah, that was a great weekend."

"Brad thought so too. He wanted us to move here. He even went so far as to check out HFPD to see if there were any openings." She went quiet for a minute, looking up at the sky and blinking her eyes. Her voice was husky when she continued. "He loved you like a brother."

"I loved him too. I miss him." He drew her into his arms. "You'll get through this, Em. We'll get through it together."

He hadn't realized Josh had joined them until he pulled them both into a group hug. "This is awesome. The gang's back together again." His best friend had never been good at reading a room.

Em elbowed Josh in the gut. Opening her mouth to no doubt give him hell, her eyes went wide. "Crap."

He followed her gaze. A red pickup was turning onto Marigold Lane.

"Go home, Cal," his sister said, pushing him in that direction.

"She's right. We've got this." Josh slung his arm around Em's shoulders. "Don't worry about Freckles. I'll keep her in line."

Cal left the two of them sniping at each other and jogged up the road to the house he shared with Raine and Izzy. As he opened the front door, he saw it through fresh eyes. They hadn't made it a home. It looked like they were just biding their time, and he wondered if that's what Izzy saw every time she walked into the house on Marigold Lane. He walked through to the kitchen. "Raine? Izzy?"

"In here," Raine called from the office at the back of the house. "I think Izzy went out with friends," she said, avoiding his gaze as he leaned against the door frame.

"I told her I was bringing Em home. I thought she'd meet us at the house."

"A sixteen-year-old will choose their friends over family every time, Cal. I don't know why you don't get it," she said, staring at the computer screen.

"I know. I guess I was just hoping she'd want to hang out with Em. I'm worried about Izzy, Raine. She hasn't been herself this past week. Did you get a chance to talk to her about it?" Izzy had read half his texts without responding to them. The other half had received short, to-the-point answers.

"When was I supposed to do that, Cal? I've spent the past two days calling everyone I can think of to donate to the trauma center. And then today, my mother and Nina dumped their news about Quinn on me."

"Look, I know you're upset about Quinn taking over as town manager." Cal walked to the desk, sitting on the edge. Something clicked with him when he said it. Maybe Raine wasn't the only one upset about Quinn's return. "Is there any chance Izzy knew he was moving to town?"

"No. I..." She shrugged. "I guess it's possible. She helped Mom out at the store last Friday when she was short-staffed." As well as being mayor, Winter owned Flower Power on Main Street. "That would have been around the time Nina shared the news with Mom. But what does that have to do with Izzy? There's no reason for her to be upset. She isn't the one whose hopes and dreams Quinn could wipe out with a stroke of his pen." She buried her face in her hands. "What are we going to do, Cal?"

"Stop worrying about it until you know you have something to worry about, which I'm almost positive you don't. Quinn is a good guy." .

Admittedly Cal had some issues with the way Quinn had cut Izzy out of his life. But he'd idolized Quinn growing up. He was four years older than Cal, and he'd been the star quarterback at Highland Falls High. He'd made it big in the NFL but he'd blown out his knee three years into what had been a stellar career. Quinn had gone back to school and had gotten his MBA. He was more than qualified for the job as town manager. "But, Raine, I think you're wrong about Izzy. I've noticed a change in her. The timing fits."

She lifted her face from her hands. "You're telling me not to worry about it as if I'm in this alone. We're in this together, remember? Or is Brianna MacLeod your priority now?"

"Don't make this about Bri. I'm as committed to the trauma center as I always was. You're the one who's worried about Quinn, not me."

"Funny thing about that. You became much more committed to the expansion after Brianna's accident."

"Stop. I'm not doing this, not now. We have to talk about Izzy. Quinn helped raise her for the first five years of her life."

Raine had been a cheerleader and as head over heels in love with Quinn as half the girls in Highland Falls. But according to Raine, he'd kept her at arm's length because of their mothers' friendship.

Apparently, things had changed between them when Raine's brother died. They'd grieved his loss together and one thing led to another. But Quinn ended their relationship soon after receiving a football scholarship. Raine hadn't taken it well. She'd started partying and dating other guys. When she'd found herself pregnant with Izzy, Quinn had stepped in and married her. Not the best way to start off a marriage, but they were together for six years.

"What does that have to do with anything? He's not her biological father. You've raised her for five years. And trust me, you've been more of a hands-on father than Quinn ever was."

Cal noticed she left out her second husband. She didn't talk about him much. Then again, their marriage had lasted only eighteen months. The ink had barely dried on her divorce from Quinn when she'd married for a second time.

"I don't know. It seems too coincidental to me. We—" His phone pinged. He pulled it from his pocket, hoping it was Izzy. It wasn't; it was Josh. He'd texted 911. "I've gotta go. But, Raine, we need to sit down with Izzy and talk about this."

"Cal! You just got here. We have to talk about how we're going to raise the—"

"I know, and I promise, this won't take long," he said, heading out of her office.

"Does this have anything to do with Brianna or your sister?" she called after him.

"No. Josh," he shouted over his shoulder before closing the front door behind him. Technically, it was true. And if he'd told her it had to do with Bri, she'd be hoofing it down the street after him. He had a feeling he was going to be dealing with enough drama.

A car pulled into the driveway as he sprinted across the front yard. Izzy got out of the back passenger side, girls' laughter and rap music following her out of the car.

"Hey, Iz," he called, jogging backward down the road. "I've gotta do something for Aunt Em, but I won't be long. How about we grab something to eat at Zia Maria's later?"

Izzy pushed her long, dark, curly hair from her face. "I'm going to a barbecue at a friend's. Maybe some other night, okay?"

He suspected she'd tacked that on because she sensed his disappointment, which he supposed was a good sign. At least she cared enough to try and appease him. "Sure, honey." He ducked his head to get a look at the teenager behind the wheel. "Is that Sam?"

"Oh my gosh, Dad. Yes, and yes he's eighteen and never been in an accident, and no, he doesn't drink and drive, and no, we're not driving around town all night." She threw up her hands. "You're so annoying!"

"I know. Sucks to have a dad who loves you." And one who'd had to perform lifesaving surgery on far too many teenagers out for joyrides. "Be home by eleven."

"I'm sixteen! I got home after midnight last night, and Mom didn't say anything."

He doubted Raine even knew where Izzy had been or when she'd gotten in. The bid for the trauma center had become all-consuming. But at least he now understood why half his texts to Izzy had gone unanswered and why the other half had received two-word responses.

"See you at eleven," he said, wincing when the front door slammed behind her.

He pulled out his phone as he jogged down the road, texting Raine.

Don't cave. Her curfew is at eleven, just like we agreed.

Pocketing his phone, he glanced at the red truck
parked behind the U-Haul. If Ellie was still there, it
meant her mother was too, and no doubt the reason for
Josh's 911 text. Cal sprinted up the walkway, taking the
stairs in a single leap.

He opened the front door in time to hear Bri say, "No.
There's nothing you can do to make it right. I loved
him. It wasn't puppy love, Mom. It was real, and true,
and deep."

The words hit him hard, and he closed the door, leaning against it. Somehow hearing Bri's passionate defense
of their love penetrated more than hearing her say she'd
loved him earlier. Then again, he was pretty sure he'd
been in shock.

"I can see that you're upset, Brianna. So perhaps now
isn't the time to discuss—"

Cal pushed off the door, following the raised voices
to the kitchen. Bri sat at one end of the kitchen table,
his sister at the other end. Ellie stood beside her mother,
the two women backed against the kitchen counter. Josh,
who stood by the patio door, looked like he was considering leaving until he spotted Cal. The women followed
Josh's relieved gaze, all except Bri, who hadn't taken her
eyes off her mother.

"Upset. You think I'm upset? How can you stand
there acting like you did nothing wrong? You ruined
my life!"

"I most certainly did not. I saved you from making
the same mistake I did. I saved you both from making
a horrible mistake." She gestured toward him. "Caleb
wouldn't have become the successful trauma surgeon

that he is or married Raine. A woman who has done more for him and his career than you ever could."

"That's enough," Cal said as he walked up behind Bri, resting his hands on her shoulders.

"Cal's right, Mom." Ellie came to crouch in front of Bri, taking her hands in hers. "I'm so sorry. I didn't know. I'll take Mom home, and then I'll come back, and we can talk."

"No. You've spent the past two days helping me with the move, and you have stuff to do to get ready for your trip. You can't make this right, Ellie. This isn't on you. It's on her."

Bri glared at her mother, who lifted her chin and said, "I'll wait for you in the truck, Elliana," and walked from the kitchen.

Bri stared after her. "I don't understand how she walked out of here looking like she was the injured party. As if she'd done nothing wrong."

"At the very least she owes you an apology," Ellie began.

Em snorted. "An apology? She should be groveling at their feet for forgiveness."

Ellie glanced at Em and Josh and then lowered her voice. "What she did was awful, truly despicable, but you know the kind of pressure she was under back then, Bri. Knowing that, can't you find it in your heart to forgive her?"

"Ellie, she's the reason any of that happened in the first place. She had an affair with a married man. And not just any married man. Dimitri Ivanov."

Cal's sister looked stunned. "Dimitri Ivanov? Your mother had an affair with Dimitri Ivanov?"

"Um, Bri, maybe we should talk in private," her sister suggested.

Apparently Bri disagreed. "Oh, trust me, it gets better. My mother got pregnant with Dimitri's child. I'll give you one guess who, and it wasn't Ellie or Jace."

Josh released a low whistle, and Em said, "Holy crap."

"I know you're hurt now, and angry, and you have every right to be, but please, please promise me you won't shut Mom out completely. We can work this out. You know we can. We're a family."

"I'm not you, Ellie. You've forgiven her for the way she treated you growing up, but I haven't. And now finding out what she did to me and Cal?" She shook her head. "I'm sorry, but I don't think I'll be able to or even want to."

"No, don't apologize to me." Ellie pressed Bri's hand to her cheek. "You didn't need this on top of everything else. What can I do to make you feel better?"

"Go on your honeymoon. That's it. That's all I ask."

"I can't, Bri. I'm sorry, but I just can't." Ellie came to her feet, reaching out to touch Cal's forearm. "I'm so sorry, Cal. If I'd known—"

"Bri's right, Ellie. You have nothing to apologize for."

Ellie glanced from him to Bri and then nodded. "I'd better go. If you need anything, just call me."

Bri watched her sister leave and then tipped her head back, looking up at him with tear-filled eyes. "I just couldn't do it, Cal. I couldn't keep my mouth shut, and now look what I've done."

"Sorry, am I interrupting something?"

At the sound of Raine's voice, he and Bri turned their heads.

She gave them a thin-lipped smile. "Your sister let me in, Brianna. I hope you don't mind."

Cal lowered his hands from Bri's shoulders as she shot up straight in the chair. "No, not at all. We, ah, were just—"

"Oh, come on, get the guilty look off your face," Em said to Bri. "It's not like you were doing anything wrong. Even if you were making out in the middle of the kitchen, you wouldn't have to explain yourself. It's not as if Raine and Cal are together."

"Cal!" Raine said at the same time Cal muttered a distracted "Em." He was having a hard time getting the image of him and Bri making out in the kitchen out of his head.

"What? It's just us. We all know," Josh said.

Raine threw up her hands. "How could you do this, Cal? You know what's at stake."

His sister answered for him. "Don't get your panties in a twist, Raine. It's not like any of us are going to say anything."

Josh snorted, clearing his throat when Raine turned on him. "No one will hear about it from me. But seriously, I doubt anyone would believe me anyway. You guys give an award-winning performance of a happily married couple."

Raine narrowed her eyes at Josh, as if waiting for the punch line. She wasn't a fan of Cal's best friend.

"They're not going to say anything, Raine. And to be honest, I feel better not having to lie to them," Cal said.

"Yeah, one for all, and all for one. We're a crew. A team. Besties for the resties," Josh said.

Bri looked at Cal, her lips pressed together, her eyes no longer glinting with tears but with amusement. Josh had always been able to make her laugh. Cal was grateful for his friend, even if that probably hadn't been Josh's intention. Em groaned. "You're so lame."

Raine rolled her eyes. "As much as I'd love to stick around for the rest of Josh's stand-up routine, we have to go, Cal. My mother invited us for dinner, and I'm hoping we can get her to rescind the job offer to"—she glanced around—"you know who."

"And here I thought you'd come to welcome me to the neighborhood," his sister said.

Raine winced, looking genuinely remorseful. "Of course I did." She walked to where Em sat and leaned in, giving her a hug. "I'm glad you're here. We'll do lunch this week."

"Sure," Em said, sounding a little sheepish for doubting Raine's intentions.

Unlike Cal, who had no doubts about why she was here, which Raine proved less than a minute later. "Okay, then, if you ladies no longer need *my husband*, we'll be on our way." Raine looked directly at Bri, staking her claim.

It didn't matter that Raine was no longer in love with him or that everyone in this kitchen was aware they were in a fake relationship. Raine saw Bri as a threat to her plan, and unlike Josh, she was very, very good at reading a room. And it looked like she'd decided that the best way to eliminate the threat was to convince Bri that she was still in love with Cal.

Knowing Bri as well as he did, he wouldn't stand

a chance of rekindling their relationship if she fell for Raine's act. The thought brought him up short. Until that moment, he hadn't realized he wanted a second chance. When he'd told Em nothing had changed, he'd been lying to himself. Everything had changed the moment he'd walked into the house and heard Bri talk about the love they'd once shared.

Chapter Eleven

♥

Bri leaned across the bed and turned off the white-noise machine on the nightstand. It was more annoying than helpful. She'd gone to bed early in hopes she'd actually fall asleep. It had been a long, emotionally draining day. But here she was, three hours later, still wide awake and staring at the ceiling. Frustrated, she threw back the covers, grabbed her cane, and got out of bed.

At least she didn't have to worry she'd wake Ellie with her nighttime wanderings. But she'd succeeded in giving her sister something else to worry about—a reason to cancel her trip. If only Bri had been able to hold back the furious accusations she'd hurled at her mother. All she had to do was keep them bottled up inside for a few more days. It shouldn't have been so hard.

She'd bottled up her shame, her guilt, her anger at herself and at Richard for the last year of their marriage. Other than her psychic sister, no one had guessed the hell her marriage had become. Everyone thought they were happily married.

Like another couple she knew.

Her hand on the doorknob, she squeezed her eyes shut to ward off thoughts of Cal and Raine. She'd spent too much time thinking about them tonight. As her mother had so callously pointed out, they were perfect together. Sometimes, the truth hurt. Cal deserved someone like Raine, a woman who was his equal. A woman who was strong, confident, and successful. A woman who, whether Cal knew it or not, was still in love with him.

"Stop it," Bri muttered, yanking open the bedroom door. Cal and Raine's relationship had nothing to do with her. It didn't matter whether they stayed together or not.

"Liar," whispered a voice in her head.

"I'm not lying," she murmured, glancing into the living room as she made her way to the kitchen. Moonlight streamed through the window, illuminating the couch where she and Cal had sat. So what if she'd gotten caught up in a what-if loop when she'd first learned the truth behind her and Cal's breakup? It was a perfectly reasonable reaction. It didn't mean she was still in love with him. It didn't mean she—

A low moan from the second floor cut off the defensive debate in her head. She turned on the hall light. Gus stood on the second-floor landing. He whined, looking behind him and then back at her, whining again.

At the sound of soft whimpers coming from one of the bedrooms, Bri moved toward the stairs. "Okay, boy. I'm coming." She used the handrail and her cane to maneuver her way up the stairs, cursing her slow, painful progress.

When the whimpers changed to pitiful cries, she gritted her teeth and took the last of the stairs two at a time.

As she reached the open door of the first bedroom, she heard a low, guttural moan filled with so much pain it nearly brought her to tears. She patted the wall and turned on the hall light. On the bed, Em tossed and turned, her blankets and pillows strewn across the hardwood floor. Gus hung back when Bri hurried to Em's side.

"No!" Em moaned, and then started screaming, "Brad," over and over again.

Bri put a hand on her shoulder. "Em, it's just a—"

Em jerked upright, flinging out her arm, hitting Bri in her stomach with such force it knocked the wind out of her. She staggered backward, using her cane to keep from falling. Once she regained her balance, she went to walk back to the bed and froze. From the doorway, Gus barked.

"Em, put down the gun. It's me. It's Bri."

Em blinked and then looked around. She reached for the bedside lamp and turned it on. "What the hell were you thinking, Bri? You don't sneak into someone's room in the middle of the night." She put the gun on the nightstand.

"I wasn't sneaking into your room. I came to check on you. You were having a bad dream." Afraid her legs were about to give out, Bri lowered herself onto the side of the bed.

Em pushed her hair from her tearstained face. "Why are you rubbing your stomach?"

She hadn't known she was, but she wasn't about to tell Em that she hit her. It was obvious she was embarrassed Bri had witnessed her nightmare. "Do you mind putting your gun away?"

"It's not like I'm going to shoot you, Bri." Her eyes narrowed. "I hit you, didn't I?"

"It was more a case of you going for your gun, and I was in your way." Bri smiled. "You're a lot stronger than you used to be."

"Physically, maybe," Em said, leaning over the edge of the bed. She opened the nightstand, punching a code into a safe. The door opened, and she placed the gun inside.

"Do you have nightmares about your fiancé's shooting often?"

"How did you know?"

"You screamed, 'No,' and then you called out his name."

Em looked away. "I have the same dream every time I go to sleep."

"Sometimes dreams are our way of processing a traumatic event. It might help if you talk about it, Em."

"You said you don't sleep at night. Do you have bad dreams too?"

Redirection, something Bri had often used in her counseling practice. She didn't want to talk about herself but she wanted Em to open up to her, and in this case, establishing common ground might work. Em was suffering, and Bri wanted to help. "I did in the beginning. I dreamed about the accident, but now it's mostly my leg that keeps me awake."

"Mostly?"

"Migraines, panic attacks, take your pick. I'm a bit of a mess."

Em snorted. "Welcome to the club." Then, looking a

little sheepish, she glanced at Bri. "I'm sorry I was such a jerk to you today."

"Which time?"

Em's eyes widened, and then she laughed. "Okay. I deserved that."

"No. I'm teasing. You were just being protective of Cal. I understand why now. And I owe you an apology too."

"For what? Your mother—"

"No. Not about that. About before. When Cal and I started dating. I put my relationship with him ahead of ours, Em. I wasn't a good friend, and I'm really sorry about that."

"Yeah, well, I took my bitchiness a little too far back then." She shrugged. "In my defense, one minute we were best friends, and in the next, it was like I didn't exist. And it wasn't only you. My brother was just as bad. I don't think I really understood what it was like for you guys. I'd never loved someone like that, not until I met Brad." She looked up at the ceiling. "How did you do it, Bri? How did you go on after you lost Cal?"

"Oh, Em," Bri said, putting her arm around her. "It's not the same. Brad died. You lost him in a senseless act of violence."

Em wiped at her eyes. "Don't tell Cal about the gun or the nightmares, okay? He has enough on his plate without worrying about me."

"He does, and trust me, I know what it's like dealing with overprotective family members. Your secrets are safe with me."

"Ellie is overprotective, but she has nothing on Cal. He basically moved in with me this summer."

"Uh, I lived with my sister and grandfather at the inn for more than a year. They were my shadows for months." And then, like when they were young, Bri found herself confiding in Em.

She told her how she'd felt smothered. How her family's constant fretting and hovering made her feel like they didn't trust her to take care of herself and how she'd begun to wonder if maybe they were right.

She buried her face in her hands and shook her head. "I can't believe I told you all that. My family's so good to me, and Ellie's sacrificed so much for me, and I sound like an ungrateful witch."

"I get it. I do. Cal actually thought I was going to hurt myself. I wanted to smack him or throw something at him, and then I felt guilty and ungrateful, and then I resented him for making me feel that way." Em sighed and looked around the bedroom, pulling a face. "I hate to break it to you, but despite you moving out of the inn and me moving here, I have a feeling your sister and my brother aren't going to stop worrying about us and smothering us anytime soon."

"You're right, and as you witnessed this afternoon, I managed to make things worse. There's no way Ellie will ever go on her honeymoon now."

"I have an idea. You help me convince Cal I'm fine, and I'll help you convince Ellie you are too, and she'll go on her honeymoon."

"Deal." Bri smiled. "But we don't have a lot of time to convince Ellie. She's supposed to leave next week."

"It doesn't look like either of us is going to sleep anytime soon, so we might as well do something productive and come up with a plan." Em got out of bed, offering Bri her hand.

Bri accepted the help while trying to hide a pained wince. She must not have done a very good job, because Em angled her head to study her. Except as Bri followed Em's gaze, she realized Em hadn't noticed she was in pain. No, what she'd noticed was far more embarrassing.

"Is that Cal's sweatshirt?" Em asked.

Bri was about to say no but then looked down at the hunter-green sweatshirt she wore over a pair of black sleep pants. There was no way she could claim the sweatshirt wasn't four sizes too big for her or that it wasn't a Highland Falls High sweatshirt. The emblem was faded but still legible. "I found it in one of the boxes. Sadie must have left it at the inn, and I packed it by mistake." A lame excuse, but she had nothing else.

"Sure she did." Em looked down at the sweatshirt she wore, lifting the neck to her nose. "This was Brad's. It doesn't smell like him anymore." Her eyes filled, and then she blew out a breath.

"After Cal and I broke up, I used to shower with Axe body wash," Bri admitted as they left the bedroom.

Em wrinkled her nose. "I remember when he went through his Axe phase. Brad wore Armani." She glanced back at the bedroom. "I'll be down in a minute."

"Ellie brought ice cream. I'll get us some," Bri said, making her way to the landing.

Josh had stuck around to help Em after Cal and Raine left, while Bri had stayed holed up in her bedroom, using unpacking her own stuff as an excuse. She'd been embarrassed that she'd aired her family's dirty laundry in front of everyone. Em hadn't come back down after Josh left, and Bri hadn't felt like eating, so she imagined Em was hungry too.

"If it's Moose Tracks, grab the carton and two spoons," Em called, her head half-buried in a box.

Bri smiled. Vanilla ice cream dotted with peanut butter cups and fudge, Moose Tracks had been one of their favorites.

Gus looked from the bedroom to Bri. As if sensing Em no longer needed him, he followed Bri to the stairs. "You might as well go ahead of me, boy. I'll just hold you up." When Gus didn't move, she glanced back at the bedroom before sitting on the landing and bouncing down the stairs on her bottom.

At a snort of laughter, she looked up to see Em grinning down at her. Throwing a leg over the banister, Em slid down, whizzing past her.

Bri laughed. "Nice. I'll try that next—" she began, startling when the door opened. Cal stood there, looking from her to his sister.

His hair was disheveled, and he wore a white T-shirt and gray joggers. He looked like he'd just rolled out of bed.

"Are you all right?" he asked, sounding far more concerned than was warranted.

"Of course we're all right. Why wouldn't we be?" Em reached out to help Bri up while scowling at her brother. "And why do you have a key?" she asked, giving Bri a *see what I mean?* glance.

Before Cal had a chance to respond, Josh ran into the house, looking equally disheveled and concerned. "You guys okay?"

Em threw up her arms. "That's it. I'm moving!"

Noticing the way Cal stared at her sweatshirt, Bri self-consciously crossed her arms. "Me too."

"No one's going anywhere." Cal leaned past Josh, looking up and down the street before closing the door.

"They're long gone. I took off after them, but I couldn't make out the license plate," Josh told Cal.

"Who's long gone?" Em asked, no longer staring daggers at her brother and his best friend.

"Not exactly sure," Josh said. "I looked out the window when all your lights came on and spotted a car parked across the road. We've had a couple of break-ins in the area so I called Cal. He's captain of the neighborhood watch."

"Okay, so let me get this straight. While Josh is basically spying on us—" Em began before Josh cut her off.

"I wasn't spying on you. I . . ." He rubbed the back of his head. "I got up to get a drink of water and noticed your lights were on. The house is lit up like a Christmas tree. What was I supposed to think?"

"That we still had boxes to unpack?" Em said smoothly before continuing. "So Marigold Lane's resident Peeping Tom"—Josh threw up his arms and walked to the couch, flinging himself onto it—"spots a car parked on the street, calls you, then chases after the car on foot, and you come running down the road to rescue us because you don't trust your sister, who is a cop and who has a

gun and who lives in the flipping house, to handle it."
Em crossed her arms. "That about cover it?"

"Okay, cut us some slack. We were worried about
you, both of you, and yeah, so maybe we overreacted,"
Cal said.

Almost certain the conversation was about to head
into uncomfortable territory, Bri said, "I'll go and get the
ice cream."

"I'll get it. You should sit down," Em told Bri.

Josh got off the couch. "I'll help." As he followed
Em to the kitchen, he said, "Are you wearing men's
cologne?"

"On a scale of one to ten, how bad is the pain?" Cal
asked as Bri made her way into the living room.

She lowered herself onto the couch. "Are you asking
about my leg or about you and Josh?"

Other than a twitch of his very fine lips, he ignored her
question and sat down. Then he reached for her legs.

"No." She batted his hands away. "You are not
massaging me. I mean, my leg. You are not massaging
my leg."

He raised his hands and backed off. "Your call, but
it would help. Or is it not just your leg keeping you
awake?" He searched her face, resting his arm along the
back of the couch behind her.

"No. Nothing else. Just my leg," she said, forcing
a smile. There was no way she was telling him that
thoughts of their broken engagement, of him and Raine,
had kept her awake. "It was a busy day."

He nodded slowly, holding her gaze. "It was."

The way he was looking at her made her pulse race.

He'd been so in tune with her feelings when they'd been together that she was afraid he could read the thoughts that had kept her awake. There was so much she wanted to say, to ask, but she no longer had the right. "Did you and your wife enjoy your dinner with Winter?"

His broad shoulders rose on a sigh. "Bri."

"Found it," Em said, walking over to the couch with a carton of Moose Tracks ice cream and two spoons in her hand. She handed Bri a spoon and took a seat beside her brother. Josh sat on the other side of Em, leaning in to scoop a spoonful of ice cream out of the carton.

He sniffed her shoulder. "I'm serious. Your sweatshirt smells like you spritzed it with my cologne."

Cal rubbed the sweatshirt material at Bri's shoulder between his thumb and forefinger. "My sweatshirt doesn't smell like me anymore, does it?"

"It's not yours. It's Sadie's." She went to lean across him to scoop ice cream onto her spoon and then realized how plastering herself over his hard, muscular abs was a bad idea. She held up her spoon. "Would you mind getting me some?"

He took her spoon, scooped up some ice cream, and then, holding her gaze, ate it. "I forgot how good this was," he said, licking his lips.

"Hey, that was supposed to be for me." She reached for the spoon. But she was having a hard time focusing on it and not his face, and she grabbed thin air.

Cal laughed. "Your aim was always off."

"That's not what you said when we played seven minutes in heaven." Her cheeks heated. She couldn't believe she'd brought up the kissing game they'd played as teenagers. Even blindfolded in a dark room filled with other people, she'd always managed to find Cal and plant a kiss on his lips.

"This is just like old times, isn't it?" Josh said. "Me and Em playing third and fourth wheel to you and Bri."

With Cal looking at her with heat in his eyes and a familiar smile on his face, it felt a lot like old times. Only he was married to someone else. Something she needed to remember.

"I don't know, buddy. I think you're romanticizing things. Em didn't hang around for long when Bri and I walked into a room, and if she did, she wasn't smiling at us like she—" He broke off at the sound of his phone ringing. Removing it from his pocket, he glanced at the screen and his brow furrowed.

He brought the phone to his ear. "Izzy. Slow down, honey. I can't make out what…" Distracted, he handed Bri the spoon and stood up. "Are you hurt?" He nodded as he listened to his stepdaughter. "Okay, that's good. Keep him talking and keep him warm. No, don't move him. How long ago did you call 911?" He gestured to Josh, mouthing, *Phone.*

Josh got up and handed him his phone. Cal nodded at something his stepdaughter said, tucking his phone between his shoulder and ear. "Okay, hang…I'm not hanging up, honey. I'm calling to get an ETA on the ambulance." He punched in a number and brought Josh's phone to his other ear. "Lynn, it's Cal Scott. My daughter's been involved in an accident on Pit Road. Two cars, multiple injuries, minor, but one sounds serious. Five minutes? Okay, thanks. Yeah, I'm on my way."

He disconnected. "Did you hear that, Izzy? They're five minutes out. I'll—" He turned at the sound of the front door opening.

Raine walked in, her dark eyes taking in the room. "Cal, we're needed at the hospital. There's been a two-car collision."

"I know. I'm on with Izzy. She's—"

Raine cried out, "No!" and rushed to his side.

Cal put his arm around her, holding her close. "She's fine. Izzy, I'm putting your mom on now." He handed Raine the phone.

Josh headed for the door. "You guys go to the hospital. Tell Izzy I'm on my way."

"Hold up. I'm coming with you," Em said, running to the entryway. She slipped on a pair of sneakers and took off after Josh.

"Friends, Izzy! You said you were staying at your friends! Not driving—"

"Now's not the time for this." Cal took the phone from Raine. "She's just upset, honey. Josh and Auntie Em are on their way to you." He paused, then nodded. "Yeah, I hear them. That's good. We'll see you at the hospital."

He disconnected. "Ambulance and HFPD just arrived."

Sobbing, Raine buried her face in her hands, and Cal wrapped her in his arms. "She's fine."

Raine shook her head against his chest. "I should have listened to you. I shouldn't have overridden you. I know better. I know better than anyone what can happen. My brother—"

Feeling like an intruder, Bri rose from the couch and made her way to the kitchen. She heard Cal comforting his wife, the low murmur of their voices, then the sounds of their footsteps. Seconds later, the door closed, and she heard the *snick* of the lock.

"It looks like it's just you and me, Gus," she said to the dog at her feet, ignoring the tiny pinch of hurt that they'd forgotten her.

Chapter Twelve

♥

Cal stood at the patio door watching Bri in the garden. The sun's rays glinted off the gold streaks in her blond hair. As she leaned over to pull out some weeds, the heavy strands fell forward, hiding her profile from view. She reached up with a dirty gloved hand to tuck her hair behind her ear. He smiled at the streak of dirt she left behind on her cheek.

Feeling like a stalker, he opened the sliding glass door. "You're up early," he said, closing it behind him.

She turned her head. "So are you. You had a long night." Shifting from a kneeling position into a sitting one on the padded cushion, she tucked her legs to her side. "How's your daughter and her friends?"

He lowered himself onto the grass beside her, feeling older than his thirty-two years. It had been a long, exhausting night. He'd finished up at the hospital an hour ago. Raine and Izzy were sleeping when he got home, and he found himself heading back out the door and walking down the street, telling himself he didn't want to wake them. It had nothing to do with that. He'd needed to see Bri.

He wanted to be right where he was now, sitting on the grass beside her. "As far as injuries go, it could have been a lot worse. The cars are totaled. Most of the kids walked away with minor injuries, cuts and bruises, Izzy included. But two of them suffered more severe injuries. It was touch and go with one of them. Sam, Izzy's friend. They're all pretty shaken up."

"I can imagine. I'm sure their parents are too. That's not a phone call anyone wants to make or to get." She looked down at her gloves, peeling them off. "You were wonderful with your daughter, Cal. And your wife."

And that was another reason why, when he'd wrapped things up at the hospital, his first thought had been of Bri and seeing her. Until then, Izzy and his patients had been his priority. But once he'd had a chance to play the events of the night over in his mind, he realized how it must have looked to Bri.

He gently clasped her chin between his fingers, turning her face to him. "Ex-wife," he said, wiping the dirt from her cheek with his thumb. "It brought back memories of her brother's accident."

"You don't owe me an explanation, Cal. It's not like we're in a relationship."

"Maybe not, but don't you think we owe it to ourselves to give us another shot?"

She seemed as surprised by his question as he was. Had he spent a lot of time thinking about his feelings for Bri since their run-in at the grocery store? Sure, he had. And after learning that her mother had sabotaged their relationship, the idea of them giving it another chance was pretty much all he'd thought about.

But he'd also convinced himself that it was too soon. That it would be better to wait until six weeks from now when everything was out in the open. It seemed operating on a boy whose chances of survival had been slim at best had put things into perspective. There were no guarantees in life. There was no perfect time, no right time. Sometimes you had to make the most of the time that you had.

"Why would you want to, Cal? My mother's right. Raine is perfect for you."

Miranda MacLeod had more than their breakup to answer for. "Your mother was grasping. She was trying to excuse what she did to us. But she can't. You were perfect for me."

"Maybe back then I was. But I'm not the girl you remember. I'm not the girl you once loved."

"I'm not the guy you remember either."

Absently kneading her thigh, she gave him a sad smile. "That's the problem, Cal. If anything, you're even more amazing than the guy I fell in love with. And trust me, I didn't think you could get any more perfect than you were back then."

"No one's perfect, Bri. Least of all me. But if I'm so amazing, why don't you want to give us a second chance?"

"It's not you. It's me. I'm a mess. I'm broken, and you can't fix me."

He reached over and pulled up a clump of weeds choking a fragile pink flower, wishing it was as easy to remove the doubts Bri had about herself and them. "You're not broken. There's nothing about you that needs to be fixed. Nothing about you that I'd change."

"Maybe not right now. But what about when I can't hike Blue Mountain Trail with you or dance with you at the Fall Festival or do half of what we used to do together?"

"You're assuming you won't get back the full use of your leg, and I don't think that's something you have to worry about. But even if you don't, none of that matters to me."

"You're forgetting the migraines and dizzy spells. Sometimes I can't get out of bed for days. Is that really what you want?"

"All I want is another chance, Bri. And I think if you're honest, you do too. Don't sabotage this, us, because you're afraid."

"I'm trying to get you to face reality, Cal. You say you don't want to fix me, but you're probably thinking of ways you can treat my symptoms and make me better right now. It's what you do. It's who you are. It's why you're a brilliant surgeon. But trust me, I know how that story plays out. I stayed with Richard, thinking I could fix him."

He bowed his head. As much as he wished there was something he could do, something he could say to convince Bri to let go of the guilt and shame she was carrying around and place the blame where it rightfully belonged, on her ex, she wasn't in the place to hear it or accept it. And there was a chance she never would be.

"You're right. I would do anything, try anything, to heal your pain. To make it so you don't suffer another single day, hour, or minute. But there's only one person who can heal what's broken inside you, Bri. And that's not me, it's you." A light, fall-scented breeze blew her hair across her cheek, and he gently tucked it back behind her ear. "I'm sorry. I shouldn't have tried to push you into something you're obviously not ready for."

As Cal let his hand fall from her face and went to stand, she lifted her gaze to his. Her eyes were tear-filled, and he crouched at her side, taking her hand in his.

"Please don't cry," he said. "The last thing I meant to do is make you cry."

She shook her head and wrapped her other hand around his fingers, stroking the faint line from his wedding band. "For years after we broke up, I used to imagine a moment just like this. You'd tell me you were wrong, and you'd beg my forgiveness, and I'd throw myself into your arms, asking what took you so long." She gave him a tremulous smile. "So maybe it wasn't exactly like this. But not once in all those daydreams—and I wouldn't be exaggerating if I said I imagined a similar moment at least a thousand times—did I ever turn away from you. I always, always, jumped into your arms with no questions asked. Simply happy that you had found your way back to me and that we had a second chance."

"What are you saying?" he asked, afraid to get his hopes up.

"I feel exactly the same way as I did in those day-dreams, Cal. And that was when I thought you'd broken my heart on purpose. Not that my mother had manipu-lated us into breaking up."

"So you're saying you want to give us another shot?"

"There's nothing I want more than a second chance

with you. But it's not the right time. You have the trauma center and your stepdaughter and Em to think about, and I have Ellie and my mother."

"We're not the same people we used to be. We both have baggage. If we wait for a perfect time, we might never get the chance. Look at Em and Brad. No one knows what life has in store for them, Bri."

"Maybe that's what I'm afraid of. I don't know if I can go through that again, Cal. Losing you was devastating. What if my mother was right? If we loved each other as much as we thought we did, she shouldn't have been able to break us up."

"We were young, and she played into our fears and insecurities." He shrugged. "Maybe we just weren't ready. It was a big step."

"But what if this"—she moved her hand between them—"what we're feeling right now, isn't real? It's just us getting caught up in the memories of what we once meant to each other and wanting to recapture those feelings. What we shared was special, magical. There's a reason why they write songs about first loves and why some people never get over them. And why it's so painful when they end."

"My love for you was real, and true, and deep." He smiled as he repeated her words back to her. "I overheard you telling your mother yesterday afternoon."

Her cheeks pinked. "And so did Josh and Em."

"Yeah, I don't think they were too surprised. At least about your feelings for me. But the feelings I had for you never really went away, Bri. And trust me, I tried my damnedest to get rid of them. I compared every woman

I met to you. And then I found one who was your polar opposite in hopes that it would work. For a while it did. So while it's possible we're looking at our past through rose-colored glasses, I don't think we are."

"I tried to love someone else too, and we both know how well that worked out."

Cal came to his feet and offered his hand, working at keeping his anger at both her mother and the man who'd abused Bri from showing on his face. "You've been sitting in the same position for too long. You need to stand up." As he helped her to her feet, she steadied herself with a hand on his arm. "You okay?"

She shook her head and moved closer to him, resting her cheek against his chest and wrapping her arms around his waist. "No. Yes. I don't know how I feel. It's a lot to take in. I never thought we'd get a second chance, and now that we have one, I'm terrified."

"Nothing in life comes without risk but I'm willing to take it if you are. We can take it slow. Spend time together here. No one has to know. Other than Em, and Josh."

She tipped her head back. "What about Raine and your stepdaughter?"

"Raine will be fine as—" He laughed at Bri's incredulous expression. "Okay, so she won't be thrilled. But as long as we don't do anything that puts the trauma center at risk, she'll just have to deal with it. As far as Izzy goes, I'd like her to get to know you before we say anything to her."

She nodded. "I'd rather we keep this just between us for now too. Or at least the five of us. I don't want to do anything that would jeopardize your relationship with Izzy or ruin your reputations. If people found out—"

He wrapped his arms around her. "How about, for right now, we take some time to focus on just you and me?"

"I'd like that." She smiled, the stress melting from her face. "Do you want to help me in the garden?"

He unwrapped his arms from her waist and brought his hands to her face. "There's only one thing I want to do with you, Brianna MacLeod, and that's kiss you."

She looked up at him, biting her bottom lip.

He went to lower his hands. "Too soon?"

She covered his hands with hers. "No. I'm just a little nervous, I guess. It's been a long time. I feel like I did right before you kissed me that summer at Bridal Veil Falls."

He remembered their first kiss like it was yesterday. They'd been swimming at the base of the falls. Em and Josh had gone off somewhere, and they were alone. Bri had climbed up on the rocks, laughing when he'd warned her that it was too dangerous. Back then, she'd been up for any challenge, and he'd taken his job as protector of his sister and her best friend seriously.

Except that summer, he'd begun seeing Bri in a new light, and he'd been working to fight his attraction. He was friends with her brother. She was friends with his sister. But the moment he looked up at her that day with the sun bathing her in a golden light, the waterfall sparkling behind her, he'd been a goner.

"Ah, so you feel like you're drowning."

She laughed. "You were the one who thought I was drowning, not me."

"What was I supposed to think? You were under the water a solid three minutes."

"Because I'd lost my bikini top."

And he'd hauled her up and into his arms, kissing her with a combination of lust and relief. A kiss that had sealed their fate. "And here we are, almost a decade later, and I've got you back in my arms. I think that's worth celebrating with a kiss, don't you?"

"I do," she whispered, and went to rise up on her toes to meet him halfway.

He moved his hands from her face, lifting her off her feet. "Wrap your legs around me."

She sighed. "You don't have to do that. My leg—"

"Didn't you say that you jumped into my arms when you imagined this moment? I'm just trying to make your dreams come true."

"You always did," she said, and did as he asked.

Wrapping one arm around her waist and one under her behind, he lowered his mouth to hers. Like that day at Bridal Veil Falls, the moment his mouth touched hers, his fate was sealed. Her lips were as soft and as sweet as he remembered. Memories assailed him with every glide of his mouth over hers, every breathy sigh she exhaled. He'd dreamed of this moment. Only his dreams hadn't done it justice. Nothing could compare with the reality of having Bri in his arms, kissing him with as much passion as he remembered.

"Dad, you have to come home. Mom's—"

He lifted his gaze to Izzy, who was standing in the open patio door, staring at him and Bri. His sister stood behind her with an *oh crap* look on her face.

Bri made a strangled sound in her throat, tearing her lips from his as she struggled to get down. "Sorry. I'm so sorry, Cal."

He'd barely steadied her on her feet when she whirled around. "Please forgive me. This isn't your dad's fault. He saved my life, and I threw myself at him. I shouldn't have kissed him. I was overcome with gratitude."

His sister, struggling to keep a straight face, said, "Yeah, don't mind Bri, Izzy. She did the same thing when she saw me yesterday. Threw herself at me when I walked through the door and planted a big kiss on me."

Izzy's eyes went wide. "She did?"

"Yeah. We hadn't seen each other in almost ten years, and she was overcome with emotion. We were best friends when we were your age."

"Oh, okay. That's cool," Izzy said, looking from his sister to Bri, who'd retrieved her cane and was making her way to the door.

"Don't worry. I won't kiss you," Bri said to Izzy, holding out her hand. "I'm Brianna MacLeod, and I'm incredibly embarrassed right now. I hope you'll forgive me."

"Sure." His stepdaughter shrugged and then shook Bri's hand. "It's no big deal."

"I'll let you and your dad talk." Bri glanced at him. "I'm sorry again, Cal."

The only thing he was sorry about was that they'd been interrupted. "Don't give it a second thought. So," he said to Izzy once Bri walked inside, "what's going on?"

Chapter Thirteen

♥

Bri shut the sliding glass door behind her and walked to the sink, resting her cane against the cupboard. "I can't believe that just happened," she said as she turned on the tap.

"The kiss or you guys getting caught?" Em asked, coming to stand beside her. She leaned over the sink, peering out the kitchen window at her brother talking to his stepdaughter in the backyard.

A kiss? Is that all it was? It certainly hadn't felt like just a kiss to her. It felt like her world had turned upside down, and she'd had plenty of experience with world-turning moments this past year. None of them good. But this? This had been a head-spinning, heart-pounding, happiness-inducing moment.

So many memories and feelings had washed over her when Cal kissed her—good memories, good feelings. Amazing feelings, actually. So amazing that they'd washed away the heavy, depressing weight that had been her constant companion for far too long. For the first time in a long time, she'd felt light and hopeful. Excited at what the future might hold in store for her.

She brought the tips of her fingers to her lips, missing the warmth of Cal's mouth on hers. It wasn't just a kiss. It was a promise of the life she could have if she wasn't too scared to reach out and grab it. But without Cal's arms around her, his lips on hers, the euphoria had faded, letting her initial doubts and fears take hold in her mind.

Em nudged her. "Earth to Bri."

"Sorry. Both. The kiss and Izzy catching us." She leaned to the side, trying to get a look at Cal's stepdaughter's face. "Do you think she believed me?"

"Probably. We see what we want to see, and you were pretty convincing." Em sighed, turning around to lean against the counter. "I'm disappointed though. I was hoping you guys were getting back together."

"Really? You hated when we were dating."

"Yeah, and I explained why last night. Jealous and feeling abandoned, remember? Now I'm just anxious to get my brother off my back. You two getting back together would do the trick. He'd be so caught up in you, he'd forget about me." She glanced at Bri. "You both looked pretty into that kiss. Are you sure there's no chance you'll get back together?"

"We talked about it," Bri admitted, mainly because she needed a sounding board. "Actually, we pretty much agreed to give our relationship another try."

"If the look on your face is anything to go by, you're having second thoughts."

She nodded, turning off the water. "I am. And if you weren't thinking how us getting back together benefits you, you'd see what I do. This has disaster written all over it."

"How do you figure?"

"I can't believe you have to ask," Bri said, drying her hands on a tea towel. "Everyone in town thinks Cal and Raine are happily married, Em. The last thing Raine wants is for it to get out that their marriage is over."

"So you keep it quiet."

"Izzy just saw us kissing."

"Yeah, but I didn't know you two were making out in the backyard. I'll be more careful next time. Check if the coast is clear before letting her in. Not that I could have stopped her today. The poor kid was on a tear. Raine flipped out about the accident and grounded her for the next two months." Em glanced over her shoulder. "I wonder if Cal will tell Izzy why Raine was so upset."

"Two months seems a little excessive, but I imagine any parent would be upset their child was involved in a car accident."

"Raine's older brother died on the same road. She didn't find out the accident was on Pit Road until Cal finished surgery."

"I didn't realize. How horrible for her."

"Yeah. Her brother had come to pick her up. She was with him at the time of the accident. Cal says she still has a hard time talking about it."

"It might help Izzy to understand and sympathize with Raine's reaction if she knew." She glanced out the window. Cal was hugging his stepdaughter, saying something that made the teenager laugh. "Cal and Izzy seem really close."

"They are. The kid adores him. Izzy and Raine have a typical mother-and-teenage-daughter relationship. They butt heads, and Cal is always there to smooth things over."

Bri had always known he'd make a wonderful father. "Which is another reason why the timing is wrong for me and Cal. Izzy needs him."

"Or are you just using her as an excuse because you're afraid of getting your heart broken again?"

"I—" She broke off when the sliding glass door opened, and Cal, Izzy, and Gus came inside.

Cal smiled, placing a basket of butternut squash on the counter. "You forgot these."

"Thanks," she said, glad to have something to keep her busy. She gave Izzy a weak smile, still mortified by what Cal's stepdaughter had witnessed. Transferring the squash from the basket into the sink, she turned on the tap.

"You don't look like you got much sleep," Cal said to Em. "Are you still having nightmares?"

Bri pressed her lips together and kept washing the squash instead of glancing over her shoulder at Em, who'd taken a seat with Izzy at the table. Bri imagined she was less than pleased with her brother's question.

"I was at the hospital half the night. How am I supposed to look? You might want to take a look at yourself in a mirror, big brother. You look like crap."

Bri snuck a peek at Cal, who was leaning against the counter beside her. The man couldn't look like crap if he tried. He was gorgeous even when he was exhausted, which clearly he was.

"Yeah, but I don't…" He glanced at the far end of the table where Izzy sat, bent down playing with Gus, and instead of continuing, pulled a business card from his pocket. "You met this guy last night. You know, the one who was talking to some of the kids?" Cal went to hand his sister the card. "Anyway, I made an appointment for you. He can fit you in this coming Thursday."

"Seriously?" Em tossed the card on the table. "I don't need a shrink, Cal. I'm fine."

"Um, is it okay if I take Gus for a walk?" Izzy asked, looking from her stepfather to her aunt.

"Good idea," Em said, coming to her feet. "I'll come with you."

"Go ahead, honey. Auntie Em will be with you in a minute. Humor me, okay?" he said to his sister once Izzy had left the kitchen. "I'm worried about you, Em."

"Well, you can stop. I'm fine, and if you don't believe me, ask Bri. She's agreed to take me on as a client."

Cal turned to Bri. "Really? I thought you were no longer practicing."

He wasn't any more surprised than Bri at the news. She turned to stare at Em and then remembered the promise they'd made to each other last night. Forcing a smile, she said to Cal, "It's not like I'm—"

"She's setting up her practice in the den. You should check it out. I'm sure she'll be overrun with clients once she hangs out her shingle."

"Babe, that's amazing," Cal said, taking Bri into his arms.

"Yeah, it really is," Em said with a hint of laughter in her voice as she headed out of the kitchen. "Don't worry, I'll give you two a heads-up when Izzy and I get back from our walk."

Bri moved away from Cal, turning back to the squash in the sink. "This isn't a good idea."

He moved behind her, putting his arms around her waist. "Why? Because Izzy caught us kissing?"

"Yes. She...oh." She moaned when he nuzzled her neck.

His lips curved against her skin. "You always liked that."

"I did, and I still do, but that's not the point." She tipped her head back. "We can't do this. It's better if we wait until everything's settled six weeks from now. It'll give Izzy time to get to know me."

"Your mom stole almost ten years from us. I don't want to wait."

"I know, and I'm sorry." She turned in his arms. "I'm not saying we can't spend time together. But I think we should spend it as friends, for everyone's sake." She smoothed her hand over his white button-down. "We don't really know each other anymore. We're different people now. This will give us time to find out if this is what we really want."

He slowly nodded. "I don't want to admit it, but you're right."

She didn't want to be right, not about this.

"As good as your excuse was, I'm not sure Izzy bought it." He smiled, tucking her hair behind her ear. "I appreciate what you did, taking the rap like that."

She brought her hands to her heated cheeks. "I'm still embarrassed she caught us."

"Stop." He took her hands from her face, bringing them to his lips. He kissed her knuckles and then, releasing her hands, stepped away from her. "You might have taken the blame, but that was on me. Not you." He blew out a breath.

"Will Izzy tell Raine?"

"Doubtful. They're not talking right now." He pulled his phone from his jeans pocket and glanced at the screen. "I probably should head back and work out a compromise with Raine."

"Em mentioned Raine's brother's accident. Did you tell Izzy?"

"I did. Raine won't be happy about it. But it's past time Izzy knew. I'm honestly surprised she hasn't heard about it since we've moved back. Although neither Winter nor Raine talk about it." He angled his head. "Would you consider taking Raine on as a client?"

"You can't be serious."

"Just a thought." He smiled. Then he lowered his head, touching his lips to hers.

She leaned into the kiss, lengthening what she belatedly realized he'd meant to be a friendly touch of their lips. She couldn't seem to help herself. She'd missed this, missed him, and she was kicking herself for putting their relationship on hold. Even when she knew it was the right thing to do.

He groaned against her lips, lifting her onto the counter. He deepened the kiss as he settled himself between her legs. The kiss they'd shared in the backyard had been more like the kisses they'd shared in the past. There'd been a tentativeness, an innocence, a gentle exploring. This kiss was very much one between the adults they'd become. It was full of want and need. As if they were making up for all the time they'd lost.

"Knock, knock."

They jerked apart, turning to see Em leaning against the wall with her arms crossed and an eyebrow raised. "You're lucky it was me who came back for Gus's leash and not Izzy, because there is no way you could pass that off as a grateful kiss."

"We would have heard her," Cal said, but Bri could tell he didn't believe that any more than she did.

"It won't happen again," Bri promised as much to herself as to Em and Cal.

Em snorted, grabbing Gus's leash from the floor. "Good luck with that."

Cal blew out a breath. "She's right. This isn't going to be easy. Or fun."

An hour later, Bri thought *not easy* and *not fun* were apt descriptions of her life at that moment. And not just because she and Cal had relegated their relationship to the friend zone. She was headed to the inn for brunch with her mother.

Em leaned forward, peering out the windshield as she pulled into the parking lot. "Ellie must be doing something right. I don't remember the inn ever being this busy on a Sunday." She glanced at Bri. "So do you want to explain why I have to come with you to brunch?"

"We had a deal, remember?" Bri said as Em parked her car. "You already put part of the plan into action. The part that benefits you. Or did you forget that you used me to get Cal off your back about therapy?"

Em grinned. "I thought that was inspired. I don't know what made my brother happier, me agreeing to therapy or you starting up a practice on Marigold Lane. But you knew I was kidding, right? You're not getting me on the couch spilling my guts."

"Really? And here I scheduled our first session for tomorrow morning at nine," Bri said as she got out of the car.

Em snorted and joined her on the walkway. "Now I know you're joking. Neither of us will be up before noon."

The door to the inn opened, and Abby walked out. She took one look at Bri and went to go back inside but Mallory blocked her escape.

Bri and Em joined them on the wraparound porch. Bri introduced the three women, adding, "Abby is the reason you and I are roomies."

"I'm sorry. I didn't know what else to do. Cal was worried about his sister—I mean, you," Abby said to Em. "And he was thrilled you had a roommate, and then Mrs. Randall canceled, and Bri said she was moving out and needed a place to rent. And Ellie was so happy you were finally moving on with your life, Bri, but she was worried about you living on your own. So this seemed like the perfect solution." Abby made a face. "Other than for the teensy issue of you two hating each other. But if you're here together, you must be getting along. You are, aren't you?"

"Yep, we're good," Em said, and Bri smiled, a smile that slowly faded as Em continued. "Bri takes care of the garden, my dog, and the cooking."

Mallory frowned. "It sounds like you're getting the better end of the bargain."

"Hey, I'm doing the cleaning and helping get Bri back

into shape. I even volunteered to let her brush up on her therapy skills. Not that I need therapy, but a friend's gotta do what a friend's gotta do, right?"

"Bri, that's wonderful." Mallory reached over and gave her a hug. "How long before you've set up an office? I'd like to refer my patients to you as soon as possible."

"Refer away," Em said. "She's setting up her office at the house."

Bri was going to kill her. Em knew exactly what she was doing, as evidenced by the smirk on her face.

"Who's setting up an office at their house?" her sister asked, coming out of the inn with a paper in her hand. She handed it to Abby. "You forgot this."

Bri gritted her teeth while pasting a smile on her face. "I'm reopening my practice in Highland Falls, just like you wanted me to."

"Oh, Bri, that's the best news!" her sister squealed, drowning out Em's choked laughter.

"We'll let you guys celebrate," Mallory said, steering Abby, who was on her phone, down the stairs.

"Okay. I'll see you tomorrow night." Ellie tugged on Bri's hand. "Come on, let's go tell Mom and Grandpa. They'll be over the moon." And maybe because Bri hesitated, the overjoyed smile on her sister's face faded. "I know you're still angry at Mom, and you have every right to—"

"I'm not too thrilled with her either," Em interjected.

"I know, and I'm not going to make excuses for what she did or how she handled it yesterday. She's had time to think about it though. She wants to apologize and try to make amends."

"Okay, but, Ellie, whatever comes out of this, you have to promise it won't impact your decision to go away. This is between Mom and me."

"I know. That's what Nate said." Ellie smiled, waving to Mallory and Abby, who were getting into a truck.

Bri stared at her sister. "So you didn't cancel your trip?"

Ellie laughed. "And miss two weeks in Scotland with my husband?"

"I think you've been played," Em said under her breath, and Bri was beginning to think she was right.

"Bri and Em," Abby called from the truck's open window. "Is it okay if I add you guys to the trauma center's fundraising committee?"

Em said, "I don't do committees," at the same time Bri said, "Sure," murmuring for the benefit of the woman now glaring at her, "We probably just have to stuff envelopes. Besides, it's for Cal."

"Awesome," Abby said. "We'll meet at your place tomorrow night, and we'll firm up the events then. This is going to be so much fun."

Chapter Fourteen

♥

I'm not going." Raine crossed her arms, tapping her black high-heeled shoe on the kitchen floor. She was dressed to impress in a long-sleeved, red wraparound knitted top and skirt, and she'd spent an inordinate amount of time on her hair and makeup. Cal knew why, just as he knew why she was now balking at the idea of attending the fundraising committee meeting at Bri's.

"You have to go." He put up his hand when Raine went to object. "How would it look if you didn't? They're doing this for the trauma center."

He hadn't seen Bri since yesterday morning. After spending half the day playing referee for Raine and Izzy—Raine hadn't been happy he'd shared about her brother's accident with Izzy, and his stepdaughter was just plain unhappy with her mother and, it seemed, the world—he'd been called into the hospital.

Sam, the teenager he'd operated on, had developed an infection. Cal hadn't gotten home until late, and he'd had back-to-back surgeries today. He was looking forward to spending time with Bri tonight. Granted, he wished they could hang out alone, but he'd take what he could get.

"It's a waste of time, and you know it," Raine said. "None of the events they're talking about are going to raise close to what we need to meet the town council's demands."

"Yeah, well, it's this or nothing. You know what David said." They'd been hauled into the hospital administrator's office this afternoon. He'd received several complaints from the hospital donors Raine had contacted, asking them to increase their donations. Two of them had canceled their automatic monthly contributions.

"He's setting us up to fail. I wouldn't be surprised if he was somehow connected to the casino consortium."

"Come on, Raine. David wants the expansion as much as we do. He just can't afford to alienate the donors, and neither can we."

"Don't you think it's funny he wouldn't share the names of the complainants with us?"

"Not really. I'm sure it—"

"If you ask me, Quinn is behind this. The timing of his appointment is certainly suspect. I wouldn't be surprised if he's in the casino consortium's pocket."

And there it was: Quinn. The reason she was dressed to the nines and the reason her nerves had gotten the better of her.

"Another reason for you to be there. You'll have the opportunity to ask him. Now let's go." He headed for the door, calling to his stepdaughter.

"I see right through you, you know. And you better hope no else does," Raine said.

"I don't know what you're talking about."

"Oh please, you'll take any opportunity you can to spend time with Bri. But I'm warning you, Cal. If anyone suspects—"

"I told you, we're taking it slow. We're friends. Izzy, come on. We're going to be late."

His stepdaughter stomped out of her bedroom. "I'm not going."

"We talked about this already. You have to regain our trust, and for now, that means no staying home on your own." He'd arranged for her to hang out with his sister if he and Raine couldn't make it home after school. "Besides, it's for a good cause, and I'm sure Em and Bri could use your help." He opened the door and ushered them outside.

"She's not going to kiss you again, is she?"

"Excuse me. Brianna kissed you? In front of Izzy?"

Cal briefly closed his eyes and then locked the door. "She was thanking me for saving her life, that's all." When neither Izzy or Raine had anything else to add, he glanced at them. They were watching a tall, well-dressed Black man getting out of a silver Mercedes a few houses down.

"I should probably stay home. I'm feeling a little queasy," Raine said.

"Me too," Izzy said.

Cal put his arms around their shoulders. "Okay, you two. I get that you're nervous to see Quinn. But he's not going anywhere, so you might as well get it over with. Besides, he's a good guy, and I'm sure he'll be happy to see you both."

Pursing her lips, Raine raised an eyebrow at him as he guided them across the front lawn.

"Especially you, Izzy," Cal amended.

Quinn looked up from beeping the lock on his fob as they approached, and smiled. "Wow, Izzy, is that you?" He walked toward them, looking intent on giving Izzy a hug.

Izzy chewed the inside of her bottom lip and nodded, glancing at her mother.

Quinn's smile faltered, but he quickly recovered. "It's good to see you. Both of you." He nodded at Raine.

"Hello, Quinn." Raine took her daughter by the hand and said to Cal, "Darling, we don't want to be late."

"You and Izzy go ahead," he said, feeling the need to apologize. He held out his hand. "It's good to see you, Quinn. It's been a while."

"You too." He shook Cal's hand, watching as Raine and Izzy walked toward the most brightly lit house on Marigold Lane. He returned his attention to Cal. "Was it something I said?"

"No. Not at all. It's been a rough couple of days, and they're not happy I made them come tonight."

Quinn nodded. "I heard about the accident on Pit Road. Must have been tough on Raine. Izzy's okay though, isn't she?"

"She is, but one of her friends is still in rough shape."

"My mother and Winter said he's lucky you were here. You and Raine." He glanced to where Raine and Izzy were headed up Bri's walkway. "I know Raine's not happy I'm here, Cal. But my mom's having some health issues, and I want to be here for her. Plus, the job interests me."

"You don't owe me an explanation, Quinn. I think it's great that you moved back."

"Obviously Raine and Izzy don't feel the same way."

"I'm not sure what's up with Izzy. She hasn't been herself these past couple of weeks, but as far as Raine goes, it all comes down to approval for the trauma center. I'm sure it's not news to you that she was upset with the financial stipulation and deadline your mother and Winter imposed."

"Yeah, they filled me in. And no matter what Raine thinks, they weren't trying to sabotage the deal. To be honest, in their place, I would have demanded the same. Actually, I feel it should have been higher."

Oh great. Cal rubbed his jaw. "Would you mind not sharing that with—"

"Quinn, my man. Great to see you," Josh said, walking across the road with his hand extended. Then he frowned, looking from Raine, who was standing under the porch light at Bri's, to Quinn. "Is this a formal affair? Did I miss the memo?"

Like Cal, he was dressed casually in jeans and a sweater.

"No, it looks like Raine and I did," Quinn said, shaking Josh's hand. Then he winced. "Sorry, Cal. That didn't sound right. You know I'd never—"

"Pft, don't give it another thought, buddy. Raine and Cal aren't—hey!" Josh said when Cal stepped on his foot.

"Aren't the jealous types," Cal finished before his best friend outed them.

"Yeah, that's what I was going to say."

Quinn frowned, looking from Josh to Cal, but was distracted by an older woman calling his name.

Cal turned. Nina and Winter were getting out of a car parked across from Bri and Em's place. "I didn't realize your mother and Winter were coming."

"Yeah. Should be a fun evening," Quinn said as he walked away. "I'll see you guys inside."

"I know, I know," Josh said when Cal turned to him. "It's just that Quinn looked like he was still into Raine, and I got to thinking that might be the answer to your problems."

"More likely increase them tenfold. And trust me, buddy. The last thing I need is more problems to deal with. It already feels like I'm living in a soap opera."

Cal didn't bother knocking when they reached the front door. He doubted anyone would hear him if he did. He walked inside with Josh following close behind. At least twenty women were sitting in the living room, some on the floor, some on foldout chairs. Raine sat on the couch with Izzy beside her. Her mother and Nina book-ended Quinn, who glanced in Raine and Izzy's direction every few seconds. Bri and Em were nowhere to be seen, and neither was Gus.

"Hi, Cal. Hi, Coach. Grab a seat," said Abby from where she stood beside a whiteboard in front of the living room window. "We're just about to hand out assignments for each of the fundraising events. Don't worry though, Cal. We only expect you and Raine to make an appearance. We know how busy you two are."

Raine smiled, looking relieved—at least she did until she happened to glance Quinn's way. The exes' gazes met and held before they quickly looked away. And Cal wasn't the only one who noticed.

Abby tapped a pointer on the board. "Okay, so because the alumni exhibition game before Friday's high school football game will draw a bigger crowd than usual, I need at least eight to ten volunteers to work the tailgate party." Abby frowned. "We seem to be missing Bri and Em. Does anyone know where they are?"

"Weren't they going to get more coffee and tea?" Ellie asked.

"I thought they were going to get more cookies and squares," Granny MacLeod said, attempting to pull herself off the floor.

"I'll find them," Cal said, ignoring Raine's warning stare.

Cal walked into the kitchen. They weren't there. He was about to check in the backyard when he heard a low woof coming from the den. "Bri, Em," he said, tapping on the door with his knuckle. He opened it. His sister was lying on the couch holding a bottle of beer while Bri was curled on a chair against the opposite wall with a glass of white wine in her hand and Gus on her lap. Cal closed the door behind him.

"Hey, get out of here. We're in the middle of my therapy session," his sister said.

He took the chair beside Bri, a small table between them, and stretched out his legs. "Really. How's it going?"

"Excellent," Em said at the same time Bri said, "Not well at all."

Cal laughed, and Em glared at Bri. "Seriously?"

Bri sighed. "Em, we have twenty women sitting in our living room. I'm pretty sure Cal has figured out what we're doing."

"Your sister thinks you're getting tea and coffee, and your grandmother thinks you're getting cookies and squares." He touched his chest. "Me, I figure you're hiding out in hopes they'll forget to give you an assignment."

"And you said all we'd have to do is stuff envelopes. That's the last time I'm listening to you," Em told Bri.

"Well, thanks to you, I have two clients starting therapy next week."

"Really? That's great, Bri," Cal said.

She glared at him and took a large gulp of her wine.

The door opened, and Raine walked in, looking panicked. "Harlan's here."

"Who's Harlan?" Em asked, swinging her legs off the couch.

"The owner of the *Highland Falls Herald*, and the man who's out to get me and your brother. And if he finds him in here with her"—she stabbed a finger at Bri—"he'll have the scandal he's looking for."

"Okay, calm down," Cal said, coming to his feet. "He's probably here to interview Abby and Quinn."

"Quinn's here?" Em asked, raising an eyebrow at Raine.

"Why are you looking at me like that?" Raine asked his sister.

"Oh, I don't know. You two were hot and heavy back in the day."

Cal gave his sister a *shut it* look. Raine was already

worked up as it was. She grabbed his hand and dragged him to the door. "You two stay right where you are. The last thing I need is Harlan thinking I had to come and retrieve my husband."

"Right, because Cal being in here with his sister and her best friend is so scandalous."

The door opened, and Josh nearly walked into Raine. "Sorry," he said, leaning around her. "Bri and Em, you might want to get out here. Ellie and Granny MacLeod have volunteered you guys for every fundraising event."

"No, don't go yet," Raine said, making a grab for Em, who darted past Josh and out of the den with Bri and Gus following at a more sedate pace.

"I'm sure you have nothing to worry about," Bri said as she edged past Raine.

Harlan glanced over his shoulder. "What were you all up to? Inquiring minds want to know." He tapped a pen on a small, black notebook.

"What are you doing here, Harlan?" Cal asked.

The other man lifted his chin toward the mayor. "Winter invited me to cover the fundraising meeting. Sounds like Abby and her committee have quite the lineup to raise money for the trauma center. You know the *Herald* is always happy to promote community events." He smirked. "You'll have to sell a heck of a lot of pumpkins and apple pies to meet your financial obligations."

Afraid Raine might punch him in the nose, Cal gave her hand a warning squeeze. "That's the thing about small towns, Harlan. They're happy to support what matters most to them."

"We'll see, won't we?" Harlan lifted his camera. "I

need some photos of our famous hometown boy. Your ex, isn't he?" he asked Raine. "First husband, second, or third? You've had so many, I can't keep them straight."

"You're taking it too far, Harlan. Knock it off," Cal said.

"A little testy tonight, aren't you? I guess it's hard having the wife's old flame move back to town. You know what? I think I'm going to do a feature on you and our famous hometown boy. Quinn." Harlan held up his camera. "Would you mind posing for a picture with the Doctors Scott?"

Raine gave Cal an apologetic glance seconds before she looped her arm through his and smiled up at him. Patting his chest with her other hand, she said, "I know you wanted to keep it quiet, darling. But I'm so excited I can't keep the news to myself for one second longer." She beamed at their audience. "Cal and I are having a baby."

Chapter Fifteen

♥

Thank you for coming with me. Both of you," Bri's mother said as she turned into the inn's parking lot, glancing at Em sitting in the backseat with her earbuds in. "I know your sister was happy we went together to see them off."

They'd driven Ellie and Nate to the airport in Asheville three hours ago in her mother's SUV. It hadn't been as bad as Bri thought it would be. Her mother had been on her best behavior.

"It's too bad Dad couldn't make it. I think Ellie was disappointed." Bri could count on one hand the number of times she'd spoken to their father in the past month. She'd been hoping he'd come and see Ellie and Nate off, as much for her sister as for herself.

Her mother parked beside the red pickup. "You know your father. His lectures and his students come first." Miranda undid her seatbelt. "But he did send her flowers."

Bryan MacLeod was a brilliant man but he wouldn't have a clue who to call or what to order, and he certainly wouldn't know Ellie's favorite flowers. Her mother had taken care of everything when they were growing up. Bri imagined her father was lost without his wife.

"Mom, admit it. You sent the flowers and said they were from Dad."

"You don't think your sister knew, do you?" her mother asked, seeming genuinely concerned.

"No. I'm sure she didn't." Bri was positive Ellie did. The sentimental note that accompanied the flowers was a dead giveaway. "She loved them. It was very thoughtful of you, Mom."

Her mother glanced at her and then looked away, blinking her eyes. "I didn't want anything to detract from her happy day. I have a lot to make up for, to Elliana and to you."

From the backseat, Em yawned and stretched her arms. "Sorry I wasn't better company. I must have been more tired than I thought. I slept the entire ride back."

Bri cast a *yeah right* look over her shoulder as she got out of the SUV, positive Em had been awake the entire time. Then again, they'd left early, and she and Em were used to sleeping in. Bri was still battling insomnia, and Em was still fighting for her fiancé's life in her dreams.

"Don't worry about it, dear. It was nice of you to join us," her mother said when they got out of the SUV, and Em came to stand beside Bri.

"Would you like to stay for lunch?" her mother asked them hopefully.

"Maybe another time, Mom. We have to get ready for the tailgate party tonight." Bri and Em were selling T-shirts before the game, with the money they raised going to the trauma center fund. It was the first of several events Bri's sister and her grandmother had volunteered them for.

"I have fond memories of the tailgate parties before the big game between Highland Falls High and Jackson County High. Your father and I used to go all the time. I'm sure you girls will have a wonderful time."

Bri didn't miss the wistful note in her mother's voice or Em surreptitiously nudging her head in Miranda's direction.

Swallowing a put-upon sigh, Bri said, "You're welcome to join us, Mom. You can help us sell T-shirts for the trauma center."

"You're sure you don't mind?"

"No, not at all." Her mother's sweet gesture to Ellie had somewhat softened Bri's lingering resentment and anger toward her, reminding her how much of the burden her mother had shouldered when they were growing up, how lonely she must have been with Bri's father's tendency to shut off the rest of the world. "You'll have to meet us there though. I'm taking Grandpa's truck."

Her mother wrinkled her nose at the red pickup. "You know, darling, you don't have to borrow your grandfather's truck. Your father—I mean, Dimitri," she quickly amended, "would buy you whatever you want. All you have to do is ask."

"You know how I feel about that, Mom." Bri leaned in and kissed her mother's cheek to make up for the sharpness in her tone. "We'd better go. We'll see you tonight."

Her mother bit the inside of her lower lip. Then she

nodded, her smile forced. "If I'm not needed here, I'll
see you there." She patted Em's arm. "Tell Caleb congratulations for me. You must all be very excited about
the baby," her mother said, casting a sidelong glance at
Bri, as if reminding her that her decision to break them
up had been the right one. Just look at the wonderful,
fulfilled life Cal had with his beautiful, talented wife.

"Thrilled," Em muttered as she joined Bri in the truck.
"Gotta give her credit, she held off giving you a jab
longer than I expected."

"And thanks to you, I invited her to come tonight.
No doubt she'll take advantage of the opportunity to get
in a few more jabs about the blessed event. I'm fairly
certain I didn't do a great job covering my reaction when
she mentioned Cal and Raine's baby news, and just as
certain she picked up on it," Bri said, putting the truck
into Drive.

"Look, I know you were upset. I was too. But Cal told
you it wasn't true. He explained why Raine did it."

"I know, and I believe him. I do," she said when Em
made a disbelieving sound in her throat.

"Okay, so why have you been avoiding him? And don't
pretend that you're not. Every time he comes over, you
find an excuse to disappear into your room or the den."

She'd barely seen him in the past four days, and it
wasn't only because she'd made herself scarce when he
was around. "He hasn't come over that much."

"Ah, so that's the problem. I didn't take you for someone who played hard to get. You never did before."

"Are you insinuating I was easy?" Bri teased, in hopes
of changing the subject.

"I'm saying it isn't like you to hold something against Cal that you know wasn't his fault."

"I'm not. Okay, so I have been avoiding him," she admitted at Em's pointed stare. "But he's busy with the hospital and the trauma center and dealing with Izzy. I don't want him to think he has to make time for me." Izzy had been more upset about Raine's announcement than all of them combined.

"If you're telling me that you've been avoiding him so he doesn't feel obligated to make time for you, I don't buy it. You know as well as I do he'd spend his every waking minute with you if he could. And don't give me that *we're just friends* bullcrap. Anyone with two eyes in their head can tell how you guys feel about each other."

"You just made my point," Bri said as she turned off Main Street. "It was bad enough when everyone thought Cal and Raine were happily married, but now they think they have a baby on the way too. We have to be more careful now than ever. It would ruin Cal's reputation if there was even a hint that there was something going on between us, not to mention ruin any chance of fulfilling the trauma center's financial obligations to the town council." Bri glanced at Em as she turned onto Marigold Lane. "Not that there's anything going on between us. We're just getting to know each other again, as friends."

"Who are you trying to convince, me or yourself?" Em asked, then grimaced. "We have company."

Bri parked behind Raine's red Toyota Camry, glancing at the woman sitting hunched over on the porch steps. "What do you think she wants?"

"How should I know? We're not exactly best buds." Em got out of the truck. "You're looking a little peaked, Raine. Morning sickness getting the better of you?"

"I can't imagine why you're not best buds," Bri murmured, following Em up the walkway.

Em laughed, and Raine glanced from her to Bri, her dark eyes filling with tears. "You're lucky to have each other. I don't have friends. I don't have anyone. Cal hates me, and so does my daughter."

Bri noticed their neighbor raking leaves. "That's just pregnancy hormones talking, Raine. You know how much Cal and Izzy love you."

Em turned to frown at her, and Bri waved at their neighbor. "Hi, Mr. Voldock. Beautiful day, isn't it?"

"Okay then. Let's take this inside." Em walked up the stairs and unlocked the front door.

"Thank you. I didn't notice him there," Raine said, following Em inside.

Bri closed the door behind her, greeting Gus with a scratch behind his ears. "Would you like a cup of tea, Raine? I have to take Gus out," she said, hoping Em would offer. Bri's leg was aching after the hours spent in the car. It didn't help that she'd been tense.

Em glanced at Gus. "I'll make the tea."

Bri sighed. She didn't know what Em's problem with Gus was. He kept his distance from Em but watched over her at night. Bri had gotten into the habit of leaving her bedroom door open. Like clockwork, Gus would alert her to Em's impending nightmare.

Bri opened the sliding glass door. "Go on, boy." She gestured for him to go outside. He sat at her feet and looked up at her like he always did. Giving in after a few minutes, Bri took a slow, painful stroll around the garden while Gus did his business.

The butternut squash and eggplant were ripe on the vines, and she was tempted to kneel down and pick them but was afraid she wouldn't be able to get up. She'd do it tomorrow.

Gus walked beside her as she made her way back to the house. "Where's Raine?" she asked Em after sliding the door closed behind her.

"In your office. I added an extra tablespoon of sugar to your tea. I have a feeling you'll need it," Em said before taking her mug and heading for the living room.

Bri made her way to the den. Sure enough, Raine was stretched out on the couch. She looked like a movie star in her wide-leg black slacks and crisp white shirt with ruffled cuffs, her dark hair perfectly coiffed, her smoky eyes expertly applied. She'd kicked off her Louboutin heels.

Bri looked down at her own outfit—sneakers, black leggings, and a slouchy black top—wondering when she'd given up caring what she looked like. She didn't have to think too hard.

Brushing aside the memory of the day she'd erased any trace of the woman who'd married Richard, she walked to the chair across from Raine and took a seat. She smiled at the other woman, who glanced at her from under the arm lying across her eyes.

"Bad day?" Bri asked, shifting in the chair as Gus climbed carefully onto her lap. She welcomed his warm weight. It soothed the ache in her leg.

Raine sniffed and nodded. "Horrible. It's been the worst week of my life, and I need your help."

"I'm not sure how I can be of help," Bri said, lifting the mug to her lips.

Raine waved a hand around the den. "You're a family and marriage counselor. It's what you do."

Bri nearly spat out the mouthful of tea. "You want me to take you on as a client?"

"Yes, me and Cal. Izzy too, if I can get her to come. My family is falling apart, and I don't know what to do."

Was Cal truly clueless or had he been lying to her all along? "So you are pregnant?"

"No," Raine said, looking horrified at the idea. "Cal and I haven't slept together in more than a year, almost two."

Bri released the breath she'd been holding, feeling disloyal for having doubted Cal for a single second.

"It's all Harlan's fault," Raine continued. "He insinuated that there was still something going on between me and Quinn. I panicked and blurted that I was pregnant, thinking it would convince everyone that Cal and I were happy and in love. All it did was make everything worse. Not only won't Cal or my daughter speak to me, but now my mother and David, the hospital's administrator, are questioning my ability to take on a project this size because I'm expecting. You have to help me, Bri. I don't have anyone else to turn to."

"I think the answer to your problem is pretty simple, Raine. Tell the truth."

"I can't! We'll be ruined. No one will support us or the trauma center if they find out we've been lying this entire time." Her eyes narrowed at Bri. "And don't tell me we shouldn't have lied in the first place. I know that, just like I know I never should have put Cal in the position to lie. But I didn't feel like I had a choice. I couldn't risk that my professional and relationship histories would be the reason our proposal for the expansion was denied. The trauma center is too important. We'll be able to help so many people."

There was a reason therapists didn't take on friends or family as clients. Not that Raine was a family member or a friend, but Cal was, and Bri was too emotionally involved to counsel Raine.

Except Bri didn't have the heart to turn her away, and the reason she didn't was because she'd heard enough of Raine's story over the past week to know that under that striking, confident persona was a wounded teenager. Raine's problematic choices and her desperation to bring a critical care facility to Highland Falls all stemmed from her brother's accident.

But this was Raine, and their relationship was strained. Bri would have to build trust between them before she could help Raine unpack her emotional trauma. "Okay, so for right now, let's see if we can't come up with a solution to—"

"You'll take me on as a client? Cal and Izzy too?"

"Why don't we just start with you for now?"

"You don't understand. They won't talk to me. They hate me. The only reason I'm here, baring my soul to you, the woman my husband is in love with, is because I love them, and I'm afraid I'm going to lose them."

"Before we go any further, I need to know if you're trying to save your marriage." Ethically, she couldn't take on Raine as a client if she was. Not to mention how painful it would be.

"No." She frowned. "I told you, I'm trying to save my family."

"Yes, but you referred to Cal as your husband, and it's not the first time."

Raine waved her hand. "Force of habit. Cal and I figured out early on that we weren't compatible when it came to marriage. We want different things in life. But that doesn't make us any less a family. I love him. He's my best friend, and Izzy loves him too. Biologically, he might not be her father, but in every sense of the word, he is. We need him. We can't lose him."

"You know Cal as well as I do, Raine. There is no one as compassionate or as kind as he is. You won't lose him. He loves you and Izzy."

"I don't know. I think I went too far this time. He was furious." Her lips flattened. "And now that I think about it, it was probably because of you."

She had a feeling Raine might be right, but that wasn't something she'd share with her. "Izzy was as upset as Cal. And that had nothing to do with me. Have you told her that you aren't really pregnant?"

"I can't. She might let it slip, and then where would I be?"

"In a better place than you are right now, if you ask me. Hear me out," she said when Raine went to object. Bri preferred helping a client come to a solution on their own, but Raine was so locked into her lies that she figured it would take too long to get her there. "You used your fake pregnancy to convince Harlan, and everyone

else, that you and Cal are happy and in love. But from
the sound of it, Cal isn't acting very loving and happy.
Am I wrong in thinking he's not doing a good job hiding
his feelings at work?"

"No, and he doesn't seem to care when I tell him
everyone at the hospital is asking if he's okay. Including
my mother and David."

"I'm glad you brought them up. If Winter and David
are questioning your ability to get the job done due to
your fake pregnancy, which, I have to be honest, offends
me on so many levels—"

"I know, right?"

Bri smiled at Raine's reaction. "But as much as it
offends us, is it possible there are others like Winter
and David who are now doubting you're up for the job?
Because if there are, I'd imagine Harlan would be only
too happy to exploit that angle."

Raine groaned. "I didn't think of that." Then her eyes
narrowed at Bri. "I know what you're doing."

"I'm not sure what you mean. I was just trying to get
clear on what you're dealing with."

"Sure you were. You want me to lose the baby." Raine
tapped her lips with a manicured finger. "You know, that
might not be a bad idea. Everyone would feel sorry for
me, including Cal, Izzy, my mother, David, and possibly
Harlan. Wow, you're a genius, Bri."

"First of all, Cal knows you're not pregnant, Raine."

"Oh, right, but he'd be happy that there was no longer
a fake baby."

"You're not going to pretend you've lost a baby, fake
or not, to gain everyone's sympathy, Raine."

"Why? It's the perfect solution."

"Not for the many women who've lost babies, it's not. I'm sure you have people on staff at the hospital who have suffered that loss, and it wouldn't be fair to remind them, or have them offer you sympathy and advice on how to deal with your grief. You, Cal, or Izzy."

"You're right," Raine huffed. "So now what am I supposed to do?"

"Hang on a sec," Bri said as she Googled *recall on pregnancy tests*. When the results came up, she smiled and turned the screen to Raine. "You just found out there was a recall on the brand of pregnancy test you used because of the high number of false positives, and you decided to take another test, which was negative."

"All right, although I would have gotten way more sympathy if people thought I miscarried."

"Not from Cal, you wouldn't. And, Raine, you're going to tell Izzy the truth."

Bri woke up on the couch in the den, feeling like someone was watching her. She turned her head. Cal was sitting on her chair, his long legs stretched out.

He smiled. "Raine wear you out?"

"No, the ride to and from Asheville with my mother did." She brought her hand to her mouth and yawned. "What time is it?"

"Time for you to get going, according to my sister." He glanced at his phone. "It's two. You have plenty of time," he said when she pushed herself into a sitting position.

"Says someone who merely has to run his fingers

through his hair before heading out the door." She raised her hand to her messy topknot. "It takes me a little longer to get ready."

He got up and came over, joining her on the couch. "You're beautiful." He tucked the wayward strands of her hair behind her ear. "Thanks for convincing Raine to come clean about the pregnancy."

"She didn't take much convincing. She loves you, you and Izzy. She was desperate to make things right."

He blew out a breath. "I'm never going to convince you that there's nothing between us anymore, am I?"

"I should have clarified. She loves you as a friend. Her best friend. Her only friend from the sound of it."

"Yeah, she doesn't make friends easily. Never has." He wrapped a strand of her hair around his finger and gave it a gentle tug. "So are you going to stop avoiding me now, or do I have to book an appointment? You spent more time with Raine today than you have with me all week."

"You'll have to check with my administrative assistant. Raine asked me to take on all three of you as clients. I said no, but I heard her conferring with Em before she left, and your sister seems determined to fill my every waking moment with clients."

"She better leave some of those moments free for me." He put his arm around her. "I want to spend time with you, Bri. I missed you this week."

"I missed you too. I'm sorry I was avoiding you." She rested her head on his shoulder and played with the button on his shirt. "Even though I believed you and knew the pregnancy wasn't real, there was something about seeing you and Raine standing there, in this house that I'd once envisioned us living in together, everyone congratulating you, so happy for you guys, that messed with my head."

"I wish you would have told me."

"I didn't realize that's what was bothering me until just now."

Em stomped into the den. "What did you say to Raine?"

Bri lifted her head from Cal's shoulder. "Sorry. Client-therapist privilege. I can't tell you."

"Well, whatever you said, she seems to think you're besties now. She wants to hang out with us at the tailgate party. She also wondered if you had one of Cal's football jerseys. Do you?"

"Um." Her cheeks heated, and she avoided looking at Cal. "I might. Why?"

"She wants to trade you Quinn's for Cal's. But you can wear Josh's, and I'll wear Quinn's."

"So you have my high school sweatshirt *and* my football jersey," Cal said as Em walked out of the den with her phone to her ear.

"I said I might."

He grinned. "Make sure you get it back from Raine after the game. You can wear it tonight when I come over."

Chapter Sixteen

♥

The sun slid behind Blue Mountain, the darkening sky streaked with purple, illuminated by the football field's floodlights where the alumni exhibition game between Highland Falls High and Jackson County High was currently under way. The air was charged with excitement and the smell of barbecued hot dogs and buttered popcorn.

Bri stood between Em and Raine in the back of the pickup in the high school parking lot with a clear view of the football field, eating a hot dog while cheering on the hometown team. They were tied, with two minutes left in the twenty-minute pre-game show.

"Look, look!" Bri cried when Cal broke away from Jackson County's defense and ran for the goal line. "Go, Cal, go!"

"Stop jumping up and down. You'll hurt your leg," Raine said. "And stop cheering so loudly for Cal. Everyone's looking at you. You're supposed to be cheering for Josh. Go, darling, go!"

"Yay!" Bri yelled, waving her hands and hot dog bun in the air instead of jumping up and down when Cal scored a touchdown. The hot dog jumped out of the bun and slapped Raine in the face.

"Oh no! I'm so sorry." Bri pressed her lips together in an effort not to laugh at the shocked expression on Raine's mustard-splattered face.

Em didn't bother trying. She doubled over laughing.

"Em, stop it, and hand me that cloth by your feet," Bri said around a gurgle of laughter.

"Say cheese, Raine." The three of them turned to see Harlan with his camera raised. He snapped the photo before they could react. Glancing at the viewfinder, he smirked. "Thanks, ladies. This one's going on the front page of the *Herald*."

Raine's face turned a vivid shade of red beneath the vibrant streaks of yellow, and she opened her mouth. Positive she planned on giving Harlan crap, Bri intervened. The tailgate party had been a huge success so far, and she didn't want anything to detract from it.

"Everyone is so used to seeing Raine as the professional and brilliant doctor she is that I'm sure they'll enjoy seeing this fun-loving side of her. Although it is kind of annoying that, even with mustard on her face, she's so gorgeous."

"You're laying it on a little thick," Em murmured, reaching past Bri to hand Raine the cloth.

Bri smiled when Harlan glanced at the viewfinder and frowned, no doubt rethinking using the photo just as she had hoped. She was about to give Em an *it worked, didn't it?* look when she noticed grease streaks from the cloth she'd handed Raine replacing the mustard stains on her face. Bri snatched the cloth from her.

"What are you doing?" Raine protested. "Give it—"

"Oh, Brianna, darling, really," said her mother, who'd returned from selling Team Trauma T-shirts. "I understand you're jealous of Dr. Scott but it's not her fault that Cal—"

Bri's eyes went wide. The last thing they needed was for Miranda to pique Harlan's interest in Bri and Cal's previous relationship. She leaned over, shoved the hot dog bun into her mother's mouth, and grabbed the unsold T-shirts from her hand. She tossed a T-shirt at Raine, and one at Harlan, while ignoring the women's stunned expressions. There was only one person's expression she cared about, and that was Harlan's.

"No charge," she said, instead of saying what she wanted to, which was *No story here.* "Sooner or later, we'll convince you to switch sides." What she needed was a distraction to extinguish the curious glint in his eyes. "You don't want to be on the wrong side of this when Em finishes her investigation into the casino consortium." She gestured to Em, whose eyes had also narrowed at her, and not in a curious way. More in a *what the heck are you thinking?* kind of way. "She's a police officer, a highly decorated police officer, and Cal's sister."

"Who do you think you are to threaten me?" Harlan blustered.

"It was more a warning than a threat, Mr. Smith. And entirely for your benefit. I'm Brianna MacLeod, in case you'd like to quote me for your paper. Granny MacLeod's granddaughter."

Harlan paled. "You're her daughter?" he asked, pointing at her mother.

"Yes, I am. Why?"

"No reason. No reason at all," he said.

She frowned as he hurried away, bringing his phone to his ear.

But she didn't have a chance to comment on what seemed like his odd reaction, because Cal, Josh, and Quinn were making their way to the pickup, followed by a cheering crowd.

To avoid having to deal with her mother and Em— Raine actually seemed thrilled with her at the moment, possibly because she had no idea her face was covered with streaks of grease—Bri joined the crowd. "Three cheers for our Hometown Heroes!" she yelled.

When Cal reached the pickup, he grinned at her. "You look like you're having fun."

She'd been having a lot of fun, and that's not something she'd believed possible a matter of months ago.

"Oh yeah, she's had a great time." Em smirked. "She's just put herself at the top of Harlan's hit list, dragging me up there with her, took out Raine with a hot dog, and nearly killed off her mother with a hot dog bun."

Cal blinked but then was distracted by a group of women waving their Team Trauma T-shirts at him, wanting his autograph, along with Josh's and Quinn's.

Ten minutes later, Bri heard Josh say, "Sorry, we've gotta wrap this up. I have a game to coach. You two going to join me?" he asked Cal and Quinn.

"Yeah, I'll be right with you," Cal said, and made a beeline to where Bri was selling 50/50 raffle tickets with Raine, Em, and her mother, who'd grudgingly accepted her apology, as well as her explanation. Now that she knew Harlan was looking for any whiff of scandal to use against Cal and Raine, her mother promised to be more careful.

"Bri, I need to talk to you for a minute," Cal said.

"Darling, Bri apologized to me and her mother. You don't have to take her to task on our account." Raine turned to Bri's mother and rolled her eyes. "He's so protective of me."

Miranda and Raine had become fast friends, which Bri found amusing while at the same time slightly worrisome.

"I'm a little busy," Bri said to Cal. It wasn't a good idea for them to be seen having a private chat, especially with her mother and Raine looking on.

She also wasn't up to him giving her grief about Harlan. Bri was a little worried about Harlan herself. The last thing she wanted was him looking into her. He wouldn't know anything about her sordid history yet; he'd only bought the *Highland Falls Herald* in December.

Izzy ran over with a group of her friends, thankfully distracting Cal, and hugged him. "You were amazing, Dad." Her friends agreed, commenting on Cal's winning touchdown.

Cal deflected their praise by heaping it on Josh and the rest of the team. Bri didn't miss Izzy's reaction when he credited Quinn's pass for winning the game. "He was okay, I guess." A cheer went up in the stands, and Izzy glanced over her shoulder.

"Hurry up, Iz," a pretty redhead said.

"Dad, can I go to Kelly's after the game? All the team will be there, and she lives around the corner from us. Please, Dad, please."

Raine looked up from selling raffle tickets. "Have you forgotten you're grounded, young lady? You're lucky I agreed that you could come to the game at all. I suggest you be satisfied with that."

Izzy flushed, and Cal shot Raine a *you're embarrassing her* look. Bri agreed that Raine could have handled it better but she didn't think Cal overriding her would be helpful either. "Are your parents going to be home, Kelly?"

"Cal!" Raine said, and Izzy shot her mother a poisonous glance.

"Yes, and my dad said to give you his number. You can call anytime. We're going to make a video for Sam, and I promise, we'll stay at my house, Dr. Scott."

Sam had been a defensive lineman for the team, and according to Josh, he'd been destined for the NFL. At least he had been before the car accident on Pit Road.

"What do you say?" Cal asked Raine. "It's for Sam."

She didn't look happy but she acquiesced with a tight nod.

"Okay." Cal entered the number Kelly gave him into his phone. "I'll pick you up at eleven, Izzy."

Izzy looked like she might argue but must have thought better of it. "Thanks, Dad." She gave Cal a hug and took off with her friends without a glance or a thank-you for her mother.

"Sounds like the game is about to begin. We better close up shop and head for the stands," Em said, no doubt in an effort to save her big brother from Raine, who was clearly peeved, as evidenced by her crossed arms and tapping toe.

Bri smiled at Cal as she walked past him to the pickup. She was a little surprised when he didn't follow her. Relieved, but still surprised. Her cell phone pinged, and she pulled it from her jeans pocket. It was a text from Cal.

Hey beautiful, don't think that smile will save you from a conversation about Harlan.

She grinned and then, biting her bottom lip, typed out her response.

How about if I wear a smile and your football jersey?

If that's all you're wearing, there won't be much talking going on.

That's a deal.

Don't tease me.

"What are you doing? Mallory and Abby won't be able to save our seats much longer." Em joined her by the truck, glancing over her shoulder. "Who are you texting?"

"None of your business, nosy." Bri slid her phone in her back pocket.

Em snorted. "Trust me, the last thing I want to see or hear about is your sext exchange with my brother."

"We weren't sexting."

Behind Bri, someone gasped. She turned. It was her mother.

"Brianna, darling, I understand women have their needs, but really, do you think it's a good idea for you to be involved with someone so soon after your marriage has ended?"

"It's been more than a year, Mom," she said, relieved her mother hadn't overheard Em mention Cal.

"Technically, it has been, but you're far from recovered. Now isn't the time to be sidetracked by a relationship. You need to put all your energy into healing." She glanced over her shoulder and lowered her voice. "Raine mentioned that you're taking on clients. Do you think that's wise? You're hardly in a place to be advising anyone about their relationships."

Em slammed the gate of the pickup. "Okay, let's go."

"Yes, I should probably go too. I promised your grandfather I'd be back in time for him and Jonathan to catch some of the game." She leaned in and kissed Bri's cheek. "Please think about what I said. I only have your best interests at heart, darling."

"Don't you dare listen to her," Em said when Bri's mother headed for her car.

"She has a point. I have no business advising anyone about their relationships." She couldn't bring herself to add *or being in one* but that didn't mean she wasn't thinking it.

"Why, because the man you were in love with and married turned out to be abusive? That's not on you, that's on him." Em linked her arm through hers, steering her around the people in line at the concession stand. "In my book, that makes you an even better counselor. You've been through it, and you've come out the other side."

Today, she'd begun to think that she had. But if her mother's comments could so easily torpedo her confidence and make her doubt herself, obviously she hadn't.

"I'll walk behind you," Em said when they reached the stands packed with cheering Highland Falls fans. Mallory and Abby waved from their seats seven rows up. Raine was sitting with them.

Bri eyed the stairs. "Maybe I should just watch from the truck."

"Get going or I'll carry you up."

Bri glanced over her shoulder, smiling at the woman with a take-no-prisoners expression on her face. "I'm glad we're friends again. I really did miss you, you know."

"Yeah, yeah, I missed you too. Now get moving."

Bri held on to the rail with one hand while tightening her grip on her cane with the other. "Remind me never to jump up and down again." She gritted her teeth as she made her way up the stairs.

"How about I remind you to do your exercises instead? She's fine. Thanks though," Em said to an older gentleman who offered Bri his seat.

"Sorry, we got here late," Mallory said when Bri finally got settled. "We left the girls with a babysitter at my place, and Teddy decided he didn't trust her to look after his sister."

Teddy was Gabe's youngest, and he adored his baby sister as much as he adored his stepmother. Gabe was standing with the rest of their boys behind the Highland Falls team. Their oldest was the team's quarterback.

Abby, who'd been bent over her phone, smiled. "Good

job on T-shirt sales, ladies. We doubled our projection. Sales from the concession stand look great too. Did you sell out of the 50/50 raffle tickets?"

"Almost." Raine held up a cash box. "I put the rest in here."

"Great. We'll sell out as soon as Josh makes the announcement," Abby said.

As if on cue, Josh walked to the center of the field with the team captain, the captain from the other team joining them. Josh raised a microphone. "Let's all give a warm welcome to Dr. Caleb Scott, the man who not only scored the winning touchdown in today's alumni game but is also spearheading the campaign to bring a trauma center to Highland Falls."

The stands on the other side of the field were crammed with Jackson County fans, who cheered as loudly for Cal as the fans from Highland Falls, which wasn't a surprise. The surrounding counties would benefit just as much from the trauma center as Highland Falls.

Bri glanced at Raine, wondering if it bothered her that Cal was getting all the credit. It didn't appear to. Raine was beaming, clapping as loudly for Cal as everyone else was. Bri admired her for that. Raine didn't need the kudos or credit. Ego had nothing to do with her need to get the trauma center built. She truly believed it would save lives.

Josh waved his best friend over. "Get out here and toss the coin for us, Cal. And, folks, don't forget to buy your 50/50 raffle tickets. They'll sell out fast."

The raffle tickets were gone within minutes.

"I can't wait to see Harlan's face when I tell him how well we did, and I can almost guarantee we'll do even better at our next fundraising event." Abby frowned at Em. "Why did you make a face when I mentioned Harlan?"

"Why don't you tell Abby and Mallory what you did, Bri?" Em said.

"Oh wow, look." Bri pointed at the field. "Highland Falls intercepted the ball." She went to stand, cheering loudly. Mostly because it was exciting but also because she was hoping to distract her seatmates.

Em tugged on the back of Josh's football jersey, forcing Bri to sit. "No jumping up and down, remember?"

"I wasn't."

"No, you were trying to get out of telling Abby and Mallory what you did," Em said, and then filled them in.

"I don't know what you're upset about, Em," Raine said. "I, for one, am glad Bri turned the tables on Harlan. He's been trying to find something to use against Cal and me for months."

"I agree with Raine." Abby patted Bri's thigh. "Good job. It's something we should have thought to look into before. And, Em, you're the perfect person to take on the job."

"I'm glad you think so, but am I the only one who's noticed the way Harlan keeps looking at Bri?" she said, nodding at the man sitting three rows down from them.

Chapter Seventeen

♥

Cal grabbed a six-pack of beer from the fridge. Josh had invited the alumni team back to his place after the game to celebrate the win.

"I think I'll stay home," Raine said.

"Come on. It'll be fun." There was nothing Josh liked more than hosting a party in his backyard. He'd installed a hot tub and a firepit this spring.

"For you maybe. You know everyone."

"Bri and Em are coming." At least he hoped they were. He thought it would be good for both of them, especially Em.

"And so is Quinn."

He should have known that Quinn was the reason Raine didn't want to attend. "We've had this conversation before. It's not like you can avoid him forever. We live in a small town, and he's taking over as town manager."

"That's not something I'm likely to forget." She picked at the red polish on her thumbnail. "Has he said anything to you about the trauma center?"

There was no way he'd share what Quinn had said the night of the committee meeting at Bri and Em's. He was just glad Quinn hadn't shared his opinion that the infrastructure price tag was too low with Raine. *Yet*, he reminded himself. Quinn hadn't shared his opinion with her *yet*.

Maybe it would be better if Raine didn't come. Except people might think she was standoffish, and that wouldn't help their cause. A couple members of the alumni team had mentioned they were Team Casino. He was hoping that, between the two of them, they could change their minds, something he shared with Raine.

She sighed. "Fine. But don't leave me on my own. You know how much I hate making small talk."

Sounds of laughter and the smell of woodsmoke from down the street greeted them as Cal locked the front door. "Great night for a bonfire," he said, looking up at the quarter moon shining in the star-littered sky.

"You and Josh think every night is a great night for a bonfire."

He smiled. There'd been a lot of pluses to moving home, hanging out with his best friend being one of them. "And Mr. Voldock obviously shares your opinion about that," he said, spotting the older man standing on his front lawn staring at the cars lining the street in front of Josh's place.

Bri and Em's next-door neighbor noticed Cal and Raine and walked their way, tapping his watch. "You'd better warn Josh to keep the noise down. I have no qualms about calling the cops on him, even if he is a member of our neighborhood watch."

"Don't worry, Mr. Voldock. We'll be shutting down by eleven." At a loud splash and raucous laughter coming from Josh's backyard, Cal decided the older man needed a reminder that his best friend was an integral part of the neighborhood watch. "Did you get my update about the car Josh spotted the other night? He chased it down but he couldn't get a good look at the license plate."

Raine, who knew how long his neighborhood watch conversations with Mr. Voldock typically lasted, took the six-pack of beer from him. "Have a good evening, Mr. Voldock. Don't be long, Cal."

"I don't know how you expect me to have a good evening with that ruckus going on," the older man muttered before turning back to Cal. "We'll catch those delinquents the next time they're in the neighborhood. Your sister has a plan."

"My sister?"

"Yeah." He jerked his thumb at Bri and Em's house. "She put up one of those porch camera thingies. Said she can get us a good deal if we get everyone in the neighborhood on board. Even offered to install them for us. Nice gal. Smart too. They both are. The other one, Bri, I think her name is. She's doing a good job with the gardens. I let Fred know," he said, referring to the owner of Em and Bri's place. "He was mighty pleased to hear it. Though you might not be pleased with her suggestion for the watch."

"Bri had a suggestion about the neighborhood watch?"

He nodded. "She thinks your sister should take over from you as captain. She didn't mean no offense by it, I'm sure. Just said how your sister is a cop and well suited for the job." He stuffed his hands in his pockets and rocked on the heels of his slippers. "So what do you think?"

He thought it was a great idea. "What did my sister say?"

"Didn't seem impressed by the idea, but I have a feeling Bri will get her on board. She told me she'd work on her. She'll probably mention it to you tonight." His mouth flattened as he glanced across the road at Josh's house. "The pair of them are over there."

"If Em is on board, I'm all for her taking over. As long as you and the rest of the neighborhood agree, of course."

"I'm sure they will. No offense, we all know how busy you are, but you're a little slow getting the newsletters out."

"None taken." Josh was the one who'd roped him into taking on the job in the first place. He'd been afraid Mr. Voldock was going to be named captain of the watch. "I'd better head over. You know you're welcome to join us." Josh would probably kill him for making the offer, but Cal thought the older man's prickly attitude was because he was lonely.

"Hmm. That might not be a bad idea. I could keep them in line." He jerked his thumb at the house on the other side of Bri and Em's. "I'll see if some of the other neighbors want to join me. I'd feel more comfortable if I had a few others my age."

"I'm sure Josh won't mind." He was pretty sure he was a dead man. "I'll see you over there." Cal jogged across the road.

As soon as he opened the gate to the fenced-in backyard,

he spotted Josh holding court by the firepit. But Cal's attention was immediately captured by the blonde in the hot tub. It was Bri, who looked as ticked with his sister as Josh would soon be with him. Cal said hi to several people as he made his way across the yard, reaching into the ice-filled cooler for a bottle of beer. He spotted Raine talking to two women in the middle of the yard. She was sipping a glass of wine and seemed to be enjoying the conversation, so he made his way to Josh.

"Hey, how's it going?" He smiled at the three women gathered around his best friend and then leaned into Josh. "Mr. Voldock and a couple of the neighbors might be dropping in."

"Yeah, right." Josh laughed, and then he looked closer at Cal. "You can't be serious."

Cal shrugged. "It was either that or he'd shut your party down in forty-five minutes."

"Fine. But they're your responsibility," Josh said, and he went back to talking to the three women. Noting the attention his best friend was giving the woman in the middle, Cal laid odds Josh would be bringing out his guitar within the next five minutes.

As he walked away, he heard Josh say, "I'll be right back. I have something I think you'll enjoy."

Cal was still laughing when he reached the hot tub. Bri pushed her wet hair back from her face. "It's not funny, Cal. Your sister is torturing me."

Em snorted. "Only you would think a couple of leg lifts qualifies as torture."

"Twenty is not a couple, and you're not my physio-therapist."

"I was laughing at Josh, not you. But working out in the hot tub isn't a bad idea, Bri," he said, trying not to get distracted by all her silky skin on display. She wore a navy one-piece bathing suit that on anyone else wouldn't be considered sexy but it'd been a long time since he'd seen Bri in anything other than sweatshirts and leggings.

"We're at a party, and you want to talk about my exercise regimen?"

"You're right. I'll save it for another time."

"Never works for me," she said, resting her head on the ledge and closing her eyes.

He smiled at her attitude and flicked a little water at her. "I'll make you a deal. Lose the cane, and I won't bring it up until your next scan a month from now."

"I can't lose my cane."

"You need to bear weight on your leg, Bri. The bone hasn't healed the way I would have expected it to."

"Thanks to the two of you, I'm no longer enjoying my hot tub experience."

He leaned into her. "If we didn't have an audience, I can guarantee you would enjoy your hot tub experience with me."

"Cal." Bri grabbed his bottle of beer and pressed it to her cheek. "Don't say things like that to me."

"Would you rather we talk about you getting me fired as captain of the neighborhood watch?"

"I want to talk about that too," his sister said. "She volunteered me without even—" Em broke off at Bri's raised eyebrow. The two of them shared a silent exchange like they used to when they were younger. And whatever Bri had silently shared with Em had his sister backtracking. "It's not as if you have the time, and I do. Plus, it's in my wheelhouse, not yours."

"You really don't mind, do you?" Bri asked, handing him back his beer.

"No, I'm more than happy to hand over the responsibility." Raine called his name. He looked to where she now stood with a group of people that included Quinn. "I better get over there."

"Uh, what are Mr. Voldock and his friends doing here?" Em asked.

Cal followed his sister's gaze, grinning at the three older men in their bathrobes and slippers. "Looks like they're coming to join you in the hot tub."

As Cal walked away, someone requested Josh play Kelly Clarkson's "A Moment Like This." Cal glanced over his shoulder and met Bri's gaze. It was their song. The one they'd planned to dance to at their wedding. He loved her as much as he did back then. He turned away, afraid someone would read the emotion on his face. Apparently, someone had. Quinn looked from him to Bri as Cal joined the tight-knit group.

"There you are, darling." Raine looped her arm through his. "I was just telling Roger how the trauma center will benefit his mother. She's in rehab."

Cal joined in the conversation but it took some effort to stay focused. He was having a hard time keeping his eyes off Bri. When she started climbing out of the hot tub, it took everything he had to stay where he was. Em reached out to help her, and he took a relieved sip of his beer. Only to choke on it when Bri bent over to pick up a pair of gray sweatpants and a sweatshirt from the ground. And it wasn't because he was worried she'd fall over.

He cleared his throat and held up his half-empty bottle of beer. "Anyone else want something to drink?" He took down their orders in his head and then made his way across the lawn.

A heavy hand fell on his shoulder as he reached the patio. He turned to see Quinn behind him. "I need a word with you. In private," the other man said.

Josh raised his eyebrows at Cal as he followed Quinn to the back door. "Someone doesn't look happy with you, brother."

"Yeah. Seems like." And Cal had a sneaking suspicion he knew why. "What's up?" Cal asked, walking to where Quinn stood in the kitchen, looking out the window.

Quinn gestured at Bri laughing with Em by the fire. "You tell me."

"You're going to have to give me a little more to go on. I'm not a mind reader, Quinn."

"I saw how you were looking at Bri, Cal. And I wasn't the only one. How could you do that to Raine?"

"You have no idea what you're talking about. So I'd suggest you keep your opinions to yourself. My personal life doesn't concern you."

"Raine and Izzy matter to me. I care about them, and I don't want to see them hurt."

"Is that right? So why did you go radio silent? Raine and I have been together for six years, and not once, in all that time, did you call Izzy or send her anything for her birthday or for Christmas. For the first five years of her life, you were the only dad she knew."

The guy looked like he'd been sucker-punched, which might have been why Josh, who'd just walked into the kitchen, said, "You told him you and Raine were done?"

Cal bowed his head and muttered, "Josh."

"What? He looked like you'd dropped a bomb on him so I figured you must have told him." Josh shook his head and reached past Quinn for a bottle opener on the counter. "And don't tell me you aren't secretly relieved, man," Josh said to Quinn as he brushed past him. "I saw the way you were looking at Raine."

"So it's true? You and Raine really are getting a divorce?" Quinn asked when the back door closed behind Josh.

"Yeah." And, praying he wasn't blowing up their dream of building a trauma center in Highland Falls, he told Quinn everything.

"I don't know why I'm surprised. It's exactly something Raine would pull," Quinn said, raising a hand when Cal opened his mouth to defend her. "I know. I understand what drives her as well as you do. Just like I know how important the trauma center is to her, and why. But if this gets out—"

"If what gets out?" Raine asked, looking from him to Quinn.

Josh needed to put a bell on his back door or stop oiling it. "Nothing," Cal said at the same time Quinn said, "Word of your and Cal's fake relationship."

"Cal! How could you?"

"It wasn't his faul—"

Cal intervened before Quinn threw Josh under the bus. He didn't think Raine and Josh's already strained relationship would survive this, and it was important to Cal that the people he cared about got along. Or at least could stand being in the same room together for more than five minutes. "It's better that we're above board with Quinn, Raine. It's going to come out eventually. We need him in our corner."

Quinn smoothed his hand over his head. "I'm not sure what you think I'll be able to do, Cal."

"Did you really expect *him* of all people to go to bat for us? He'd be happy if the trauma center falls through. He sees the casino as a cash cow." Raine headed for the front door, yelling over her shoulder, "Don't bother coming home tonight, Caleb Scott!"

"Raine, I have to pick up Izzy at—"

"I told her she could stay at Kelly's. That's what I came to tell you, only to find out you were in here ruining our lives!"

"She hasn't changed much, has she?" Quinn said when the door slammed behind her.

"She's not right about you supporting the casino, is she?"

"No, and I don't plan on saying anything about this to anyone. But, Cal, you've gotta know this isn't going to end well."

"If we can meet our financial obligations in the allotted time frame, we should be able to weather the storm."

"And if you can't?"

"We'll cross that bridge when we come to it. So what was with your reaction earlier? Because Josh was right, you looked stunned when I mentioned that you hadn't... You didn't just cut Izzy out of your life, did you?"

"No. Like you said, for the first five years of her life she was mine. I loved that kid. Raine told me my calls upset her, so I stopped. But I kept sending her money for her birthday and for Christmas, updated my contact information in the cards, and let her know that I loved her and would always be there for her if she needed me." He swore under his breath. "Raine never gave them to her, did she?"

Cal shook his head. "I'm sorry, man. I had no idea."

Quinn looked away and blew out a breath. "No wonder Izzy hates me. She thinks I abandoned her."

Which was no doubt the reason why Izzy hadn't been herself these past couple of weeks. "I know it's a big ask, but can you hold off on confronting Raine? It might go better if I talk to her first, and obviously, she's not open to talking to me tonight."

"Yeah, okay," Quinn agreed, although he didn't look happy about it.

Cal didn't blame him. "Appreciate it, and don't worry, Izzy is my number one priority. She needs to know you didn't abandon her, and I'll make sure that she does, whether Raine likes it or not."

Quinn ended up leaving after that, saying he wasn't in the mood for a party. Cal felt the same, especially after heading into the backyard and discovering that Em and Bri had left. He hung around for a bit and then let Josh know he was leaving, saying goodbye to the rest of the guests before heading over to Em and Bri's.

"You guys got room for one more?" he asked when his sister opened the door. "Raine kicked me out."

"She kicked you out?"

"Yeah, she's ticked I told Quinn about our little arrangement."

"Sounds like she's more than ticked, big brother." Em pulled him inside, glancing up and down the street as she did so. "What about Izzy?"

"Raine told her she could stay at Kelly's, and before you suggest it, I can't stay with Josh. He has company." Cal toed off his sneakers and crouched beside Gus, giving the dog a scratch behind his ears.

"Could have called that as soon as he brought out his guitar," Em said, closing the door. "It was his signature move in high school."

"Yeah, looks like he's ready to put himself out there again." Cal straightened and walked into the living room with Gus following behind him.

It didn't appear as if his sister and Bri planned on going to bed anytime soon. A fire crackled in the fireplace, an episode of *Grace and Frankie* was paused on the TV screen, and from the sweet smell wafting from the two mugs on the coffee table, they were enjoying some hot cocoa.

He sat on the couch. Gus jumped up, sending a cautious glance at Em before settling in beside him. "Where's Bri?"

"I wondered how long it would take you to ask. She's grabbing a shower." Em rolled her eyes at Gus and took a seat on the couch. Bringing one of the mugs to her lips, she looked at Cal over the rim. "Go. I know you want to, and I'd actually like to watch this episode in peace."

"Bri still talk while she's watching TV?"

"Talk? She never shuts up."

He laughed and headed for Bri's bedroom. From behind the en suite bathroom's closed door, he heard the blow dryer. He rapped on the door. "Bri, it's me."

The blow dryer turned off, and she opened the door. Her cheeks were flushed, her long hair a bright, shiny cloud around her face. She pushed it from her eyes. "Hi."

He smiled. "Go back to what you're doing. I just wanted to let you know I was here."

"My hair's dry." She tightened the belt of her white robe. The warm, humid air that followed her from the bathroom smelled like her—an intoxicating blend of lavender and mint. "Is everything okay?"

"It depends on how you look at it, I guess. Raine kicked me out." He told her what had transpired in Josh's kitchen. "So I need a place to stay for the night, and I thought I'd stay here."

"Here? With me?"

"I was thinking I'd sleep on the couch, but if you're willing to share your bed with me"— he sat on the end of the mattress, reaching out to draw her between his legs— "I'd be more than happy to take you up on the offer."

"I don't know if that's a good idea, Cal. We agreed—"

"To take it slow and start as friends?" He nodded, resting his hands on her hips. "I know we did. It just feels like we're wasting time. It's not as if my feelings for you are going to change. You've been through a lot this past year, but you're still the beautiful, sweet, compassionate woman I fell in love with."

She cupped the side of his face in her hand, stroking his cheek with her thumb. "I'm not so sweet or so trusting anymore."

"That's not a bad thing. You're older and wiser." He turned his face, kissing the palm of her hand. "I love you, Bri, as much as I did, maybe more."

"I love you too. I always have, and I always will." Her gaze flicked from the bed to him. "It's not that I don't want you to sleep with me. I do. I really do want to make love with you. It just feels wrong somehow. I don't know why, maybe because, technically, you're still married."

"I guess I should have been clearer. I can't say I don't want to make love to you, because I do. Desperately. But what I really want to do is the one thing we never got a chance to. I want to spend the night with you. I want to fall asleep with you in my arms and wake up in the morning with you next to me."

"I'd like that too. Very much. But right now, I'd like you to kiss me."

"I think that can be arranged."

Chapter Eighteen

♥

Bri woke up to her phone ringing on the nightstand. She was still half asleep, and it took a moment for her to recognize the ringtone. Her sister was FaceTiming her. Finally! Bri leaned over and grabbed the phone, accepting the FaceTime call at the same time a deep voice beside her said, "Babe, don't—"

Bri's eyes went wide as she realized where she was and who she was with, and her sister's smiling face appeared on the screen. Bri plastered what she hoped was a happy and not a panicked smile on her face while ensuring that Cal didn't appear on the screen. "Ellie! Wow! You're in Scotland! Isn't that amazing?" She pressed her nose to the screen in hopes of blocking out the side of Cal's face, pretending she was trying to get a better look at the view. "Is that a castle in the background?"

"Move back from the phone, Bri. All I can see is your nose smushed against the screen."

Bri fake-laughed, nudging the bare, muscular leg of the man half-groaning, half-laughing beside her. "Better?" she asked as she pulled back from the screen.

"No. Farther. I want to see who's in bed with you, and it better not be who I think it is."

"I don't know what you're talking about." Out of the camera's view, she tossed the comforter over Cal's head, leaned on him, and then gave her sister a look at the bed. "See, nobody here. You must have seen Gus. So, tell me, have you seen any handsome Highlanders? What am I saying? You have Nate with you. Of course you're not looking at other men."

"Stop babbling. You're giving yourself away, and would you mind moving your elbow? It's in my ear," said the muffled voice from under the comforter.

"That was not a dog in your bed, Bri. And I know when you're lying to me."

"Ellie, you promised never to read my mind! Get out of my head right now," she said, panicked by what her sister might see. She was having a hard time not thinking about the brief, slightly bleary image of Cal with his messy bedhead and chiseled, beard-stubbled face or how incredible his warm, muscular body felt pressed against her.

"I don't have to read your mind to know you're lying. You're blushing. Caleb Scott, I know that's you in my sister's bed so stop hiding."

He sighed and went to toss back the covers but Bri wasn't giving up, not yet, and tried pushing him off the bed. "I'm trying really hard not to be offended here, but I'm willing to give you a pass on account of jet lag," she said, using the heels of her feet as leverage. The man was an immovable mountain. There was no budging him.

Or changing his mind, apparently, because he pushed

off the covers and that handsome face of his appeared on-screen beside her. As did a delectable view of his broad shoulders...and bare chest! Bri shifted, angling herself across his front in order to hide that part of him from view, which resulted in her face tipping up, looking like she wanted him to kiss her. Which at any other time she would.

"I can explain, Ellie. It's not what it looks like," Cal said, shoving his fingers through his hair.

The movement distracted Bri. He had really great hair. It was kind of annoying how good he looked first thing in the morning. Then she remembered where she was and who she was talking to. "You know what, we don't have to explain anything to you, Ellie. You have to stop treating me like your baby sister. I'm almost thirty."

"And Cal's a married man!"

"Oh right. I forgot about that."

"You forgot he's married? How could you forget he's married, Bri?"

"Traumatic brain injury?" she said.

Looking like he was fighting back a smile, Cal took the phone from her. Then he proceeded to tell her sister about his arrangement with Raine.

She could tell by her sister's doubtful expression that she was as worried about the fallout as Bri, and she took the phone from Cal. "Don't worry about me. It will be fine. Now show me the view and tell me what you've done so far." She and her sister talked for another five minutes, ending the call with *I love you*s and a promise to talk later that night. Her sister didn't have to say *without Cal around*. She'd let her off too easy for Bri to think they wouldn't be discussing this further.

"Well, that was a fun way to start the day," she said, returning her phone to the nightstand. She rolled on her side to face Cal. "I'm sorry. I didn't think."

"It wasn't exactly the wake-up I was looking forward to," he said, tugging her into his arms, "but it's better Ellie heard about it from me."

"I suppose," she said, snuggling closer. "But what if she slips and accidentally says something to my mom? Or to Abby, Mallory, or Sadie?"

"If it happens, we'll deal with it. It's not like any of them would say anything anyway." He reached for his phone on the nightstand. "I didn't realize it was so late. I'd better get going. I want to be home before Izzy."

Raine had called Cal late last night to apologize for kicking him out.

Bri smiled and patted his chest. "Good thing you're well rested. Just remember what you told Quinn when he called to set up your family meeting today." Raine hadn't been his only late-night phone call.

"You mean what *you* told me to say." He angled his head. "Any chance you want to come over and mediate?"

"None at all." She laughed at the face he made. "You'll be fine."

"I'd be even better if I could spend the morning here with you." He brushed his lips over hers before getting out of bed.

She stretched, enjoying the view. He'd stripped down to his boxers last night. She wore his T-shirt and her

panties to bed. "So would I, but I'm surprisingly ener-
gized this morning. It must be the hot tub. I haven't slept
through the night in I don't know how long."

"You sure it was just the hot tub?" he asked, leaning
over her with a wicked grin on his face, caging her
between his arms.

She linked her hands around his neck. "You might
have had something to do with it."

"Might have?"

"I don't want you to get a—"

She was interrupted by Em, who called through the
closed bedroom door, "You two have four minutes,
maybe three, to get decent." The front doorbell rang.
"Okay, so she was moving faster than I gave her credit
for," Em added, then yelled, "Relax. I'm coming."

"Go, go," Bri told Cal, changing her mind a second
later when a thought came to her. "Wait. Maybe you
should stay here until we know who it is. Otherwise,
we're going to have to come up with a reason for you
being here at nine in the morning."

"How about I was here helping you with your exercises?" He raised an eyebrow when she got out of bed to
grab a pair of jeans from the closet. "You do know you
should be doing your stretches before you get out of bed,
don't you?"

"This is hardly the time to discuss my stretching
routine, Cal. Your sister is about to let someone in, and I
can guarantee exactly what they'll think when you come
walking out of my bedroom."

"You in that T-shirt would raise more eyebrows than
me walking out of this bedroom."

She frowned and looked down at herself. She was braless under his white T-shirt. "Right." She pulled a red-and-black flannel shirt off a hanger and put it on, combing her fingers through her hair.

"You might want to brush it. You have seriously sexy bedhead going on." He cocked his head as he opened the door. "Never mind, it's just Raine."

"Never mind, it's just Raine?" she repeated. "How is me having bedhead not a problem when we're going to greet your wife?"

"Ex-wife, and you forgot the seriously sexy part." He gave her a hard, fast kiss. "And trust me, she doesn't care as long as we're circumspect."

"Em, let me pass. I know Cal slept over, so I have a fairly good idea where Bri is, and I don't care. This is an emergency!"

Cal shot Bri an *I told you so* look over his shoulder as he walked out of the bedroom. "What's going on?"

"What's going on is Quinn just showed up at our door with coffee and my favorite pastries from Bites of Bliss, and he's...he's being nice to me!" She threw up her arms with a dramatic flourish.

"And that's a problem, how?" Cal asked.

"You wouldn't understand. And I didn't come here to talk to you anyway." She marched past him and took Bri by the hand. "I need a session with my therapist, if you don't mind."

Cal laughed, pressing his lips together when Bri shot him a glare, raising his palms as if this wasn't exactly what he wanted. "Cal should probably join us, Raine."

Raine sighed. "Fine," she said, then glanced at Em, who looked like it was taking everything she had to remain upright. Gus leaned against her as if propping her up.

And that's when Bri realized Em must have stayed awake the entire night so her brother didn't discover she was still having nightmares. Bri felt horrible but thought it might have been for the best. Maybe now Em would open up to her about her fiancé's death. She couldn't go on like this.

"I'll have a cup of that tea you made for us last time, Em. It was delicious."

"Would you like some pastries to go with it?" Em asked.

"That would be lovely, thank you," Raine said, obviously missing the sarcasm in Em's voice.

Her brother didn't. "I'll take care of it, Freckles. Why don't you go back to bed? You look like you had a rough night."

Em shrugged. "You know what I'm like when I'm on a case."

"You're on a case? What case?" Cal asked, frowning.

"The one Bri volunteered me for, remember? The casino consortium. I think I'm getting close to figuring out who's behind it."

"Really? That's incredible. You can fill me in while I'm making the tea," Cal said.

"Okay, you guys. Aren't you forgetting something? Quinn," Em said when the three of them looked at her blankly. "He's—" The doorbell rang. She glanced at the alarm system's camera and grinned. "Never mind. He's here." She opened the door. "Hi, Quinn. Come on in. So,

Bri, should I invoice them separately or give them the family rate?"

"Actually, as much as I'd love to take you all on as clients, I can't. My business isn't registered yet. So honestly, Raine, I shouldn't even be working with you." Raine's face fell, and she looked like she might cry. "But that doesn't mean I can't listen, as a friend," Bri quickly amended.

Raine beamed, half-dragging Bri along with her to the den.

"Raine, slow up," Cal said. "Bri doesn't have her cane."

"Because someone told me I shouldn't use it anymore, remember?" Bri reminded him.

"She's fine." Raine opened the door and ushered Bri inside. "Now go away," she told Cal, closing the door in his face. She glanced at Bri. "I didn't hurt you, did I?"

"No." She looked at Raine and shook her head. "How do you look like that at nine in the morning?"

"Like what?" Raine looked down at her long cream cashmere sweater and the brown suede leggings she'd paired with brown knee-high boots as if she didn't look like she'd stepped out of a fashion magazine.

"Stunning." She waved her hand at Raine's hair and now smiling face. "You're in full makeup and your hair looks like you just came from the salon. Do you always look like this on a Saturday morning or were you going out when Quinn arrived?"

As Bri had hoped, the compliments relaxed Raine. She'd also meant every word of them. But Raine tensed right back up at the mention of Quinn.

She sank down on the couch and stretched out,

covering her eyes with her forearm. "I may have taken extra care knowing he was coming over. We can't all be like you, Bri. Some of us need to look good to boost our confidence. You're confident no matter what you look like." She lifted her arm and glanced at Bri. "That didn't come out the way I meant it to. You're effortlessly beautiful. You don't care what other people think. I admire that about you."

Bri had once put as much effort into her appearance as Raine. Except, for her, it hadn't been about impressing anyone or boosting her confidence. She'd just loved pretty clothes and dressing up. But Richard had been all about using her appearance to impress others while at the same time ensuring that it conformed to what he deemed suitable for his wife to wear—expensive, conservative clothes in dull, boring colors.

It had started slowly—a gift of clothing for a business dinner or a night out or because he'd seen it in a store window and thought of her. It wasn't long before her entire wardrobe had been replaced. A part of her personality erased. She rubbed the red-and-black flannel shirt between her fingers. Maybe it was time she took back that part of herself.

She returned her attention to Raine. "My first thought when I saw you at the grocery store was *There's a woman who has it all together.* You came across as strong and confident, a woman who got what she wanted. And you know what, Raine? It had nothing to do with how you looked. I mean, you were obviously beautiful and put together like you always are, but it was more than that. It was the vibe you gave off."

"It's all an act."

"So your clothes, the makeup, the hair, they're like a suit of armor? A mask you wear?"

She nodded. "Yes."

"Who's under the suit of armor, Raine? Who's under the mask?"

And just like that, Raine's armor cracked, revealing the teenager who blamed herself for her brother's death, who blamed herself for the actions of her father, a man who, unable to cope with his son's death, abandoned her and her mother. The heartbroken teenager who was looking for love wherever she could find it after Quinn, her first love, left Highland Falls. The pregnant teenager who felt shamed by her family and her friends but desperately wanted to keep her baby. The pregnant teenager who'd accepted the marriage proposal of the boy she still loved, despite believing the only reason he'd married her was because he felt sorry for her. And when Quinn, struggling to come to terms with the end of his NFL career, shut her out, she'd left him before he could leave her.

Everything, every hurt, the guilt and the shame, poured out of Raine in huge, gasping sobs.

When the sobs eventually subsided, Raine sat up and buried her face in her hands. "I'm so embarrassed. I have no idea where all that came from."

"I think you've been holding everything in for far too long, Raine. Thank you for trusting me enough to open up," Bri said as she got up from the chair. She picked up the box of tissues from the side table and made her way to the couch. She sat beside Raine, offering her the box.

Raine took several tissues and dabbed at her eyes, looking up at the knock on the door.

"Sorry," Cal said, walking in with two cups. He stopped to stare at Raine. "Why are you crying? What happened?"

"Thanks for the tea, Cal. You can leave it on the table." Bri nodded at the door, encouraging him to leave.

He put the cups on the table, but instead of leaving, he crouched in front of Raine, taking her hands in his. "Talk to me. Tell me what's wrong. Is this because of me and Bri? Or Quinn. Is this about Quinn?"

Bri sighed. "Cal, would you mind giving us—" She broke off when Quinn walked in with a pastry box from Bites of Bliss.

"Sorry. I thought you might like…" He trailed off, staring at Raine, and just like Cal, he put the box on the table and came to her side. "I won't say anything to Izzy. The last thing I wanted was to make you cry."

Unlike Cal, Bri couldn't say Raine's tears had nothing to do with Quinn. Still…"Okay, you two. You're interrupting my session with Raine, and despite what you both seem to think, men aren't the only reason women cry."

"Why's she crying then?" Cal asked, clearly unimpressed with her answer, adding for Raine, "Whatever it is, we can fix it."

Quinn nodded. "Just tell us what you need us to do."

"Raine doesn't need you to fix things for her, Cal. And it isn't her job to tell you what you need to do, Quinn."

"Well, what are we supposed to do?" Quinn asked, looking as unhappy with Bri as Cal was.

Bri got up from the couch and walked to the door. "Leave."

Raine snorted a laugh into another tissue and then looked at Bri. "It's okay. They can stay. We have to talk about Izzy anyway."

As Cal and Quinn went to sit on either side of Raine, Bri gestured to the chairs. "No. You over there, and you over there."

It was important that Raine feel comfortable letting herself be vulnerable and honest, and Bri didn't see that happening with Cal and Quinn bookending her on the couch.

Cal fisted his hands on his hips, raising an eyebrow at her. "She's upset."

"My session, my rules. If you don't like them, you can leave." Bri took a seat beside Raine. "As much as this is about Izzy, it might be helpful for Quinn to understand why you ended your marriage, Raine." Bri smiled and took her hand. "But only if you're comfortable sharing that today. It's entirely up to you."

Raine glanced under her lashes at Quinn. "Okay."

Bri gave her hand an encouraging squeeze. "And not a peep out of either of you until she finishes. This is about Raine, not you."

For the most part, Quinn and Cal abided by her rule, although they both seemed to share the we-can-fix-it gene and weren't pleased whenever she corrected them. But it was a minor flaw. They were both kind, empathetic, caring men, and Raine and Izzy were lucky to have them in their lives, which Bri shared with them when she ended the session an hour later.

"I don't know how to thank you," Raine said, hugging Bri as she opened the door to the den.

Em looked up from where she sat at the kitchen table, working on her laptop. Bri smiled at the sight of Gus curled up at her best friend's feet. He'd finally broken through Em's defenses.

Tapping her finger on three printed invoices, Em said, "You can pay her."

"Em, we talked about this. I can't charge for my services until I've—"

"I registered your business last week." She pointed at an official-looking document beside her laptop.

Raine, Quinn, and Cal each went to pick up an invoice. Bri covered them with her hand. "No, this was on the house."

"Em's right, Bri. You should be charging for your services," Cal said. Then he grinned. "Although Quinn and I should get a break—you hardly let us talk."

"With the amount of work it took for Bri to keep you two in line, I think she deserves double," Raine said. "And you more than earned your fee with me. Please let me pay you."

"How about you take me shopping instead? Me and Em."

"Hey, leave me out of it," Em muttered.

"I'd love to, and the three of us can do lunch afterward."

As Bri walked them to the door, she and Raine worked out a date for shopping and her next appointment.

"I'll meet you guys at the house," Cal said, closing the door after Quinn and Raine. "So how big a jerk was I? Don't hold back," he said, taking Bri into his arms.

"Maybe a tiny bit of one, but I knew where you were coming from. And I'm sorry if I came off a little harsh. Raine's my client, and my job is to make her feel safe."

"And you're incredibly good at your job. I'm glad I got the opportunity to see you at work. You're impressive, Bri. You really are."

"Thank you. I forgot how much I enjoyed counseling, how rewarding it can be."

"So you really are opening a practice here?"

"I don't think your sister is going to give me much choice." She rose up on her toes and kissed him. "You'd better go. Izzy will probably be home by now."

"You sure you won't reconsider joining us?"

"I have faith in you, in all three of you. You'll be fine. You out of anyone can identify with how an abandoned child feels, Cal. Raine can too. But I'm here if you need me."

"Thanks." He gave her a long, lingering kiss before releasing her. "I'll see you later. Don't forget to do your stretches."

She raised an eyebrow.

"Yeah, yeah, I know, but you're going to have to deal with it, beautiful. It's my job to take care of my patients, and it sucks for you that not only are you my patient, I'm also in love with you. So if there's something I think you should be doing that will speed up your recovery, I'm going to tell you. Even if it means ticking you off." He opened the door.

"I can almost guarantee you'll be ticking me off."

He winked. "Think how much fun we'll have making up."

Bri was still smiling when she entered the kitchen. Em was on the phone, her eyes following Bri as she poured herself a cup of tea. She held up the pot. Em shook her head. "Thanks for your help, Sadie."

That was a surprise. She wondered why Em was talking to Sadie and why she seemed to be avoiding Bri's questioning gaze.

"Yeah. I'm not looking forward to it. I will. I'll tell her. Thanks again." Em disconnected and scrubbed a hand over her face. "You'd better sit down for this." She pushed out a chair with her foot.

"What's going on?"

"With some help from your cousin, I've figured out who's behind the casino consortium."

There was only one reason Em would have her sit down. Bri knew the person. And there was only one person she knew who had the funds and the inclination to back a casino in Highlands Falls. "It's Dimitri, isn't it?"

Chapter Nineteen

♥

Bri was right. Dimitri was heading up the casino consortium. "How am I supposed to tell Cal and Raine that my father is behind the casino?"

Em shrugged. "It's not like you knew. Besides, it has nothing to do with you, and the trauma center was approved."

"If they meet their financial obligation to the town." She moved her cup of tea around on the table. "I'd never say anything to Cal and Raine, but, Em, it's a lot of money to raise."

"Yeah, I know. I didn't want to say anything either. Abby was excited about the amount they raised yesterday, but it's a drop in the bucket. Any chance you can get Dimitri to back down?"

"We've only met a couple of times so I don't know him all that well. But my guess is no. He's a businessman through and through, and he's extremely proud of what he's accomplished."

"Yeah, but you're his daughter. Didn't your mom say he'd give you anything you wanted?"

"She did, but she was talking about money. And even if that was something I'd do, which it isn't, I couldn't. I'd feel disloyal to my dad if I took anything from Dimitri."

"Even if you could give it to Cal and Raine for the trauma center?"

She groaned. "I never thought of that."

"Maybe you could get Dimitri to pull out of the casino consortium and make a donation to the trauma center. Cal and Raine saved your life. You'd think he'd want to reward them. He's like a gazillionaire, isn't—"

Someone rang the front doorbell, cutting off Em. From under the table, Gus gave a sleepy *woof*. "What do you wanna bet it's Izzy? They probably weren't getting anywhere with her so they decided to let the counselor extraordinaire work her magic. I can't say I blame them. Teenagers aren't easy to deal with, especially angry, hurt teenagers."

"I'm glad you have so much faith in me."

Em picked up her phone to check who was at the door and made a face. "Okay, so it looks like you'll have a chance to ask Dimitri about the casino sooner than we thought."

Bri's stomach dropped to her toes. "He's here?"

"Yep, and so is your mother." Em turned the phone. Bri's mother stood beside Dimitri on the front porch, a chauffeur-driven limousine in the background.

"I don't want to do this today. Maybe if we stay quiet, they'll go away." Bri's visits with Dimitri were uncomfortable. A painful reminder that she wasn't a MacLeod. That she wasn't really her father's daughter.

They rang the doorbell again, and Gus scampered out from under the table, barking.

Em glanced at her phone. "I don't think they're leaving anytime soon. You might as well get it over with. Who knows? Dimitri might surprise you and back out of the consortium, and you'll be this week's Hometown Hero."

"Or villain," Bri said, pushing back from the table. Em was right. As much as she didn't want to do this, she didn't have a choice. She had to do it for Cal.

"You look like you're going to a funeral," Em said, sprinting past her to corral Gus.

"Yes, mine, when Raine finds out *my father* is behind the casino consortium."

Em laughed as she led Gus into the kitchen by his collar. "Do you want me to make more tea?" she called over her shoulder.

"No thanks. I'm hoping they're not staying long." The doorbell rang for a third time, followed by an impatient knock. "I'm coming!"

When she reached the door, Bri took several calming breaths and smoothed a hand over her hair. A wasted effort, she knew, but a force of habit whenever she saw her mother. No doubt the first words out of Miranda's mouth would be about Bri's unseemly attire.

But instead of the judgmental commentary she'd prepared for, her mother gave her an apologetic smile and a hug. "I'm sorry," she whispered against Bri's cheek. "Your fath—Dimitri found out you'd moved, and he insisted we visit."

"It's okay," Bri whispered back, surprised by her

mother's confession. She sounded uncomfortable about their surprise visit, which was odd, given that her mother had been the one who'd instigated their father-daughter visits in the past. But now that Bri thought about it, her mother hadn't pressured her to spend time with Dimitri in the last few months.

Bri moved away from her mother and offered Dimitri an awkward smile. "Hi." She couldn't bring herself to call him *Dad* or *Father* but it seemed rude to call him *Dimitri* to his face.

He took her by the shoulders, leaning in to kiss first one cheek and then the other. He was a handsome man with a thick head of wavy, silver hair. His light blue eyes were the only thing he'd passed on to her. She looked more like her mother.

Em joined them and introduced herself, inviting them inside. Bri couldn't believe she'd left them standing on the front porch.

Dimitri stepped into the entryway, taking Em's hand between both of his. "Thank you for taking care of my daughter. I hope you will not be offended, but I had you investigated. A father worries, you understand. But you are well qualified to keep her safe."

"Em is my friend. She's not here to take care of me or to keep me safe. I can manage that on my own, thank you. And you had no right to have her investigated." Her mother's apology made more sense now.

"On that, I am afraid we shall have to agree to disagree. I am a wealthy man, Brianna. Some people might try to use you to get to me." His tone of voice was genial, but there was no mistaking the thread of steel beneath it.

He closed the door and gestured at the living room. "Miranda, please." He followed her mother into the room.

They sat on the couch side by side, a study in gray. Her mother wore a white blouse and gray slacks, while Dimitri wore a well-tailored gray suit.

As Bri took a seat in the chair by the window, Em said, "Would either of you like a cup of tea?"

"That would be lovely," her mother said, and Dimitri agreed.

"I'll help," Bri said, feeling as uncomfortable as she always did seeing her mother with Dimitri and not her father.

"No, you sit. Your leg, I can see that it still pains you. Your mother will help your friend." He glanced at her mother and lifted his chin.

Bri stiffened. As she'd noticed during previous visits, Dimitri's old-world manners matched his views on a woman's place in the world. "My leg's fine, thanks. Mom, you sit," Bri said when her mother went to stand.

"All of you relax. It's a couple cups of tea. I think I can handle it." As Em walked out of the living room, she glanced over her shoulder and mouthed *Casino* at Bri.

Dimitri followed Bri's gaze and nodded. "I see Harlan was not wrong. You have discovered my involvement in the casino. I am impressed."

"It would have taken me longer if Bri's cousin Sadie didn't help unravel the shell corporation," Em said, sharing a glance with Bri.

She imagined the pieces of the puzzle had fallen into place for Em like they had for her. Harlan's reaction to

Bri's revelation about who she was now made sense. He must have called Dimitri and shared the news right away. Dimitri hadn't come to check out Bri's new place. This was about the casino.

Her mother stared at Dimitri, clearly surprised by the news. "I didn't know you were involved with the casino. You never said anything to me."

He waved his hand as if it were none of her concern. Bri gritted her teeth at the dismissive gesture, raising an eyebrow at her mother.

Which Dimitri obviously noticed, because he said, "I apologize if I sounded dismissive toward your mother. It was not my intention. But my business has nothing to do with her."

"Except that it does," Bri said. "It impacts our family and friends, this community. Everyone who believes that we need a trauma center. I would think you out of anyone would understand that, Dimitri. If it weren't for the doctors who spearheaded the initiative, Cal and Raine Scott, I wouldn't be here, and neither would your son."

Adrian Ivanov had been seriously wounded last year while attempting to take her sister hostage. Nate was the one who'd shot him.

"But you both survived, thanks to the very skilled attentions of the Doctors Scott. And I do not believe they are planning on leaving Highland Falls anytime soon. So it is a moot point, is it not?"

"No, it's not, and you would realize it wasn't if you took the time to review their plans for the trauma center."

"Brianna—" her mother began.

Dimitri patted her mother's knee. "It is all right, my dear. I will let her disrespectful tone pass. Our daughter, she is obviously very passionate about this."

Bri was about to take umbrage with his comment when Em returned with the tea.

"Here you go." She placed the tray on the coffee table in front of them. Retrieving a cup and saucer, she walked over and handed it to Bri. "Tripled up on the sugar this time."

"You should have added alcohol," Bri muttered, and Em snorted.

Dimitri stirred his tea, tapping his spoon on the edge of the cup before returning it to the tray. "I assume by your passionate defense of the trauma center that next you will ask that we withdraw our proposal to build a casino in Highland Falls. Am I correct?"

"Actually, no. You're not. The trauma center has already been approved."

"Ah, I see. You wish me to donate the funds to cover the infrastructure costs that they are required to pay or the approval you speak of will be null and void in a matter of weeks. I am afraid this is something I cannot do."

"I don't under—"

He snapped his fingers, cutting Bri off. "Please do not interrupt me. Your brother—"

"Do not snap your fingers at me and do not call your son my brother. He held my mother and my sister at gunpoint. And nearly shot you, which you seem to have forgotten."

Dimitri turned to her mother. "While our daughter did

not inherit my looks, it appears she inherited my temper. So as this is something I understand, I shall once again allow your rudeness to pass. But please do not disrespect me again."

"Likewise," Bri said, refusing to be quelled by the glint of temper in his eyes. She gestured for him to continue. "You were about to tell me, us, why you refuse to financially support the trauma center."

He bowed his head as if striving for control, raising it a few seconds later. "I made a generous donation to the hospital last year in thanks for the Doctors Scott saving your life and your... Adrian's life. And while I understand your feelings toward my son, the blame for what transpired that day lies with me, not him. My affair with your mother hurt Adrian deeply, as did my inattention after my daughter died. I was consumed by the need for revenge, and I neglected him. My wife's family gave him solace, and then they used him to get to me, stoking his jealousy, his belief that I would will my fortune to you. He always believed I favored his sister over him. So when he learned of your existence, he feared that once again, he'd be on the losing end of my affection. The casino, it is my way of making amends."

"So you're financing the casino but it's your son's baby," Em said.

"That is correct."

Bri's mother gasped. "You're doing all this for Adrian? The man who threatened me, blackmailed me, and nearly shot me, my daughter, and you?"

"He has changed. I have gotten him help."

Bri was shocked. "He's out of prison?"

Dimitri nodded. "I did not press charges. How could I when my wife's family was to blame? And myself, of course. I have much to atone for."

"But he was involved in the drug trade with his mother's family," Bri's mother said.

"He had a very minor involvement and was manipulated by his uncles. He turned state's evidence for immunity. With great risk to himself, I might add."

"Why here? Why not somewhere else?" her mother demanded, clearly upset.

Dimitri appeared taken aback by her mother's harsh tone. Frowning, he said, "The cost of the land here is relatively cheap, but the real selling point was the growth of Highland Falls tourism in the past two years. The other areas we looked at could not compete."

Tourism had increased exponentially in Highland Falls thanks to Abby. Bri wondered how she'd feel when she learned that, indirectly, she was the reason the consortium had set their sights on Highland Falls.

Bri's mother shook her head. "I don't care. Put your casino anywhere else but here. This is my home!"

"Why are you behaving this way, my dear? I do not understand why you are so upset."

"You don't understand? You don't understand," her mother repeated, her voice rising on a hysterical note. "Your wife spent years tormenting me. I lived in fear for more than two decades. I put my family, my daughters, through hell because of her. Because of *your* family, I didn't know a moment's peace. Until the day I read her obituary in the paper. But then your son took over. He's just like his mother, and I won't have him anywhere near my family. Do you hear me? I won't!" she practically screamed. She was pale and visibly shaking.

Until that moment, Bri hadn't understood how deeply traumatized her mother had been for all those years. She got up, handing her teacup to a shocked Em, and walked to the couch. Bri sat between her mother and Dimitri, putting an arm around her now sobbing mother. "I think it would be best if you leave, Dimitri."

He nodded, placing his teacup on the tray. "I am sorry for the pain my family has caused you, Miranda. I could have put a stop to it had you told me, but you did not. You kept me in the dark about everything, including my daughter."

"No. You don't get to put this on my mother. She's suffered enough. If you ever cared for her, you'd do as she asked and find somewhere else, somewhere far from here, to build your son's casino."

"Perhaps had I known how she felt about this earlier," he said as he came to his feet, "I could have, but I am afraid it is too late. The casino will go ahead as planned."

Her mother raised her gaze. Her eyes were no longer filled with tears or fear. They were scarily determined. "No. It won't. Because I'm going to do everything in my power to ensure that the trauma center raises the funds they need by their deadline."

"I understand," he said, giving her mother a sad smile.

"No. I don't think that you do. Not only am I going to help with the fundraising, Dimitri, I'm going to make sure everyone knows you and your son are behind the casino, and exactly what Adrian is capable of. I'll tell whoever will listen what your son and your wife's family did to me."

"You are emotional, so for now, I will let your threat slide. But I warn you, Miranda, if you follow through with your threats against my son, life will become very unpleasant for you."

Her mother released a harsh laugh as she rose to her feet. "You can't do anything worse to me than your son and your wife already have. You're not the only one who will do whatever they have to in order to protect their child, Dimitri. I've spent my life trying to protect mine. And I believe with all my heart that your son poses a danger to my daughters and to this town, and I will do whatever I have to do to protect them." She walked past Dimitri and opened the door. "Leave. Now."

Dimitri glanced at Bri. "Please, for your mother's sake and for your own, make her see reason. If the story were to come out, she is not the only one who would be shamed—so will you."

"Really? That's how you see it?" Bri said, limping to her mother's side. "You and your son, your wife, are completely blameless?"

"I can see there is no reasoning with either of you." He straightened the cuffs of his white dress shirt and then nodded. "You leave me no choice. My lawyers will be in touch."

"You'll be hearing from my lawyer as well," her mother said.

"Save your money, Miranda. My lawyers are very good at what they do. There is nothing you can legally do to stop the casino."

"I wouldn't be so sure of that. My husband was a well-known and extremely well-respected trial lawyer before he went into teaching. But I'm not suing you to stop the casino, Dimitri. I'm suing you and your son and your ex-wife's estate for pain and suffering on behalf of me and my family." She smiled at Dimitri's stunned expression and then shut the door in his face.

Equally stunned, Bri stared at her mother. "You're going to sue him?"

With a decisive nod, her mother got her purse off the couch and pulled out her phone. "If your father believes I have a good case, I most certainly am."

Bri watched her mother walk away with her phone pressed to her ear.

"Dimitri's wrong, you know," Em said, picking up the tea tray. "You didn't inherit his temper. You inherited your mother's."

Bri groaned. "Don't joke about it. This is serious, Em. She just threatened him, and I don't think he takes threats well, and he has oodles of money."

"Yeah. It was pretty awesome. Your mom totally rocked, and so did you."

Bri angled her head as her mother's voice came from the kitchen. She mustn't have gotten through to Bri's father, because she was talking to his mother, and sharing what had just transpired. "You might not think she rocks when half the town shows up in our living room within the next hour."

Forty minutes later, Bri sat on the stairs. It was easier than walking to the door every five minutes to let someone in. Em joined her, glancing at the women already packed into the living room. "I thought you were exaggerating when you said half the town would show up."

"Nope. This is what happens when Granny puts the Highland Falls phone chain into action."

They looked up when the door opened. Izzy walked in with a backpack slung over her shoulder and a duffel bag in her hand. "I can't stay under the same roof as my mother, Aunt Em. She lied to me. All she's ever done is lie to me. I hate her! Please, can I move in with you?"

"I don't know, Iz. It's not really a good—"

The teenager's shoulders sagged, and her face crumpled.

"You're more than welcome to stay with us, Izzy," Bri said, shrugging at Em's *you can't be serious* stare. "We have an extra room and a bed."

Izzy rewarded Bri with a grateful smile. "Thank you."

"It's no problem. Second room on your right." Bri smiled, gesturing behind her.

As Em went to follow her niece up the stairs, she leaned into Bri. "No problem? How do you think Raine and Cal will feel about this?"

"I'm sure they'll be fine with it," she said, feeling a little less confident now that she thought about it.

"Looks like you're about to find out what my brother thinks," Em said, nodding at the door.

As soon as Cal walked inside, Izzy shouted down the stairs, "I'm not going home! Bri said I can stay here."

The conversation in the living room stopped, and everyone turned their way. "Maybe we should talk outside." Bri ushered Cal out the door, closing it behind them.

"What's going on?" he asked as Bri limped to the

porch swing and sat down. "You didn't really tell her she could stay, did you?"

She patted the cushion, and he joined her.

"Bri?"

"Just give me a minute. It's been an eventful morning." She tipped her head back, looking up at the blue sky through the red and yellow leaves, breathing in the smell of autumn and woodsmoke. She appreciated that he didn't pressure her to talk. He stretched out his long legs, gently rocking the swing. He didn't interrupt her when, five minutes later, she told him about her mother and Dimitri showing up, and everything that had transpired.

When she'd finished, he blew out a low whistle. "Eventful is an understatement."

"I'm sorry, Cal. I had no idea he was involved with the casino."

"Don't apologize. It has nothing to do with you."

"Logically, I know that. But I can't help feeling if it wasn't for me and my family, your and Raine's dream of building a trauma center wouldn't be at risk. And then there's what my mom did to us."

"Are you having second thoughts about us?"

"No, but I thought you might be."

He glanced at the living room window. "If we didn't have an audience, I'd show you that's not something you have to worry about."

"Even if I told Izzy she could stay with us?"

"Okay, I'm not going to lie to you, I wish you would have talked to me first."

She nodded. "I should have talked to you first, and I'm sorry. It's just that she was so upset, I agreed without thinking. I guess I identified a little too strongly with how she was feeling. It wasn't that long ago that I didn't want to live under the same roof as my mother because of her lies."

"Yeah, Iz pretty much shut down the second Raine admitted Quinn hadn't abandoned her, and that she was the one who'd kept them apart. She didn't give Raine a chance to explain why. She wouldn't listen to me or Quinn either."

"I'll try talking to her tomorrow, and if she's open to it, you, Raine, and Quinn can come for dinner. We can do an informal family therapy session."

"So no sleepover for me tonight, I guess." She wrinkled her nose, and Cal smiled. "You didn't think about that when you told Izzy she could stay, did you?"

Chapter Twenty

♥

Bri glanced at the teenager digging beside her in the garden, wondering how to broach the subject of Cal, Raine, Quinn, and Josh coming for dinner. She chided herself for being selfish. Just because she'd missed Cal last night didn't mean she should push Izzy before she was ready.

"You're a big help, Izzy. I never would have gotten the flower bed weeded without you. Your Aunt Em doesn't like getting her hands dirty."

"I can hear you, you know," Em said from where she sat on a lounge chair reading, Gus sunning himself at her feet.

It was another beautiful autumn afternoon. The musky-sweet smell of fall was heavy in the air.

"And for the record, I'm allergic to weeds." Em got out of the chair. "Anyone want something to drink before I go install cameras for half the neighborhood?"

"I'm good, thanks," Bri said. Izzy passed too, and they both told Em to have fun. She responded with an eye roll.

When the patio door closed behind her and Gus, Izzy asked, "Is Aunt Em okay?"

"She's doing better. Why do you ask?"

"I heard her last night. She was having a nightmare."

Bri considered making an excuse but decided to go with the truth. "Em isn't ready to talk about what happened with her fiancé yet. Once she is, her nightmares should lessen. But let's keep that between us, okay? Your dad worries about her, and he has enough to worry about right now. Besides, Em really is doing much better."

"You mean me, don't you? My dad's worried about me."

"That's what dads do, Izzy. They worry about their kids."

"Not all dads do," she murmured, and then glanced at Bri. "Are you like a doctor or a lawyer? Like if someone tells you something, you have to keep it confidential?"

She nodded. "I'd never share anything that a client told me during a session."

"You mean I have to like lie on a couch and talk to you to keep it just between us?"

Bri smiled. "No. I'd keep anything you told me confidential, Izzy. Is there something bothering you?"

"Other than my mother lying to me about Quinn, you mean?"

"Yes, other than that. But you can talk to me about that too, if you'd like. I can relate a little to what you're going through with your mom."

"Your mom lied to you too?"

"She did, and she'd lied to me for a very long time, and it was really hard when I learned the truth."

"What did she lie to you about?"

If her mother went through with her plan, it wouldn't be long before everyone in Highland Falls knew. So Bri figured Izzy might as well hear it from her and told her how she'd felt upon hearing the news her life had been based on a lie.

"Whoa, that's awful. But your mom was here yesterday, and you guys seemed okay. How did you forgive her?"

"To tell you the truth, up until yesterday, I was far from okay with my mom. I pretended that I'd forgiven her for my sister's sake but my mom is the reason I moved out of the inn. I couldn't bear to live under the same roof with her."

"I wanted to pretend I was okay about it for my dad's and Quinn's sakes, but I was just too mad at my mom to fake it."

"It's better that you're honest about your feelings. I should have been more honest about mine. If I had been, I might have resolved my issues with my mom a lot sooner."

"What do you mean?"

"Yesterday, I got some insight into why my mother kept her secret, which I sort of already knew, but I also got a better understanding of just how difficult it had been for her. The only thing she was really guilty of was trying to protect me. I might not agree with how she went about it, but it helps to understand why."

"Why do you think my mom didn't tell me Quinn still loved me and hid his cards and presents from me?"

"Okay, so this is a tough question because I'm your mom's therapist."

"You are?"

"I am, and without breaking her confidence, I can tell you one thing for sure: your mom loves you very much."

"Does she talk to you about my uncle? 'Cause I think the accident really messed her up. My dad thinks so too, and so does Quinn."

Bri didn't say anything. She just smiled.

Izzy nodded. "I get it. You can't talk to me about that. I'm glad my mom's talking to you though. You're the one who made her tell me she wasn't really pregnant, aren't you?" Izzy sighed. "It's okay. She told me you did."

Bri wasn't about to confirm or deny. Izzy was a smart kid. Bri wouldn't put it past her to figure out a way to get her to share something she shouldn't. "You were really upset when your mom announced that she was pregnant that night. Do you want to tell me what that was about?"

Izzy leaned over and pulled a clump of weeds out of the vegetable bed, the sun shining on her long, dark, curly hair. One day she'd be as beautiful as her mother. "It's kinda embarrassing."

"I shared some pretty embarrassing stuff with you, and you didn't judge me, did you?"

"I guess not." She shook the dirt off the clump of weeds, tossing them in the pile. "I was upset because the baby would be my dad's real kid. I thought he'd love it more than he loved me."

Bri knew exactly how Izzy must have felt, and her heart ached for her. That had been Bri's biggest fear when she'd learned she was Dimitri's daughter. She worried that her dad would love her less, knowing that she wasn't really his. And she was almost thirty, not sixteen.

"You may not be Cal's biological daughter, but you are the daughter of his heart, and no one will ever take your place." And as Bri reassured the teenager sitting beside her of her stepfather's love, she knew the man who'd been her father for nearly thirty years, a man who was as kind and as good as Cal, loved her too. And the tiny hole in her heart that had opened the day she'd learned the truth about her paternity stitched itself back together again.

"He loves me more than my real dad, that's for sure," she said, glancing at Bri from under her lashes as if gauging her reaction.

"I didn't realize you had a relationship with your biological father."

Izzy snorted. "I don't. He's married, and he didn't want his wife to know about me. They have a couple of kids, and he's a pastor or something." She shrugged. "He told me not to contact him again. I guess he was worried I'd ruin his squeaky-clean reputation."

"I'm so sorry, Izzy. That must have been really difficult for you. Did you contact him recently?" she asked, thinking back to the changes Cal had noticed in Izzy. He'd assumed they had to do with Quinn, but maybe they hadn't.

"A little over a year ago. I tracked him down after my dad moved out, and it kinda felt like no one wanted me." She must have realized what she'd said, and her eyes went wide with panic. "Please don't say anything. No one's supposed to know my parents are separated."

"First of all, we already agreed this conversation was confidential. So I'm not going to share anything you don't want me to. But, Izzy, I know your mom and dad are legally separated." She didn't know how Cal and Raine would feel about it, but she felt it was important Izzy knew there were other people she was close to who knew the truth. It might help ease the burden of keeping her parents' secret if Izzy had friends and family she could open up to. "Your Aunt Em and Josh know too. And so does Quinn."

"Oh my gosh, are you kidding me? They're going to ruin everything."

"No, we've all promised to keep it quiet. Even though some of us are worried about the fallout when the truth eventually comes out." Namely her.

"That won't be a problem if you guys keep it to yourselves."

"You don't think so?"

"Nope. I still have a few weeks to convince my parents they're meant to be together."

Bri worked to keep her reaction from showing on her face. She didn't know why she was surprised. It was natural for children to want their parents to stay together—even adult children, she thought, thinking about herself and her siblings. She imagined that for Izzy, who'd had a somewhat unconventional upbringing, those feelings would be magnified tenfold.

Izzy sat back on her heels. "You're a family and marriage therapist, so that kinda makes you a relationship expert. Do you have any advice on how I can keep my parents from getting a divorce?"

"It doesn't work that way, Izzy. My clients come to me to try and save their marriages," she said, uncomfortable with the direction their conversation had taken. It was highly inappropriate and unprofessional for her to be offering Izzy advice about Cal and Raine's marriage. But where the Johnson-Scott family was concerned, she couldn't seem to help herself. "How about you tell me why you think your mom and dad should stay together?"

"Because we're a family," Izzy said, and then she began listing the reasons why Cal and Raine shouldn't divorce. Except Izzy's reasons had nothing to do with her parents' relationship—they had to do with Cal and Izzy's relationship. Something Izzy must have realized on her own because she added with an almost desperate edge in her voice, "They're best friends. My mom needs my dad, and so do I."

"You are a family, and your mom and dad are best friends. None of that will change if your parents go through with the divorce, Izzy. Cal loves you, both you and your mom."

"It will so change. My dad will meet someone, and she won't want me hanging around, and then they'll probably get married and have kids."

Given her experience with her biological father and with Quinn—even though, as they now knew, his abandonment hadn't been intentional on his part—the possibility Cal would abandon her too must have felt very real to Izzy. Bri wished she could alleviate the young girl's fears. The last thing she'd do is come between Cal and his stepdaughter. But besides the fact that it wasn't her place to say anything, she had enough experience to know that Izzy wouldn't be happy to learn Cal and Bri were together.

"Your dad would never let that happen, Izzy. But for what it's worth, my advice is to talk to your parents. Tell them how you feel." Cal had been worried Izzy was confused about his and Raine's relationship, and clearly she was. This was something he needed to know, and Bri had boxed herself in. She'd told Izzy she'd keep their conversation confidential, and she wouldn't break her promise.

"They'll just say the same thing they always do. That they love me and that I'm their priority and that nothing will change. But it will. We won't really be a family anymore."

"It will be different, and change is hard, but the great thing is that you live in a small town so your mom and dad will still live close to each other. I wouldn't be surprised if your dad found a house on Marigold Lane."

"Unless the trauma center doesn't go through. If that happens, my mom will do what she always does. She'll make us move, and my dad won't be able to stop her."

Bri couldn't deny that she made a valid point. Whenever one of her marriages ended, Raine picked up stakes. "Ninety percent of the things we worry about never happen, Izzy." But something she'd said earlier worried Bri, and she felt it needed to be addressed. "You mentioned that you felt like no one wanted you after reaching out to your biological father. Do you still feel that way?"

Izzy yanked out several blades of grass, rubbing them between her fingers before tossing them into the air.

"Even though my mom pulled that crap on me and Quinn, and this trauma center stuff is making her crazy, I know she loves me, and I know my dad loves me, 'cause he tells me all the time, and I think Quinn probably does too, 'cause he said he does."

"A mom and two dads who love you? Sounds to me like you won the parent lottery."

Izzy raised an eyebrow. "You have met my mother, haven't you?"

Bri laughed. "I have, and you've met mine. They're a lot alike, your mom and mine. They're not perfect. They've made mistakes, and they've hurt people. But I'm sure you have too. I know I have. None of us is perfect, Izzy."

"So you think I should forgive my mom?"

"I can't tell you what to do. That's up to you. But I can tell you that, by forgiving your mom, you're not absolving her of the hurt or harm she caused you. Your feelings are legitimate, and you're entitled to them. But the anger and resentment, those feelings of wanting to get even with someone who's hurt you, they aren't easy emotions to carry around. And the best way to release them is by forgiving the person who's hurt you. Forgiveness is a gift, Izzy, a gift to yourself."

"Have you forgiven your mom?"

"I'm working on it." Bri peeled off her gardening gloves. "It's not easy. At least I don't find that it is. You should probably talk to my sister, Ellie, about forgiveness. She's a pro."

"I'd rather talk to you. You're easy to talk to."

Bri smiled. "I'm glad you think so. And I hope you'll

still like talking to me when I tell you that I invited your mom, dad, Josh, and Quinn to come to dinner tonight." At Izzy's groan, she said, "If it's too soon, we'll do it another time. It's entirely up to you. Your dad wasn't happy that I let you stay here, so the invitation was me covering my butt. It's on me, not you."

"No. It's okay. I can't avoid my mom forever, and at least I'll have you there to back me up."

"If you'd like, we can go over what you want to say to your mom while we're making dinner," Bri said as she struggled to her feet. She'd been sitting in the same position for too long, and she no longer had the benefit of her cane to get herself off the ground.

"I'd like that, thanks." Izzy offered her a hand, looking over as Cal walked outside. "Hey, Dad, I hear you guys are coming for dinner tonight." Izzy left Bri's side to give him a hug and glanced over her shoulder. "Is it okay if my dad stays and helps us make dinner?"

The last thing she wanted was to be stuck in the kitchen with Cal and Izzy. Bri didn't trust Cal not to give their relationship away, and it wasn't like she could warn him about Izzy's matchmaking plans for him and Raine. "Sure. No pressure though, Cal. I know how busy you are."

He frowned. "No, I'm good. What was that about?" he asked Bri once Izzy walked inside.

"Nothing."

"Really? Because it sounded like you didn't want me helping out in the kitchen."

"I just thought Izzy might find it awkward. We're going to work on what she wants to say to Raine. And she might want to say something to you . . . and Quinn."

"Are you sure that's all it is? Izzy didn't—"

"She's my therapist, Dad. She can't tell you any-thing so stop pumping her for information," Izzy called through the open kitchen window.

"I'm not."

Izzy raised an eyebrow.

"Okay. But you know you can talk to me about any-thing, kiddo."

"Yes, Dad. Are we starting dinner now or do I have time to take Gus for a walk?" Izzy asked Bri. "I want him to meet my friend Kelly's labradoodle."

"I'm sure Gus would love that. Your dad has to help me pick the ingredients from the garden so we probably won't start making dinner for at least an hour."

"Cool." The tap went off, and they heard her calling for Gus as she closed the window.

"Izzy seems to be doing better than yesterday," Cal said.

"Despite everything she's dealt with, Izzy is an extremely well-adjusted kid, and that's to your credit. Yours and Raine's. She knows she's loved, and that's half the battle."

"I'm happy to hear that, and I'm glad she felt com-fortable opening up to you." He leaned back, his gaze roaming her face. "But I have a feeling you're holding something back."

"Nothing that I can share with you unless Izzy gives me permission to."

"Come on, Bri. She's only sixteen. If it's something Raine and I should know—"

"A sixteen-year-old who is well aware of her privacy

rights, as are you, Cal. And even if I wasn't a therapist, I wouldn't break her confidence unless the information put her at risk. But I suggested that she talk to you and Raine about it because it is something you need to know."

"Don't you think I should be the one to judge if it puts her at risk or not?"

She just looked at him, and he sighed. "Fine, but is there anything we can do to help her deal with whatever it is she's dealing with?"

"Other than reassuring her that she's loved and that that won't change when you and Raine divorce? Not really."

"I knew it. This goes back to when Raine and I separated the first time, doesn't it?"

"We have about forty minutes to ourselves. Do you really want to waste it trying to get information out of me that I'm not going to give you?" she asked, wrapping her arms around his neck.

"Are you seriously trying to distract me by kissing me?"

"I am." She smiled. "Will it work?"

"I'm not sure. I guess it depends on the kiss."

She was about to give it her best shot when a voice brought her head around.

"What are you two doing?" Mr. Voldock called over the fence, a note of censure in his voice.

"I...tripped in a hole. Thankfully, Cal was here to catch me before I fell." She patted Cal's chest and stepped away from him, avoiding looking at him because he seemed to be struggling not to laugh. "Are you having a problem with groundhogs? Because we're having a problem with them here. They're digging up the backyard."

Mr. Voldock inched up to get a better look over the fence. "Fred used to have trouble with them. It's the garden that attracts them. There's probably a couple of traps in the basement. Or if you want, I can shoot them."

"I'll just set up the traps. Thanks for the offer though. Now I'd better get harvesting ingredients for our dinner. Cal and his wife are joining us tonight," she said in hopes of eliminating any remaining suspicion from Mr. Voldock's mind.

"Might be a good idea to get Em to put one of those motion thingies in your backyard. You wouldn't want the groundhogs getting at your pumpkins. Looks like you got yourself a couple of prize winners there. Are you entering them in the Fall Festival?"

"Maybe I will. They are doing really well."

"Word of advice. Don't tell Ted down the way if you are. He wins every year, and he wouldn't appreciate the competition. Last time Fred's pumpkins looked as good as those ones, they went missing the night before the Fall Festival."

"Thanks for the warning. I'll be sure to keep it to myself."

"It's a little scary how fast you came up with a believable excuse," Cal murmured as they waved goodbye to Mr. Voldock.

"You should be glad that I did. That was too close for comfort. No more kissing in the backyard." She limped to the basket under the apple tree and turned to hand it to Cal. "Do you mind picking eight tomatoes for me? The bigger, the better. And I need onions, and some basil. Eggplant too."

"I don't mind but I do mind that you can't do it yourself because you obviously were gardening for too long." He raised an eyebrow. "And this time, you can't distract me with a kiss."

Which is how Bri found herself doing her stretches on the grass while Cal deposited the ingredients for their dinner into the basket.

Chapter Twenty-One

♥

A toast to the cook." Cal smiled at Bri from the opposite end of the dining room table and raised his glass. "I didn't believe you when you said I'd love eggplant lasagna, but you were right. I do. This was the best meal I've had in...I can't remember when."

"Thank you, darling," Raine said as she raised her glass, joining Cal, Em, Quinn, Izzy, and Josh in toasting Bri.

"Mom, you don't cook."

"I know, but that's not the point." Raine smiled at Bri. "Cal's right. The meal was delicious."

Everyone echoed Raine's praise, and Bri blushed, looking uncomfortable with the compliments. "Thank you, but I can't take all the credit. Izzy and Cal helped."

"I helped. Dad was too busy sampling the food."

And trying to kiss Bri when Izzy wasn't looking. He'd also quietly suggested that it might be a good time to let Izzy know that they were together but Bri had reacted as if he'd suggested they make out in the kitchen naked. He didn't know what the problem was—not with making out in the kitchen naked, obviously, but with sharing how they felt about each other with Izzy. She was clearly comfortable with Bri and enjoyed hanging out with her.

"He was sampling a few other things too," his sister said, then laughed when Bri shot her a *shut it* stare.

"I think we should toast Izzy for being so open and honest with her feelings. That's not easy, and she did a great job," Bri said, raising her glass.

They all smiled and toasted Izzy, who'd decided she wanted to air her grievances about Raine keeping Quinn from her before the meal was served.

"I think Raine deserves a toast too," Quinn said, raising his glass and sharing an appreciative smile with Raine.

Izzy's narrowed gaze moved from Quinn to her mother, and then she looked at Cal. "Don't you want to make a toast to Mom, Dad?"

"Uh, yeah, I guess." He raised his glass. "To Raine."

Izzy motioned for him to continue, so he repeated what Bri had said about Izzy.

"That's kind of lame, Dad. You just repeated what Bri said about me. Don't you want to tell Mom how proud you are that she took responsibility for her actions? That wasn't easy for her, you know."

"I know it wasn't, Iz. And I am proud of her."

Izzy nudged her head at her mother, and Cal held back a sigh. "I'm very proud of you, Raine. I know that wasn't easy, for either of you."

"Thank you, darling," Raine said at the same time, giving Cal a *what is going on with her?* look.

He shrugged. He honestly had no idea. He glanced

at Bri, wondering if she might know, but she avoided his gaze. Something he'd noticed her doing a lot of tonight.

"You know, Dad, you and Mom will be super busy once the trauma center gets approved, and you won't have time to take a holiday. Why don't you take Mom away for a romantic vacation? She deserves a break, and so do you. I can stay with Aunt Em and Bri."

Cal and Raine shared a shocked glance, Josh's eyebrows shot up under his hair, Em choked on her wine, and Quinn slowly lowered his glass from his mouth. And for the first time that night, Bri looked at Cal and held his gaze. He briefly closed his eyes as things fell into place. Izzy wanted him to stay with Raine. Something she'd no doubt shared with Bri, which explained why Bri had been acting like they were nothing more than friends, and not very good ones at that.

Either Izzy didn't notice their reactions or she chose to ignore them. "Maybe you could go back to Cabo. They had an amazing time there on their honeymoon," she told her stupefied audience. "You should see their pictures. Mom, don't you have some on your phone?"

"Um, no, I don't think so. It was five years ago, darling."

"I have pictures of your mom's and my wedding on my phone if you want to see them, Izzy," Quinn said.

"How do you still have pictures of us on your phone? It was sixteen years ago," Raine said.

Quinn shrugged. "I uploaded the photos of us, us and Izzy, anytime I updated my phone. It's not like I have a lot of other photos anyway."

Cal could tell Izzy was torn. Quinn and Raine's time together was a missing part of her life, and one that she was obviously curious about. But maybe because, like Cal, she sensed Quinn still had feelings for her mother and she saw him as a threat to the happy ending she was hoping for, she looked away when Quinn turned the screen to show Raine.

"I look so young. So do you," Raine said to Quinn. "And that dress. And my hair." She made a face. "Someone should have told me how ridiculous I looked."

"You didn't. You looked beautiful," Quinn said, holding Raine's gaze. If Cal had any doubts how Quinn felt about Raine, or about Raine's feelings for Quinn, they were vanquished with the look the couple exchanged.

"Is it just me or did the temperature go up about twenty degrees in here?" Josh waggled his eyebrows at Cal, which spoke to his best friend's inability to read a room, or in this case, Izzy.

"Hey, what was that for?" Josh asked Em, who had obviously kicked him under the table given that he was leaning over rubbing his foot.

Bri glanced at Izzy and pushed back from the table. "Why don't we take this into the living room? Izzy, would you mind helping me with the tea and coffee?"

Izzy chewed on her bottom lip, casting a worried glance at her mother and Quinn.

Raine tore her gaze from Quinn and practically jumped off her chair. "I'll help too."

"Come on, Iz, let's go cut the apple pie you and Bri made," Em said. "Raise your hand if you want pie and ice cream."

Cal and Quinn raised a hand, and Josh raised two, which made Em roll her eyes and Izzy laugh. A subdued laugh, but a laugh nonetheless.

"So what about it, guys? How does a double wedding sound?" Josh asked.

Cal bowed his head. The tension was so thick you could cut it with a scalpel. He had no idea how Josh didn't sense it. "Brother, do me a favor and don't share those thoughts when they bring out the dessert."

Quinn put down his glass of wine. "After I tell you why I was running late, I can almost guarantee Raine is more likely to want to kill me than marry me."

So he'd been right. Quinn was still in love with Raine. But obviously, like Josh, Quinn hadn't noticed Izzy's reaction. Probably because he'd been focused on Raine.

"Sounds like we might need alcohol for this announcement," Josh said.

"Yeah, and lots of it." Quinn smoothed a hand over his head and glanced at Cal. "Remember the night of the committee meeting when I told you I would have expected the infrastructure costs to be higher? Well, it seems I was right. I crunched the numbers, and they are too low. My mother had based it on quotes she'd received three years ago when they'd looked at expanding the hospital."

"How low is too low?" Cal asked.

"A hundred thousand."

Cal swore under his breath.

"But the town council agreed on the amount. They can't go back on it now," Josh said.

"They can, and they will. I had to inform them of the discrepancy. They're voting on it as we speak."

Cal had been saving for a place of his own for a while but there was no way he could cover that kind of shortfall. He still had student loans to repay while keeping enough aside to help out Em, and he'd already donated ten thousand to the infrastructure fund. So had Raine.

"I wish I could help, buddy. But the hot tub tapped me out," Josh said.

"I'd help if I could, Cal. But it would be seen as a conflict of interest. I have to stay neutral. At least until you've met your financial obligations."

Raine walked toward the living room with a tray of tea and coffee, glancing back at the dining room table. "What's wrong?"

"Nothing. Everything's good." Cal pushed back from the table and went to take the tray from her.

"Cal, she needs to know," Quinn said.

"Know what?" She looked from him to Quinn.

"Why don't you sit down, Raine?" Quinn said.

"It can't be that bad, can it?" she asked Cal as she slowly lowered herself onto the couch.

Cal sat beside her. "It's not great news. But you know what, we've faced worse odds than this before. We can do it again."

"Cal's right, Raine," Quinn said.

"Would one of you just tell me what is going on?"

Cal nodded at Quinn to go ahead and break the news at the same time Quinn nodded at him to do the same.

Josh shook his head at the two of them and said, "There was a shortfall of a hundred thousand dollars on the infrastructure costs, and you guys have to cover it.

Or you will once the council votes on it. Who knows though? Maybe they'll vote in your favor."

Raine grabbed her purse and shot off the couch.

"It's a closed-door meeting, Raine. They won't let you in," Quinn said.

"Let them try and keep me out." She frowned at Cal. "What are you waiting for? Come on."

"Raine, it's a waste of time. They won't let us in. We're better off staying here and figuring out what we're going to do," Cal said.

"Fine. If you won't come with me, I'll go by myself."

"Mom, where are you going?" Izzy walked toward the living room with two plates of apple pie and vanilla ice cream in her hands.

Cal looked at Raine, trying to convey that she needed to stay for Izzy's sake. Tonight was a big deal for Izzy. She'd been honest about how she was feeling— obviously not about everything, but he didn't know many sixteen-year-olds who would have been able to share their feelings like she had. She'd also been proud of the pie she'd helped Bri make.

Either Raine didn't notice him trying to get her attention or she didn't care. "I have to go to the town hall and stop the council from ruining everything." She bent her head to dig in her purse, missing the disappointed look that came over Izzy's face. "I need a lawyer, that's who I need." She took out her phone.

"Raine," Bri said from where she stood behind Izzy. When Raine looked her way, Bri nodded at Izzy. "The pie and ice cream won't wait, but I'm sure whatever you need to talk to the town council about will."

"You don't under—"

"Izzy made the pie especially for you. She said it was your favorite."

Raine looked at her daughter and finally seemed to get what Bri was trying to tell her. She put her phone away, smiling as she walked to the couch. "It is. Did you really make it for me, darling?" she asked when Izzy handed her a plate.

Izzy shrugged. "It's no big deal."

"I beg to differ," Bri said as she made her way to the chair by the window. "My pie crust has never turned out this good, or my apple pie, to be honest."

"Kiddo, Bri's right. This pie is amazing."

"Dad, you say that about anything I make," Izzy said, coming to sit beside him.

"Your brutally honest aunt doesn't, and this is really, really good. And I don't even like pie," Em said from where she sat cross-legged on the floor beside Bri. "You should enter this in the apple pie contest next weekend."

Everyone but Izzy agreed it was a great idea.

"I don't know. I didn't do it all by myself. Bri helped."

"We'll do it together. Maybe we can get your mom to help," Bri said.

Izzy laughed. "No way. My mom burns water," she said, and then entertained everyone with stories about Raine's cooking disasters, of which there were many.

Raine was a good sport about it and offered a few stories of her earliest attempts at cooking, sharing a laugh with Quinn, who she'd nearly sent to the hospital with food poisoning in the second week of their marriage.

"We were lucky we lived over this amazing Italian restaurant or I would have starved," Quinn said, reminiscing with Raine about their first apartment together.

Cal caught Bri's eye and gave her a grateful smile. This was the kind of night he'd wanted to give Izzy: family and friends gathered together, sharing memories and laughs over a great meal. And Bri had made it happen.

"Don't sit there looking so smug, big brother. You've had your share of cooking disasters. Remember the year Mom had to work on Thanksgiving and you decided you'd make the turkey? He left everything inside the bird, and then he forgot to set the timer and went to play football with Josh. It looked like the turkey in *Christmas Vacation*," Em shared.

"Hey, I was fifteen, and it didn't look that bad."

Josh laughed. "I remember that. You guys ended up at our place for dinner, and I had to listen to my mom talk about how wonderful a son Cal was for an entire month."

Izzy angled for more stories about him from Josh, but Cal had gotten a glimpse at the time. "Sorry, kiddo. Time to call it a night. You've got school tomorrow."

"Come on, it's only nine thirty. Just a little longer. Please."

Cal might have given in if Raine hadn't stood up. "Your dad's right. You have homework, and he and I have to figure out how we're going to come up with the funds to cover the extra hundred grand Quinn tacked onto the infrastructure bill, which will probably take us all night." She glanced at Cal. "Do you think it's too late to call Abby?"

"Okay, you're making it sound like I'm personally responsible for this," Quinn said, no doubt in response to the mutinous look Izzy shot him.

"A hundred grand more than what you already have to pay?" Em shook her head. "There's no way you guys can..." She trailed off when they all looked at her. "Ignore me. I'm a pessimist. Just ask Cal. I'm sure it will be fine." Her expression said it would be anything but fine.

"That's not fair. They can't do that. I'm calling Grandma," Izzy said.

"Izzy, there's nothing your grandmother can—" Cal began before Raine cut him off.

"Go ahead, darling. Call your grandmother. Maybe she'll listen to you."

"Raine, that's not fair to your mother," Quinn said, and not surprisingly, Raine turned on him.

Cal had wondered how long it would take before the feelings she'd been holding back for Izzy's sake came out. Worried it was going to devolve into a shouting match because apparently Quinn wasn't about to stand there and take Raine's crap, Cal tried to intervene. "Look, let's not ruin a nice evening. This isn't anyone's fault. It is what it is, Raine."

"What it is, is the town overcharging us to pay for their incompetence. This is your mother's mistake, Quinn, and don't think—" At the sound of a shrill whistle, Raine stopped talking and looked around.

Bri waved her hand. "I know I'm short and easy to overlook, but I've been trying to get your attention for the past five minutes."

"Do you have a whistle in your pocket or was that you?" Josh asked.

"Me and my two fingers." She wiggled them at him.

"Impressive. I could use you at my practices. I'm always losing my whistle."

"Whistles? We're talking about whistles when we're at risk of losing everything we worked for?" Raine said.

Bri sighed. "That's what I've been trying to tell you. I'll cover the shortfall."

Cal stared at her. "It's a hundred thousand dollars."

"I know. And I'm okay with that."

"I'm not," Cal said. "It's too much, Bri. As much as we appreciate the offer, I can't let you do it."

Raine threw up her arms. "What are you doing? Bri has very generously offered to cover the shortfall." She walked over and hugged Bri. "Don't listen to him. Of course we accept, and you have our undying gratitude."

"Mine too," Quinn said, taking her hand between his. "I never would have heard the end of it."

Cal waited until the others had finished thanking Bri and were heading out the door before taking her aside. "I'm not comfortable with you doing this. We'll talk when I come back."

"It's too risky, Cal. What if Mr. Voldock or one of the other neighbors see you? Em hooked up their porch cameras today."

"It's okay. I'll come through the backyard."

"You're going to hop the neighbors' fences?"

"You say it like I'm fifty, not thirty-two. I'm still in pretty good shape, you know."

"Trust me, I'm not worried about your physical

prowess. I'm worried someone might think you're an intruder and shoot you. Namely Mr. Voldock."

"I'm willing to take the risk if it means spending time alone with you. I missed you last night."

Behind him, his sister sighed. "Would you just go? You're letting the cool air in. And Bri's right. Be careful. I was checking the fence the other night, and Mr. Voldock came out with his shotgun."

Two hours later, Cal was second-guessing his plan, and not just because Mr. Voldock had a shotgun. The neighbor two doors down from Bri and Em had a dog, and not a small one. It was too dark to make out the breed, but he didn't need to see the dog to know he'd lose a limb if it got hold of him.

Cal snuck out the gate of the neighboring backyard and crept around the front, hiding behind bushes to make it to the house beside Bri and Em's unseen. He couldn't risk darting across the front yard, because his sister had inconveniently installed cameras on their front porch and the one across the street.

He carefully opened Bri's neighbors' gate and crept into their backyard, only to have the yard light up like it was two in the afternoon. He sprinted across the yard, the dog from the house next door barking its head off. Grabbing the top of the fence, he got one leg over, when the neighbors' patio doors opened, on both sides.

Cal threw his other leg over a little too quickly, lost his balance, and fell into Bri's garden. He lifted his head to see his sister and Bri standing at the patio door watching him, the two of them laughing like they were twelve.

"You're lucky you didn't land on one of the pumpkins, Cinderella," his sister said as she let him in. "Bri's entering them in the Fall Festival."

"Har har," he said, glancing at the clock on the kitchen wall. Sure enough, it was midnight. As he took off his muddy sneakers, the front doorbell rang. Em took out her phone and showed him and Bri the screen, bringing a finger to her lips. She brought up the alarm app.

"Hi, Mr. Voldock. Everything okay?"

The older man squinted up at the camera. "Motion detectors went off next door, and the dog is barking its fool head off. Thought I'd better check and make sure you ladies were all right." He held up his shotgun. "You want me to go check the backyard?"

"Thanks for the offer, Mr. Voldock, but I already did. A couple of raccoons were having a party in the garden."

"All righty then."

Em thanked him again, closing the app after telling him to have a good night.

"Don't move until I shut off all the lights and close the curtains, and I hope you have a better plan for getting out of here unseen than you did for getting in here," his sister said.

He didn't. "I'll come up with one."

"Cal, as much as I want you here with me, it's an unnecessary risk. Mr. Voldock could have shot you," Bri said when he joined her on the sofa ten minutes later. The drapes were closed, the TV was on low, and his sister had gone to bed.

"It's a risk, but not an unnecessary one. We need to

talk about you donating a hundred grand to the trauma center, and Izzy."

"We're not talking about Izzy. I made her a promise, and I plan on keeping it. You and Raine will have to deal with her expectations." She blew out a breath. "And that's all I'll say about that, which is more than I should have said. As for me covering the shortfall, I've thought it through, Cal. I did well on the sale of my practice. I can afford to donate the money. A few weeks ago, I wouldn't have. I didn't know what I was going to do with my life. I didn't see myself going back into counseling, and I needed a nest egg in case I didn't work for another few years. But thanks to you and your family..." She grinned, and he laughed. "I remembered how much I love it, and I've regained some of my confidence. I'm pretty good at what I do."

"No 'pretty good' about it. You're a great therapist, Bri. It's what you were meant to do."

"I think so too. So now that I've decided to reopen my practice here, I feel comfortable donating the money. I want to help, Cal."

"Even if you have your doubts we'll meet our target by the deadline?" Earlier that day, she'd made a face when he'd mentioned how much money they'd raised at the football game. When he'd called her on it, she'd reluctantly admitted her concerns about them meeting their fundraising goal.

"That was the new me talking. In case you haven't noticed, I've become a bit of a pessimist. I'm working on it though. Maybe one day, I'll be the Bri you remember and fell in love with."

"I loved the girl you used to be, Bri. But I'm in love with the woman you've become. I wouldn't change a thing about you."

"I can think of a few things you'll want to change."

"Are you going to start listing all the things that you think are wrong with you? Because you know——"

"No. I was going to remind you about my mother and Dimitri."

"Trust me, I can forget anything when I'm with you."

"Then how about you make me forget?" she said, wrapping her arms around his neck and tipping up her face.

"I can do that." He smiled and did his best to make her forget everything except for how good they were together.

At a faint whimpering coming from the second level, he lifted his head. "Is that——"

"It's Gus," Bri said, sounding breathless. She patted his chest and then got off the couch, taking his hand and pulling him to his feet. "You should go before we get carried away."

She had a point but... "I was going to give it another hour. I want to make sure Mr. Voldock is——"

"It'll be fine. Just crouch down and run really fast," she said loud enough to wake the dead as she steered him toward the door. She shut off the porch light, opened the door, and pushed him outside with a smile and a whispered "I love you."

He frowned at the closed door and then, remembering Mr. Voldock and his shotgun, ducked down and did as Bri suggested.

Chapter Twenty-Two

♥

Oh my gosh, Bri, you look amazing. Did you cut your hair?" Ellie leaned into the screen. "You have makeup on. What have you done to my sister?"

Bri had seen the same thing Ellie did when she was sitting in the hairstylist's chair. But it had nothing to do with the stylist shaping her hair or adding baby-blond highlights or the mascara, blush, and lip gloss Bri had put on.

The woman looking back at Bri in the mirror at the beauty salon resembled the woman she used to be. Her eyes were no longer shadowed with lack of sleep. Even before the stylist had worked her magic, her hair had regained its shine and bounce. Her face had filled out, and her skin glowed. She was happy and fulfilled. She had a sense of purpose again, and more important, she'd gotten a second chance with the man she loved.

"That would be 'What has Raine done to your sister?'" Em said over Bri's shoulder.

Bri had her phone propped against the backsplash on the kitchen counter while she took the apple pies out of the oven. Izzy had just left to get ready for today's fundraiser at the apple orchard. She'd spent the morning making pies with Bri.

"Raine took me and Em out for lunch yesterday and surprised us with a makeover. Look how great Em looks." Bri took off the oven mitts and picked up the phone. "Isn't her hair amazing? The shag is back—well, a modified shag. And don't you love her highlights?"

Em's full lips thinned. "You might want to ask your sister why Raine was feeling so generous."

Bri gave her best friend an *I can't believe you'd out me* look. Em shot back an *I can't believe you forced me into it* look.

"You stopped seeing Cal?" her sister guessed.

"No. I didn't stop seeing Cal. Why would I…okay, I know what you mean but we explained all that to you." Bri pushed aside her concern about Izzy's matchmaking scheme. She hadn't given up on her parents' marriage. She was positive all they needed was time away together. And just as positive she had to keep Quinn away from her mother.

"I'll give you a hint," Em chimed in. "There are a hundred thousand reasons why Raine was feeling generous."

"A hundred thousand reasons? I think I'm missing something," her sister said.

"Don't pay any attention to Em," Bri said, walking out of the kitchen. "So tell me, is Scotland everything you dreamed it would be? I can't believe you've been there a week already."

"I'll tell you, if you tell me what Em is talking about."

"I'm making a donation to the trauma center, that's all. Now your turn," Bri said, sitting on the couch.

Her sister frowned and then her eyes went wide. "You donated a hundred thousand dollars?"

"Yes, but I'll be fine, Ellie. I've opened my practice here for real now. I saw four clients this week, and I have five appointments booked for next week. Besides that, Cal and Raine saved my life. I owe them."

Em joined her on the couch. "You'd better not let my brother hear you say that. He'll rip up your check."

"You know that's not the only reason I'm doing it, Em. The trauma center will bring jobs and opportunities to the area. Highland Falls and the surrounding counties need a trauma center a heck of a lot more than they do a casino."

"Aha," Em said. "I knew there was more to this. You'll do whatever you have to do to ensure the casino doesn't get built."

"She'll have to get in line behind our mother," Ellie said. "Have you talked to Mom today?"

"No." Bri had talked to her yesterday when the story broke in the *Herald*. Harlan had gone on the offensive, doing a three-page exposé on Dimitri, the casino, and his relationship with her mother. Needless to say, it painted Dimitri as the saint and her mother as the sinner. Abby had arrived at the inn twenty minutes into Bri's call with her mother, and the two of them were working on a story that countered Harlan's version of the events. "Why?"

"You know Dad. She was having a hard time getting him to return her calls, so she was heading home yesterday afternoon. I haven't been able to reach her today."

"She's planning on coming to the fundraiser. I'll talk to her then and let you know what's up. Do you think Dad's going to take on the lawsuit?"

"I'm not sure, and I'm worried how she'll react if he doesn't."

"She'll be upset, but she won't back down. She'll find another lawyer to take it on."

"I know, and that worries me a little. I'd rather she focus on helping raise money for the trauma center than on going up against Dimitri."

"I think she has to do it, Ellie. You weren't here. You didn't see how she reacted when she found out Adrian would be running the casino. She was deeply traumatized by what he and his mother put her through." A message came through on the fundraising committee's group chat. "Sorry, Ellie. We have to get going. Abby wants us there early to help with the setup."

"Okay, hang on. I have to show you something. I found a handsome Highlander for you." She handed her phone to Nate, who appeared on the screen in a kilt.

Bri laughed. "Look at you! You look amazing in a skirt, Nate," she teased.

"Ha ha. You're as funny as my brothers-in-law." He glanced over his shoulder. It looked like they were in a clothing store. She caught a glimpse of Ellie at the register. Nate followed her gaze and changed the angle of the camera, and her sister disappeared from view. "You didn't mention the story in the *Herald* to Ellie, did you?"

"No. Mom and I agreed to keep it from her. We didn't want her cutting your honeymoon short. But how did you find out?"

"Sadie gave me a heads-up. It took a lot of convincing to get your sister not to change our flights when she heard about Dimitri and Adrian's involvement in the casino. If she knew they were attacking your mother in the press—"

"Mom felt bad she told Ellie about Dimitri's involvement. She was upset, and she didn't think how the news would impact her."

"Understandable, and I have a feeling your sister won't be happy when she finds out we've been keeping this from her, but I don't want her upset right now."

"Don't worry, Nate. I'll make sure she doesn't hear anything from me. But you might want to confiscate her phone. Abby's going to feature Mom on her podcast this coming week."

"Like she'd let me take her phone. Don't worry, I'll figure something out. Sorry about that," he said to another customer and moved out of their way, giving Bri a clear view of her sister, who held a tiny pink kilt in her hand.

Bri gasped. "You're having a baby!"

Nate winced. "Keep it down. She wants to surprise you."

"Aw, my sister's going to be a mommy, and you're going to be a daddy. I'm so happy for you, Nate. For both of you." She sniffed back tears.

"Here come the waterworks," Em said. "You'd better tell Ellie you lost the connection or she'll figure out your secret's been blown, Nate."

"Good idea." He frowned. "You okay, Bri?"

"Mm-hmm," she managed, smiling through her tears. "I'm just so"—sniff—"happy."

Em ended the call. "Those are an awful lot of tears for someone who's just heard they're going to be an aunt. What's going on?"

It took a few minutes for Bri to get her noisy sobs under control. "You have no idea what Ellie did for me, what she sacrificed for me, Em. All I've ever wanted was for her dreams to come true, and seeing her now, happy and in love and expecting a baby, I guess it hit me that she got everything she's ever wanted."

"Are you sure that's all it is?"

Bri wiped at her damp cheeks. "What do you mean?"

"I know you're happy for Ellie. But are you maybe a little bit jealous too? Let me finish," she said when Bri opened her mouth to protest. "No one wanted kids as much as you. You and Cal. That's all you guys ever talked about. You had names picked out. You guys had your life together all planned out, and then..." She shrugged. "I'm not a therapist, but maybe you're grieving what could have been. What should have been."

Bri couldn't talk, her throat clogged with emotion as fresh tears trickled down her face. "I'm sorry. I shouldn't have said anything," Em said, taking her hand in hers.

"Maybe you should be a therapist. I don't think I've ever let myself grieve the loss of the dreams Cal and I had for our future. I got caught up in the anger and the hurt and then shoved everything deep down inside." She gave Em's hand a gentle squeeze. "Don't do what I did. You and Brad had dreams too. You need to grieve—"

"Oh no, you're not turning this on me. I'm good." She got up off the couch. "We're going to be late helping Abby set up as it is."

Bri glanced at the time on her phone. "No. We should make it on time."

"You haven't seen your face. I figure it'll take at least half an hour." She narrowed her eyes at Bri. "Maybe an hour."

"Oh my gosh, I can't look that bad." She switched the camera on her phone to selfie mode. She could barely see her eyes through the swelling, and what little she could see of the whites was red.

They arrived at the apple orchard two hours later. It had nothing to do with vanity; Bri didn't want to explain to Cal why she looked like she'd been crying for a week. If she had to, she was afraid she'd start crying again.

"By the way," Em said as they got out of the truck in a field that was filled with parked vehicles, "I told Izzy and Raine that you had a migraine."

They'd arrived at the house an hour ago to pick up the pies. Bri had been lying on her bed with cucumbers on her eyes. The teabags hadn't worked.

"Great," Bri said. "Just what I want Cal to hear."

"Hey, I had to come up with something. Your other bestie was heading for your bedroom, coming to pick out an outfit for you to wear." Em glanced at Bri as they headed across the field. "I'm not sure what you're wearing will get Raine's stamp of approval. She wanted you to wear that dress she made you buy."

"I like this outfit." She had on a soft knit pumpkin-orange sweater with butterscotch suede leggings and calf-high leather boots that Raine had picked out for her, deeming them to have the proper support. Bri bought them because they looked good, and more important, they were comfortable. Although she would have preferred that they had a heel. "And who wears a dress to an apple orchard?"

"Raine, that's who," Em said, lifting her chin at the entrance where the woman in question stood greeting people standing in line.

"Raine can get away with anything." It was true. She looked amazing and not the least bit out of place in a camel suede wraparound dress and cowboy boots.

"You better hope we can too, because here comes Abby."

The petite redhead sprinted toward them, darting past a car. Abby never walked when she could run. Bri wished she had some of her energy. And a leg that actually worked, she thought on a sigh. No matter what Cal said, she doubted she'd ever run again.

"I'm so sorry we're late," Bri said when Abby reached them.

"Don't apologize. I'm just glad you could make it. Are you doing okay? Raine said you had a migraine."

"I'm good now, thanks."

"Really? Are you sure?"

Bri shot Em a *thanks a lot* look as she forced her lips into a wide smile. "Absolutely."

"Awesome. Because you're on the stage in fifteen minutes."

"I'm on the what?"

"Stage. You know, for your check presentation." She made a face. "Raine didn't tell you?"

"No. She must have forgotten."

Abby nodded. "I'm sure she did. Anyway, it's a great

idea. We're hoping your generous donation will spur others to give as well." She looked around and lowered her voice. "And we really need a few big donors to step up to the plate. I haven't told Raine and Cal, but I'm a little nervous we won't reach our target in time."

"Now who's your best bestie?" Em said when Abby hurried off after giving Bri directions to the stage, which was set up in front of the red barn. "Come on, it won't be so bad."

It was bad. Bri had to walk up four stairs to the stage, which wouldn't have been a problem except that whoever had been on the stage before her had mud on their boots, and Bri slipped on the last step. She would have fallen on her face if Cal, who'd been walking toward the stage, didn't sprint up the stairs and grab the back of her sweater to keep her upright.

"Thanks," she murmured before limping toward the center of the stage where Abby now waited for them.

Cal stopped her with a hand on her arm, coming around to look down at her. "Are you okay? Raine said you had a migraine. Did you have a dizzy spell when you were coming up the stairs?"

"Cal, stop making a fuss over her. Everyone is looking," Raine said through a clenched-teeth smile as she joined them on the stage, waving at their audience.

The check presentation was a bit of a blur, lots of smiles and gushing from Raine and Abby too. Cal was a little more subdued, probably because he was concerned about her, and his frowning sidelong glances in Bri's direction earned him an elbow from Raine. Their audience didn't seem to pick up on the undercurrent. They were too busy clapping and cheering and calling for a speech from Bri, which she pretended not to hear.

Abby handed her the microphone. "Just a short one. It's great publicity, and the press is here."

She was right, and it wasn't only Harlan standing in the front row. Abby had ensured the media from surrounding counties had come out, including the female hosts from the local radio station, who were clearly enamored with Cal.

Bri took the mic, smiled, thanked the audience, and then thanked Cal and Raine. "If it wasn't for the two of you, I wouldn't be alive today. But that's not the only reason I donated to the trauma center. The expansion isn't just about caring for victims of life-threatening accidents. As wonderful a hospital as we have now, we don't have the equipment or the staff to provide pediatric care, substance abuse screening and intervention, rehabilitation for stroke and heart patients, or prevention and public education."

Several people in the audience shouted their support, calling out the name of a family member who would benefit from the services Bri had outlined.

She smiled and continued. "A level-one trauma center will provide all that and more. Not to mention attracting specialists and surgeons of Cal and Raine's caliber." A loud cheer went up in the crowd for Cal and Raine, and Bri clapped with them. Once the cheering died down, she added, "Radiologists, anesthesiologists, nurses, and frontline workers too. People who will live and shop in our communities, and pay taxes too. But Cal and Raine and everyone who works at Highland Falls General can't do this on their own. They need our help. So please, donate. No donation is too small. Every bit helps." She smiled, acknowledging people clapping and cheering, including Cal and Raine, and handed the mic to Abby.

As they went to walk off the stage, Raine hugged her with tears in her eyes. "I knew you'd be amazing, and you were. Thank you."

Bri hugged her back. "I meant everything I said, Raine. I hope it helps." Bri laughed when Raine murmured to Cal, "Don't you dare hug her."

He rolled his eyes and hugged her anyway, whispering against her cheek, "Meet me in the corn maze after the pie judging."

"I don't think that's a good—" She was drowned out by Harlan and members of the press shouting questions at Cal and Raine. Afraid someone would ask about her accident, Bri ducked away, escaping into the crowd.

Em and Izzy caught up with her, congratulating her on her speech. "Nice way to counter Harlan's argument about the money the casino would bring to town without mentioning the casino," Em said.

Bri laughed. "Harlan didn't seem as happy with my speech as Cal, Raine, and Abby."

"Yeah, you might want to stay out of his way."

Izzy tugged her hand. "It's almost time for the pie judging. They're set up in the apple orchard."

Bri glanced down the long, tree-lined dirt road. "I'll never make it in time. You guys run ahead."

Izzy pointed at a horse-drawn wagon parked near the entrance. "If we hurry, we can catch a ride."

They made it just before the wagon pulled away, which was a good thing because the judging was under way when they got there.

"Dad and Mom are going to miss it." Izzy took her phone from her jeans pocket.

"It might be hard for them to get away from the press, but don't worry. We'll record it," Bri said.

"There's my dad," Izzy said, waving Cal over.

Bri smiled. She shouldn't have doubted Cal. He'd never let the press stand in the way of him being there for Izzy.

"And your mom," Bri said, spotting Raine running after Cal.

"We didn't miss it, did we?" Cal asked, giving Izzy a hug.

"Nope. They're just about to announce the winners," Izzy said, holding up her crossed fingers.

They all did the same.

"And our third-place winner is Izzy Johnson! Congratulations, dear. Come and get your ribbon."

"Would you guys stop cheering so loud? It's just third prize," Izzy said as she returned with her ribbon.

"Uh-oh, some of the white-haired ladies aren't happy they were beaten by a teenager, Iz." Em nodded at a cluster of older women, glancing at Izzy while talking among themselves.

"They'll be really unhappy next year when we win first place, won't they, Bri?" Izzy said.

"Absolutely. But I think third place is awesome."

As the second and first place winners were announced, Raine said, "I bet you did come in first but they didn't want to upset their friends. Whenever I see them, the five of them are always together."

They all laughed, and Raine said, "What? It's true."

The judges invited everyone to sample the pies.

"Why don't we check out the maze? Everyone's busy eating pie. We'll have it to ourselves," Cal said.

Everyone but Raine and Bri thought that was a good idea.

"I'm going to check out the winning pies. Harlan's going to meet me here for an interview, so don't be long. You too, darling," Raine said to Izzy. "I want him to get a picture of you for the paper."

Bri reluctantly went with them. She didn't want Harlan to corner her for an interview. She doubted Raine would save her. She'd want the added publicity.

"Dad, you and Bri go in at this end," Izzy said, pointing at the opening closest to them. "And Auntie Em and I will go in at the other end." Taking Em by the hand, she took off at a run. "You can't start until we text you though," she called over her shoulder.

"Cal, this is crazy. Someone's going to see us," Bri murmured as they walked to the entrance of the maze.

He looked around and then took her hand, pulling her in among the seven-foot stalks. "I don't care." He ducked off the path and wrapped his arms around her. "I'm crazy about you, you know."

"I know but, Cal, what if—"

He lowered his head and kissed her, a kiss that obliterated her fear that they'd get caught. "Headache gone?" he murmured against her lips.

"Mm-hmm, all gone," she said, pressing against him.

He smiled, deepening the kiss, and she lost herself in the feel of his mouth on hers, his hands tangling in her hair.

Her first indication that something was wrong was when his shoulders tensed beneath her hands, and then she noticed she was kissing him but he wasn't kissing her. She heard a click, and a softly muttered curse from Cal. Then someone dragged her away from him.

"How dare you! How dare you throw yourself at my husband!"

The blood drained from Bri's face as she slowly turned to face Raine, Harlan with his camera raised, and the two women from the radio station.

"Raine, stop—"

Raine ignored Cal, yelling at Bri, "Do you think your donation entitled you to seduce my husband? Is that what you think?"

Her heart began to race. It felt like they were closing in on her, their faces blurring before her eyes. She struggled to catch her breath, to say, "I'm sorry. I'm so sorry."

"Everyone back off," Cal said, reaching for her.

She wrenched free of his hands, pushing her way through the crowd and out of the maze, only to come face-to-face with her parents, who stared at her in confusion.

"Brianna, darling, what's wrong? What happened?"

"I'll tell you what happened," someone said. "She got caught making a move on Dr. Scott by his wife. Threw herself at him, is what I heard."

Her mother gasped. "Brianna, no, how could you? He's a married man. Did you learn nothing from my mistake?" Her mother pressed a hand to her mouth. "I'm so ashamed of you right now."

Her mother's words didn't hurt as much as the disappointed look in the eyes of the man who stood behind her. Bri ran, stumbling and tripping, desperate to get away from the disappointment in her father's eyes, the shame in her mother's, and the disdain in all the others'.

Chapter Twenty-Three

♥

Bri!" Cal called after her, but she ignored him, pushing her way through the crowd. He wondered if she even heard him. She looked like she was having a panic attack.

He went to go after her but Raine grabbed his arm. "Cal, no. Let her go."

"What's going on? What's all the yelling about?" Em said, making her way toward them with Izzy on her heels.

"Your sister-in-law caught Brianna MacLeod making a move on your brother. Looks like the apple didn't fall far from the tree," Harlan said.

"Shut up," Em snarled, and then turned to Cal. "Where's Bri?"

Before he could answer, Raine intervened, putting on a show for their audience, no doubt afraid Cal or his sister would blow her cover as the wronged wife. "She left after I caught her kissing my husband. I can't believe she would do that to me." Raine sniffed, accepting a tissue from one of the radio hosts.

Izzy looked from her mother to Cal. "No. Bri wouldn't

do that. She's Mom's friend. She's her therapist. Tell them, Dad. Tell them it was a mistake."

"Does this look like a mistake to you, kid?" Harlan asked, pressing the Playback button on his camera.

"Get your camera out of her face," Cal said, pushing Harlan back. "This is on me, Izzy. Not Bri." He wouldn't let Bri take the fall for this.

"No, Cal. Don't," Raine pleaded, shooting a desperate look at their growing audience.

"No, let him finish," Harlan said. "I for one would like to hear why this is on him, and I'm sure I'm not the only one. Did you make a pass at her, not the other—?"

The crowd that had gathered in the maze parted for Raine's mother. "Cal, what's going on? Someone said Brianna MacLeod made a pass at you?"

"No. She didn't." He took Raine's hand and Izzy's. "Winter, we have to talk."

Raine pulled her hand from his, frantic. "No, Cal. Please, please, don't do this."

"I'm sorry, Raine. But this has gone on long enough. And I'm not about to let Bri pay the price."

"Damn straight you're not," his sister said. "I'm going after her."

"Why are you blaming my dad? It's Bri's fault," Izzy said, her face crumpling as she looked at the adults surrounding her. "She's ruined everything."

Em held his gaze. "Make this right, big brother."

Cal nodded and released Raine's and Izzy's hands, wrapping an arm around his stepdaughter's shoulders as Em sprinted off in the opposite direction. "It's going to be okay, Iz."

"No." She shook her head. "No, it won't."

Raine curled her fingers around his forearm. Reaching up on her toes, she whispered in his ear, "Izzy's right, Cal. Think about her. Think about me. The trauma center and everything we've worked for. Bri will understand."

Raine was right. Bri would sacrifice her reputation for them. And for one second, as he took in Izzy's heartbroken expression, he considered taking the easy way out. But he couldn't do it. No matter what came of this, he had to tell the truth. He had to protect Bri from the fallout. Somehow, he'd make Izzy understand.

Cal guided Raine and Izzy out of the corn maze to where Winter waited for them.

Miranda MacLeod came to stand before them, wringing her hands. "Cal, Raine, I'm so sorry. I can't believe my daughter would do something like this. Maybe it's because of her head injury? I've heard it can change someone's personal—"

Cal would have stopped her sooner but he'd spotted Bri's father standing behind her with his fisted hands jammed in his pockets. Cal briefly closed his eyes, thinking what that must have done to Bri. If he'd thought he could do what Raine wanted, seeing Bri's parents would have changed his mind.

"Mrs. MacLeod, Bri didn't do anything wrong. This is on me, me and Raine. You might as well come with us. I can explain everything." He headed for a storage shed behind the tables that were set up for the pie judging. The sooner he got this over with, the better.

"Would someone please tell me what's going on?" Winter said as she opened the door to the shed.

"Give me a second, okay?" He didn't want to tell Izzy with an audience.

Raine, looking like she was going to her execution, followed Bri's parents and Winter inside. Cal glanced around. A crowd was still gathered near the maze, a couple people looking their way. They weren't within hearing distance, and there was no sign of Harlan, so he felt safe talking to Izzy here.

He placed his hands on her shoulders. "I'm sorry you had to find out about me and Bri this way. I should have told you sooner. I wanted you to get to know her first."

"So it's true? You love her?"

"I do. Your mom knew, Iz. I didn't go behind her back. I was up-front with her from the beginning. I'm just sorry I wasn't up-front with you, and even more sorry that we weren't up-front about our impending divorce with everyone else."

"So all of this was an act." She waved the third-place ribbon in his face. "Bri didn't really care about me. She just wanted to spend time with you. Everything was about you. You and her."

"That's not true, honey. Bri was worried about how this would affect you right from the start."

"If she was so worried about me, she should have stayed away from you. She's wrecked our family. She's wrecked everything!"

"Izzy, no. Our family isn't—"

She wrenched away from him. "I hate you! I hate her!" she cried, crumpling the third-place ribbon in her hand. She threw it on the ground and took off.

"Izzy, wait!" He needed to go after her and make this

right but he also needed to set the record straight with Winter and Bri's parents.

He pulled his phone from his pocket. His sister picked up on the first ring. "Em, are you still here?"

"Yeah. Bri took off with the truck. She's not answering her cell."

He rubbed the tips of his fingers on his forehead, cursing himself for being an idiot. None of this would have happened if he hadn't dragged Bri into the corn maze. He'd wanted to make sure she was all right, and then, like it always happened when he was around her, he couldn't resist holding her and kissing her. "I told Izzy about me and Bri. She's upset. She took off. I'm worried about her."

"I'll find her."

"Thanks, Em. I'll meet you at my jeep. I'm parked three rows from the entrance."

As soon as he disconnected from his sister, he texted Bri.

I'm sorry. I love you. I'll make this right.

He opened the door to the shed and walked inside. Winter and Bri's parents stood beneath a bare lightbulb. Raine stood by herself, tucked into a corner as if trying to fade into the background.

"You all might as well take a seat." He gestured at the bags of corn and apples. Once they were seated, he told them how Izzy had reacted when he and Raine announced their impending divorce and he'd moved out, why they'd decided to come home, and why Raine felt the need for them to continue to appear like they were living as a happily married couple.

Winter turned to Raine, who'd remained standing, her arms wrapped around herself, her face tearstained. "How could you lie to us like that? What were you thinking?"

Cal got defensive on Raine's behalf. "A better question might be why did Raine feel like she had to lie, and why did I feel like I had to go along with it? I'm not making excuses for what we did but you and David have something to answer for too. The trauma center was Raine's baby, her dream, her vision. She's a brilliant doctor, and she'll make a damn fine administrator, and I don't know how you can't see that. She should have been able to come to you on her own and pitch her proposal. She doesn't need me, and we certainly don't need to be married to make the trauma center a success."

Winter sighed. "I wish she had come to me about this before, because I'm not sure how we're going to get out of this mess."

"I did come to you, Mother," Raine said, her voice husky from crying. "I pitched my proposal for the trauma center to you seven years ago. You brushed me off."

Winter bowed her head, nodding. "I'm sorry. You're right, you did." Winter stood and went to Raine, taking her hands in hers. "But I will stand by you and Cal now. I don't know if we can weather this storm. Harlan will use it to his advantage. But I've been mayor of this town for a very long time, and that should buy us some goodwill. We should probably go meet with David now. We have to get ahead of this."

Cal glanced at his phone. Bri hadn't responded to his

text, and there was nothing from his sister about Izzy. "I can't. I have to go to Bri." He left *and find Izzy* unsaid. He didn't want to worry Raine.

"Of course." Winter looked at Miranda and Bryan, who'd sat quietly through everything. "I'm so sorry Bri had to be drawn into this."

Raine went to Bri's parents. "I hope you can forgive us. Forgive me. I've never had a friend like Bri. She's an amazing person and therapist. She's helped me so much, and I...I didn't know what else to do. Please tell her how sorry I am, Cal."

He nodded and turned to leave. A heavy hand came down on his shoulder. "You will make this right for my daughter."

"I will, sir. I love her. I always have." He glanced at Raine, thinking that wasn't fair to her.

"It's okay. I know you loved me too. Now go. Go to Bri."

Cal had barely gotten a foot out the door when his cell phone rang. It wasn't Em telling him she'd found Izzy or Bri telling him she loved him too. It was the hospital. Raine's phone also rang. Three firefighters had been injured battling a warehouse fire outside of town. He immediately thought of Josh and called his cell. Josh didn't pick up.

"I'm sure he's fine," Raine reassured him as they made their way to the field and their vehicles. "It's not like he can answer the phone if he's in the middle of fighting the fire."

"I hope you're right," he said as they reached the field. He searched for Em and Izzy among the rows of vehicles. Jogging to the jeep with Raine keeping pace, he called his sister. "Any luck?"

"No. Someone saw her talking to a couple of kids five minutes ago. She might have gotten a ride with them."

He told Em about the fire, leaving out that he hadn't been able to reach Josh. "I have to go to the hospital. I'll catch a ride with Raine and leave the keys to my jeep on the rear wheel well."

"I'll take one more look around here, and then I'll drive around town and see if I can find her. You guys should start calling her friends."

"What's going on?" Raine asked when he'd disconnected.

Cal didn't have a choice. He had to tell Raine that Em couldn't find Izzy.

She reacted exactly as he expected her to, blaming him. "This wouldn't have happened if you'd just done as I asked," she snapped.

"None of this would have happened if we'd been honest from the beginning."

"So now it's all my fault?"

"Blaming each other isn't going to help us find Izzy or deal with the fallout from this." He attached the keys to the magnet in the rear wheel well and then straightened. "Give me your keys. I'll drive, and you call Izzy's friends."

By the time they pulled into the hospital parking lot, Raine had spoken to all of Izzy's friends. No one had seen her. Cal texted Em to let her know, trying not to let his mind go to worst-case scenarios.

Em called as he was walking into the hospital. "I got

through to Bri. I'm picking her up. She's going to help
me look for Izzy."

Raine raised an eyebrow, and he shook his head.
She nodded and strode past him, heading to Emergency.
She'd organize the patients in order of priority and
arrange a medevac if the hospital wasn't equipped to
handle their injuries.

"I don't know if that's a good idea, Em. Izzy blames
Bri for all of this."

"Yeah, I kinda realized it was a bad idea myself but
it was too late to take it back. Bri blames herself. She's
beside herself that Izzy's missing."

Cal swore under his breath. The last thing he wanted
was for Bri to feel guilty about this, but there was nothing he could do about that right now other than ask Em
to reassure Bri that she wasn't to blame.

"I have a feeling alleviating Bri's guilt about any of
this will be a challenge, one I doubt even you're up for."
And maybe sensing that wasn't something Cal needed
to hear right now, she said, "But you know me. I'm a
pessimist by nature."

A familiar voice called his name. He blew out a
relieved breath upon seeing Josh walking his way in his
turnout gear. "I have to go. It sounds like I'll be heading
into surgery so I'll be out of reach for a couple hours."

"I've got this," she assured him.

"I know you do. And I appreciate it. I'm glad you're
here. I'm glad you're home."

"Me too, big brother. Because someone has to look out
for you. You've gotten yourself into a hell of a mess."

"Tell me about it." He disconnected and took in Josh

with an experienced eye. "It looks like you've dislocated your shoulder again."

Josh nodded and told him what happened. The warehouse had come down, and two of the firefighters had been trapped in the wreckage. Josh had managed to pull them to safety. "He kept saying he can't feel his legs, Cal."

"All right. You go and get yourself looked after." Cal waved a nurse over, leaving Josh in her care, and then headed to emergency.

Josh was pacing the hall when Cal got out of surgery five hours later. "You should be home resting," Cal said.

"Is he going to make it?"

"He has a long road ahead of him, but yeah, he should make a full recovery."

"Thank God. His wife and kids are in the waiting room."

He nodded. "Raine told me. I'm going to talk to them now." He looked up to see his sister walking toward them. "Did you find Iz?" he asked when she reached them, steeling himself for her answer.

"What do you mean? What's going on with Izzy?" Josh asked, looking from him to Em.

"You didn't fill him in on what went down at the apple orchard?" Em asked Cal.

"I've been a little busy here. Did you find her?"

Em nodded. "Yeah, she was drinking at the pit. And just FYI, she is not a nice drunk or a happy one."

This was not news to Cal. Izzy had begun hanging out with a rough crowd and drinking after he'd moved out. It was the reason he'd moved back in with them and the reason they'd decided to relocate to Highland Falls. "Was Bri with you when you found her?"

"Yeah, and that went over even worse than I expected. I put Izzy in your office with a garbage can close by. One of the nurses offered to check on her."

"Is Bri here?"

"Uh, no. I dropped her off at the house. I didn't think it was a good idea for her to be anywhere near you. Things have gotten—"

Josh interrupted Em. "Would one of you tell me what's going on?"

Cal quickly filled him in.

"Oh man, that's all kinds of messed up."

"It's gotten worse." Em pulled her phone from her pocket, turning the screen. The headline on the *Herald*'s home page read "Like Mother, Like Daughter," and underneath was a photo of Cal and Bri kissing in the corn maze.

Cal wasn't a violent man. He'd spent the past ten years living by the credo "Do no harm." But at that moment, he wanted to pound the crap out of Harlan. "I'll kill him," he muttered.

"Get in line," Em said.

"Did Bri see this?"

"I don't think so but I'll head home now and confiscate her phone."

The three of them turned as a nurse approached, her lips pressed in a thin, judgmental line. "You're wanted in Dr. Warren's office," she said to Cal, and then walked away.

He was shocked. He was well liked and respected

by everyone at the hospital. "Bri might not have seen Harlan's article but some people obviously have."

"Do you want me to stick around?" Em asked, her eyes narrowed on the nurses gathered at the end of the hall, looking their way.

"No, I'd rather you go home. Bri needs you. I'll be there as soon as I find out what David wants." After seeing that headline, he had a fairly good idea. He felt sick at the thought that David might withdraw his support of Cal and Raine heading up the trauma center.

Em's phone pinged with an incoming text, and she glanced at the screen. "You have got to be kidding me."

"What's wrong?" Cal asked.

"Nothing." She pocketed her phone before he could read the screen. "It'll be fine. I've gotta go," she said, and headed down the hall at a brisk pace.

"I can sit with Izzy if you want," Josh offered.

Josh wouldn't take no for an answer, and Cal had no choice but to give in. He couldn't waste time arguing with his best friend. Cal checked on Izzy, who was asleep on the couch. He crouched beside her, covering her with a throw.

"Go away," she muttered, turning her back on him.

He hesitated, and Josh held the office door open. "I've got her. Go do what you have to do."

Cal nodded and grabbed his phone off his desk. "Text me if you need me." After checking on his patient in the recovery room—his reception there wasn't as chilly—he headed for David's office. Raine and her mother were there. Neither would look at him, which he figured didn't bode well for the outcome of the meeting.

"I hear your surgery went well," David said, looking as uncomfortable as Cal felt.

"It did." He glanced at Raine. "Izzy's in my office."

"I know." She picked at her nails. She must have been at it awhile because there was barely any polish left.

"We might as well get to it. Raine and Winter have apprised me of the situation, and I think we've come up with a solution."

"Really?" Maybe his sister's pessimism had rubbed off on him. He'd been prepared for the worst.

"Yes. Although I must tell you, it gives me no pleasure. You are one of the finest surgeons I've ever met. Everyone at Highland Falls General has the utmost respect for your skills and admiration for you personally. As do I."

Cal stiffened. What the hell was happening here? He glanced at Raine, but she wouldn't look at him. Neither would Winter.

David continued. "You have to believe me when I say, if I could see any other way out of this, I'd gladly take it. But I think Raine is right. The only way for the hospital and trauma center to survive this scandal is for you to resign."

"Resign. You want *me* to resign?" The blood roared through Cal's veins. "This was your idea?" he asked Raine. "Look at me. You don't get to sabotage my career without telling me why."

"Cal, calm down. This wasn't an easy decision to come to," Winter said, reaching out to pat her daughter's hand.

"Yeah, it doesn't sound like either of you had a difficult time throwing me to the wolves."

"What did you want me to do, Cal? Throw my career away too? Throw away any chance we have of getting the trauma center built? Did you read the article in the *Herald*? Harlan paints me as the wronged woman. People will sympathize with me, with me and Izzy, and that sympathy will garner added financial support for the trauma center. Or at the very least, we won't lose support."

"At Bri's and my expense." He got up from the chair and walked to the door. He had to get out of there before he said something he'd regret. "You'll have my resignation by the end of the week and not a moment sooner. I have a patient in recovery and two that I'm monitoring."

"I respect your concern for your patients, but I think it would be better for everyone if your resignation was effective immediately," David said.

"Push me, and you'll be talking to my lawyer."

David's Adam's apple bobbed. "A week will be fine."

"Cal, wait." Raine grabbed the office door before he slammed it behind him. "Don't you see? This is the only option we had. This will blow over in a month or two, and then I can rehire you."

"We? I had no say in this. You cut me out and went behind my back."

"This isn't my fault. It's yours! You had to know the risk you were taking kissing Bri but you went ahead and did it anyway. It's like you were trying to get caught."

Her observation brought him up short. He was so sick of pretending, of lying to everyone that maybe subconsciously he had wanted to get caught. "Maybe you're right. Maybe I did. But I never would have expected you to turn on me. What happened to *we're in this together*? I guess we were only partners when it benefited you." He turned and walked away.

Chapter Twenty-Four

♥

You're not going anywhere. You're overreacting," Em said, scooping the clothes still on their hangers from Bri's arms.

Bri lowered herself onto the side of the bed and rubbed her thigh. She never should have tried running from the maze on her leg. But she'd been too emotional to think straight, the looming panic attack shutting off her brain. She'd been numb to everything but the damage her actions had caused.

It wasn't until she'd reached the truck that she'd been overcome by debilitating pain. She had no idea how'd she'd made it home without throwing up or crashing the truck. There had been a part of her that had wanted to keep driving. She couldn't face anyone in Highland Falls, not after today. She didn't blame Raine. She was just trying to protect their reputations, and the trauma center.

Bri squeezed her eyes shut in an effort to block out the faces of her mother and father but it was Izzy's face, the accusations she'd hurled at Bri when they'd picked her up, that she couldn't shake.

"What I'm doing is ensuring that you can continue living here," Bri told Em. "Maybe if I'm gone, Mr. Jones will back down."

Their landlord had called half an hour ago. He'd given them two weeks' notice without any explanation. It wasn't until Em had finally caved and shown her the story that Harlan had published online—"Like Mother, Like Daughter"—that Bri had realized why.

It was while reading the article that Bri had also realized what she had to do. She just hadn't been able to bring herself to tell Em. She had to tell Cal first.

Em turned from rehanging the clothes in Bri's closet. "He can't kick us out because he thinks you had an affair with a married man. I wouldn't be surprised if Cal and Raine are clearing everything up as we speak. He was heading to a meeting with the hospital administrator when I left. Once they tell everyone that they're separated and getting a divorce, you'll be in the clear."

Bri didn't share Em's unusually optimistic outlook. If Cal and Raine were going to come clean about their fake relationship, they would have done so by now. But they had too much at stake professionally. And then there was Izzy.

At the sound of the front door opening, Bri's heart began to race. She knew who it was even before he called out to her and Em.

"Crap." Em grabbed the opened suitcases off Bri's bed and tossed them into the closet. "Don't you dare tell him Mr. Jones gave us notice," Em warned as she closed the closet doors. "We'll deal with it. Cal has enough to worry about. Back here," Em called out.

Bri got off the bed, steeling herself for what she had to do. No matter what Cal said, no matter how much she loved him, she had to do this.

"You look like crap, big brother," Em said when Cal walked into Bri's bedroom. "I'll give you guys some privacy. Gus needs to go for a walk."

Cal nodded, his gaze roaming Bri's face. "Are you okay?"

She shook her head. She wasn't, and she'd be far from okay after she did what she had to.

He came to her and took her into his arms. She let herself hold him one last time, wishing they had forever. She'd fooled herself into thinking that this time they might.

He brushed his lips over the top of her head. "I'm sorry. I promise. I'll make this right."

She moved away from him. "You can't, but I can."

"What are you talking about?"

"I'm leaving, Cal. I'm leaving Highland Falls. It's for the best. If I'm not here, the controversy will die down. It'll be easier for you to repair your relationship with Izzy if I'm not around."

He stared at her, a muscle ticking in his clenched jaw. "So that's it? I don't get a say? You're just going to walk away from what we have?"

"If I stayed, you'd be torn between me and Izzy. Your professional reputation will be ruined. People will pull their donations from the trauma center. Read the comments section of the *Herald* if you don't believe me. I love you too much to let you suffer because of me."

"You have no idea how much I love you if you think

for one minute that I won't suffer if you leave me." He released a harsh laugh and shook his head. "And my reputation you're so concerned about protecting? Don't worry about it. It's already ruined," he said, and then he told her that David had demanded his resignation and why.

"No. You can't let them do that, Cal. Call David. Call Raine and Winter. Call them right now." She reached up, fisting her hands in his shirt, desperate for him to understand. "Don't you see? If I'm not here, you can put the blame on me. You can say I threw myself at you, just like Raine said. I'll be the bad guy in this, not you. People will sympathize with you and Raine. You and Izzy—"

"Stop," he grated out, taking her hands from his shirt. "Stop pretending this is about me."

"But it is about you. I—"

"No, it's not. At least be honest with yourself, Bri. You're looking for a way to punish yourself. You're looking for an out, and now you found one."

"How can you say that?"

"Easy. You're willing to walk away from what we have without a fight. That pretty much says it all, doesn't it?"

"We can't fight this, Cal. Too many people have already been hurt. Think of Izzy."

"I can't do this. You've already made up your mind," he said, and then he turned and walked away.

"Cal, please. Don't leave like this," she called after him, wincing when the front door slammed shut. Her legs went weak, and she once again lowered herself onto the edge of the bed.

She didn't know how long she'd been sitting there when Em burst into the bedroom. "What the hell happened? What did you say to Cal?"

The words tumbled out of Bri. She had to make Em understand. If she could convince Em, Em could convince Cal that Bri was doing this because she loved him.

Em scooped up her hair, holding it on the top of her head. "I can't believe how stupid I was. I knew you'd break his heart again."

"How can you not see that I don't have a choice?"

"Keep telling yourself that." She looked around the room. "Text me when you're leaving. I'll be staying at Josh's until you do."

"Em, please. You don't have to leave."

She didn't look at Bri. She walked away with Gus trailing after her, the front door slamming shut behind her. Bri heard it open moments later and wiped the back of her fingers across her cheeks, relieved that Em had returned. She didn't want to leave like this.

But it wasn't Em. "Honey, it's Dad. Where are you?"

She got off the bed and met her father in the hall. He took one look at her and opened his arms. She walked into them and sobbed against his chest. He smelled like Old Spice and old books. "I've ruined everything, Dad."

He wrapped an arm around her and guided her into the living room. "You sit down, and I'll make you a cup of tea."

That was her dad's answer for everything. Mostly he used it to avoid having a conversation but apparently that had changed. "It'll take a few minutes for the water to boil," he said, returning from the kitchen to take a seat beside her on the couch. He put his arm around her. "Now, why don't you tell me what's got you so upset?"

"You were there, Dad." At his frown, she said, "The apple orchard?"

"Yes, but Cal cleared that up." He told her what had taken place in the shed. Something Bri hadn't known. "He told us he loved you and that he was going to make it right."

"I know he wants to. But he won't be able to if I'm here." She told him everything that had transpired in the past few hours. "I broke it off with Cal. I'm leaving Highland Falls."

"Now why would you do that, honey? He loves you, and it's obvious you love him."

"I know he does, and I love him too. But sometimes love isn't enough. This is bigger than us."

"I'd be the first to admit I'm no expert when it comes to relationships, but it seems to me you're sacrificing your relationship with Cal because you think you're to blame for this, and from everything I've heard, that's far from true." He rocked her against him. "You do have a habit of taking the blame for things that aren't your fault, you know. You did the same thing as a little girl." He smiled. "Remember the time your brother knocked over the glass of milk onto my laptop, and you took the blame because it was your glass of milk he'd spilled? Or the time your sister broke the vase and you took the blame because she'd been chasing you."

The kettle whistled, and her dad got up from the couch, looking at her with a sad smile. "I know you kids think I walk around with my head in the clouds, and admittedly

I do spend a lot of time in my mind, but there are some things that even I haven't missed. I know you think you're to blame for the rift between Ellie and your mother and the rift between me and your mother but you aren't. You need to let it go, honey. Just like it's time you stop blaming yourself for your fall last year."

Bri stared after her father as he walked to the kitchen. That was the longest speech he'd ever made. He was a quiet, contemplative man who rarely gave advice, so when he did, Bri and her siblings took it to heart. And if her father was right, maybe Cal was too. Maybe she was punishing herself. Maybe deep down inside where her guilt and shame lived, she believed she didn't deserve to be happy.

As she contemplated the story she'd been telling herself for the past year, her father returned with two cups of tea. Handing her one, he took a seat. "Thanks, Dad," she said. "Where's Mom?"

"She's at the inn. She was ashamed of how she reacted this afternoon at the corn maze, and then she saw the story..." He trailed off and took a sip of his tea.

"I saw the story that Harlan posted online. It's not Mom's fault."

"She was worried you'd be upset with her. She knows how difficult all this has been for you."

"It's been worse for her than it has been for me. Is she still planning on going on Abby's podcast with her side of the story?"

"I've asked her to hold off for now."

"Because of the lawsuit?"

"Yes. I'd like to find a way for your mother to feel

heard and to have her experience validated without going to court."

"You don't think you can win?"

"I have no doubt we can. Your mother kept everything—the threats, the photos—all meticulously documented. The evidence can't be disputed." He rubbed a hand up and down the side of his face. "She suffered in silence for a very long time. I worry how she'll handle a trial. I didn't protect her then. I want to protect her now."

"Dad, it's not your fault. Dimitri's family are to blame."

"For the trauma she suffered, they are. But I wasn't a very good husband, honey. There was a reason your mother looked for love from someone else. I was too absorbed in my work. I'm afraid I wasn't a very good father either."

"Don't say that. You're a wonderful father."

"If I was, I would have realized how the truth about your paternity affected you. I assumed you'd know that it changed nothing for me. But last week your grandmother told me I have to stop burying my head in the sand and start seeing what's going on around me. And I realized maybe you needed me to tell you how much I love you and that, in my heart and in my head, you're my daughter. You're my baby girl, and I don't care what a blood test says."

Tears welled in her eyes, and she managed a wobbly smile. "I love you too, Dad."

He put his teacup on the coffee table and wrapped an arm around her. "I'm going to do better. With you kids and your mother."

"You and Mom aren't getting a divorce?"

"No. We're starting over with a clean slate. I've given my notice, we're selling the house, and we're moving home to Highland Falls." He smiled. "Your grandfather gave us some land on the lake, and your mother and I are building a house."

"You and Mom are building a house...together?" she asked, unable to keep the skepticism from her voice. "Like from the ground up?"

Grinning, he nodded. "We'll probably need counseling for our marriage to survive so you might want to book a standing appointment once a week for your parents."

She laughed, hoping he wasn't serious. The idea of acting as her mother and father's mediator held little appeal. "I'm happy you and Mom are giving your marriage a second chance, Dad. It'll be nice having you here in Highland Falls. Granny will be thrilled, and so will Ellie."

"Nice enough to get you to reconsider leaving town?"

Their family would be together again and would soon be welcoming a new member. Bri wanted to be here for that but how could she stay when it would bring nothing but heartache to Cal's family? But wasn't she doing the same thing to Cal and to Em if she left? To her own family and friends?

"I don't know, Dad."

"You've had an emotional day. Why don't you sleep on it before you make a decision?" His cell phone rang, and he retrieved it from the pocket of his brown tweed jacket. "It's your mother," he said, bringing the phone to his ear.

"Miranda, calm down. I can't understand a word you're saying." He winced and glanced at Bri. "I see. I'm sure it was upsetting. You told him what?" He pinched the bridge of his nose between his thumb and forefinger. "I thought we agreed you'd hold off on the podcast." He nodded in response to whatever her mother said. "Yes, you do. I'm not saying that you don't but I . . . maybe you should talk to Bri." He handed her the phone with an apologetic wince.

"Hi, Mom. What's going on?"

"The last thing you need to talk about are my problems with Dimitri. You have enough to deal with. Are you okay, darling? I've been worried about you, but I thought you'd prefer talking to your father. He did talk to you, didn't he? He didn't just get you a cup of tea and pat your knee, did he?"

"No, Mom," she said, struggling not to laugh. "Dad and I had a nice chat . . . and a cup of tea. You're welcome to come over, you know." Dealing with her mother's problems would be easier than dealing with her own. She needed a distraction.

"Really? You wouldn't mind?"

"Of course not." And thinking how concerned her father was about her mother going to trial, a concern Bri shared, she said, "If you're open to it, I'd like to ask Dimitri to join us."

She glanced at her father, who gave her a relieved smile and patted her knee. "I'll make more tea," he said, and got up from the couch.

"Why on earth would you invite him? He called me, you know. He read that inflammatory article online, and he had the gall to blame me. The sanctimonious—"

"On second thought—"

Her mother talked right over her, giving voice to every wrong she felt Dimitri and his family had committed against her, and then she totally surprised Bri by saying, "You're right. Call him. It's about time he had a face-to-face with your father. He'll put him in his place."

"Mom, I'm not sure this was a—"

"I'll see you shortly, darling. I just have to make a few notes before I come."

Bri stared at the phone. What had she done? Nothing yet, she realized. She'd tell her mother she couldn't reach Dimitri, which she shared with her father a few minutes later.

"It's up to you, but I don't see any other way to get your mother to drop the lawsuit." He lifted a shoulder. "It might be good for me to get a few things off my chest too."

And that's how, an hour later, Bri found herself sitting in her den/office beside her mother on the couch, with Dimitri and her father across from them in the chairs.

"I have a few ground rules before we get started," she said. "First, I'm here not as your daughter but as an unbiased mediator. I won't take sides. I will also end the session if there's name-calling, blaming or shaming, or emotional outbursts of any kind. Everyone will get a chance to talk so I expect you to listen respectfully and not interrupt. And as hard as this is to do, given the emotion on all sides, try not to get defensive." She looked around. "Does everyone agree to abide by the ground rules?"

The three of them glanced at each other and then nodded. "Great. So, Miranda, if you feel comfortable—"

"I don't like when you call me Miranda. I'm your—"

She sighed. "For the next hour, you're not my mother. You're a client. Now, are you ready to get started?" Her mother glanced under her lashes at the two men sitting across from her. Bri took her hand. "If you don't want to do this, that's okay. No one is here to judge you. Just remember that Bryan loves you, and at one time, Dimitri did too. And you love Bryan, and at one time, you also loved Dimitri. So focus on that, focus on the love you all shared, and go from there."

Her mother sniffed and looked down at the paper she held clutched in her hand. It contained a long list of wrongs by Dimitri and his family. Bri released the breath she'd been holding when her mother folded the paper in half and tucked it in the pocket of her jacket.

Her dad met Bri's gaze and smiled. They might just get through this after all.

Two hours later, they'd gone through two pots of tea and a box of Kleenex. It was emotionally draining for all of them, Bri included. As much as she'd tried to stay objective, it was difficult when her parents, all three of them, had openly shared their hurt and heartache. But it had been worth it, especially for her mother.

She'd had her pain and suffering validated, and more than that, she'd forgiven Dimitri, who'd been moved to tears. He'd agreed to remove himself from the casino consortium, assuring them that a casino wouldn't be built in Highland Falls without him bankrolling the bid. Her mother had agreed to drop the lawsuit, refusing Dimitri's offer of financial reparation for all that she had suffered. It had never been about the money for her.

Her parents said goodbye to Dimitri, and Bri walked him to the door. "Thank you for coming tonight. I know that wasn't easy for you."

"Nor for you. I hope in time you can forgive me too," he said as he opened the door.

"I do forgive you. And I hope you can forgive me."

Dimitri's brow furrowed. "There is no reason for me to forgive you."

"We didn't get off to a very good start. You made several overtures, which I rejected. And I'm sorry if I hurt you."

"There is no need to apologize. You were shocked and hurt when you learned you were a result of my affair with your mother. I understood your reaction." He gave her a sad smile. "I understand if you would prefer for me to stay out of your life. You have a family who loves you, and that is all I could ever ask for you."

For all his wealth and power, she suspected Dimitri was a lonely man. "Actually, I was hoping we could start over. You're part of my family too."

His face lit up with a smile. "I would like that. I would like that very, very much." His chauffeur got out of the limo and came around to the passenger side. "I will call you, and perhaps we will meet for lunch."

"I'd like that." She leaned in and kissed his cheek.

Her parents joined her at the door, waving goodbye to Dimitri. "Your father and I planned to leave for Durham first thing in the morning to get the house on the market, but we can put it off if you'd rather. I don't like leaving you on your own right now."

"No, I'm fine. I've never been on my own before. It might be just what I need to get some clarity."

"If you need us, we're only a phone call away." Her father leaned in to kiss her forehead. "Your mother and I are proud of you, honey."

"We are." Her mother kissed her cheek. "You're a wonderful therapist, darling." She patted her husband's chest. "Thank goodness, because Lord knows we're going to need one to survive building this house. Can you believe your father actually wants a log cabin?" Her mother shuddered, and her father ushered her out the door.

Bri waved goodbye to her parents, smiling as her mother kept up a running commentary of what she wanted in the house all the way to their car. As Bri went to close the door, she glanced across the road at Josh's house and considered going over to talk to Cal. But his jeep wasn't there. Maybe it was a good thing. She still hadn't decided what she should do.

The house was quiet without Em and Gus, and Bri's heart ached a little at the loss. She sat on the couch, picking up the remote control. She put it back down and did what she'd advise her clients to do. She sat with her emotions. She didn't try to push them away or shut them down like she'd done for the past year. She let the images play out in her mind, surprised when the memories of Richard's abuse and her near-fatal fall didn't trigger a panic attack.

He was the one person she'd yet to forgive. At the

thought, her heart began to race, but then the conversation she'd had with Izzy came back to her. Forgiving Richard wasn't about him; it was about her. She inhaled for a count of four, held it for a count of seven, and then blew out for a count of eight. She repeated the pattern several times, and her anxiety began to ease.

"I forgive him," she whispered to the empty room. She expected to feel a lifting of her spirits but she didn't feel any different. And that's when she realized that, in truth, the one person she'd yet to forgive was herself. She opened her mouth to say the words but they jammed in her throat. She tried two more times with the same result and was about to give up. But then she saw Cal as he'd looked tonight when she told him she was leaving, and she gave it one last try.

"I forgive you," she whispered to the little girl who'd always felt the need to take the blame. "I forgive you," she murmured to the young woman who'd allowed herself to be manipulated into thinking she didn't deserve Cal's love. "I forgive you," she said to the woman who'd allowed fear to silence her and keep her in an abusive marriage that almost ended in tragedy, a woman whose only responsibility for the accident that nearly took her life was that she'd tried to protect herself. The paralyzing weight of guilt and shame she'd been carrying with her for what felt like forever slowly lifted.

She deserved to be happy. She and Cal deserved their happy ending. The hard part would be convincing Cal that he could trust her with his heart. Cal...and Izzy.

Chapter Twenty-Five

♥

Someone knocked on the door to Cal's office, and he looked up from the open file on his computer screen. "Come in."

The door opened and one of the surgical nurses stepped inside. "Dr. Scott, do you have a minute?"

"Sure." He closed the file on the screen, resisting the urge to rub his eyes. He'd been working almost around the clock for the past five days trying to wrap up his case files and ensure his remaining patients were well looked after when he left.

Several other members of his surgical team followed the nurse into his office. "What's going on?"

"You're leaving, for one," someone in the back of the group said. A dark-haired resident came forward and placed a piece of paper on his desk. "We've signed a petition asking that Dr. Warren rehire you."

"Thank you." He glanced at the signatures on the paper. There were more than he expected, considering the cold shoulder half the staff had been giving him.

"We appreciate the lengths you and your wife—

ex-wife, I guess," the resident corrected herself, "were willing to go to for the trauma center. Some people might not understand why you kept the status of your relationship under wraps, but we do."

"What exactly do you mean by 'keeping the status of our relationship under wraps'?"

"Everyone knows, Dr. Scott. Your wife—"

"Ex," a voice in the back corrected the nurse.

"Right, ex-wife. Anyway, Dr. Johnson-Scott wrapped up her press conference half an hour ago. She's resigned."

"Raine resigned?"

"Yes, and there's a petition started to reinstate her too. We need you guys. The hospital won't be the same without you."

"Thank you for your support. I appreciate it, and I know Raine will too," he said, trying to wrap his head around the idea that she'd come forward and told the truth. He'd barely spoken to her. At first, he'd been furious, but in the last few days, he'd been too busy to seek her out. "I'm sure Dr. Warren has several good candidates to choose from. This is a great hospital, and you're one of the best surgical teams I've worked with."

They spent a few minutes trying to convince him to stay on, and then several of their pagers went off and they cleared out, closing the door behind them.

Just as he picked up his phone to text Raine, the door flew open, and Izzy stormed into his office. "Dad, you have to talk to her. We have to change her mind. She can't do this!"

"Iz, what are you doing here? You're supposed to be in school."

"School? Really, Dad? Mom is going to ruin my life, and you're worried about me being at school."

"Okay, stop pacing. Come and sit down and tell me what this is all about."

"Weren't you at her press conference? It's all the kids at school can talk about."

"I wasn't. I just found out about it now." He got up and came around his desk, crouching beside her. "I'm sorry, honey. That must have been embarrassing for you." Leave it to Raine not to think about the consequences of outing them to the press. The least she could have done was prepare Izzy. He would have appreciated a heads-up himself.

"I don't care what the kids at school think."

"You don't?" This was new.

"No, my friends have my back."

"That's good. I'm glad they do. They're a great group of kids." Better than the ones Em had found Izzy drinking with at the pit. Thankfully, there hadn't been a repeat. Izzy had been remorseful the next day. Remorseful and hungover. Cal had been lucky his sister had been available to be there for Izzy while he wrapped things up at the hospital. Raine had been working even longer hours, according to Izzy.

"You don't get it, Dad. Mom texted me twenty minutes ago that we're moving." Blinking back tears, Izzy crossed her arms. "It's not fair. I'm doing good in school, and I like my friends. I'm not moving again, Dad. I won't. She can't make me."

He reached behind him for the box of tissues on his desk and handed them to Izzy. "Don't cry, honey. I'll talk to your mom. We'll work this out."

"She won't listen to you. The only person she listens to is Bri." At what must have been his skeptical expression, she said, "It's true. Remember the fake pregnancy? If it wasn't for Bri, Mom would probably be walking around with a pillow stuffed up her shirt."

His smile faded as he thought of Bri. He still couldn't believe she'd left him. His schedule had been his salvation. Anytime he had some downtime, all he did was think about her, and what might have been if she hadn't given up on them. He reached for the phone several times a day, wanting to talk to her, needing to hear her voice. But he'd stop himself, afraid of what she'd say. The only way he'd gotten through the past five days was by hanging on to the hope that once she had a chance to think about it, she'd change her mind.

"Honey, Bri's gone. She left Highland Falls five days ago."

He hadn't seen her leave. He'd been going over to talk to her later that night to try and convince her to stay. But Em had told him she'd seen her leave with Dimitri. Apparently all three of her parents had arrived at the house on Marigold Lane. Dimitri had probably whisked her off to Europe, getting her as far away from Cal as possible. They'd blame him for ruining her reputation. They wouldn't be wrong.

"What are you talking about? Bri didn't leave, Dad."

"She did. Aunt Em saw her leave."

Izzy rolled her eyes. "Dad, Bri spends half the day in her front yard raking leaves. I'm pretty sure she's hoping to see you."

"Are you sure it was Bri?" he asked, afraid to give into the tidal wave of hope rising inside him.

"Yeah. I saw her this morning when I left for school. She said hi to me." She ducked her head. "I pretended I didn't see her."

"Iz."

"I know, but I was embarrassed. I don't remember exactly what I said to her last weekend, but I know I was pretty mean."

"Bri wouldn't hold that against you, honey." No, she'd blame herself. "Come on, let's go. Your aunt has some explaining to do." He shut down his computer, calling his sister as he locked up his office.

"Hey, I was just going to call you," Em said. "Did you hear the news?"

"That Raine resigned or that Bri never left Highland Falls?"

"Oh, that."

"Em, how could you?"

"Easy, big brother. She's broken your heart twice. No way am I letting her break it a third time."

He ushered Izzy out the hospital's front doors. "Did you really think I wouldn't find out she was still in town?"

"It's been five days, and you didn't notice. And it's not like she goes anywhere. So who ratted me out?"

"Iz. Raine not only resigned, she's moving. Izzy thinks Bri is the only one who can change her mind." He got in the jeep and started the engine, waiting for Izzy to put on her seatbelt before pulling out of the parking lot. "Did Josh know Bri was still in town?"

"Um, maybe."

Cal shook his head. "I don't believe you guys."

"We were trying to protect you."

"Explain that to Bri."

"Fine. I'm tired of cleaning up after you and Josh anyway."

"Are you seriously thinking of moving back into the house after you pulled this?"

"Uh, yeah, it's my house too. And if you're going to be stupid enough to trust Bri with your heart again, you need me there watching your back."

"Dad, stop. Look, it's Bri," Izzy said, pointing at a woman crossing the grocery store parking lot. Cal did a double take. The blonde walked across the parking lot with a confident stride, despite her limping gait.

By the time he pulled into a parking space, Bri had disappeared inside. "Aren't you coming with me?" Cal asked as he unbuckled his seatbelt but Izzy didn't do the same.

He was barely resisting the urge to run into the store. He felt the same level of anticipation as when he was a kid and he knew Bri was coming to town, only it was magnified tenfold.

Izzy shook her head. "You talk to her first. Tell her I'm really sorry I was mean to her."

His foot on the asphalt, he glanced over his shoulder at Izzy. "Are you sure about this, Iz? We haven't talked about how you feel about Bri and me." To be honest, he hadn't seen the need. As far as he knew at the time, he and Bri were over. And apart from grabbing a couple of hours to spend with Izzy, they hadn't had a lot of time together. "You were pretty upset with us."

She shrugged. "I thought maybe you and Mom would stay together. It was stupid. I didn't know you and Bri were engaged when you were young and that her mom broke you guys up. Aunt Em told me after we dropped off Bri that day. At least I'm pretty sure that's what she said. I was kind of, you know, wasted when she was giving me crap about giving you guys a hard time."

"We were engaged, and I loved Bri. A lot. I still do, and I hope she feels the same way about me. If she does, I'm going to ask her to marry me. Not right now, but one day. And I need to know you're okay with that, Iz."

"What if I'm not?"

"Then I guess I'd put off asking her until you were."

"Really? You'd do that for me?"

"Of course I would. I love you, and I want you to be happy."

"I want you to be happy too, Dad. And I can tell Bri makes you happy, even if I didn't want to admit it. Do you think she'll mind me hanging around though?"

"You got to know Bri pretty well. What do you think?"

"She'd probably be okay with it."

"No *probably* about it. There's nothing she'd want more than you in our life, kiddo. In fact, I'm pretty sure she'd be as unhappy as I would if you didn't want to spend time with us."

"If we can't change Mom's mind, you guys might have me living with you full-time, because I'm not moving, Dad."

"We'll cross that bridge when we come to it, but that's fine with me, honey. And I'm sure Bri will feel the same."

"Okay, but, Dad, Bri broke up with you. So maybe you shouldn't get ahead of yourself."

Izzy was right. What if the reason Bri had stayed in Highland Falls had nothing to do with him? His stomach bottomed out at the thought. "But you said it looked like she was hanging out in the front yard waiting for me."

"Yeah, but I could be wrong. Maybe she just really likes raking leaves."

"How did she look when you saw her?"

"Not as bad as you, that's for sure."

Cal glanced at the grocery store, wondering if he should wait until she got home. But he didn't want to wait another thirty minutes to see her, to talk to her. Even if their reunion didn't go the way he hoped, he needed to know. "I won't be long. Do you want me to pick up anything for dinner?"

"Nah, Aunt Em said she has eggplant lasagna." Izzy grinned. "Aunt Em doesn't cook. Bri must have left it for you."

"Your Aunt Em and I are going to have words." Because while it was clear Bri had been trying to reach out to him, it was just as clear his sister had been blocking her at every turn. And he could only imagine how that had made Bri feel, which meant he'd have some making up to do.

"Wish me luck, honey." He smiled at Izzy's thumbs-up and sprinted across the parking lot. He spotted Bri as soon as he walked into the grocery store. She was just finishing up in the produce aisle.

"Bri," he called, walking toward her. She ignored him. He blew out a breath. She wasn't going to make it easy for him, and he didn't blame her. He reached out a hand, resting it on her shoulder. "Bri, I can ex—"

She gave a startled scream, jumped, and threw up her arms, shoving the grocery cart away from her. She whirled around to face him. "Cal, you just about gave me a heart attack," she said, removing the earbuds from her ears.

"Sorry, I—" He broke off at a man's shout, raising his gaze in time to see Bri's runaway cart plow into the toilet paper display.

"Not again!" said a voice that he now recognized as the manager's.

"Please tell me my cart didn't just take out the toilet paper pyramid."

He smiled down at her. "Don't worry, I'll take the rap."

She didn't return his smile. She simply said, "Thanks" and then walked over to her cart. Apologizing to Stan, she began picking up the packages of toilet paper and restacking them.

"Go do whatever you have to," Cal told Stan. "We've got this."

Stan looked from him to Bri, who was now studiously ignoring Cal. "You sure?"

Cal nodded and picked up a package of toilet paper, waiting for Stan to move away before saying to Bri, "I thought you left town."

"I live across the road, Cal. How could you not know?" She shook her head. "Never mind. It doesn't matter."

"It does. It matters to me. Would you just give me a minute to explain?" he said, taking a package of toilet paper from her and tossing it onto the pile. He put his hands on her shoulders, turning her to face him. But instead of explaining, he said, "You look amazing." She did, and that worried him.

She frowned. "You don't. You look exhausted."

"Yeah, because I am. The only time I've left the hospital is to spend an hour or two with Izzy and grab a few hours' sleep. Which is why I had no idea you were still in town." He decided to keep his sister's part in it to himself. "Do you really think I would have avoided you if I'd known you were here?"

"You were angry, Cal."

"Yeah, I was. Angry and hurt, and I didn't react well. In my defense, I'd just been asked to resign from a job I loved. But that didn't compare to the thought that I'd lost you again, Bri."

"You never called me or texted me. I sent over an eggplant lasagna four days ago."

"I didn't know about the lasagna until a few minutes ago, and I didn't call you or text you because I didn't want you to tell me it was over."

"When you didn't come over after I left the lasagna, I was afraid to text or call you for the same reason. Not to mention Em made it clear my calls wouldn't be welcome." She lifted her arm. "I've spent so much time in the front yard raking, hoping to see you, that I actually have muscles." She lowered her arm and nodded at her cart. "Today I decided I was going to suck it up and make you apple dumplings and sit on Josh's doorstep until you came home, but I saw Izzy this morning and had second thoughts."

"She told me. She feels bad about how she acted. She's the reason I found out you were still here." He told her about Raine resigning and how Izzy hoped Bri could convince her not to move.

"Oh, Cal, it's all such a mess. If—"

"Don't you dare take the blame for this, Bri. None of this is your fault."

"I know. And as much as I missed you, the time on my own has been good for me. It's given me a chance to work on myself and my healing." She smiled. "I feel like the old me again."

He smoothed his hands down her arms and brought them to her hips, drawing her closer. "You look like the old you. Any chance the old you wants to pick up where we left off and turn back the clock ten years?"

"You want to date again?"

"Actually, I was thinking we'd skip over the dating part and go right to the engagement."

"You're asking me to marry you?"

He glanced at the pile of toilet paper rolls lying around them and laughed. "I guess it's not the most romantic place to propose."

She looped her arms around his neck. "I don't know. If I hadn't run into the toilet paper pyramid that day, and you hadn't been here, we might not have gotten a second chance with each other."

"Eventually we would have found our way back to each other. You and I were always meant to be."

She lowered her arms from his neck. "I love you, and I'm so happy right now that I want to kiss you, but we're drawing attention, and I don't think that's what either of us needs right now." She smiled. "Any chance you want to continue this at home?"

"Do you even have to ask? But just out of curiosity, was that a yes?"

"Do you even have to ask?" She looked around, reached for a package of toilet paper rolls, and then held it to the side of her face, hiding them from the curious onlookers.

He leaned in and kissed her, murmuring "I love you" against her lips.

Chapter Twenty-Six

♥

Three weeks later

Cal and his sister walked across the Village Green carrying Bri's entry in the Great Pumpkin Contest. The last place he wanted to be was at the Fall Festival with half the town in attendance, but Bri was running late, and she didn't want to miss the entry deadline. She was holding her first meeting with the support group at the community center.

The grounds were packed with people checking out the vendors selling arts and crafts while eating sausages and funnel cakes from the concession stands, feet tapping and heads bobbing in time to the music coming from the main stage.

Cal kept his head down as he and Em wove their way through the crowd, hoping to escape notice. It wasn't as bad as it had been those first couple of weeks, but he still ran into people wanting to share how ticked they were at Raine and him. Bri didn't escape their censure but she was surprisingly blasé about it these days. Probably because she was able to do the job that she loved and her practice was thriving.

Cal was still out of work with no prospects. He knew all he had to do was pick up the phone and GW would take him back in a heartbeat but he wouldn't ask Bri to move, and there was Izzy to think about.

When it came to his personal life, he couldn't be happier. He was marrying his one true love, Izzy was happy and doing well, he'd forgiven Raine, and she'd agreed to remain in town. Em also had decided to stay in Highland Falls. So yeah, he wasn't about to pull up stakes or ask anyone else to. He just had to figure out what to do with his life. And while volunteering with the county's emergency medical services kept him busy, he missed his patients and his surgical team and coworkers at Highland Falls General. And a paycheck.

"Please tell me Bri doesn't think she has a chance of winning," Em said as they approached the sign-up table for the Great Pumpkin Contest.

"I'm pretty sure that she does," he said, eyeing the competition. Three of the giant squashes would have needed more than two people to carry them. They would have needed a crane.

"Cal!" a familiar voice hailed him as one of the organizers showed them where to place the pumpkin.

Abby ran up to him as he and Em carefully lowered Bri's pumpkin onto the crate.

"Hey, Abby. What's up?" he asked, reminded of another reason he didn't want to be here today. Later that night—at the dinner and dance—the trauma center's fate would be sealed. They'd announce whether or not the fundraising goal had been reached from the stage where a pipe band now performed.

"The radio hosts from *Good Morning Highland Falls* want to interview you."

"Ah, no thanks. I've had about all the negative coverage I can handle."

One of the organizers handed him an entry form, which he signed.

The man glanced at Bri's pumpkin and grinned. "It doesn't stand a chance in the weight category but it is a pretty little thing."

"It's not that little," Em said. "It has to weigh at least two hundred pounds."

He nodded at the three giant squashes. "Those weigh between eight hundred and a thousand pounds each. But like I said, it's a pretty little pumpkin so you never know. It might take the prize for most beautiful."

Abby pressed her palms together. "Please, Cal, they feel bad about their coverage and want to make it up to you. An interview with you might be just what we need to meet our target."

"You're really that close?" Cal asked as he moved out of the way of another pumpkin grower—an adorable pint-sized pumpkin grower who proudly deposited her baby pumpkin on the table. So much for Bri's chances of winning most beautiful pumpkin. The little girl had it in the bag.

"Well, no, we're seventy-five thousand short of our goal," Abby admitted. "But your patients love you, and so do your coworkers."

In the end, Cal reluctantly agreed to do the interview.

It might be a lost cause but it was one he truly believed in, which he shared ten minutes later with the hosts of *Good Morning Highland Falls*. The interview went well, and they'd drawn a fair-sized crowd who were mostly supportive. Cal thanked the two women and their audience and then made his way to where his sister and members of Bri's family waited for him.

"If that doesn't raise the money to cover the infrastructure funds, I don't know what will, laddie," Bri's grandmother said.

"From your lips to God's ears, Granny MacLeod," Cal said, thinking it would take a miracle for them to meet their target.

Bri's grandmother glanced at someone in the crowd and patted his arm. "Don't worry, I have a good feeling about this."

"And I have good news," his sister said, holding up her phone as they made their way en masse to the pumpkin judging. "I have an interview at HFPD at six." She grimaced. "Crap, I'm going to be late for Bri's sur…" She trailed off at Ellie's wide-eyed stare.

"Bri's what?" he asked, looking from Bri's sister to Em.

"Oh, look, there's Bri," Em said, sounding relieved.

Bri waved from where she stood among the other contestants and crossed her fingers.

Cal smiled, forgetting about anything other than the woman he loved. He held up his hand and crossed his fingers.

"She really does think she has a chance." Em sighed. "I guess I shouldn't be surprised. She always was the most optimistic person I've ever known."

Cal and Ellie shared a smile. They'd gotten their old Bri back.

She didn't win, but not surprisingly, Bri was thrilled with her third-place finish for most beautiful pumpkin. The adorable pint-sized grower had an equally adorable brother, who came in second. His sister came in first.

As the sun set behind Blue Mountain, Bri stood on the front lawn of the house on Marigold Lane, surrounded by friends and family. Cal stood beside her in front of the *For Sale* sign, wearing a blindfold. "Babe, can I take this off?"

"One more minute." She was stalling. She was nervous about how Cal would react to her surprise.

"I get how it's a big deal for you guys that our divorce was finalized today, but I don't think today is a day for celebrating," Raine said from somewhere behind Bri.

"Mom!"

Raine sighed. "I'm happy for Cal and Bri, Izzy. You know I am. It's just that, in a little more than an hour, they're announcing whether or not we raised enough money for the trauma center to be approved, and we all know that didn't happen. So excuse me if I'm not jumping for joy that Bri is about to—"

Izzy covered her mother's mouth before she spilled the beans.

Bri's engagement ring twinkled in the fading sunlight as she placed the *Sold* sticker on the *For Sale* sign. "Okay, you can take it off now."

Cal removed the blindfold and looked down at the sign. Everyone cheered and clapped their hands. Everyone except Cal. "You bought the house?"

"We should probably head to the Village Green," Josh said, obviously sensing his best friend wasn't overjoyed with Bri's surprise. "The dinner starts in twenty minutes." It wasn't long before everyone else cleared out, offering subdued congratulations as they headed for their cars.

"You're upset," Bri said, walking to the porch and taking a seat on the stairs.

Cal joined her, taking her hand in his. He brought it to his lips. "I'm not upset. I love this house as much as you do." He lifted a shoulder. "I don't know, call me old-fashioned, but I would have liked to contribute."

"You will. I don't plan on making the mortgage payments on my own."

"Babe, I don't have a job, and it won't take all that long to go through my savings." He glanced at her. "Did Dimitri give you the money for the down payment?"

"No, you know how I feel about that. I wouldn't ask him for money."

"So how did you come up with the down payment? Did you renege on your donation to the trauma center? I wouldn't blame you if you did."

"I thought about it when David forced you to resign. But I feel as strongly as you do that we need a trauma center here." She looked down at their joined hands. "Do you remember when I told you that being alone when we'd broken up was good for me?"

"I don't like to think about those five days, but yeah, I do. What about it?"

"I wasn't in a good place when my divorce was being negotiated, and I realized that I didn't stand up for myself. I let Richard and his lawyer bully me out of my fair share. So I contacted Richard and his lawyer and demanded that I get what I was entitled to and threatened to sue if they didn't meet my demands."

"Babe, that's awesome. I'm proud of you."

She rested her head on his shoulder. "I'm proud of me too. But to be honest, the conversation didn't go well. They laughed at me."

"The bastards."

She smiled. "They stopped laughing when I told them they'd be hearing from Dimitri and his team of lawyers."

He laughed. "Good for you."

"I got what I asked for with interest. I used it for the down payment." She rubbed her thumb on his. "I wanted to surprise you but I should have talked to you about it first."

"No, not now that I know where you got the down payment. Standing up to Richard to get what you deserved was a really big deal. It makes the house even more special."

"So you're happy?"

"Couldn't be happier. No wait, I take that back. I'd be happier if we stayed home and celebrated in bed with a bottle of champagne. What do you think?"

"It sounds like a wonderful idea but—"

"Awesome." He stood, bent down, and scooped her into his arms. "This is the practice run for when we get married," he said as he carried her over the threshold.

She kissed him. "You cut me off. I was about to say it's a wonderful idea but we'll have to wait until we come home from the Fall Festival. I know how difficult it will be for you, Cal, but it's important we be there."

Em ran past them and pounded up the stairs. "Sorry I'm late. Interview went long. I'll be five minutes. Don't leave without me."

Gus joined Bri and Cal at the bottom of the stairs. "Wait. Did you get the job?" Bri called up to her.

"Of course I did. It doesn't start for a couple of months so you guys are stuck with me and Gus."

An hour later, they arrived at the Village Green. The trees were strung with mason jars filled with miniature lights. To the left, tables were draped with white linens. Pots of fall flowers decorated the stage and surrounded the dance floor in the middle of the green. To the far right, a blazing bonfire warmed the crisp night air.

Abby ran over and hugged them. "I'm so glad you guys made it."

"How does it look? Did they meet the target?" Bri asked, thinking it better that they be prepared.

"Thanks to your interview with *Good Morning Highland Falls*, we raised twenty-five thousand dollars, Cal, but I'm afraid it's not enough. We still have a shortfall of fifty thousand dollars." She nodded at the stage. "Winter's going to announce that we didn't reach the goal in the next few minutes. She thought it would be better to get it over early, and I think she's hoping it will encourage more people to donate before the night is over. Even if it does, there's no way we'll reach our target."

Bri hugged Abby. "I'm sorry. I know how hard you've worked these past six weeks."

Cal thanked Abby for all she'd done. The smile on his face was strained. Bri took his hand. "You okay?"

she asked as they walked to the table Abby had directed
them to before she ran off again.

He lifted her left hand. "You agreed to marry me,
and we got the house we always dreamed of. What do
you think?"

"That this is a difficult night for you."

"It's not easy," he admitted. "But it would have been
a lot harder if I didn't have you by my side."

"I love you."

He smiled down at her, the strain leaving his face. "I
love you too."

They sat with their family and friends. They needed
three tables to accommodate all of them. It took at least ten
minutes for them to greet everyone and assure them that
Cal was thrilled with the house. Bri leaned forward in her
chair. "Granny, where's Mom and Dad?"

"Haven't got a clue. They said they were heading this
way after we left your place."

Cal grabbed the bottle of wine from the middle of
the table and poured Bri and her grandmother a glass.
"Looks like they're getting it over with now," he said,
nodding to where Abby walked onto the stage.

Abby introduced Winter, who looked as dejected as
all of them felt.

"Excuse me. May we say a word?" a man asked,
raising his hand as he walked toward the stage with
another man and woman. Bri squinted against the glare
of the stage lights. "Wait a minute. That's my mom and
dad and Dimitri."

Bri gave her sister a *what's going on?* look. Ellie
shrugged and lifted her hands.

"Don't look at me," her grandmother said. "I have no idea what they're up to."

"Thank you, Ms. Mackenzie. My name is Dimitri Ivanov," he said, addressing the audience. "As some of you might now know, I was behind the casino consortium. I withdrew my support and financing several weeks ago. I...we"—he gestured to her mother and father—"thought that without the casino as an option, the trauma center would have a chance of raising the necessary funds. But today while attending the Fall Festival, we learned that was not the case."

His announcement was met with audible disappointment. Dimitri nodded. "We shared your disappointment. I am sorry, I should introduce you." He waved her mother and father closer. "This is Bryan and Miranda MacLeod. The three of us are the proud parents of Brianna MacLeod, soon to be the wife of Dr. Caleb Scott, the man who saved her life, and a man who has our greatest respect and profound gratitude."

Bri sniffed, and her grandmother handed her a napkin. Cal wrapped his arms around her, drawing her back to his chest.

"As does Dr. Raine Johnson," Dimitri continued. "They both were instrumental in our daughter's recovery. And it is for this reason that we are donating a million dollars to a cause that is near and dear to our hearts—the trauma center."

"No fricking way," Josh said, and around them, people burst into applause.

Other than Josh, and apparently her grandmother, who had a smug smile on her face, their entire table

was stunned. Bri was in shock, and Cal seemed to
be too.

Dimitri held up a hand, silencing the crowd. "We do
have one caveat though. One I do not believe the mayor
or hospital administrator will have difficulty agreeing
to." Winter and David joined Dimitri and her parents
from the other side of the stage.

"With a million dollars at stake, I don't think there's
anything we'll deny you," David said to titters of
laughter.

Dimitri smiled. "Our request is that Dr. Raine Johnson
heads up the expansion and that Dr. Caleb Scott leads the
trauma team. As I'm sure you'll agree, you won't find a
more qualified or respected surgeon than Dr. Scott."

"Done. Cal, Raine, can you come up here, please?"
David said, waving them to the stage.

Cal stood up, leaning in to kiss Bri before heading for
the stage, offering an arm to Raine.

Everyone at their family and friends' tables stood
and cheered as Cal and Raine joined Dimitri and Bri's
parents on stage. They gave a short speech thanking Bri's parents, everyone who'd worked tirelessly
fundraising for the past six weeks, and all their supporters and donors.

"Raine and I would also like to thank our daughter
Izzy for putting up with us. One day, in the not-too-
distant future, we hope she'll be working with us at
Highland Falls General. And I'd like to thank my beautiful fiancée, Bri, for handling the backlash she faced over
our relationship with grace, strength, and kindness."

Bri pressed a hand to her heated cheek, thinking Cal

had taken it a bit far but she appreciated the point he was trying to make.

Cal and Raine were mobbed by well-wishers, and it took at least half an hour for them to make it back to the table. Cal smiled and offered her his hand. "They're playing our song. Dance with me."

And that's what they did. They danced to "A Moment Like This" by Kelly Clarkson. They certainly wouldn't win a dance contest—Bri was hardly a graceful dance partner—but she didn't care. She was in the arms of the man she loved, surrounded by family and friends, a bright and happy future stretched out before her.

About the Author

Debbie Mason is the *USA Today* bestselling author of the Highland Falls, Harmony Harbor, and Christmas, Colorado series. The first book in her Christmas, Colorado series, *The Trouble with Christmas*, was the inspiration for the Hallmark movie *Welcome to Christmas*. Her books have been praised by *RT Book Reviews* for their "likable characters, clever dialogue, and juicy plots." When Debbie isn't writing, she enjoys spending time with her family in Ottawa, Canada.

You can learn more at:
AuthorDebbieMason.com
Twitter @AuthorDebMason
Facebook.com/DebbieMasonBooks
Instagram @AuthorDebMason

Can't get enough of that small-town charm?
Forever has you covered with these heartwarming
contemporary romances!

AT HOME ON MARIGOLD LANE
by Debbie Mason

For family and marriage therapist Brianna MacLeod, moving back home to Highland Falls after a disastrous divorce feels downright embarrassing. Bri blames herself for missing the red flags in her relationship and thus worries she's no longer qualified to do the job she loves. But helping others is second nature to Bri, and she soon finds herself counseling her roommate and her neighbor's daughter. Bri just wasn't expecting them to reunite her with her first love...

THE BEACHSIDE BED AND BREAKFAST
by Hope Ramsay

Ashley Howland Scott has no time for romance as she grieves the loss of her husband, cares for her young son, and runs Magnolia Harbor's only bed and breakfast. Ashley never imagined she'd notice—let alone have feelings for—another man after her husband was killed in Afghanistan. But slowly, softly, Rev. Micah St. Pierre has become a friend...and now maybe something more. Which is all the more reason to steer clear of him.

RETURN TO CHERRY BLOSSOM WAY
by Jeannie Chin

Han Leung always does the responsible thing, which is why he put aside his dreams of opening his own restaurant to run his family's business in Blue Cedar Falls, North Carolina. But when May Wu re-enters his life, he can no longer ignore his own wants and desires. Garden gnomes are stolen, old haunts are visited, and sparks fly between the pair, just as they always have. Han and May broke up because they wanted vastly different lives, and that hasn't changed—or has it?

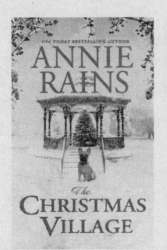

THE CHRISTMAS VILLAGE
by Annie Rains

As the competition heats up in the Merriest Lawn decorating contest, Lucy Hannigan can't help feeling like a Scrooge. Her mom had won the contest every year, but Lucy isn't sure she has it in her to deck the halls this first Christmas without her mother. But when Miles Bruno, her ex-fiancé, shows up with tons of tinsel, dozens of decorations, and lots and lots of lights, Lucy begins to wonder if maybe the spirit of the season can finally mend her broken heart.

DREAMING OF A HEART LAKE CHRISTMAS
by Sarah Robinson

To raise enough money to start her own business, Nola Bennett needs to sell "the Castle," her beloved grandmother's historic house, and get back to the city. But Heart Lake's most eligible bachelor, Tanner Dean, rudely objects. He may be the hottest, grumpiest man she's ever met, and Nola has no time to pine over her high school crush. But sizzling attraction flares the more time he spends convincing her the potential buyers are greedy developers. Will Nora finally realize that this is exactly where she belongs?

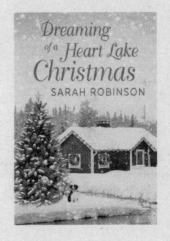

Discover bonus content and more on
read-forever.com

SUGARPLUM WAY
by Debbie Mason

Aidan's only priority is to be the best single dad ever, and this year he plans to make the holidays magical for his young daughter. But visions of stolen kisses under the mistletoe keep dancing in his head, and when he finds out Julia Landon has written him into her latest novel, he can't help imagining a future together. Little does he know that Julia has been keeping a secret that threatens all their dreams. Luckily, 'tis the season for a little Christmas magic.

A LITTLE BIT OF LUCK
(2-IN-1 EDITION)
by Jill Shalvis

Enjoy a visit to Lucky Harbor in these two dazzling novels! In *It Had to Be You*, a woman's only shot at clearing her tarnished name is with the help of a sexy police detective. Is the chemistry between them a sizzling fling...or the start of something bigger? In *Always on My Mind*, a little white lie pulls two longtime friends into a fake relationship. But pretending to be hot and heavy starts bringing out feelings for each other that are all too real.

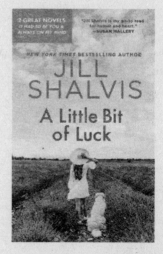